SHOW OF FORCE

Visit us at www.boldstrokesbooks.com

By the Author

Hostage Moon

Show of Force

SHOW OF FORCE

by
AJ Quinn

2013

ISBN 10: 1-60282-942-X
ISBN 13: 978-1-60282-942-8

This Trade Paperback Original Is Published By
Bold Strokes Books, Inc.
P.O. Box 249
Valley Falls, NY 12185

First Edition: September 2013

Credits
Editor: Ruth Sternglantz
Production Design: Susan Ramundo
Cover Design By Sheri (graphicartist2020@hotmail.com)

Acknowledgments

Special thanks to Rad for inspiring me and making me want to be a better writer. To Ruth Sternglantz, editor extraordinaire, for being so very good at what you do, and for being willing to teach me and help me tell a better story. To the amazing team at BSB who work to make all of this possible. To JP for sharing all those stories about life as a navy pilot—even the ones that made me blush. And especially to the readers for your encouragement and support. It's both an honor and a pleasure to share my stories with you.

Dedication

To BJ, for so many reasons and more.

PROLOGUE

February 16
1800 AST
USS Nimitz (CVN 68)
Northern Arabian Sea

It was into a warm mid-February evening that Lieutenant Commander Evan Kane stepped out of the squadron ready room. The winds were light, cloud cover minimal, and the setting sun had painted the horizon in glowing shades of orange and gold. It promised to be a great night to fly, and she was eager to get the mission underway.

Following close behind her, she could hear her wingman, Deacon Walker, giving some good-natured grief to a nugget—a new pilot on his first deployment. She wanted to keep her mind focused on the mission, and for a moment or two, she remained silent. But she finally had to shake her head and laugh as the trash talk escalated. The kid would learn soon enough.

As her long stride took her into the noise and bustle of the flight deck, she realized she was hyperaware of everything around her. The constant scream of aircraft engines. The inescapable smell of jet fuel that filled every breath. The flow of action. It was almost, she reflected, as if, like the nugget, this was the first time she'd ever been here.

Except, of course, this was not her first cruise. She'd been on the flight deck of a carrier untold times, day and night, in good weather and bad. And, unlike the nugget, she was at the top of her game.

During this last deployment alone, Evan had flown countless sorties to and from the operating areas in Afghanistan. Each mission lasted between five and seven hours and necessitated refueling by air force tankers while en route. And between takeoff and landing, she provided close air support to US and coalition forces on the ground.

Sometimes that meant performing strafing runs while under antiaircraft fire. Still other times, she'd been called on to use the sensors on her F/A-18 to locate possible improvised explosive devices or roadside bomb positions.

Lately, many of those missions had included loud and low show-of-force passes over insurgency areas. In the lexicon of close air support, the maneuver was a nonlethal display of power intended to signal enemy forces that the ground troops were not alone.

It was all part of the job.

A job that was coming to an end.

Tonight's mission had the distinction of being her last. After this mission, and all the intervening years since she'd walked into Aviation Officer Candidate School as a fresh-faced college grad, she was finally going home.

Stepping onto the four-and-a-half acre flight deck, she walked with cautious familiarity as sailors and aircraft moved about in a tightly choreographed ballet. Not just a cliché, it truly was poetry in motion.

She wasn't surprised to find Dave Riley, the air wing commander, standing near her aircraft. They'd met years earlier while training in Fallon, Nevada prior to her first deployment, and they had served together a long time. Dave had always been supportive, pushing, stretching, and encouraging her to be the best. He had also done everything in his power to convince her to stay in the navy. But he had finally accepted her decision to walk away.

Without saying a word, he fell in beside her as she completed her last preflight walk around. He then stood at attention and crisply saluted her. She returned his salute and watched him turn on his heel and leave the area.

Alone once again with her thoughts, Evan quickly slid into the seat of her F/A-18 and strapped in. She was on the clock as she went through her takeoff checklist, then followed direction and lined up at one of the *Nimitz*'s four catapults, collectively capable of launching aircraft from the flight deck every thirty seconds.

With canopy down, engines turning, and ejection seat armed, she patiently awaited her turn. A yellow shirt—an aircraft director—gave her the signal to start rolling forward, and she followed the wands until she was parked behind the jet-blast deflector, which protected her from the jet twenty feet ahead about to take off.

Evan tensed, felt the adrenaline flow increase, and forced her muscles to relax as she double-checked her trim settings and her ejection seat and ensured all radios, navigational aids, and data links were turned on while an engineer gave a final check. As he ran clear, he gave her the signal to go to full power.

Evan complied. She heard the roar of the engines reverberate, felt the aircraft quiver in anticipation of takeoff. Seconds ticked by, and then she saw the yellow shirt snap a smart salute. She returned the salute, her response telling the CAT officer both pilot and aircraft were ready for launch. An instant later, she pressed her head against the seat, slammed the throttle to full afterburner, and was catapulted into the evening sky.

God, she would miss this, she thought fleetingly, as she cleared the deck. The exhilaration. The camaraderie. The sheer joy of flying. But the moment quickly passed, and she turned her focus to the immediate business at hand. Raising the gear and shutting off the lights, she ascended rapidly as the giant carrier receded below her and her wingman joined her in the darkening sky.

They were four hours into the mission when the call came in. A marine unit doing reconnaissance had run into unexpected resistance. Under heavy fire, they had requested air support, and a ground controller wanted the two strike fighters to send a sign—a show of force—to the marines and the Taliban fighters.

She signaled Deacon to follow, and the two jets dropped down, skimming over the massive, snowcapped mountain range. They used the jagged mist-covered mountains and valleys as cover, trying to avoid detection and surface-to-air missiles.

As they approached their target, Evan banked and aligned her aircraft, diving before pulling level and accelerating into the canyon, broadcasting her proximity with an extended engine roar. Deacon followed suit.

What happened next came without warning.

A surface-to-air missile hit her starboard wing.

The sound was paralyzing and her world exploded into chaos.

Her F/A-18 shuddered and smoke began to fill the cockpit, while the instrument panel lit up like a Christmas tree with flashing warning lights. She quickly lost altitude and speed and groaned under the g-forces.

Not good.

Already the aircraft had become unresponsive, and in those fleeting seconds, as time slowed to a crawl, Evan resigned herself to the fact that on her very last mission she would be abandoning her aircraft. Ejecting into a no-man's-land of cliffs and rocks and ice, far from help and the possibility of a quick rescue.

Automatically, her hands moved in a sequence of actions reinforced through years of continuous repetitive training. She tightened her harness straps, cinched down her helmet, and got ready to take the ride of a lifetime. And then she was out of time.

It was going to be close. With her aircraft disintegrating around her, she grabbed the pull handle of her ejection seat.

After an explosion caused by the canopy separating, she was blasted into the cold and eerie silence. She had barely begun her descent when something struck her helmet. It hit hard, shattering her visor.

She never lost consciousness, not quite, but everything blurred. Her head exploded with pain and cold air rushed in. Something wet ran down her face and she thought she could taste copper.

Dazed, disoriented, her vision dimmed, and her last conscious impression as she hurtled toward the ground was of being surrounded by snow. Tate loved snow, she remembered dreamily as she descended through the clouds.

Just before she slipped into unrelieved blackness, only one thought was on her mind.

I'm sorry, Tate. I'm so sorry.

Chapter One

Seventeen months earlier
September 21
1900 AST
Manama, Bahrain

Everything in Tate McKenna's world was irrevocably altered on the evening of her thirty-third birthday. It happened the moment she caught her first glimpse of Evan Kane in the grand ballroom at a by-invitation-only embassy party honoring the US secretary of state's visit to Bahrain.

Under normal circumstances, Tate went grudgingly or outright avoided these formal affairs. But for some inexplicable reason, she had put up only a token resistance when reminded by a colleague this was a must-attend function, especially given her job as a correspondent for the Middle East news bureau entailed covering the guest of honor's tour through the region.

So she pulled out the little black dress she saved for occasions such as this and contemplated putting her shoulder-length hair up before deciding to leave it loose. She added a hint of scent and put a smile on her face. Twenty minutes later, she braced herself as she entered the ballroom, prepared to spend the next few hours watching an assortment of diplomats fawn over the secretary of state.

The room was brightly lit and echoed with the clatter of crystal and laughter and the sounds of countless muted conversations. The dignitaries and guests in attendance milled throughout the ballroom, their voices competing with the strains of music from the orchestra.

Almost immediately, a waiter wandered by with a tray of full champagne flutes and Tate gratefully swept up a glass. As she brought the champagne to her lips, it was a husky laugh that first caught her attention. Transfixed by the sound, she scanned the nearby crowd, looking for its source.

And then she saw her and literally froze, the glass hovering near her mouth.

It wasn't as if she was unused to seeing an American military presence. Marines at parade rest stood guard at every embassy she'd been in. Bahrain was also home to the roughly one thousand land-based navy personnel at the headquarters for the Fifth Fleet, which directed operations in the Persian Gulf, Red Sea, and Arabian Sea. And Tate was aware the USS *Nimitz* had just arrived in the Gulf.

But for some reason, the three naval officers cutting across the room—two men and a woman—stood out with poster-child perfection in their dress whites. Then again, maybe it was just the woman who cast a magical spell and captured her attention, because over the next few seconds, the two male officers beside her ceased to exist, while the woman seemed to offer the potential of changing her evening from one of tedium to one promising endless possibilities.

She was stunning.

There was an unconscious arrogance in the set of her shoulders, and she moved with the languid, easy grace of a woman who knew what she was doing—and could handle anything that came her way. Tate watched as she moved through the crowd, charmingly mingling with the savvy of someone well used to these events, and when Tate saw a smile tug at the corners of her beautiful mouth, she was certain she'd never seen anything as sexy in her life.

She was at least five-ten, possibly more, and lean, with narrow hips and long, endless legs. And her dark, nearly black hair was styled in one of those hypershort cuts that just looked sinfully sexy. Maybe because it bordered a bewitching face that was instantly unforgettable. High, slashing cheekbones, dark eyes, and a lush mouth. Actually, make that an incredible mouth, curving upward in a kind of lazy smile, framed with twin dimples that flashed each time she smiled.

Evocative as hell. It was also a face that gave the impression she was hiding a wealth of secrets and made Tate want to unveil every single one of them, until she discovered who the officer really was.

It took Tate a moment to recognize the nearly instantaneous and overwhelming sweep of raw desire that enveloped her, and she almost stumbled as the realization dawned. Her mouth became dry and she was aware of an indefinable, primal attraction that had nothing and everything to do with the pleasure of simply watching the officer as she cut through the crowd.

As Tate followed her with her eyes, swallowing grew increasingly difficult. And as a small, pleasant ache settled between her thighs, Tate wondered if anyone else in the room was suddenly thinking of hot, hungry mouths and sweat-dampened skin.

The thought startled her. She would not have described herself as an impulsive woman, nor was she normally given to flights of fancy. Especially not while on the job.

But the naval officer seemed like every fantasy, every dream played out. She was every wish personified, and Tate had not been involved with anyone for a very long time. A deadly combination.

Who are you, and why can't I take my eyes off you?

Tate shook her head in silent bemusement. She was accustomed to relying on her instincts when it came to people, and she was rarely wrong. But she had never experienced anything quite like this. She was actually breathless.

"See something interesting?"

Tate turned around, bringing her face-to-face with Jillian Cordell, smiling as she drew near. "Maybe," Tate replied, looking back for an instant until she was staring once again at the naval officer. "Do you know who she is?"

A tiny blond dynamo in a flame-colored silk dress, Jillian was considered direct, focused, and disciplined by everyone who knew her. She was also a seasoned foreign service officer and came with a reputation that could walk into a room about ten minutes before she did.

As two individuals went, Tate and Jillian couldn't have been more different. But in spite of those differences, Tate would be eternally grateful Jillian had taken a new and relatively inexperienced correspondent under her wing when Tate had first arrived in the Middle East. And for reasons neither of them fully understood, the two women connected and had quickly become friends.

Jillian nibbled from a small plate of hors d'oeuvres she was holding as she attempted to follow Tate's line of sight, and Tate knew the moment she saw the navy officer. Jillian made no attempt to hide the fact she was staring and her smile widened.

"Mercy," she whispered reverently. "If you're looking at tall, dark, and oh-my-God-she's-gorgeous in the dress whites, she makes me want to fall to my knees and beg. And, no, I don't know who she is, but I'm thinking now would be a good time to change that."

Tate shook her head. "Uh-uh. I'm thinking now would not be a good time. At least not for you, my friend." She smiled to ease any potential sting in her words. "Besides, she's much too young for you," she added, knowing Jillian had recently turned forty-two while guessing the lieutenant in question was most probably only in her midtwenties.

Jillian laughed. "I don't think so. If you look at the insignia on her uniform, there's a half stripe between the two full stripes. She's a lieutenant commander, and that should put her somewhere around thirty years of age. Not too young at all."

"Okay, she just looks young."

And delicious. Desire, stronger this time, spiked through her again as Tate continued to follow the lieutenant commander with her eyes. She was faintly surprised by the involuntary reaction, causing Jillian's sarcastic retort to fade into the din of the ballroom.

She shook her head. She hadn't felt this kind of immediate response to a woman since—she paused and grinned to herself—well, since never.

Jesus, I need to get it together. Or I need to get laid.

She tried to keep an eye on the striking brunette but momentarily lost her as she was swallowed by the crowd. Maybe that was a good thing, she told herself. Her job was to cover the secretary of state. She was here to work, not to find a lover or rediscover her previously dormant libido.

But then the naughty little voice inside her head beckoned. Why couldn't she do both? Especially if it was just for one night. She could keep it simple. Easy. No regrets. No looking back. And it was her birthday, after all. What could it hurt?

A sudden, wicked-sounding laugh broke her train of thought. She turned back toward Jillian and found her gazing intently across the room with an odd expression on her face.

"Something funny happening?"

"Well, I could be wrong, honey," Jillian drawled softly, her look guileless as she indicated with a nod of her head. "But if that delectable-looking officer is still of interest, you may have some serious and unexpected competition."

Tate looked across the ballroom, and while conversations in multiple languages swelled around her, she watched in stunned silence. The sexy but nameless commander had just approached the secretary of state, waited silently as she completed the conversation she was having with the US ambassador, and then extended her hand as if it was the most natural thing in the world for her to do.

Clearly visible from across the room, Althea Kane's initial irritation lasted mere seconds. In the next instant, her face paled, and she appeared to be almost in shock as she looked up and finally brought the tall, young officer into focus. And before security staff could respond to the apparent breach in protocol and intervene, Kane accepted the proffered hand and allowed the commander to escort her onto the dance floor.

Tate stared in unabashed fascination as the two women assumed an open embrace and silently waited for the music. Once it commenced, they began to move fluidly around the dance floor, executing a series of long, elegant steps and complicated footwork with apparent ease, as if they were born to it.

For the next several minutes, Tate was unable to concentrate on anything other than the passionate dance playing out for all to see. In fact, many of the couples on the dance floor ceased their own movements and simply stood, blatantly staring.

When the music finally concluded, the two women stood motionless in the midst of the crowd, oblivious to the applause their performance had spontaneously generated. The young naval officer released Secretary of State Kane and took a step back. There was a brief exchange of words, followed by another long, seemingly endless minute while the two women simply looked at each other without saying anything.

And then the commander saluted smartly, turned, and disappeared like a chimera into the crowd, leaving Althea Kane staring into the empty space where she had been.

Jillian shook her head. "Jesus, that was not only incredible, it was ballsy as hell. Who the hell is she?"

"I don't know, but I intend to find out." Draining her glass, Tate handed it to a passing waiter and replaced it with a fresh drink. "Don't wait up for me," she added softly.

"One question before you go. What makes you think she's interested in women?"

"What makes you think she's not?"

"Go, Tate." Jillian applauded softly. "And happy birthday."

Right, Tate thought. *Let me make a wish.*

With a determined smile, she began to cut through the crowd, moving unerringly toward the balcony where she had last seen the navy commander before she disappeared.

Escaping the heat and noise of the crowded ballroom, Evan released a sigh of pure pleasure the moment she stepped outside. The night was quite warm, but she welcomed the relative quiet of the balcony.

Voices and laughter were all but indiscernible. Only the music filtered through, soft and seductive as it flowed gently around her, while the air carried the scents of the lush plants, twisting vines, and the many exotic blooms in the garden below.

It was a near-perfect night. The moon, almost full, rode a sky crowded with stars, while the air was filled with promise. After weeks at sea in a crowded floating city where the air was filled with the scent and sound of the jets continuously taking off and landing, this was bliss.

She breathed deeply, raised her eyes and stared out into the vast and endless night sky, feeling the beauty of the moment stir her. Far above, the canopy of distant lights flirted seductively with her. And as she counted the stars, she lost herself among them.

Minutes drifted away. But at some point, something—a scent or a sound—intruded, and she became acutely aware another person now shared the darkness with her. A woman standing to her left stared out into the night sky. A faint breeze drifted across the balcony, and Evan caught the allure of her scent. Something subtle, maddening. Or maybe it was only her imagination.

She chose, for the moment, to say nothing. Instead, she waited while the other woman walked toward the edge of the balcony and leaned over the railing. As she looked out, a soft sigh escaped her. And, after another few seconds had passed, she turned and smiled in Evan's direction.

The sexy redhead in the little black dress. She'd noticed her earlier. A classic beauty. Delicate features, flawless skin, and dazzling green eyes.

Evan schooled her expression as heat swirled through her, maintained a cool and calm exterior while her heart rate increased, and deep inside, she recognized a surge of cautious speculation.

"Do you mind the company or would you prefer to be left alone?"

Initially, Evan didn't say anything. But, finally, she responded with a smile. "I daresay your company would always be preferable to being alone with my thoughts."

Her voice was low and smoke edged and soft as the night. Liquid sex. Tate felt an odd combination of chill and heat as the sound of the commander's voice flowed over her like a silken caress. It was a voice meant for endless nights, and she found herself more aroused. Further proof, if she needed it, confirming it had been much too long.

A shiver coursed down her spine, and though she warned herself not to do it, Tate lowered her gaze until it fixed on the commander's sensuous mouth. Just long enough to wonder if it would be as soft as it appeared. Or taste as sweet.

Her heart slammed and her throat tightened as she forced herself to meet the commander's eyes. "You're being very gracious, but I would have thought after being on board a ship—with, what is it? four or five thousand sailors?—you might prefer the solitude."

"Good guess. Actually, the *Nimitz* has a crew of roughly fifty-seven hundred."

"And what's your role in that horde, Commander?"

A smile came and went. "Air wing."

"That means…?"

"I'm a pilot. I fly an F/A-18E Super Hornet."

Intrigued, Tate sipped her champagne and considered the information before nodding quietly. A navy fighter pilot certainly fit with the first impression she had of the young commander. The keen intelligence in her eyes. The aura of self-assurance she had projected while mingling in the ballroom. The elegance with which she had moved as she approached Secretary Kane and led her onto the dance floor. The fluid grace she had demonstrated once she got there.

"What's it like to fly?"

There was no hesitation. "Awesome. When the seas are rough, the deck is pitching, and you're a thousand miles from the nearest ground-based landing strip, it's the scariest thing you'll ever do. You know if you run into a problem, the only option is going to be ditching your aircraft into the ocean." She paused then smiled. "But on a night like tonight, when you get high into the sky, it tastes like freedom and feels like you can all but touch heaven."

A poet. Tate could hear the passion in her voice, and her smile, as it widened, was magnetic. Good God, what would this woman be like on full power?

She hadn't finished the thought when her eyes were drawn to the commander's hands—beautifully shaped, strong hands with long, slender fingers—and Tate realized she was imagining how it would feel to have those hands stroking her body.

Jesus. She usually had better control over her thoughts than this. Tate cleared her throat, as if that could somehow help clear her mind, as well. "Are you any good?"

"I am very, very good."

Tate laughed and tried to ignore the double entendre. "I was talking about being a pilot."

"Of course. So was I."

"Of course you were. And being a pilot means you'll have a call sign you go by," she mused out loud. "Dare I guess what it might be?"

"Don't bother." A grin preceded the soft response, and the commander's expression became filled with wry amusement. "It's Dancer."

"Oh, that's perfect." Tate smiled with sheer delight and then tilted her head, staring for a moment as the commander's mouth continued to tempt. "And that tango, by the way, was absolutely…it was amazing. Where on earth did you learn to dance like that?"

The commander didn't answer her for the longest time. Instead, she looked at Tate intently and seemed to be weighing her words carefully. Finally, she appeared to come to a decision and shrugged. "Would you believe me if I said my mother taught me?" she asked, laughter shimmering just beneath her voice.

"Sure. Why not?"

"Good, because it's the truth."

Tate considered her response but didn't press. "Well, you certainly got my attention. But why are you out here? Did you get tired of dancing?" she asked, assuming the commander would have had plenty of partners in the crowded ballroom after the performance she had given. "I thought fighter pilots were all about work hard, play hard."

"We can be, but I guess tonight I'm just not in the mood." She cocked her head slightly to one side and their gazes held once again.

"Then what are you in the mood for, Commander?"

They stared at each other speculatively for another long, pensive moment. The commander's eyes—not dark, as Tate had previously thought, but rather a storm-cloud gray—were luminous now, appearing almost silver, and even in the low light Tate could see the interest sparked in her smile. Another thrill raced through her body.

"If we're speaking frankly, I'd like to ask if there is anyone in your life right now," the commander said in that dangerously sexy voice, while moving infinitesimally closer.

"Why would you want to know that?"

"I'd like to know if there's anyone who would be upset about anything that might happen between you and me. Like, perhaps, the very attractive blonde you were standing with earlier."

The words hung suspended in the air between them. Tate felt her mouth grow dry once again as the realization hit. While she had been observing the commander, the commander had clearly been watching her in return.

Tate's heart rate quickened until it was beating so hard she was sure the commander could hear it. She was equally certain somewhere in the back of her mind she could hear a bell clearly pealing a warning as she hovered on the edge of temptation.

It had been so very long since she had experienced any kind of visceral response to another person—and never before with a total stranger. She felt overwhelmed by a sudden desire to kiss this unknown woman. Wasn't that what this moment called for? *Wasn't that why you followed her out to the balcony?*

"That's quite a segue, Commander," she said finally, fighting the smile that tightened her lips. "To answer your question, the attractive blonde's name is Jillian and she's a very good friend. But just a friend. So, no, there's no one. Not at the moment. And there hasn't been for a long time."

"Are they all fools?"

Everything went still inside her as Tate stared blankly, blinking quickly, her chest rising and falling. She paused long enough to brush the curtain of overgrown bangs out of her eyes and set her drink aside. "That's sweet. But it's also not very subtle. Are you always this direct?"

The commander's face held amusement, and the corners of her mouth twitched with a grin. "I'm sorry," she said, although she didn't sound particularly sorry. "But then I wasn't trying to be sweet. Or subtle. I've discovered life's much too short, and I have other things on my mind."

Tate stared at her through narrowed eyes. "Other things?"

Her smile widened. The twin dimples flashed as she stepped closer and, in a smooth and no doubt practiced move, she slid a hand up to cup Tate's neck and brought her face closer. "That's right. For example, I suddenly find myself preoccupied, wondering what your mouth tastes like. Why do you suppose that is?"

She leaned closer still, her lips mere inches from Tate's while her fingers brushed Tate's cheek. Warm. A feather touch that sent a shock wave through her.

She stopped with their faces barely three inches apart and looked at Tate through nearly closed eyes. Hovering on the edge of temptation, Tate met her gaze and was filled with a slow, simmering awareness. Her heartbeat continued to pound, and she felt nearly overwhelmed by the sense of inevitability that came over her.

Driven partly by instinct and partly by burning desire, Tate closed the remaining distance, bringing their lips together and filling with a stunning sense of absolute rightness.

One taste and she was hooked.

Tate had never been kissed like this. As if kissing her was all that mattered. As if nothing else and no one else existed.

The closer she got, the closer she wanted to be, and finally, she gave herself up to it. They fit against each other perfectly, and she was slowly seduced by the commander's mouth.

A sweet moan of approval encouraged Evan, and she briefly deepened the kiss before drawing away. In that moment, something inside her changed. Something that had been previously dormant, as if waiting for this moment and this particular woman's touch in order to awaken. Heat bloomed on her skin and in her blood.

She had to force herself to breathe. She was keenly aware of her rapid heartbeat and her quickening breath. And because her hands began to tremble, she moved back slightly, creating the illusion of distance. She reached for her drink and finished it.

Her lips still tingled where they had connected with those of this unknown woman. But she had chosen to let the kiss play out. Closing her eyes for just a moment, the sensation continued to wash over her. The redhead's taste, unexpected yet familiar, rushed immediately to her head. She tasted like champagne and temptation.

Intoxicated with the taste of her, the feel of her body, Evan leaned closer once again. Nipped at a tempting bottom lip, momentarily dragging it between her teeth. "I think we should leave now and continue this at your place," she whispered, keeping her voice soft and intimate.

"My place?" Moonlight reflected in clear green eyes as they opened with surprise. "Why my place as opposed to—oh, I don't know—a hotel room? I mean, we are currently standing on a balcony in a five-star hotel."

"We can do that if it's what you really want, but I get the distinct feeling you might feel more comfortable if you're on familiar ground."

"Like at my place?"

"Mm-hm. If we're at your place, it puts you in control, and you can always kick me out if you decide you've made a terrible mistake inviting me in."

"And would I be...making a terrible mistake?"

"No."

She cupped the delicate face in her palm. Kept her tone light. Casual. But when their eyes met, she found what she was feeling wasn't quite so casual.

"Please don't break my heart by saying no," Evan whispered and loaded her request with an irresistible challenge. "Please say yes."

"This is crazy," Tate murmured.

Even as she said the words, something sizzled in the air between them. Something told Tate that sex with this navy commander would not be a civilized affair. Instead, it would be hot and uninhibited. Mind-blowing and incredibly intense.

For the first time in forever, she knew what it meant to want something. Something primal. Something forbidden and dangerous. And she badly wanted to acquiesce. "Did I mention it's my birthday?"

"Oh, that's perfect. Happy birthday, beautiful lady. And all the more reason for you to go a little crazy with me. Let me be your birthday present. Let me fulfill all of your birthday wishes."

Tate chewed on her bottom lip and bit back a groan. "Shouldn't I at least know your name?" she asked, skimming against her, aching for even closer contact.

Everything changed in the span of a heartbeat.

Tate had always considered herself quite good at judging people. But in that instant, she couldn't read the curiously shuttered expression that suddenly crossed the beautiful face only inches from her own. Nor could she read the dark, smoky eyes. Uncertain what had just happened, she silently waited.

"It's Evan."

"Evan." Tate tried it on, liked how it fit. She drew her lips nearer. "Is that a first name or a last name?"

The smoky eyes appeared almost black. Evan's nostrils flared and the pulse at the base of her throat appeared to go into overdrive. "Kane," she whispered. "My name is Evan Kane."

The effect on Tate was nearly instantaneous. She froze with her lips less than an inch away from their intended target.

Kane? Oh Jesus, please. Please say it isn't so.

A frown creased her brows and she bit her bottom lip. "I know this is going to sound ridiculous, and I'm probably going to hate myself for asking, but I think I need to know. By any chance, are you related to Althea Kane? As in Secretary of State Althea Kane?"

Evan sighed. "She's my mother."

Before Tate's eyes, Evan Kane's seductive mood visibly shattered and conflicting emotions flashed across her face, hot and quick. Her expression darkened, and for an instant, there was something in her eyes, but she looked down before Tate could tell what was going on.

Even though she hadn't actually moved, Tate could feel the tremor beneath her skin and knew she was losing her. Could almost see the barriers closing down around her. *She expects me to walk away,* she realized and wasn't entirely surprised.

Knowing Althea Kane was her mother, it was probably the right thing to do. It was certainly the smart thing to do.

As a reporter, Tate knew regardless of the inroads Althea Kane had made, there would always be people unhappy with the president's choice for secretary of state. Just as she knew what could happen if the wrong person saw her with Evan Kane and correctly surmised what was happening. The potential fallout could wreak havoc with all of her carefully made career plans.

With a sigh, she leaned back, willed herself to relax, and acknowledged that from a pragmatic perspective, she should stop things from progressing before it was too late.

She might have even followed through if she hadn't felt the flutter of Evan's pulse. And if she hadn't heard the accelerated beating of her own heartbeat as she remembered the taste of Evan's mouth. Heat speared through her like lightning, and in that singular moment, Tate understood there was no turning back from the fierce need that grabbed her and held her in its grip. She could only think of her need to possess—and be possessed.

Evan's relationship to Althea Kane didn't matter, Tate decided with her last rational thought, as she slowly let out the breath she'd been holding and mentally switched off her internal alarm.

Sometimes words were overrated. She stopped any further protest or withdrawal by slipping her hands up behind Evan's neck and tugging her closer. Finally, without any hesitation or thought, she guided Evan's mouth to hers and kissed her.

Thoroughly.

Completely.

"I can live with that," she said against Evan's lips, barely recognizing her own voice. "And the answer is yes."

Evan raised an eyebrow as she stared at Tate, her expression inquisitive and confused. "Pardon?"

Tate exhaled a ragged breath. Feeling strangely disconnected, she tried to remember who she was—a woman who didn't, as a rule, indulge in casual sexual encounters. At the same time, she couldn't help but wonder how long it had been since she'd heard another woman's sigh. Or felt another woman's heat. Or tasted another woman's passion. And the truth was casual sexual attraction was light-years removed from the feelings hammering away in her chest.

Because, oh God, if sin could be tasted, it would taste like Evan Kane.

"How about I don't care if your mother can arrange it so the only reporting opportunity I'll ever find is covering afternoon traffic in rural Nebraska. My name is Tate McKenna and I want you, Evan Kane. As much as I think you want me," she said, before she crushed her mouth to Evan's.

CHAPTER TWO

W hen Tate awoke after a brief, dreamless sleep, the bedroom was dark. The air was still, and only the faintest light bled through the one small window, soft and indistinct. Vaguely sore, tired from too little sleep, she rubbed a hand over her face and blinked several times. But as her eyes adjusted to the darkness, she caught herself smiling.

To her right, she could just make out the woman in bed beside her, and she stayed very still so as not to wake her. In repose, Evan's breathing was deep and even, and the thin light enabled Tate to see the steady rise and fall of her small breasts.

She'd said yes.

Tate sighed, basking in the afterglow as her body remembered and ached.

At that moment, Evan shifted in sleep, and the top sheet slipped off her hip. Gazing at her with appreciative eyes, Tate was struck once again by her beauty.

She was perfect. The stunning face, damp and flushed from the heat. The warm, smooth skin. The long, lean, subtly muscled body. Just looking at her made Tate shiver, and her breath caught as moments from the previous night flashed in her mind.

Last night had been so damned good.

Happy birthday to me.

No, last night had been beyond incredible. Spontaneous combustion. The first time had been fast and hard and had sent her directly over the edge, but the second time…

The fire between them had raged on, and the night had dissolved into a mindless blur of pleasure. She could still hear herself whimpering, grabbing Evan's hair, arching into her wickedly skillful mouth and begging her. Please, please, *please.*

Evan had focused her seemingly boundless energy on learning Tate's body. Taking the time to explore what made her tremble, what made her ache and hunger, what made her come apart.

At times she had been edgy and intense. Other times, she'd been surprisingly acquiescent. Not exactly submissive, just seemingly content to let Tate lead, willing to follow her instructions not to move while Tate took her time devouring her.

And still other times, she had been gentle and sweet and funny. Tate couldn't remember ever having laughed so much while making love.

She had been thrilled to discover how responsive Evan was. How her body moved as pleasure filled her. How she had moaned Tate's name.

I want you, Tate. Again. I'm not nearly done with you.

She smiled.

They had made love repeatedly and with wild abandon, and Tate had felt something she hadn't expected to feel in what was supposed to be a one-night stand. It had felt right and had made her think impossible thoughts…like extending whatever this was beyond one night. But now, as night waned, she knew that would be impossible.

She could think of all the reasons she shouldn't see Evan again. All the reasons why it wouldn't work. They were two very different people, focused on careers that came with long, uncontrollable work hours. Extended absences. And then there were the dangers inherent in their jobs.

Her smile faded.

She loved her job. Passionately. Had known since she was ten that she'd wanted to be a journalist and counted Kate Webb, Martha Gellhorn, and Marie Colvin among her inspirations. And she had pursued the education and constructed a career plan that would get her where she wanted to be.

Standing as a witness. Documenting the truth demanded by history. Filing stories of courage, endurance, and the impact of war on ordinary people.

Contrary to what some believed, she wasn't naive. She knew the dangers inherent in her job. But she'd never wavered, despite the lure of safer, more secure jobs. And after focusing on her career for the last ten years, she liked where she was and had no regrets.

The only flaw in her plan, as she saw it, was she'd never learned the art of balancing career and relationships and, in fact, had failed every time she tried. Failed rather painfully the last time out, and being no fan of pain, she was in no hurry to try again.

She didn't have a specific timeline in mind. One day she hoped she'd find the right woman. A partner for life. But not right now—or for the foreseeable future. For now she needed to stay focused.

As much as she loved her work, other challenges beckoned, and she knew she had one more year in her—two at most—doing frontline reporting. Until then, the best she could hope for were occasional nights like this.

Hot, unforgettable nights. No strings, no commitments, and no emotional entanglements. Anything more than that was simply out of the question. And getting involved with someone like the daughter of the secretary of state certainly wasn't part of the plan.

There was only one problem. She never would have thought a one-night stand could become so addictive so quickly. And having been with Evan Kane on this one occasion, it was inconceivable she wouldn't be with her again.

It was certainly something to think about.

Turning onto her side, Tate spent the next few minutes intoxicated by Evan's fragrance, feeling her warmth burn against her hotter than any sun. And when she could no longer fight the silken allure, she leaned up on her elbow and traced the perfect symmetry of Evan's face.

Warm. Smooth. Flawless.

It was the face of an angel with a devilishly sensuous mouth. Damp strands of short dark hair clung to the moisture at her temples, and her long dark lashes stirred as they cast shadows over her cheekbones.

Tate savored the moment as a fresh jolt of desire sizzled through her. *Jesus, but she's so damned beautiful.* It was all she could think as she touched and tasted again, enjoying the sleepy warmth of her.

She tasted like ambrosia and felt like heaven. She stroked the silky texture of Evan's bare arm. So soft on the surface, but she could also feel her strength as muscles tensed and shifted just beneath her skin.

Evan sighed contentedly and was already smiling before she opened her eyes and saw Tate.

"Hey, beautiful lady," she said. "I thought I'd dreamed you." She wrapped her arms around Tate's neck, pulling her closer. "But reality works out so much better, don't you think?"

The predawn light was as soft as the slight breeze sifting through the window when Evan slipped quietly out of the bathroom. Her body was still pleasantly tender from a night of uninhibited passion, but she was freshly showered and fully dressed, with her short hair finger combed and smelling faintly of vanilla from Tate's shampoo.

Last night had amazed her. Adrenaline fueled, like standing in the path of an inbound jet. Tate's taste lingered still and, for a minute, the memories of the two of them intimately tangled flashed through her mind.

But it had also been a long time since she'd spent the entire night with a woman, and she wasn't sure what to expect of the morning after.

She paused, settling against the door frame when she caught sight of Tate standing by the window looking lost in thought. Her eyes were nearly closed, but Evan could tell she wasn't relaxed, noting the tension in the tightly controlled set of her shoulders.

She watched Tate push her hair out of her eyes, turning just enough to reveal her face in profile, and Evan found herself captivated all over again. She knew one thing for certain. With her hair sleep tousled, her eyes shadowed, and her lips soft and slightly parted, Tate looked every bit as beautiful in the dim light of morning as she had under the glittering chandeliers in the hotel ballroom.

"There's something unbelievably sexy about the line of a woman's bare back," she murmured in quiet appreciation.

Tate turned abruptly, causing her hair to swirl around her shoulders like a cloud of silk. Control slipped for an instant and the startled expression on her face swiftly changed, showing flashes of both delight and uncertainty.

"I thought you'd gone."

Evan ignored the sudden dryness in her mouth and shook her head. "No, still here. I hope you don't mind, but I helped myself to your shower." She gave a quick grin. "Just in case I run into anyone, I thought it best if it didn't look like I'd spent the entire night—well, doing exactly what we were doing last night."

Unexpectedly, Tate blushed. She cast her eyes around the room, and as if suddenly realizing she was naked, she crossed the room and slipped back into bed.

Evan wasn't certain how to interpret Tate's actions and gave her a long contemplative look. The heated blush covering a great deal of fair skin was the curse of a redhead. Still, she couldn't recall the last time she had seen a woman blush.

"Hey, what's going on?"

Tate merely shook her head as she slowly raised her eyes. "I'm sorry, I'm being an idiot."

Evan moved toward her, but when she laid a hand on Tate's shoulder, it was shrugged off, causing her to step back. "Tell me what's wrong."

"It's nothing. Trust me." Tate paused, seemed hesitant to continue. "It's just—damn, I'm sorry. I thought I could do this, but it seems I don't know how."

"How to do what?"

With a visible effort, she pulled herself together. Calm again, detached, she looked at Evan. "It's been a long time since I've been with anyone, and it seems I no longer know how things are supposed to end."

"Does it have to—Oh, you thought I'd left while you were still sleeping."

Tate looked away but didn't try to argue. Encouraged, Evan leaned closer. "You were sleeping so soundly I didn't have the heart to wake you when I got up. But trust me. I had every intention of waking you before I left. If for no other reason than to tell you last night was amazing. And to tell you I want to see you again."

Tate blushed once again. Closing her eyes, she held herself very still. There followed a long silence, but when she opened her eyes, she managed a rueful smile. "You don't have to say any of that. I don't need promises," she said softly. "I'm just glad you're still here. It'd be nice if you stayed a little longer, but I'm not looking for more than that."

Evan arched a brow. Tilting her head, she continued to silently gaze at Tate with those fascinating, inscrutable eyes, looking away only for an instant as she glanced at her watch, a complex aviator's timepiece that gleamed dully on her wrist. "Damn, I'm sorry, but I—"

"It's all right, Evan. I understand."

"No, I don't think you do." Evan shook her head and her mouth curved with the faint trace of a smile. "Let me try this again. Tate, if this was a different place and time, I would get back in your bed and we would make love until you forgot all about whatever's causing those shadows in your eyes."

"That would work."

"Good to know. Now tell me what's bothering you."

Tate swallowed. "It's just…this wasn't supposed to happen, and I can't afford the complication right now."

"But it has happened, and it doesn't have to be complicated. People become lovers every day. We're simply two adults who happen to want each other."

"It's not that simple."

"But it can be, and another time, I'd be happy to debate the issue. The only problem is it's nearly morning and staying any longer is a complication neither of us can afford. Bahrain may be one of the more tolerant nations in the Middle East, but traditional religious mores still view what we did in this room as immoral. There are no concessions made, regardless of my last name or how long a shadow my mother happens to cast. In fact, who and what I am makes me a more likely target for attention."

Of course. And she's not just the secretary of state's daughter, she's a navy officer. A pilot. Tate sat upright on the bed, the sheet gliding like water over her naked skin and pooling at her waist. Even if a person overlooked her sexual preferences, Evan Kane was a woman navigating a dangerous, testosterone-fueled, male-dominated world.

Message received. Loud and clear. Tate grimaced as she thought about it.

"Please, don't be angry with me," Evan said softly.

"I'm not angry. I just can't believe I've not given any thought to where we are or who you are and how this might affect you. And I should have, given I've been living and working in the Middle East for several years."

Tate hesitated before looking up at Evan once again. "At the moment, I also happen to be covering your mother's official sweep through the region. I'm not certain, but…damn, I'm pretty sure I told you that at some point last night. At least I hope I did."

"You did. Don't worry. I'm well aware you're a reporter."

"Good, but it does beg the question, doesn't it? If this"—Tate indicated the two of them with one hand—"is putting you at risk, why did you suggest it last night? Why did you spend the night with me?"

Evan looked at her with a startled expression. "I would have thought it was obvious."

Tate crossed her arms over her chest and waited, her gaze fixed on Evan.

"Since you need to ask, you should know it had a lot to do with seeing you from across the ballroom last night and thinking you had the most incredible green eyes I'd ever seen."

Tate's brows lifted.

"And maybe because who I was had nothing to do with the fact you wanted me as much as I wanted you," Evan added. "Should I continue?"

Tate knew she was being drawn in. Fascinated. But she sensed there was something else that remained unsaid. "No. But maybe I need to be certain. Is this—what we did—going to create any kind of personal problem for you?"

Evan shook her head. "No. The pilots in my squadron only want to know I'll be there for them when it's all on the line. As for anything else—it's just never been an issue."

"What about your mother?"

"That's even less of a problem."

"Why's that?"

"Because we live by a simple rule established some time ago. As long as I don't embarrass her, what I do and who I do it with isn't even a blip on her radar." Without shifting her gaze from Tate, Evan's face became so expressionless she might have been thinking of anything... or nothing at all. "You look surprised. It might help if you understand. Other than last night, Althea and I haven't spoken—I mean, we haven't had a normal exchange or conversation that didn't end up with harsh words and bruised feelings—in longer than I care to remember."

Tate thought back to the image she had of Althea Kane, looking pale and shocked as a tall navy commander offered her hand and led her onto the dance floor. "No offense, but why the hell not?"

"Because Althea and I fundamentally disagree with some of the choices I've made in my life."

"What does that mean? What did you do that could have been so bad?"

Evan simply looked at her and shrugged. "Althea wasn't exactly happy—no, that's not right—I guess you could say she disapproved of my decision to enlist in the navy."

Tate tried to remember what she knew about Althea Kane's family but quickly realized there wasn't a lot. Somehow Althea and her equally high-profile husband had managed to keep their private lives and, more specifically, the lives of their children away from the media glare. Beyond knowing the power couple had two children, possibly in their twenties, Tate really knew nothing about them. She turned to Evan, looking for clarity.

"I'm not sure I'm following any of this. To my knowledge, your mother has spent most of her career in service to her country. There was even a rumor some time ago she might throw her hat in the ring and go for the top job, but instead she came out in support of Max Renfield."

"All true."

"Then what could possibly be wrong with one of her children choosing to do the same by serving in the military?"

"It's a long story." Evan laughed. "Really, it's the kind of story that's best saved for a rainy afternoon accompanied by a couple of bottles of wine. And we don't have that much time right now. Maybe we can try again another time."

There was a protracted pause as both women looked at each other. Tate finally broke the seemingly endless silence, exhaling with a nervous laugh. "Maybe," she said faintly. "Long stories are usually the best kind. And maybe I'll even spring for the wine."

One eyebrow rising, Evan gave Tate a level stare. "Sounds like a date."

"Maybe." Tate shifted uncomfortably, aware that somewhere in the middle of this conversation, things had changed and she might have just agreed to see Evan again. She took a deep breath. Then another.

"Tate, tell me something. Other than one night of really great sex, what do you think is happening here?"

"I honestly don't know." Tate cleared her throat, folded her arms across her chest, and decided there was no turning back. "You need to understand the kind of person I am. I've never been capable of no-strings sex. Nor have I ever jumped into bed with a woman I just met, so you're a first for me."

"I like the sound of that."

Tate released a small laugh. "Don't let it go to your head, Commander. And don't get me wrong. Quite obviously I'm not exactly an innocent. But for the longest time now, my career has come first. And if by chance I meet someone, normally I like to get to know a woman before making the physical leap. I'm really not into the one-night stand thing."

"It's not."

"It's not what?"

"It's not a one-night stand. I'd like to think of this simply as the first night of many."

Tate swallowed and fought the surprise that swept through her. "Oh, really," she said dryly.

"Yes, really," Evan replied. "Look, I don't want to push you or complicate your life. And I certainly don't want to take this anywhere you don't want it to go. But while I have no idea where things between us could go, I'd like to find out."

Tate remained silent for a moment. "I'm not sure what you're really saying."

"For now, I'm just saying I don't want it to end when I leave this room. I can appreciate how important your career is to you. At the moment, mine also happens to take up a great deal of my time and energy. But I'd still like to see you again."

"Is that a fact?"

"I never say anything I don't mean."

"Good to know."

"It should help that I'm doing back-to-back sea tours. It means I'll be in the region for at least the next year."

"As it happens, my plans have me staying with the Middle East bureau at least one more year. But still—"

"Tate." Evan stopped her gently. "I appreciate that between your schedule and mine, the circumstances are far from ideal. But I'm also pretty sure we can work around it."

She was doing it again, Tate realized. Tempting her with something that simply couldn't be. She tried again to set things straight. "I don't think you understand. My job…my last relationship ended rather badly because of it."

"If your last girlfriend couldn't cope with what you do, that was her problem. Her loss. Believe it or not, I've met women who weren't crazy about the idea of getting involved with a navy pilot with an eight-year service commitment."

"Really?" Tate found herself suppressing a laugh. "I find that hard to believe."

"I know, sad but true." Evan smiled as she threaded her fingers through Tate's hair and gently cupped her neck. "So why don't we just take things as they come and not look for complications?"

Tate found herself distracted by the gentle touch of Evan's hand. "Complications?"

"That's right. And if we're going to have any chance of seeing each other again, I've got to get out of here now, before someone sees me. Because while you may not have had any idea who I was when we first met last night, there are others, like Ambassador Connors, as well as half a dozen members of Althea's staff, who have known me since I was a child."

Tate found herself nodding. "Can I get you something to eat before you go? I'm pretty certain I've got some kind of cereal. Or I might be able to come up with some toast if you're not too picky about best-before dates."

"Um—thanks, that's okay. I'll just grab a coffee from somewhere on my way back to the *Nimitz*."

"Coward. Didn't your mother ever tell you that breakfast's the most important meal of the day?"

"Are we talking about Althea?" Evan arched an eyebrow, her expression bright and amused. "You've met my mother, haven't you?"

Tate laughed. "Good point. What was I thinking?"

Without breaking eye contact, Evan leaned closer and kissed her, more gently than ever before. Her mouth was soft and sweet and hungry, and Tate pressed her lips together to hold on to the taste. Stared and tried to memorize the gray of her eyes and how they reflected her laughter.

"Life's all about timing, beautiful lady," Evan said, brushing the backs of her fingers across Tate's cheek.

"Keep your eyes open and make sure you catch the third wire, Commander."

Evan grinned. "Every chance I get. And you keep your head down, McKenna. Especially around my mother." With languid grace she rose, sent one last smile over her shoulder, and then walked out of the room. The door closed gently behind her.

CHAPTER THREE

When Evan walked out of her flat, part of Tate wanted to pull the covers over her head and sleep for the rest of the day, while another part resisted the urge to jump up and watch Evan leave her building. Worse, after only a few minutes, she found she was already missing the sound of Evan's voice. Not a happy discovery and something she would have to consider and deal with sooner rather than later.

But reality beckoned.

Shaking her head, she untangled the sheet wrapped around her waist and got out of bed. After taking a couple of extra-strength ibuprofen for the headache that was brewing behind her eyes, she padded to the bathroom looking forward to a long, cool shower. And by the time she had dressed and made her way to the embassy, she felt almost human.

The buzz among the staff was palpable.

"What's happened?" she asked absently, continuing to replay her night with Evan while trying to pour coffee into a mug without spilling any.

An embassy staffer looked up. "There was a bombing at a club around three o'clock this morning. How the hell did you miss it, McKenna?"

Instantly alert, Tate looked up. "A bomb? Jesus, how bad?"

"Bad enough. Five dead. Fourteen injured, including several crew members from the *Ronald Reagan*."

"Shit."

"All shore leave was canceled effective immediately, and all navy personnel have been recalled to their ships," Jillian added softly as she entered the room. She paused and the conversation resumed around her while she regarded Tate, then gave a slight grin and wiggled her eyebrows suggestively. "I'll assume by the tired but smug oh-so-satisfied look you're wearing this morning, the commander more than lived up to expectations before leaving you to return to her ship."

There was a momentary silence as Tate considered an appropriate answer. "It was, um, I had—" She locked eyes with Jillian, felt herself blush, and smiled sheepishly. "God, it was amazing. I had a wonderful time."

"I'm happy for you. I applaud your taste in women. And a part of me is insanely jealous."

"Only part of you?"

Jillian's eyes changed, darkened. She wasn't smiling anymore as she closed the distance between them. "I'm not sure if I'm stepping in where I don't belong, and if you want me to stay out of it, I will. But I had a chance to learn a few things about your commander after you left last evening."

Tate nodded, knowing precisely where the conversation was leading. She lifted her chin slightly and gave a philosophical shrug. "I'm well aware of who she is, Jillian. In fact, I knew who she was before I made up my mind to leave with her, and it made no difference to me."

"Really?"

"It was a personal decision."

"Did you give any thought to what it might look like? A reporter taking the secretary of state's daughter home from an embassy party?" Jillian's voice was soft as she continued. "The daughter spending the night with you? Tate, she's public property. What the hell were you thinking?"

That I wanted her and it's nobody's business who ends up in my bed. Tate considered her response as she toyed with her coffee mug, then thought about Althea Kane and her take-no-prisoners reputation.

"Do you think this is going to create a problem with my job? Should I talk to the bureau chief about finding someone to cover for me for the duration of Kane's tour through the region? Preferably before she has me reassigned to McMurdo Station?"

Jillian's expression softened. She gave a small laugh and shook her head. "I don't think you need to start packing for an extended visit to Antarctica."

"What makes you say that?"

"Because your reputation as a journalist is that you're fearless, passionate, and very good at what you do." She paused and took a deep breath. "But also because I understand, last night's tango notwithstanding, relations between mother and daughter are in the strained and not speaking category, and they hadn't seen each other for quite some time. At least, that's the gossip from Kane's staff. So you don't need to get someone to cover for you."

Relief washed through her. "Good to know. I happen to like my job."

"But, Tate, as your friend, I have to ask. Do you know what you're doing?"

Tate remembered the taste of Evan's mouth, the soft sounds she made, the way her body moved and arched against her. Remembered and wanted. "Do I know what I'm doing?" she repeated. "No, not at the moment."

Jillian sighed and shook her head once again. "I think you're crazy. I also happen to believe what you do in your private life, with Evan Kane or with anyone else, is no one's business."

Tate sensed there was more, beyond a friend's reluctance to give unsolicited advice. "I hear a *but* coming," she said lightly. "What is it?"

"You're both intelligent women. If last night was just a one-night fling and you're never going to see the very hot commander again, then no harm, no foul."

"That's great, except Evan said she wants to see me again."

"And what do you want?"

Tate frowned and pressed her lips together as she stared at Jillian. "I honestly don't know." Feeling a surge of frustration, she blew out a breath. "I don't deny I feel a strong physical reaction to Evan—I mean, hell, you've seen her. You also know I'm lousy at relationships and I'm not ready to go down that road again. But I don't know if I can do a no-strings, just-sex kind of thing."

Given their friendship, her response could hardly be surprising and was enough to make Jillian smile. "Sweetie, you're not lousy at relationships. You just haven't met the right woman."

"I'm not looking for the right woman."

"I know you're not. And until you do, if you're going to consider a purely physical relationship, I can't think of a better choice than the made-for-sin Lieutenant Commander Kane."

Tate narrowed her eyes. "Are you seriously *encouraging* me?"

"Sure, why not? You liked her, didn't you?"

"Yes, but that doesn't mean it will work."

"Why not?"

"Because—" Tate bit back the sarcasm about to roll off her tongue. "Look, let's just forget about this conversation, okay?"

But Jillian waited expectantly and wouldn't let her off the hook. "Tell me why it won't work first."

"Because, damn it. My job makes things complicated. You've seen it firsthand. The odds are high she'll get leave and want to get together. But it will be like it's always been. I'll be unavailable because I've gone to Cairo or Benghazi or Kabul on some story. And after a couple of tries, no matter how good the sex is, she'll grow tired and move on."

"I agree it's bound to happen at some point," Jillian countered mildly, "but I'd think if anyone is going to understand the unpredictable nature of your job, it's a pilot serving on the *Nimitz*. Isn't she just as likely to be unavailable when you have an urge to get together?"

Tate opened her mouth to protest and then stopped as she realized Jillian was right. Well, damn. What was she supposed to say to that? Turning, she narrowed her eyes and stared at her sharply. But all Jillian did was smile blandly.

"Let me know how it works out," she said before she slipped out of the room.

❖

The moment she stepped on board the *Nimitz,* Evan was met by three fellow pilots—Deacon Walker, J.D. McNeely, and Will Jones— all sparking with an as yet unidentified energy. Not necessarily a good sign, she mused, but after the night she'd spent with Tate, she doubted if anything they said could dampen her mood.

Brow lifted, she smiled. "A reception committee? How sweet."

Of the three men facing her, she'd known Deacon the longest. He was not only her wingman. He'd been her closest friend since she'd abandoned graduate school and joined the navy. The scowl he sent her was therefore rendered meaningless.

"Commander," he said, casually saluting. "About time you got back. The captain wants to meet with us ASAP."

"Oh?"

"Yeah, scuttlebutt has it he wants us to participate in some high-level exercises with a group of air force pilots from the UK and Saudi Arabia. He's waiting to hear you think we're up for it and won't embarrass the US Navy."

Because she recognized the gleam in his eye, Evan narrowed her own. "Does that mean I won't have to spend the next two weeks serving as Landing Signal Officer while a bunch of nuggets do carrier qualifications?"

Deacon almost managed to maintain a straight face. "Why yes, ma'am, I believe it does."

"Cool." Evan grinned. "Do I have time to get changed?"

Jones responded, "Hell, no. Doesn't pay to keep the captain waiting. He might pass this opportunity on to someone else, so you're just going to have to see him looking like you spent the night with some gorgeous woman screaming out your name." He paused for effect before grinning and adding, "Of course, I say that with the utmost respect, Commander."

"He's just jealous because you score with the ladies more than he does," Deacon said.

"Everyone scores with the ladies more than Jones," McNeely said dismissively.

"Unfortunate, but true," Jones conceded. "But if the commander would be willing to give me some pointers—"

"What?" Evan choked on a surprised laugh and felt her face heat but wasn't certain if it was embarrassment or annoyance. She shook her head, muttered something inventive, and blew out a breath. "Sorry, Jones, but that's one discussion we'll never have."

"I don't believe your suggestion is anatomically possible," Deacon said with a laugh as he fell in step beside her, while Jones and McNeely quickly walked ahead. "Don't mind Jones. He's been jealous ever since you hooked up with that sexy British pilot when we were in Tokyo."

"Julianna Spencer."

"That's the one." He paused and glanced at Evan. "Since the Brits are involved, I wonder if the lovely Captain Spencer will be part of the upcoming exercise."

Considering, remembering, Evan looked away. "That would make it interesting. She's a hell of a pilot."

"That's it? No interest in revisiting a past conquest?"

"Not particularly."

Something in her face must have given her away, although Evan would have sworn she kept it blank and unreadable. She felt Deacon's questioning gaze and silently cursed. He knew her—too well—and there was something about the way he looked at her that could always get to the core. Immediately, she tensed, closed up. And he saw it.

"Evan?" He lowered his voice. "Is everything all right? Did something happen last night after you left the embassy party?"

Ten seconds passed, then twenty. "Maybe. I guess so." She swallowed. "All I know is I met the most amazing woman." Her voice trailed off and she shook her head helplessly.

"The sexy redhead?"

She responded with a quick nod. "No smart remarks?"

"Never crossed my mind, Commander." But the corner of his lips quirked.

"Smart-ass. Don't know why, but I've always liked that about you."

Deacon said nothing, but his grin widened.

Evan struggled not to smile back at him, ended up laughing instead. "Damn it, Deacon. Don't grin while I'm trying to figure out how I got in over my head so quickly."

Obediently, Deacon wiped the smile from his face. "Sorry." He watched her a moment longer. "Are you thinking about seeing her again?"

Evan shook her head. Saw the disappointment in Deacon's eyes. "Don't need to think about it, I know I'm going to see her again. Just have to figure out the when and how."

She hadn't meant to say it aloud, nearly jolted at the sound of her own voice as she watched Deacon's grin flash.

"I'll be damned," he said softly.

Yeah, except the lady wasn't certain she was interested. Now all Evan had to do was figure out how to convince Tate to give her a chance.

❖

A full week flew by before Tate had the opportunity to try and learn more about Evan Kane. Seven grueling, chaotic days spent breathing the dust and sand and detritus of thousands of years as she chased interviews and stories throughout a troubled region.

Finally, exhausted and alone in her tiny flat, she lit a candle, poured herself a glass from the bottle of California red Jillian had managed to score for her, and allowed herself to decompress. The wine eased the dryness in her throat and reminded her of home. And in the gathering darkness, as she circled a finger around the top of her half-full glass, she watched the candle's flame reflected in the wine and thought of Evan.

At the moment, she had more than enough on her plate professionally, yet as hectic as the past week had been, Tate had found herself constantly distracted by thoughts of Evan. Too often for her own peace of mind. She had also spent an inordinate amount of time wishing she would hear from her. A voice mail or an e-mail. Anything that would let her know Evan was at least thinking about her.

No one had ever captured her interest the way Evan Kane had managed to do. And the ache was amplified each time she heard or saw military jets flying high overhead. Or each time she saw someone in a navy uniform.

Or each time she breathed.

But there had been no call, no e-mail, and Tate began to wonder if, despite Evan's assurances to the contrary, the night they had spent together had indeed been a one-time occurrence. One night of hot sex and nothing more. If that was the case, she'd gotten exactly what she'd wanted.

She didn't bother asking herself why it bothered her. Why it mattered. She only knew it did and she was too tired to deny it.

It was possible her usually flawless memory had exaggerated Evan's appeal. But no. Evan's appeal was undeniable, and Tate remembered the pull with perfect clarity. Just thinking about her—the laughing eyes, the sensuous mouth—tugged at her. She wanted to feel the attraction again, to enjoy it, to understand it.

Still the question remained. What did she really know about Evan Kane?

She was drop-dead gorgeous. She was bright, laughed easily, and could dance the tango like no one she had ever known. She was adventurous and uninhibited.

And, damn it all, Tate was unbelievably attracted to her.

Acting on impulse, she reached for her laptop and initiated a search before she could question her own motives too closely. Maybe if she could relegate the enigma that was Evan Kane to a tidy little niche in her mind, she could forget about her and move on. But as long as there were so many unanswered questions, Evan would continue to linger in her thoughts.

Three hours later, she sat in the darkness, surprised by how limited the information available actually was. Considering how often they themselves made the news, Althea and Robert Kane had quite clearly done an admirable job of protecting their children's privacy.

But not completely. Completely was impossible in the information age, Tate thought, as Evan's image stared back at her from the computer screen. The photograph she was looking at was her favorite of all the images she'd come across. It had been taken at a party political fundraiser, when Evan would have been perhaps eighteen.

She had a face photographers would love. But there could be no question Evan was even more striking in person than in her pictures, Tate decided. Because of her vitality. Her intelligence. Her humor. In person, she was irresistible.

At the time the photograph was taken, her face had been framed by a tumble of long ebony hair that gave her a wild, sexy look—a free spirit in the midst of political movers and shakers. Wearing a slim-fitting Alexander McQueen with a plunging neckline, diamonds sparkling in her ears, Evan looked sleek and sophisticated. Her angular face might be younger, but she was instantly recognizable. There was no mistaking the luminous gray eyes, the high cheekbones, and the boldly sensuous mouth flanked by the twin dimples.

Her smile was full and beckoning. Provocative.

Through the wonders of Google, Tate learned Evan Kane had been educated at private schools in Europe and Washington and had graduated from Stanford with a degree in aeronautical engineering. She'd been everywhere by the time she was seventeen and spoke seven or eight languages, with Farsi, Arabic, Mandarin, and Japanese among them. With those skills and her mother's connections, it was a wonder no one in Washington had reeled her in yet.

There were also numerous hits on her brother Alex—a twin— described as an out-and-proud artist who was rapidly making a name for himself in the West Coast art scene.

She continued to sit, staring at the photograph without moving until long after the candle burned out.

The flowers arrived two days later, a crystal vase filled with roses and Asiatic lilies in varying shades of yellow and orange. Inexplicably touched by the gesture, Tate tried to remember the last time anyone had sent her flowers, but nothing came to mind.

The card simply read *Evan*. Perhaps more was unnecessary, she mused, especially when she could Google the language of the flowers in the delicately beautiful arrangement.

The lilies symbolized feminine sexuality, while the roses spoke of passion.

Yellow for the promise of a new beginning. Orange for desire.

Are you trying to tell me something, Commander?

CHAPTER FOUR

It was more than two full weeks after the embassy party before Tate finally received the telephone call she'd been alternately dreading and hoping for.

"Hello, beautiful lady."

She would have recognized that voice anywhere. In automatic response, Tate's heart jolted and began to beat just a little faster. "Commander, I was just thinking about you."

"Were you? Good thoughts, I hope."

"I was thinking I wanted to thank you for the flowers, but I didn't know how to contact you. They were beautiful, so thank you."

"I'm glad you liked them." Evan's pleasure reached out across the distance. "It was a bit of a challenge getting them to you, since I didn't actually have your address, just a vague recollection of where your flat is located. But I believed getting them to you was necessary."

"Why is that?"

"We've been flying simulated dogfights and strike missions for the past couple of weeks with a group of air force pilots from the UK and Saudi Arabia—a kind of high-speed hide-and-seek."

"Sounds like fun."

"It has been. But it's also been unbelievably challenging and intense with very little downtime, and that's meant I haven't had a chance to call you. And I didn't want you to think I'd forgotten about you. So I hoped the flowers would let you know I was thinking about you, and maybe when you looked at them, they might make you think of me. Maybe help you remember."

"I'd have thought of you anyway," Tate responded honestly. *In fact, I've not been able to stop thinking about you. But I still don't know what that means. I just know I'm not ready to tell you that, Commander. At least not just yet.*

"I'm glad you've been thinking about me because I find myself free for the next seventy-two hours." Evan's voice dropped hypnotically as she continued. "And I'm really hoping you might see your way to spending some of those hours with me."

"How many hours, exactly, were you hoping for, Commander?"

"As many as I can get. I'm not greedy, but you've got to know I'll take all of them if I can."

There was a pause the length of two heartbeats before Tate could bring herself to speak. Long enough to tell herself to slow down and think about what she was doing. Long enough for her to reject her own advice. "Do you want to meet at my flat? Do you remember how to get there?"

"I've a better idea. You meet me. I'm at the Ritz-Carlton. Room six one four."

Tate closed her eyes and swallowed. "I understand room service at the Ritz is excellent."

"Is that a yes?"

"I can't get away for at least another hour—two at the most."

"I can wait."

"Then why don't you make yourself comfortable?" Tate said, her voice barely above a whisper. "And maybe try to have a nap because I don't think you'll be getting much sleep tonight."

Evan laughed. A low, sexy rumble.

Tate immediately felt herself become damp and fought to contain a moan. "I'll be there as soon as I can."

"I wasn't supposed to be the one to join the navy," Evan said when she finally shared her story with Tate. "It was supposed to be my brother, Alex. We're twins, but it was meant to be his destiny, as the firstborn and only son."

It was late in the evening and the light in the room had grown diffused, the shadows long. They had spent the better part of the previous day and night reconnecting. Patience forgotten, they had come together hungrily, quickly sliding into each other's skin. Hands touching, bodies straining, mouths greedy for more.

Now they sat cross-legged on the bed in a tumble of sex-warmed, twisted sheets while sharing a bottle of wine. Evan noted with amusement that on an empty stomach, the effects of the smooth merlot were nearly instantaneous, leaving her feeling faintly lightheaded.

But, strangely and maybe for the first time, she wanted a woman—she wanted Tate—to know, to understand who she was. The wine simply made it easier to talk.

In vino veritas…In wine there is truth.

"I'm not sure how much of this is public knowledge, but as far back as you want to go, every generation of Kanes has served their country in the military. Specifically, in the navy. My father served just as his father did and his father's father before him. Generation after generation, good little sailors all."

"Okay." There was a faint echo of confusion in Tate's voice. "But—"

Evan shrugged. "But when it came time for my father's son to step up and continue the time-honored tradition, sadly Alex turned out to be a poor candidate for military service."

"Because he's gay?"

Evan silently studied Tate, measured. "You've been doing research," she chided softly. "That's cheating."

Tate flushed. Her lips parted, and for an instant, just the tip of her tongue showed between her teeth. "I'm sorry."

Over the rim of her nearly empty wineglass, Evan watched Tate's eyes drop as she looked away. "It's okay, Tate," she said, keeping her voice low and even. No censure. "You're a reporter. I would think it's in your DNA, and I should have expected no less."

Putting the wineglass down on the small bedside table, she closed her eyes and held up a hand, allowing a long moment to pass in silence as she gathered her thoughts. "So, yes, because he was gay, but it was more than that," she said. "You've got to remember ten years ago, open homosexuality was still banned in the US military, and Alex knew he'd never be able to go back in the closet. He'd been out since he turned fifteen, and by the time he turned twenty he was completely and proudly open about his life, had fallen madly in love, and was in the midst of establishing a solid reputation as an artist."

"In other words, he didn't exactly fit into the military mold," Tate summarized succinctly.

"Right."

"But weren't you also—? Or didn't you know?"

"Oh, I knew." Evan smiled wryly. "But after the challenges my parents were put through dealing with Alex's very public coming out, mostly because of Althea's political aspirations, it was decided—I decided—it would be best for everyone if I just remained discreet."

"That had to be hard for you."

"It wouldn't have been my first choice, and at first it seemed so damned inauthentic. But I quickly realized the only thing that really mattered was the people who were important to me knew the truth. My family. My friends. And when the whole family drama began about who would serve in the military, it proved to be rather fortunate. I knew Alex would never survive any of it. Certainly not life in the navy. But I knew I could."

"What did Alex have to say?"

"He wanted me to tell our parents that neither of us was prepared to fulfill what was in his opinion an outdated family tradition."

"But you couldn't do that to them," Tate guessed, quiet acceptance in her voice.

Evan felt slightly stunned by her statement—and maybe a little pleased. "No, I couldn't. So I enlisted."

"What happened?"

"My father, needless to say, was shocked when he found out what I'd done. He told me he understood why I did it and said he was proud of me. But he also knew I would end up serving in a war zone, and he begged me to do whatever I had to do to stay alive."

"And your mother?"

"Althea was another story," Evan said reluctantly. "She refused to accept my decision. We had words. Angry words. And then we simply stopped speaking."

"I don't get it. What was the problem?"

"I think, in part, the problem is rooted in an archaic belief she has that military service is an obligation meant to be fulfilled by the male side of the family. Someone must have forgotten to tell her a Y chromosome isn't really a requirement. Go figure." She gave Tate an irreverent grin. "But, more importantly, Althea's always needed to be in control, and I dared to embrace a different kind of life than she envisioned for me."

"What was it she wanted for you?"

Evan thought about it then shrugged. "I don't honestly know. Something in the foreign service, I suppose. We never actually talked about it, and by the time she found out I'd enlisted, it was much too late for her to do anything about it."

"How the hell could she not know what you were doing?"

"Tate," Evan began gently, "I don't know what kind of family environment you grew up in—"

"I'd say it was a pretty ordinary one. I'm an only child. My father's a doctor, has a busy family practice. My mother works for my dad, manages his office. But, mostly, at least while I was growing up, she was a stay-at-home mom. She attended every parent-teacher meeting and went to every basketball and softball game I ever played."

She searched Evan's face for a second or two then sighed. "I know you're going to argue your mother was different, and I get that. I've met her. But, Jesus, Evan. She was still your mother."

Evan gave an eloquent shrug and smiled in spite of herself. "The definition of motherhood is subject to debate when it comes to Althea. It's not that she didn't love us. She did. Alex and I always knew that. But her priorities were always a little different. And the point is life happened. Politics happened."

"Politics trumped motherhood?"

"What can I say? Althea was busy being the attorney general and weighing her options for higher office. As far as she was concerned, her job with her children was done. Alex was in San Francisco painting, and I was supposed to be safely tucked away in graduate school, not at Aviation Officer Candidate School." She fell silent as she picked up her wine and finished it.

Tate shivered. "Well, I for one am glad you chose the path you took. Otherwise I never would have met you. We wouldn't be…here. Like this. But maybe you could have chosen something that doesn't have you landing a jet at night on a moving runway the size of a postage stamp in the middle of the Arabian Sea. Or maybe didn't put you directly—"

"In the line of fire?"

"Well, yeah."

"You do know your job's dangerous too, don't you?"

"Of course, but I try not to think about it. Otherwise, I wouldn't be able to function. But while we haven't known each other long, I know I don't want to report how Lieutenant Commander Evan Kane, the daughter of the secretary of state, was shot down while flying a mission."

"I'm sorry about that," Evan said quietly. "I really am. I don't mean to put you in that position."

"Do the risks bother you?"

"Not really. I know there's no margin for error, but I've trained for every contingency, and I know I'm doing something that matters. It also happens I love to fly. I've had my private pilot's license since I was seventeen, and if I had to join the navy, it just made sense to do it as an aviator. Just think of all the cool planes I get to play with."

She saw a glimmer of a grin on Tate's face.

"And, truthfully, I wasn't really thinking about risk when I made my decision. I was simply trying to find a solution I could live with, while ensuring Alex didn't have to compromise who he is." She hesitated before continuing more slowly. "But I also think it's part of why I've avoided getting involved with anyone. At least until I could finish my service commitment. Geography alone can be a relationship killer, and I never thought it would be fair to anyone."

Tate gave her a sharp look, her eyes searching, and there was a subtle change in her expression as she held her gaze. "And now?"

"And now," Evan repeated, and tipped her head back to grin wickedly. "Now the clock's ticking and I'm coming down to the wire. Tick-tock. It won't be long until I complete my service commitment. Close enough to start thinking about all the possibilities life has to offer beyond the navy, don't you think?"

She could feel Tate's heartbeat pick up, see it accelerate in the pulse at her throat. "Could be," Tate murmured and quickly changed the subject. "Have you really been flying since you were seventeen?"

"Twelve, actually. But the law said I couldn't get my license until I turned seventeen. I'll have you know I restored a 1942 Tiger Moth from the ground up while I was doing my undergrad. I still have it, although it's in storage."

"Am I supposed to know what a Tiger Moth is?"

"It's a two-seater biplane. They were originally built by de Havilland in the 1930s and 1940s and used as trainers by the British Royal Air Force."

"A biplane? Like the Wright brothers flew?" Tate's eyes widened. "Are you crazy?"

"What are you implying? You think it's okay for the US Navy to trust me with an eighty-five million dollar aircraft, but I can't be trusted to fly an old biplane? Keep that up, McKenna, and I won't take you flying when we get home."

Tate blinked. "You're going to take me flying?"

Evan nodded and gave Tate a flicker of a grin.

"When we get home?"

"You're not planning on staying in Bahrain forever, are you?"

Tate shook her head and stared at Evan. "You're going to take me flying in your biplane." A statement, not a question.

"Trust me, you'll love it."

"Why is that?"

"Because there's nothing like the thrill of open cockpit and wind-in-the-wires flying. Instead of high and fast, it's low and slow, like flying in slow motion. But it's absolutely magical and you'll believe you've gone back in time to the golden days of aviation, when flying was an adventure."

"My God, you're a romantic."

Evan simply smiled.

Chapter Five

As March prepared to roll into April, Tate was presented with an opportunity to go to Afghanistan to interview a Taliban commander—a man who had fought the Soviets in the eighties and was now a key leader in an increasingly virulent insurgency.

Under normal circumstances, she would have seized the opportunity with both hands. But her still-evolving relationship with Evan had made her increasingly aware of how precious life was and how fragile it could be. She could no longer prevent the unbidden thoughts that had her envisioning a possible future with Evan in it, and much to her chagrin, she found herself questioning if the assignment was worth the risk.

She remembered early days in her career, fearlessly flying to Iraq in pursuit of a story, being embedded for a brief time. Driven by the great sense of responsibility that came with being there, covering the war. Being on the front line in the desert somewhere west of Basra, under attack from artillery and rockets.

The experience had at times been exhilarating, other times simply terrifying. But the aftermath had also left her sensitive to the impact her risk taking had on those closest to her. Her parents who had said little at the time, but eventually confessed how much they had worried each and every day she was in Iraq. And the girlfriend who had ended their relationship shortly after Tate's return, saying she couldn't handle the stress of worrying whether or not Tate would make it home alive.

It hadn't been enough to stop her from returning to Iraq, which she had done three times. But the nature of conflict was different in Afghanistan, and the threat to both soldiers and the reporters who rode in their armored vehicles or patrolled with them had expanded.

There were still RPGs and bullets, but there were also suicide bombers and IEDs—the deadly improvised explosive devices that destroyed limbs and lives indiscriminately.

Was a story worth taking the chance of not coming home? Was it worth rolling the dice with roadside bombs?

As she weighed the pros and cons of taking the assignment, she wondered if her hesitation might not also be because she was starting to feel she had seen and done enough. Maybe it was time to let someone else take up the challenge along with the responsibility.

She desperately wished she could talk to Evan and get her thoughts on the matter. But Evan was currently out of reach somewhere in the northern Arabian Sea, most likely flying strike missions over Afghanistan. She viewed Evan's unavailability as simply par for the course, part of the package that came with becoming involved with an active-duty pilot.

But a hell of a package she was, Tate mused wryly. All nearly six feet of hot, lean, gorgeous woman. That she also came with intelligence, humor, style, and class seemed like an excess of riches, but Tate wasn't complaining.

It was the intelligence she missed the most right now. As a naval officer with several sea tours behind her, she was certain Evan would have been able to offer an insightful and unique perspective. But it just wasn't meant to be.

Finally, after several sleepless nights and numerous abortive attempts at decision making, she sought Jillian out for a serious heart-to-heart conversation. Jillian, as usual, was candid and to-the-point.

"You're never going to entirely eliminate the risk, Tate. You know that as well as I do. All you can do is manage it down to what you believe is an acceptable level and hope for the best. So take a second here and think things through."

They were both silent for a long moment, and in the silence Tate estimated that the hours she would spend as a potential target were few, calculated that the risk was slim, and concluded the story she was pursuing was worth reporting.

"Now ask yourself this," Jillian said quietly. "If you don't go, will you look back and regret it?"

Tate knew then she'd found her answer. She still felt uneasy, but as she explained, "I have to go. In part because I'm the one they're willing to talk to. But mostly because if reporters aren't brave enough to go into a war zone, then truth truly does become the first casualty."

She was rewarded with a beaming smile. "I never doubted your decision. Your courage is one of the reasons I care about you, and because I do, I need you to promise you'll keep your head down and try not to take too many risks."

"I won't. I promise to be alert and aware at all times."

"You'd better be." Jillian's expression softened. "Now what do I tell the hot and sexy Commander Kane if she happens to come by and you're not around?"

"Just tell her where I am," Tate responded with her customary honesty. "She'll understand."

❖

Evan would understand all of this better than most, she thought again after she'd been in Afghanistan for almost two weeks.

She'd been covering the recent increase in attacks against government forces and NATO-led troops when one assault left more than twenty dead. Among those killed was a BBC reporter Tate knew and whose work she respected immensely—a harsh reminder of the risks faced by those committed to telling the story.

Feeling deeply conflicted and off balance, Tate barely had time to react, let alone grieve, when she was taken on a confusing odyssey through switchback dirt roads to an unidentified location where she could conduct her interview. She had expected no less, as the insurgents wanted to ensure she'd be unable to reveal their location to the US military. It was just a case of bad timing.

After two days in a hardscrabble village, the job she had come to do was complete. The interview finished, she was left standing alone in the baking heat, sweltering under body armor and a Kevlar helmet. Waiting to meet up with a military convoy that would provide her ride back to Kandahar.

It couldn't happen soon enough. She was exhausted. Physically. Mentally. Emotionally. Her head ached, the twin Nikons around her neck had become unbearably heavy, and all she wanted was to get to the airport, catch the first flight back to Bahrain, and fall into Evan's arms.

Or at least that was the way it was supposed to work. In reality, she had no idea where Evan was at the moment or if she was anywhere near Bahrain. The thought further disheartened her. Made her question her judgment yet again in attempting to have some kind of relationship with Evan. Was she drawn to Evan *because* she was unavailable? God, she hoped not.

The convoy picked her up just after dawn. In spite of the early hour, the temperature was easily in triple digits. But as she gazed at the marines she was travelling with—a mix of seasoned vets and young soldiers led by a twenty-five-year-old lieutenant—they seemed surprisingly informal and relaxed in spite of having encountered heavy fighting earlier in the month.

Their friendly banter helped pass the time, and several willingly shared their stories. One young corporal eyed her speculatively before offering to be her personal escort for the duration of her stay in Kandahar. Amid ribald comments and laughter, Tate gently turned him down, not bothering to point out that at barely nineteen he was almost fifteen years younger than she was. He took her rejection good-naturedly, smiled, and seemed about to say something.

And then the world exploded.

Tate thought it was a dream when she first opened her eyes. She blinked, disoriented, as the thick black smoke billowed and swirled all around her, stinging everything it touched.

Blinking hurt. Breathing hurt. Jesus, everything hurt. Her head was pounding, keeping pace with the wild staccato of her heartbeat, and she could feel warm blood running down her face and into her mouth.

But even as she forced down the panic, she was too busy fighting all the things fear was doing to her to do more than swipe at it.

She heard a voice, then a second. Drifting through the smoke and haze. Talking softly. She tried to block them out, but then a shadow took shape as it crouched beside her. A medic, his fingers on her wrist as he checked her pulse. His hands were gentle, but firm enough to hold on when she tried to push him away.

"Keep still," he ordered.

"I'm fine." Her voice was rough, her throat dry, but she managed to get the words out between quick gulps of air.

"Why don't you let me be the judge? Since you're the only civilian in sight, I'm guessing you're the reporter, but I can't remember your name."

"McKenna...Tate McKenna. It's April tenth and Queen Latifah's the president."

"Cool—glad you remember. I'm Carter." The medic grinned as he undid her flak jacket. "So, McKenna, I need to check you out before you move anything."

"What—no date first?"

"You can buy me dinner later. Do you think you can move the fingers on this hand for me? Can you squeeze my hand?"

The thought was agonizing, but she flexed her fingers, faintly alarmed at how much effort was required for such a simple task. She grimaced as the pain radiating up her arm intensified.

"You're doing good."

Easy for you to say, she thought but didn't say anything because all she really wanted to do was scream.

"Now your left hand. Can you move your fingers?"

She did her best, wiggling her fingers in spite of the pain she was in. Her best turned out to be good enough because Carter the medic didn't ask her to do anything else. Grateful, Tate closed her eyes, as he bound her right arm with gauze and tape, and felt the wind as it picked up.

She tried to distract herself from whatever the medic was doing by looking over his shoulder. Almost immediately, her eyes fell on a young marine lying in the sand several feet away, his chest covered in blood.

It took a moment before she realized she was looking at the corporal who'd been flirting with her earlier. Boomer. That was what the others had called him. Nineteen year old Boomer from somewhere, South Carolina.

"I think he needs your help more than I do."

Carter glanced over his shoulder then shook his head.

Tate looked away and dug for composure. More than ten years of reporting hadn't inured her, nor had it made accepting death any easier. Emotions warred through her and the tears came unbidden.

Shuddering once, she blanked everything out of her mind but the moment. She was singed, she was bleeding, and she was bruised. But she was alive.

While Carter cleaned a wound on her leg, she fought past the nausea and disorientation and began to take stock of her surroundings. She was sitting on the ground, leaning against a piece of the armored vehicle she had been riding in minutes—or possibly hours—earlier.

Someone moaned. It might have been her, but as she glanced around, she quickly realized it could be any one of the half dozen similarly dazed and bloodied people sitting in the midst of sand and twisted wreckage.

As the reality of her situation hit her, and in spite of the heat, she started to shiver. *Shock's setting in*, she mused. And then she jolted as she felt the prick of a needle in her arm. *Damn, I hate needles.* Looking up, she met Carter's gaze. "What was that?"

"Painkiller. Kind of like morphine except it's a non-opiate so it won't slow your breathing." He continued checking her as he spoke. "I know you've got to be hurting. But you took a bit of a blow to your head, so I don't want to give you too much of anything until we know what we're dealing with. I just want you comfortable enough to travel, okay?"

Tate nodded.

"How are you feeling?"

"I know I've felt worse, but I can't remember when."

"Any double vision?"

"No."

"How's the headache?"

"Bad enough." She started to shift, then thought better of it, cursing under her breath as the aching in her head intensified. "Oh shit, everything hurts. What the hell happened?"

"The vehicle you were in hit an IED." Carter shook his head as he efficiently went about the business of patching her up. "Could be Taliban, could be something left over from the Soviets. Damned near impossible to tell."

"The experts say Afghanistan is one of the world's most heavily mined countries," Tate mused absently. "They estimate there could be anywhere from five to ten million landmines buried here."

Carter whistled softly. "You don't say. Well, all I can tell you is we have one less mine now. The first three trucks in the convoy ran over the same spot before the vehicle you were in hit it."

"My lucky day."

"It is. You're still alive."

Tate understood but couldn't help thinking about a nineteen-year-old boy who would never know twenty. Anything else she might have said was lost by a sudden burst of gunfire, followed by the thunderous blasts of falling mortar rounds. It was somewhere in the distance, but still much too close for comfort. The sound spooked her, but the medic seemed not to notice.

"How close? How long before they get here?"

"You don't need to worry. The lieutenant has called for air support and the medevac choppers will be here in a few minutes to take you to Kandahar."

"Air support?"

Carter nodded. "Navy fighters routinely perform high-level sweeps in this area. They'll be here before you know it, and they'll take care of whoever's out there."

Minutes later, four jets roared overhead, weapons firing. Initially, Tate could hear the insurgents returning fire, but seconds after that, the ground fire ceased.

"A sight for sore eyes," Carter said. "Awesome, aren't they?"

Yes they were, Tate silently agreed and would have said something, but the edge of her vision was starting to blur and she could see the darkness closing in. She turned her head, trying to find relief from the headache, then closed her eyes, too tired and battered to do more.

But there was still something she needed to know. "Those fighters…where did they come from?"

"The *Nimitz*."

Tate thought about that, and even as she felt herself fading, she wondered if by chance Evan had been one of the pilots flying above her. The possibility made her feel better even before she heard the welcome sound of the approaching medevac helicopters. That was good, she thought.

And then her world faded to black.

Chapter Six

Kandahar, Afghanistan

Evan tried not to think about what she might find as she quickly made her way to the main entrance of the hospital. But it was impossible to shut everything out, and her heart hammered painfully at the realization Tate was hurt and receiving treatment somewhere inside the trauma center.

For the past six weeks, flight operations on the *Nimitz* had been running nearly round the clock, and for eighteen hours a day, she'd been constantly on the go. Most days, it meant attending flight briefings and flying sorties over Afghanistan twice daily.

That, in turn, meant keeping a watchful eye on her team, especially the nuggets, while still maintaining constant focus on waypoints, radio frequencies, fuel plans, locations of refueling tankers, emergency divert fields…*and, oh yeah, trying to avoid task saturation.*

She normally thrived under pressure. But the schedule was as intense as it was brutal, and she had taken to declaring it a good day if she and her team made it back to their respective racks at the end of each day.

It was why, for eighteen hours a day, she'd been too busy to think about Tate.

But for the remaining six hours at the end of each day, even as she tried to sleep, Tate was all she thought about. She wanted to see her. Be with her.

She had an upcoming thirty-day leave and she'd originally made plans to spend the time with Alex. But that was months ago. Before Tate. Now she wanted to spend her leave with Tate.

She could, of course, do both, simply by asking Tate to join her in Chamonix.

Alex would love it. He'd been clamoring to meet Tate ever since Evan had let slip she'd met someone. She could already see Tate and her brother becoming fast friends. And being able to spend her leave with Tate would go a long way to making her final sea tour more bearable.

But there was a challenge.

In his last e-mail, her father had let her know he would see her in France and was looking forward to spending a few days with both his children. Under normal circumstances that would be great. She missed her father. Except there was a better-than-even chance he would bring Althea with him in another attempt to reconcile mother and daughter.

Her father wouldn't understand her reluctance wasn't about reconciling with her mother. And she didn't know how to explain. It was a simple matter to introduce Tate to Alex. But the situation grew infinitely more complex when it came to introducing Tate to her parents. Especially when Althea already knew her—as a reporter.

She'd been weighing her options before this last sortie. Wondering if she should simply let Tate decide if she was up to it. If she was even interested.

When the call came in to provide air support to a convoy in trouble, fuel levels were running low and she'd already been scanning the horizon looking for the tanker. So once the ground situation had been resolved, the decision to divert to Kandahar Airbase rather than tank and return to the *Nimitz* was an easy one.

It was after she'd landed, while talking to the base maintenance chief, that she discovered a reporter had been injured in the convoy she'd been called to support. There was a heart-stopping instant before she could ask, "Did you happen to catch a name?"

Unable to accept assurances Tate hadn't been badly injured, Evan made her way to the base hospital and left Deacon to look after arranging an overnight billet for them. Just before she entered the building, she caught sight of her reflection in a window and groaned softly. There were visible signs of fatigue carved into her face, her hair was damp with sweat and badly in need of a cut, her flight suit was sun faded, and her boots were coated with salt from weeks of being at sea.

She wouldn't make a great impression, but she needed to see Tate.

Thankfully, the hospital was quiet. A medic, handing out food to an Afghan family waiting for a doctor to see them, pointed to his right when she inquired about Tate. Twenty feet down the corridor, she found her sitting on a bed behind a privacy screen. Drawing the curtain aside,

Evan hesitated, looking Tate over to assure herself she was still in one piece.

She'd acquired a tan since Evan had last seen her and it looked good on her. Her hair was up in a twisted knot, but some of the strands had escaped and hung loose, curling around her neck. Her lips were parted, and she seemed to be struggling to balance a tray on her lap while trying to eat one-handed.

It was then she saw Tate's right arm was bandaged, and then she noticed the bruising above Tate's right eye. There were no other injuries immediately evident, but the look of pain on her face was unmistakable, and she looked surprisingly fragile.

A single heartbeat became two and then two more, but Evan found herself unable to speak. Instead, she took an aching breath and continued to gaze at Tate. Allowing her eyes to linger on Tate's lips, Evan was suddenly struck by a memory of what it was like to kiss her, and a shiver worked through her body.

No other woman tasted like that. No other lips felt like those. No other kiss made her feel as much. Tate's touch could make the world disappear, making her feel as if they were the only two people in it.

Biting back a sigh, she swallowed past the dryness in her throat and hoped her voice would still function. "Looks like you could use a hand."

Tate looked visibly startled and their eyes met with an almost palpable intensity. But as recognition set in, there was an immediate change in her expression. Evan was going to remember that look of joy—pure and unfettered—for a long time.

"Evan? Oh my God, what are you doing here?"

"I was hungry." She scanned the tray, sniffing at the aromatic cheese and tomato sauce appreciatively. "Is that vegetarian pizza?"

Tate's laughter was soft and spontaneous. She held out a slice, almost succeeding in sending the tray crashing to the floor.

Evan reached over in time and grabbed the hapless tray, then leaned in, took a bite, and nodded her approval. "Not bad at all."

"For you, I'm more than willing to share. It's actually not bad considering it's hospital food. When I can get some in my mouth without dropping everything else, that is…sorry, I'm rambling. God, I've missed you."

"I've missed you too."

Evan could feel Tate watching her for a moment, weighing whatever she was going to say. Their gazes locked and fenced before Tate spoke again. "Earlier today…that was you overhead, wasn't it? Dealing with those insurgents?"

"All in a day's work. I'm only sorry I couldn't do more—beyond providing support after the fact." Evan gave her a tight smile as she cut a piece of pizza and fed it to Tate. She waited patiently for her to swallow before offering another piece, continuing to feed her until Tate put her good arm up in surrender.

"No more, please. But thank you. If you hadn't come along, I'd have ended up wearing it."

"As I said, just doing my job."

"It's more than that," Tate said softly. "You saved our lives today. You'll be my hero forever." She began to shake as if just recognizing the enormity of what had happened earlier.

Evan took the tray and set it on a table before she wordlessly sat down next her, pulling Tate into her arms. She felt a brief splash of hot tears and held her gently. With her thumbs, she brushed away the tears, then continued to stroke her cheeks. "Don't think about it," she whispered. "You're all right, that's all that matters."

For the next few minutes, she continued to hold Tate in her arms, stroking her and whispering soft, comforting words. Finally Tate eased out of her arms, leaned back, and gave a hesitant smile.

"Sorry about that. The doctor did say there was a good chance my emotions would be all over the place after what happened, and he was right. Every time I think about it, I start to come undone. But I'm all right for the moment."

"Okay. If I ask, will you tell me how you're really feeling?"

Tate blinked, and Evan could see she was uncertain how to answer. But as she tilted her head, her eyes narrowed, revealing even that small movement hurt.

"I'm okay—really." She sank into the bedding and fought back a tired yawn. "I've got some stitches in my arm and some of my bruises have bruises, but everything seems to still be attached. My only problem right now is the doctor gave me something lovely for the pain just before you got here and it's making me sleepy. And they want to keep me overnight for observation because I got hit in the head."

"Were you unconscious at any time?"

"Maybe, but only for a minute or so."

"Tate—" The pain darkening Tate's eyes stopped her. Without saying another word, Evan reached for her hands. Slowly she turned them palm up, revealing scrapes and bruises. She placed a gentle kiss on each palm, felt an overwhelming surge of emotion, and willed her voice not to shake. "I'm sorry. I think I panicked earlier when I found out you'd been in that convoy and you'd been hurt." She cleared her throat when she heard how raw her voice sounded. "I feel better now that I've seen you for myself. But you're tired and in pain if your eyes are telling me anything, so I should go and let you get some sleep."

Visibly wilting, Tate grabbed onto her hand as if seeking an anchor in a storm, clearly not wanting to lose the connection. "I'm sorry. I'm tired and I know I'm fading on you, but please don't go. Not yet. Can you stay a while longer?"

Exhaustion and thoughts of sleeping in a bed vanished. "The maintenance chief's currently working on my plane, so I'm not going anywhere until morning." Evan gently squeezed the fingers entwined with hers and leaned in, placed a kiss on Tate's lips. "Go to sleep, beautiful lady. I'll still be here when you wake up."

❖

Evan shifted uncomfortably in the hospital's vinyl-covered chair, pulling her knees to her chest and setting her chin on them. The good news was the doctor had been by and Tate would be allowed to leave in the morning. The bad news was it would be light soon.

It meant all too soon, Tate would be leaving the hospital, and she would be flying in the opposite direction, back to the *Nimitz*. Except she didn't want to leave.

Not without talking to Tate first.

"Evan?" Her name was a hoarse whisper on Tate's lips.

Gratefully vacating the chair, Evan moved to the side of the bed, reaching over to gently push locks of sweat-dampened hair off Tate's forehead. "I'm right here. Do you need something?"

"Just to see you." Her voice sounded sleepy and sexy. "You stayed."

"You asked me to."

Tate stared at her in the dim light and blinked. "I just realized something. I never thought I'd say this to you, but you look like hell."

Evan laughed a little at that. "Thanks."

"I'm serious. I can see you've lost weight, even though you probably thought I wouldn't notice. You also look exhausted and in need of two or three days of sleep. Why aren't you sleeping?"

"Too wired, I guess."

"But you've got to fly back to the *Nimitz*…sooner rather than later, I would guess. How are you going to do that? How are you going to keep safe if you haven't slept?"

"Tate, please don't worry. I can find my way back to the Nimitz with my eyes closed. Otherwise I'll be in for a long, cold swim and the navy frowns when we drop their toys into the water."

"Hey, don't joke about it," Tate responded in a strained voice.

Evan mentally swore. "I'm sorry. When I'm tired, my mouth moves before my brain engages. As for how I look, it's actually pretty normal for me at the end of a sea tour."

"Except you're doing back-to-back six-month tours. Jesus, Evan. How are you going to survive?"

"Actually—" She took a breath and straightened a little, figuring she'd put off the inevitable long enough. "I just need to survive another few days and then I can R and R to my heart's content."

"Why is that?"

"I've a thirty-day leave coming up before I start my final tour."

"Oh?" Tate's eyes narrowed.

"Alex and I rented a chalet in Chamonix—" She'd intended to tread carefully, but the flare of disappointment suddenly evident on Tate's face came as a moment of clarity and was all the encouragement she needed. "Do you ski?"

Tate nodded stiffly.

"The skiing in Chamonix is unbelievable." She paused, feeling a shudder of uncharacteristic nervousness. "Um, you need to know my father—and probably Althea as well—will be there for at least a couple of days sometime during the second week, but I'd really love for you to join me if you could see your way to coming anyway. Still, I'll understand it if you can't."

Tate remained silent for a long, uncertain moment. When she finally spoke, her voice maintained an edge. "Are you asking me to spend your leave with you? To meet your brother and your parents?"

There was no room for hesitation. "Yes."

"To be open with your family about the fact we're involved—in a relationship?"

Evan nodded, took a breath, and waited.

"Okay."

Evan felt a measure of calm descend. Leaning closer, she gently kissed Tate's mouth. It lasted for only a heartbeat, but it was the only thing she could think to do. She didn't want Tate to voice her reservations. Kissing her was a much better and far more enjoyable idea. And it tasted like heaven.

CHAPTER SEVEN

February 16
1800 AST
Manama, Bahrain

With her frustration level mounting, Tate stared at her laptop.

She was supposed to be putting the finishing touches on a story, but nothing was coming. It had been like that all day. She'd been unable to concentrate, unable to slow the driving beat of her heart, conscious only of the date.

Today was a red-letter day.

Sometime last night, more than two-and-a-half months after her last sea tour was supposed to have ended, Evan had finally flown her last mission. Sometime today she was scheduled to catch the mail flight off the carrier and fly to Bahrain.

Tate had made plans to celebrate Evan's homecoming.

They would make love. Reconnect. At some point, they would have a nice meal. Then they would talk. In that order. And sometime during the course of their conversation, Tate intended to make it very clear they were meant to stay together.

There had been enough separations in their relationship to last a lifetime, and when Evan returned stateside, she intended to go with her. Be by her side. It was time—well past time.

She expected Evan wouldn't be surprised.

Evan had understood her fears, better than Tate had understood them herself, and had shown remarkable patience. Waiting for Tate to open her heart and let her in. Showing her how wonderful—and pleasurable—her life could be if she only took a chance on a navy pilot whose service commitment was finally coming to an end.

Well, here she was. Ready to take that chance. It frightened her, more than a little, that she'd come to care so much. But she was smart enough to accept this was where she'd been heading from the start.

All day long, it was all she'd been able to think about. Daydreaming to the exclusion of everything else. Conjuring up images of Evan. And they came easily, as they always did.

But then, Evan was never very far from her thoughts. In her mind, she was always laughing, radiating energy. Always beautiful, with a face created to haunt dreams.

Tate smiled as she remembered the last time they'd gotten together. Evan had somehow managed to get a brief leave and had called unexpectedly, asking if she could drop everything and meet her in Germany. Tate hadn't needed to be asked twice, and they had spent five glorious days and nights in a small hotel. Ordering room service and then forgetting to eat. Forgetting about the world that existed beyond the confines of their hotel room...

The time apart never seemed to lessen Evan's effect on Tate.

She continued to fascinate and tempt. Just looking at her always took Tate's breath away and she grinned, not bothering to contain her anticipation as Evan exited a taxi and crossed the street toward her.

Her throat tightened as she watched long, jeans-clad legs swallow the short distance in that fluid stride she had. Her chest started to pound as she saw Evan's mouth curve upward in that perpetually sexy, unrepentant smile. And she felt the full impact as she watched a mischievous gleam appear in Evan's eyes.

Oblivious to the traffic and people and rain, Evan laughed as she reached Tate. Dropping the small duffel bag she'd been carrying over one shoulder, she swept Tate up in her arms, holding her as though she would never let go.

"Hello, beautiful lady."

"Hey, yourself."

Tate inhaled deeply, breathing in the fresh smell of rain and the delectable scents emanating from a nearby restaurant. A moment later everything receded and there was only the faint, tantalizing scent that was distinctly and uniquely Evan. More aura than perfume, it had always drawn Tate in. Smiling and brimming with unbelievable happiness, curiously alone in the midst of a crowd, all Tate could think was how wonderful it was to have this chance, this moment. To laugh, to touch, to love.

She wanted to make the most of the time available to them before Evan had to return to her ship. Until then, they had five endless days without deadlines and distractions.

Five glorious days and nights, having Evan's mouth there for the taking.

The first taste was never enough to satisfy Tate, but she knew she would have five days to try and get her fill. Enough to last until the navy finally released Evan from responsibilities and duty.

"Is this all you've brought?" she asked, reaching for the small duffel bag.

Evan looked at her, a frank grin shaping her mouth. "And here I thought I'd overpacked."

Tate pondered her comment seriously and then started to laugh. "Yeah, you're probably right."

Still laughing, still touching, they barely made it up to their room. The door had hardly closed before Evan's hands moved along Tate's ribs, brushing her breasts lightly through her shirt, undoing buttons as fast as she found them. Between searing kisses, their clothes fell away, until they were skin to skin. Pale curves and silken shadows.

"Slow down," Tate whispered. "We can take our time."

But even as she tried to set a slower pace, tried to prolong the pleasure, Evan would have no part of it and there was no staying the inevitable.

"Ah, Tate, it's been too long," she whispered, her mouth hungry and desperate as if she would never get enough. Somehow sighing and tasting in the same breath. "We can do slow later. I promise. As many times as you like. Right now, I need you hard and fast."

Evan took control of the pace with the arch of her body. She created a sensual fog that clouded Tate's mind until all she could think about was the sweet taste of Evan's mouth, the soft silk of her body, the scent of their combined desire. And then driving, hot, and insatiable, she began to move against Tate with urgency and greed, with searching fingers and a wickedly talented mouth.

Evan had no inhibitions, and when they came together, she was like a fire consuming everything in her path. She instinctively knew how to find the spots that made Tate weak. The ones that made her cry out with pleasure. The ones that made her quiver with need.

A liquid heat filled Tate as deliciously long fingers slid inside her, taking her breath away as her body responded, leaving her blind to everything but the moment and Evan's touch. And then she couldn't think anymore. She gasped out a litany of need as Evan took her to the edge and held her suspended before covering her mouth and swallowing her cries with a searing kiss as she came apart.

She collapsed, her body limp, damp, exhausted. And when the last tremors had flexed through her, she finally opened her eyes to find Evan's slanting cheeks and sensuous mouth mere inches away. Her eyes were dark and shadowed, while her sultry midnight voice whispered, "Now we can do slow and easy."

In that moment, as the soft voice danced along her spine, Tate understood the truth she'd been ignoring for months. She was in love with Evan. And had been for a very long time. *The knowledge was both terrifying and exhilarating.*

Tate blinked slowly, her mind cloudy and filled with memories. Long after the feel and taste and scent of Evan had faded into memory, she'd continued to remember, to ache. It was what had enabled Tate to hold on—to survive—until now. She glanced at her watch when she noticed the darkening sky beyond the window, wondering when she would hear from Evan. Time ticked inexorably forward, and eventually the room was dark save for the small lamp that burned on the table.

When the much-anticipated knock finally came, she pushed off the sofa so hard she nearly stumbled in her eagerness to get to the door. "Evan—"

She found Jillian standing there.

Tate pushed disappointment aside and smiled. "Oh, hey, your timing's perfect. I've been going crazy waiting for Evan to show. Come on in and keep me company until she gets here, would you? Can I get you a beer?"

"Tate."

"Or do you want wine instead? I think I still have some of that red you like so much."

"Tate," she said again, this time softer. Quieter.

Tate froze midway to the small kitchen, her back to Jillian. She felt cold all over and was filled with an inexplicable dread. "Don't—"

"Tate."

Slowly she turned toward Jillian, who was still standing by the door. She took stock of her face, noted her eyes were red, her features stricken. *Oh Jesus.* The world slowed, her vision blurred, and she felt her heart start to break.

"Please don't," she begged as a thousand emotions crashed over her. If she didn't let Jillian say anything, she wouldn't have to listen as someone told her what she already feared in her heart. *She's not dead. She can't be.*

"Tate, I need you to listen to me. Early this morning, two Super Hornets were shot down near the Pakistan border."

"No—"

"I'm so sorry, Tate. The navy has confirmed Evan was one of the pilots. The other was a lieutenant named Deacon Walker. I—I wanted to tell you before you heard it from someone else."

The words shook Tate hard, tearing a sob from her throat as her world came apart. "But they're looking for them, aren't they?"

"Search-and-rescue teams were launched just after dawn," Jillian said, "but the area they went down in is as bad as it gets. The navy confirmed an emergency beacon was initially picked up by satellite, but it went silent too quickly to be much help. And the closest eye witnesses on the ground reported no one saw either pilot eject."

"That doesn't mean anything." Tate blinked away tears. She heard the fracture in her voice, felt the burn in her throat. "There's still a chance. I mean it, Jillian. It's not in Evan to give up. We shouldn't give up, either."

Jillian looked at her, just looked, and remained silent.

The thought that Evan was somewhere in Afghanistan…hurt… dying…or dead…"No. Please, God—"

The strength gave out in her legs and her knees hit the floor.

Evan and Deacon Walker were listed as missing in action—they were only presumed dead. And for Tate, the days that followed became nothing more than a jumble of vague images and dreams. Voices and movements. Impressions of people.

For the first time in years, Tate found herself praying to a God she hadn't quite believed in since she began covering wars. She prayed for a miracle more times than she cared to admit. But no matter what promises she made or what sacrifice she offered, no miracle was forthcoming.

Miracles didn't exist. Reality did.

Several days after the media reported two navy jets had been shot down during a night mission in Afghanistan, a video appeared on the Internet. Alleged to have been released by a group claiming responsibility, the black-and-white video was a propaganda coup for the insurgents as it immediately went viral.

It also removed any doubt that might have lingered about the fate of the two missing pilots.

Tate had no desire to watch the video. But it garnered such intense coverage from every major news outlet there was no escaping its near-constant airplay. And each time she saw the video, or heard another talking head expressing an opinion, Tate was conscious only of a tearing sense of loss as she tried to keep from being crushed by the weight of her own emotions.

The horrific images opened with the silent approach of the two Super Hornets. They had been conducting what the military described as a show of force. It was a tactic that had been used countless times, an action meant to intimidate—a display of readily available strength.

But clearly, on this particular night, the insurgents had been waiting.

The moments that followed illustrated the sequence of events with startling clarity. Two surface-to-air missiles were shoulder-launched seconds apart, using what the experts called MANPADS—a man-portable air-defense system—which could be had for as little as a few hundred dollars on the black market.

All Tate would remember for days afterward was seeing the shower of flames as the first missile struck the lead aircraft—Evan's jet—with lethal accuracy. A few seconds passed and then the fighter exploded in a blast that filled the screen, lighting up the black night.

What the experts couldn't determine was whether it was the wing from Evan's aircraft, as it sheared off, or the second missile that brought down Walker's jet. *What the hell difference did it make,* Tate wanted to scream as she struggled against the mounting evidence Evan had died in that fireball.

Because the search-and-rescue missions found no evidence either pilot survived. And the SEAL team which eventually managed to survey the crash site found only burnt wreckage consistent with the two missing aircraft, strewn over an inhospitable mountainous region.

Sometime during the second week of March, the navy officially called off any further recovery missions, and Evan and Walker's status was changed to KIA/BNR: killed in action/body not recovered.

And on a cold and gray Washington afternoon, the flag-draped casket beside the open grave sat empty.

After the funeral, Alex gave Tate the flag presented to him at the conclusion of the service. Meticulously folded thirteen times into the symbolic tri-cornered shape with no red or white stripe evident, leaving only the blue field with stars.

On behalf of the President of the United States and the Chief of Naval Operations, please accept this flag as a symbol of our appreciation for your loved one's service to this country and a grateful US Navy.

"I don't know how to do this," she whispered to him. "I don't know how to go on without her. I loved her but I never told her. Now I don't know how to say good-bye. I don't think I can."

She could see pain evident in Alex's eyes and grief etched on his face. But he had no advice to offer. No answers. What he had was a letter Evan had left in his care, written just before leaving Chamonix to begin her final deployment.

It was her just-in-case letter. A letter Tate never intended to read. And then, having read it, she reread it so many times the edges became curled and it was in danger of falling apart.

My beautiful Tate—

Believe me when I say I'm sorry. I know I promised you I'd
stay safe. But if you're reading this, it means I broke my word
to you. Please forgive me and understand it was a promise I
never meant to break. At the time I wrote this letter, I never
truly believed I would give you cause to read it.

I know you're hurting. But if it helps, I always hoped
to eventually meet my end without regret. And though it was
much shorter than I'd hoped, it turns out there's not a lot I
would have changed about my life.

I regret I never made things right with Althea. We got a
good start on putting the hurt and anger behind us those few
days we were together in Chamonix, and it was always my
intention to fix the rest once I got home. But now it looks like
I won't be getting the opportunity. When you see her, please
make sure she and my father know I loved them both very,
very much.

My second regret is not getting a chance to say good-
bye to Alex. He was and always will be the other half of
me, so there's no need to tell him I love him. He knows.
Just as he knows how much I love to fly. But you may need
to remind him that flying an F/A-18 was a thrill I wouldn't
have experienced if I hadn't joined the navy. Don't let him
grieve for too long. And get Nick to help if Alex gives you
a hard time.

As for you, beautiful lady, I only regret you and I never
got the chance to discover how far we could take what's been
happening between us since the moment we met. You made
me so very happy for what we've had and hopeful for what
was still to come. More than anything, I wanted to see things
through with you. I just know it would have been amazing.

Be well, Tate. And when you think of me, know that all
of my life was good. But the best part of my life was you.

Evan

Tate closed her eyes, unable to stop the searing pain that tore
through her. Because it was then it finally hit her. Evan was truly gone.
She might have screamed—she wasn't sure—as she buried her face in
her hands and wept.

CHAPTER EIGHT

Puget Sound, Washington

As the days flowed following Evan's funeral, Tate found she was unable to fill the void in her life. She was certain the world went on around her just as it had before. But the longing to be with Evan again—just one more time—never left.

Finding it too painful to go back to the life she'd known in Bahrain, she chose to remain stateside. Well-meaning friends tried to assure her the passage of time would lessen her pain and cautioned against making rash, life-altering decisions. But Tate knew this particular decision had been a long time coming.

Since Kandahar.

For the sake of those closest to her—especially her parents—she tried. Mostly she avoided people. And when she couldn't avoid, she put on a brave front.

Alex understood. And although he was struggling with his own grief, it was Alex and his partner Nick who finally saved her. Three weeks after the funeral, as dawn was breaking over the city, she awoke to find Alex at the door of her DC hotel room.

"How'd you find me?"

Alex shrugged. "You're registered under your own name, and I'm persistent. Jesus, look at you—you're skinny and pale. Why are you hiding, Tate?"

"I don't know what else to do." Her throat tightened and bittersweet tears choked her voice. "I'm sorry. I'm not really good company. It's just that sometimes I swear—"

"You swear what?"

"Sometimes I swear I've seen Evan." Tate felt foolish. "In a passing car. Or on the street...or in a crowd."

Alex didn't say anything. He just watched her with smoky gray eyes so like his sister's and appeared to understand.

"I start to call out. But she's never there, of course."

Alex closed his eyes. "I miss her too. Most days I feel like I've lost part of myself, like half my soul is missing, and yet I don't feel like she's really gone. Does that even make sense?"

"Come home with us, Tate," Alex said, "with me and Nick. I think Evan would have liked it, and maybe between the three of us, we can figure it out."

She'd stayed with Alex and Nick until she felt strong enough to be on her own. And until Alex felt strong enough to let her go. They then helped her find a place of her own, barely a mile away as it turned out. A beautiful house with soul-soothing views of Puget Sound and the Olympic Mountains.

Work helped. She began writing again, mostly articles providing insights into American foreign policy. She was also writing the book she'd been working on forever. Now seemed as good a time as any to see if she could finish it. But at the end of each day and long into each night, there was no escaping reality. She knew she had to find a way to move on. But she would have to stop thinking about Evan first, and to do that, she would have to stop breathing.

Releasing a soft sigh, Tate pushed away from her laptop, deciding to call it a day. She poured a glass of wine and on her way through to the deck for what had become a daily ritual, she paused to turn up the volume on the music softly playing in the background.

As the sultry Latin rhythms of the Buena Vista Social Club came through the speakers, she felt her throat tighten. The music evoked a memory of a long forgotten afternoon and Evan trying to teach her some intricate dance steps in her tiny flat in Bahrain.

God, Evan, I miss you.

As the day waned, Tate sat on the end of the deck, legs hanging over the edge looking out at the water while, overhead, the gulls wheeled and cried.

The scent of rain hung in the air, but she didn't mind. She was enjoying both the wine and the tranquility of the late afternoon when the stillness was disturbed by the recognizable beat of a helicopter. She watched as the aircraft drew near, hovered momentarily, and then much to her annoyance, it set down in the vacant field across the road from her home.

Son of a bitch, that's private property. My private property.

She got up and started to walk over, intent on giving the errant pilot a piece of her mind when she froze. Stared in disbelief as Althea

Kane stepped down, ducking under the still rotating blades before straightening and walking toward her.

"Tate, I hope you don't mind my dropping by unannounced, but I need a private word with you. I thought this might be the simplest way, rather than dragging you to DC."

Tate nodded and tried to control the conflicting surge of surprise and concern. Without another word, she led the way to her house, her nerves brittle enough to snap.

❖

"It's Evan. She's alive."

The instant the words were spoken, Tate's world shifted on its axis. She forgot how to breathe. Hope bloomed, tentative, in the remains of her shattered heart. And if Althea said anything else in the moments that followed, her words failed to register.

If it had been anyone else, Tate would have said this was a cruel hoax. But this wasn't just anybody speaking to her, and she couldn't contain the flicker of hope that once again coursed through her body and awakened her soul.

This was Althea Kane. The secretary of state. Evan's mother.

And Tate desperately wanted to believe her.

She crossed her arms and finally looked at Althea. Was it possible? What was she supposed to say? How was she supposed to respond?

Althea appeared not to notice her dilemma. Instead, she reached into her bag and pulled out a disc, which she swiftly thrust into Tate's hands. "Six days ago, a video was delivered to a CIA outpost near Kandahar," she said in a curiously flat voice. "It came through a regular contact."

"And—?"

"An insurgent cell has proposed a prisoner exchange. They've identified eight detainees awaiting transfer to an American facility. They want them released and, in return, have offered to return two US pilots."

Tate licked her lips and cleared her throat, but couldn't find a way to ask.

Thankfully, Althea did not seem to require the question. "There are only two missing American pilots," she said softly. "Evan and her wingman, Lieutenant Deacon Walker."

Tate pressed her lips together as her fingers tightened around the disc. "What's on the disc?"

"Proof of life."

Tate walked toward her laptop, still open on the table by the scattered files where she'd been working earlier. Althea wouldn't be here if the information hadn't been vetted through unimpeachable channels. She wouldn't be sharing the disc if she didn't somehow believe it provided absolute proof her daughter was still alive.

"Tate?"

She turned at the sound of Althea's voice, hearing her despite the constant waves of grief and hope breaking over her as her head spun in wonder. Althea had handed her a reprieve. A second chance. Already, she could feel her world begin to right itself.

Because if Evan was alive, she would move heaven and earth to bring her home. And then she was never letting her go.

Tate slipped the disc into the drive, entered a couple of quick keystrokes, and stepped back. She crossed her arms, fingers gripping her elbows as if to hold herself together. And with her jaw tightly clenched, she watched the screen flicker to life.

The image was grainy, the lighting dim. As her eyes adjusted to the jerking motion of obviously handheld equipment, the camera zoomed in, focusing first on a young man—maybe in his late twenties or early thirties—with shaggy dark blond hair and old haunted eyes. He was wearing a flight suit and was seated stiffly in a wooden chair, his arms tightly bound in front of him. Was this Deacon Walker?

The camera paused, lingered, and then panned slowly to the right.

A woman sat slumped in a wooden chair, her chin resting on her chest. Dark hair shrouded her face, rendering it all but invisible.

It could be Evan. At least it was a possibility Tate couldn't disregard, even though she still couldn't wrap her mind around it. But then again, the grainy image scrolling across the screen could be that of any dark-haired woman.

The image shook as a hand came into view, grasping the woman's head by the hair and pulling it upright, revealing her face. The camera zoomed in and Tate couldn't control the rush of anger. Rage. Helpless fury.

Evan.

Her name reverberated in her mind. Not a figment of her imagination. Not a ghost from the past or a manifestation of her dreams. Bruised. Gaunt. Obviously ill, her eyes unfocused and glazed.

But very much alive.

Unable to look away from the image on the monitor, Tate could see the cuts and bruises marring her beautiful face. Her eyes fixed on one particularly ugly bruise before finally noting the newspaper held in her tightly bound hands. She looked up at Althea, once again silently asking questions.

"It's the front page of the *New York Times*. It's dated seven days ago." Tate felt Althea sigh before she spoke again, her voice a whisper of pain and sorrow. "Did Evan ever tell you I once offered to meet with the Secretary of the Navy on her behalf? I told her I could get her out of her remaining service commitment. Do you know what she said?"

Tate shook her head.

"She told me I had always been myopically focused on my career to the exclusion of everything else, including my children, and she didn't expect or need me to change and jeopardize anything on her behalf at this late stage in the game. She wasn't a child—hadn't been one for quite some time, in case it had escaped my notice—and she didn't need me to protect her."

"I'm sorry." Tate didn't know what else to say.

"Don't be sorry, Evan was right. But that's not what's important now." Althea's expression seemed sad, almost wistful.

"Tell me how I can help."

"I know I have no right to ask you to put yourself in danger. And yet that's exactly what I'm here to do. I'd like you to go to Afghanistan. To be there during the exchange."

Tate was too shocked to do anything more than stand there and stare. Her throat tightened and her breath stalled in her chest. "The exchange will be a military operation. They won't allow—"

Althea smiled wearily. "Believe it or not, Tate, I do have influence. Your presence has already been approved and transport to Afghanistan has already been arranged. You just have to say yes."

"Yes."

The rain that had been threatening all day finally started to fall, and as drops splattered against the window, Tate peered sightlessly into the thin mist. She could hear the mournful sound of the ferry horn in the distance. And for the first time, the horror and pain of losing Evan began to recede. "So what do you need me to do to make this happen? What's our plan to bring Evan home?"

CHAPTER NINE

Near Kandahar, Afghanistan

"It's going to get a little rough, folks. Just hang on tight and enjoy the ride."

The pilot's disembodied voice had barely registered before the C-130 Hercules began to lift and dive, like an insane roller coaster. Tate was terrified of roller coasters. Strapped into a jump seat along the wall of the plane's belly, she gritted her teeth, clung to the heavy webbing that made up her seat, and did her best to survive. But surviving gracefully was proving to be a difficult if not impossible task. The aircraft was designed to carry passengers. But it had never been designed to carry passengers comfortably.

The Kevlar over her jeans and T-shirt simply added to her discomfort.

Turning her head slightly, Tate saw a grimace flicker across the face of the foreign-service doctor who had been assigned to travel with her. *Greg Turner, wasn't that his name?* He was a tall, lean man of about forty, clean-cut with a tanned complexion. At the moment he appeared to be fighting back a wave of nausea as he swiped at the sweat trickling down his face.

"I hope it won't be much longer," he said, shouting to be heard.

I hope so too, Tate thought and nodded vaguely.

It had taken three adrenaline-fueled days to pull it all together—a miracle that owed its existence to the grace of God and Althea Kane's connections. But while the combination of endless logistics, frayed tempers, and jet lag had long since sapped her strength, the drone of the engines and the shaking aircraft made sleeping impossible.

This was Afghanistan. A place where the enemy sometimes looked like a friend and would be quite happy to kill you.

And the enemy didn't only fire missiles. According to the intelligence reports she had read prior to leaving the US, insurgents were known to target incoming aircraft with machine guns, which helped to explain why they were ordered to wear Kevlar.

The aircraft emptied within twelve minutes of the wheels touching down. The soldiers and equipment they'd flown with were picked up and taken by ground transport to unknown destinations. That left Tate and the doctor standing alone under a blazing sun beside the runway.

Exhausted from the flight but almost giddy with anticipation, Tate pulled sunglasses out of her backpack. Slipping them on, she waited for her eyes to adjust to the brightness, using the time to try to clear her head and focus. She also tried pinching the bridge of her nose in a futile effort to vanquish the tension sitting there.

"Headache?"

Tate nodded and tried not to think about the fact that other than catnaps, she hadn't slept in nearly forty-eight hours.

"It's going to be a long day. Can I give you something for it?"

"Thanks, but no. I'm good," Tate replied, her eyes never leaving the distant horizon, knowing the end of her nightmare was near. Evan was out there. Closer than she had been in months, although still far enough away to cause concern.

A cloud of dust heralded the arrival of a small military convoy that included several armored personnel carriers. Tate's heart rate spiked, and she watched them with a critical eye, knowing the soldiers in the convoy were charged with escorting her safely to and from the prisoner exchange. More importantly, they would be responsible for ensuring Evan's safety once they got her back.

Before the dust had settled, an army major exited the lead vehicle. "Ms. McKenna? Dr. Turner? I'm Major Campbell." He extended both hands, offering bottles of ice-cold water. "My team is standing by as soon as you're ready."

The major projected a quiet competence Tate found reassuring, especially since she wasn't in a position to accept anything less than a win today. She gratefully accepted the water and drank deeply, trying to ease the dryness in her throat.

When she lowered the half-empty bottle, her eyes were immediately drawn to an approaching civilian in jeans and a faded desert-camouflage T-shirt, ambling slowly from the convoy. And then she started to laugh.

Jackson Thomas Dupree's face was as apple-pie wholesome as the last time Tate had seen him, in Kuwait almost three years earlier. His thick, unruly hair was sun bleached nearly white, and with his slow, lazy stride, he resembled a laid-back surfer. But he was one of the sharpest CIA tacticians she had ever met, and his presence had Tate beginning to believe they would really pull this off.

"Damn, but it's good to see you, JT. I can't tell you how happy I am to see you here."

"You look good, Slim. Real good." His drawl still carried a trace of what had once, a long time ago, identified his connection to Louisiana. "And you don't look all that crazy. So you want to tell me what the hell you're doing getting mixed up in this? I thought you were smarter."

Tate shrugged. "This one's personal. Evan Kane is—she's a good friend. A really close friend."

"Jesus, Slim, you like to live dangerously, don't you?" He stared at her a moment longer, then nodded toward the line of waiting vehicles and military personnel. "But it don't matter none as long as you know what to expect."

"And what's that?"

"It should take us just over two hours, if all goes well, to get to the exchange site. But the roads around here are among the most dangerous in the country." JT scratched the faint stubble on his chin. "And convoys are popular targets, particularly VIP convoys. Personally, I'd have liked our chances better getting in and out by chopper, but we couldn't get that bastard Khalid to agree. I'd swear he just wants to see us sweat a bit first."

The mere mention of Khalid caused Tate's shoulders to stiffen. The dossier she'd received through one of Althea's staff indicated no one trusted the young insurgent brokering this deal. Probably because, although born in Helmand province, he was the son of an American engineer currently living in Oregon.

She could feel JT watching her, sensed his concern. "I'm aware of the risks," she said finally.

JT cocked his head, then shrugged and grinned. "Then I think our two pilots have waited long enough. If everything goes according to plan, we should have all of you safe and sound in Germany by early evening."

❖

Once onboard the sand-colored Humvee, Tate sat in the front opposite JT, watching while the doctor moved to the rear of the vehicle. Glancing over her shoulder, she saw the vehicle had been modified to serve as an ambulance.

"You've got all the bases covered."

"Hope so. Word has it both packages sustained some damage a couple of days ago," JT said. "We don't really know how bad, so we just want to be prepared."

"Damaged? They're hurt?" Tate choked on the words. "Why the hell wasn't I advised before now?"

JT shrugged. "I've been told they tried to escape two days ago. Unsuccessfully, and the damage occurred when they were recaptured."

Fear and fury hummed hot in Tate's blood. "Why the hell would they try to escape? After all this time, why now?"

"I can't answer that," JT said, "but I'm guessing they had no idea an exchange had been negotiated. Once we get back to the air base, we've got a team of top-notch medical people on standby, and a medical transport waiting to take Commander Kane and Lieutenant Walker to the hospital in Germany."

A sharp, frustrated sound escaped Tate. Squeezing her eyes tight, she shook her head.

She just wanted to have one more chance with Evan.

Was that too much to ask?

As the convoy progressed deeper into the lawless lands of southern Afghanistan, Tate reached for another bottle of water, trying to stay hydrated in the already oppressive temperature. Through dust-covered windows, she could see the landscape shimmer in the late-morning heat as the sun baked the earth below it. Heat mirages rose in waves and, from time to time, she could make out the bombed-out hulks of tanks scattered across the rugged landscape. Rusted symbols of the Soviet failure to occupy Afghanistan in the 1980s.

But slowly the landscape changed, and instead, it started to resemble something out of *Star Wars*. Dun-colored nomad settlements made up of ancient mud buildings began to appear sporadically. Still, Tate could see no evidence of villagers. Just ghost villages, collapsed mud walls, and an oppressive eerie silence.

"How much longer?" There were nerves in her voice, and hearing them irritated her.

"Maybe another twenty minutes or so."

Swallowing dryly, Tate rested her head against the seat. "Do you suppose they have any idea who they've got? Who they've been holding all this time?"

"I wouldn't think so. If Khalid knew who Evan Kane was, he'd have asked for a hell of a lot more than the eight losers we've got in the transports behind us."

"He'd have gotten it," Tate said with certainty. "He didn't have to threaten to behead them."

JT cursed softly. "He didn't mean anything by it. That's just his way of doing business. In any case, as near as we can tell, Khalid's cell has only had Kane and Walker for a little over a month."

Releasing a long, jagged breath, Tate sat up straighter. "They aren't the ones who shot them down? Is that what you mean?"

"According to the intel we've managed to gather, Kane and Walker got traded between two cells about five weeks ago."

Tate inhaled sharply.

JT sighed. "Tate, you need to look at it from their perspective. Life here has very little value, and Kane and Walker are just commodities. They got traded for RPGs. Or maybe potassium chlorate. Ammonium nitrate. Whatever someone needed to make more IEDs. The fact they were perceived to have some value is probably the only thing that's kept them alive all this time."

Tate's lips compressed into a thin line. The thought of Evan being traded for a rocket propelled grenade made her nauseous.

A short time later, the convoy came to a full stop as they topped a small rise. Pulling up just behind one of the lead vehicles, JT motioned for her to follow him.

"Whatever you do, don't walk on the shoulder. Better still, stay behind me, walk where I walk, and keep your eyes peeled for any signs of recently disturbed earth," he cautioned.

Tate nodded and slowly eased out of the Humvee. Shoving her hands into her pockets, she followed JT, then waited as he conferred with Campbell. After a brief discussion, JT surveyed the area ahead through high-optic binoculars.

"I'd say they're ready for us." He paused as a marine handed Tate binoculars for her use. "Now we just have to wait for their signal to proceed."

Tate felt the trail of perspiration trickle down her back, and she bit her lower lip as she surveyed the scene. She could see a group of hard-eyed men dressed in baggy cotton trousers, loose cotton tunics, and traditional rolled round-topped hats and armed with what looked like assault rifles.

No one else was visible.

After almost a minute had passed, one of the men separated himself from the group. He was young, Tate noted, as she zoomed in on his face. But even from a distance, his expression seemed to lack any emotion. It made her stomach recoil. She couldn't read his lips, but it appeared he was issuing instructions. As if to prove her right, another man stepped out from a nearby hut and into her line of sight, dragging two people, bound, limping, and tethered behind him.

And then everything stopped.

Tate hung suspended in the moment. Unable to breathe. Unable to move. Unable to speak.

Then she was breathing again, feeling again. Her heart jumped, her eyes filled, and she felt herself come apart a little. Weak-kneed and dry mouthed, she forced herself to remain calm as first Deacon Walker and then Evan came into focus.

It was only then she knew, finally, and with absolute certainty.

This was real.

Evan was really alive.

Chapter Ten

Evan flinched.

She bit back a cry when the rope binding her wrists chafed against already raw and bleeding skin as she was dragged to her feet. Blinking, she tried to bring her surroundings into focus. Tried to see where they were taking her as she was pulled from the mud hut. But the brightness of the sun made her head throb almost as badly as the pain radiating from her leg.

Aware only that Deacon was being pulled just in front of her, she abandoned her efforts to see where they were going and tried to let the guard they'd nicknamed Moe pull her along. But with her hands tightly secured and her balance compromised, she had to struggle to stay on her feet and stumbled behind him.

The guard paused, drew closer, and looked down at her impassively, then dragged her off the ground. The movement brought forth a wave of dizziness, caused her stomach to roil, and she found herself wanting nothing more than to surrender to the combination of exhaustion and pain and fever. Wishing she could sink back into oblivion where nothing mattered.

"Are you ready to die today?"

Evan shuddered involuntarily at the sound of the soft voice.

Khalid. She recognized his scent. Knew the pain his touch brought. Her heartbeat instantly accelerated until its wild, erratic pounding resonated in her ears. She felt perspiration trickle down her face, drip down her back, and tried to keep perfectly still. Almost didn't breathe.

But it didn't help.

She hated that he could still do this to her—hated that after all this time, he could still elicit any kind of fear response. A conditioned stimulus, she'd decided. Like Pavlov's dogs.

But she hated it. Almost as much as she hated him.

She drew a fortifying breath, found the strength to lift her chin in defiance, and issued a deliberate response, even as she told herself that sarcasm wouldn't be appreciated. But she was so very tired of his games, and with her body already battered and bruised, she didn't think Khalid's likely retaliation would make much difference. Maybe she simply wanted to feel something other than fear.

"Let me make sure I don't have any other plans first."

Or maybe she just wanted to know she still existed.

In either case, it was the wrong thing to say. Without preamble, he backhanded her, bloodying her mouth. Pain shot through her, wringing a sharp gasp from her lips as she felt something explode in her head and then reverberate through her body. But before she could do more than stagger back under the force of the blow, he hit her again, this time dropping her to her knees.

She would have cried out if she could have drawn a breath. But as it was, she was well past the point of caring. Dazed and disoriented, she heard Deacon call her name, thought she saw him struggle against the guards holding him back. An instant later, she felt the hard barrel of Khalid's assault rifle against her temple, and she froze, refusing to give him the satisfaction of struggling. Fighting to hold back the sound that rose in her throat.

"Would you have me execute you here and now?" Khalid's face was emotionless, as always. His question sounded calm, almost reasonable.

But Evan could still feel his rage. It was always there, held barely in check. Her own anger started to surface in response, but she held it at bay. He wanted to kill her and she was helpless to stop him. She remained still, waiting to see what he would do.

From somewhere beyond her line of vision, he produced a jug of water. Immediately forgetting his question, Evan heard only the sweet sound of the water sloshing inside the container. Her eyes were drawn to the condensation clinging to the sides of the jug, mesmerized by the sight of the fat drops that fell, only to evaporate in the heat before they could touch the ground.

Bastard. She watched Khalid drink deeply and she could only stare at the water dribbling down his chin and swallow painfully.

Khalid smiled.

"Do you still believe someone will save you from your fate, Commander? Should I behead you now and prove you wrong? Is that what you want? Do you want me to decapitate you and send your head home to your lover?"

Evan stared back, unblinking. Chills racked her body in spite of the sizzling heat. She knew most of the cuts on her torso and the bullet wound in her leg were infected. Knew under the present conditions, without any antibiotics, it constituted a death sentence. And until now, she had thought it likely the infection would do her in before Khalid could finish her off.

But now it appeared he had changed his timetable. Quite possibly, she'd reached the end of the line. She bit her lower lip, worked to keep her emotions at a distance, then dug deep and squared her shoulders.

"You could have made this easier on yourself by cooperating with me," he told her. "Now it seems we've run out of time."

Uncertain what he meant, she remained silent. She could feel the warmth of blood pooling at her knee and knew the wound in her leg had opened again. Her vision blurred and the fever was making her mind slow. But she knew she would die here.

She closed her eyes.

God, she really didn't want to die here. She wanted to see Tate again. Alex. Her parents. She hadn't survived all this time so Khalid could kill her now.

No, she had no intention of dying. Not here or anywhere else.

Please.

It was a one-word prayer.

❖

The sight of Evan threw Tate off balance, but she couldn't risk looking away, not for a single second. She was fearful Evan would simply disappear. Afraid she had not really been there. Terrified she had been made real solely by the power of a wish.

Everything inside her grew still, and the flood of sensations was almost like the first time they'd met. The same rush of awareness. Her mind clouded with emotions and images of Evan.

With her hair sweat soaked and clinging to her forehead as she reached for release.

Smiling as she stood on skis on a sunlit mountaintop just before beginning her descent.

Trembling with the joy of finding her alive, it took Tate almost a full minute before she could focus on what was wrong with this picture.

Yes, that was Evan standing less than a mile away. But she was swaying on bare feet. Her hands were bound in front of her and there was a rope wound around her neck, the end held by one of the men gathered there. As Tate brought her into sharper focus, she could see multiple signs of violence. Evan's lip was split and swollen, and dark bruises shadowed her cheeks. Her head was bowed uncharacteristically, and her shoulders were hunched beneath a filthy and sweat-stained tank top no longer recognizable as white.

Her flight suit, stained with dirt and possibly blood, hung on her thin frame, held together by the twist of rope that also bound her hands. The sleeves had been ripped off allowing Tate to see numerous bruises and cuts in different stages of healing, as well as a filthy bandage covering one arm from elbow to shoulder.

From out of nowhere, a different image superimposed itself in Tate's mind. A photograph of Evan a reporter friend had taken while embedded onboard the *Nimitz*. Evan had been standing on the flight deck, dressed in her green flight suit with her helmet tucked under one arm.

She had looked incredibly beautiful. A warrior out of time, with her dark hair windblown, and a half smile on her lips. The glow of the setting sun was slanting over her and reflecting on the gleaming Super Hornet behind her.

The image had made the cover of a national magazine under a banner that proclaimed the new US Navy. It had also singlehandedly done more to increase enlistment than any other recruitment strategy.

But as Tate stared at Evan now, she realized there was no resemblance between the woman in the photograph and the one standing a mile away under the harsh Afghanistan sun. This Evan was barely recognizable. She looked beaten. Beyond exhaustion and beyond defeat. And the knowledge tore at Tate.

"That's Khalid," JT said, indicating the man who had separated himself from the group. Tate watched as he approached and said something to Evan.

It was evident Evan didn't like whatever had been said to her, but Tate saw something else, as well. She might be down, but Evan Kane was not out. Tate could tell by the set of her shoulders, the defiant lift of her chin as she spoke back. By the flash of restrained anger visible on her face.

Khalid retaliated immediately. With a movement so swift Tate barely saw it coming, he backhanded Evan. He struck her quickly a second time, dropping her to her knees without a sound. She could see Walker struggle weakly, only to freeze an instant later as Khalid pressed his weapon hard against Evan's temple while clearly saying something to both of them.

This time, Evan didn't move. Didn't say anything. She simply bowed her head and closed her eyes, the move submissive, yielding. She remained silent and so still she no longer appeared to be breathing.

Oh God, this has to stop.

Scarcely able to breathe, Tate whimpered deep in her chest as panic bolted through her and her mind tried to process what she was seeing. Her world tilted.

She had not come all this way only to stand by helplessly and watch as Evan was executed. Anger welled up inside her and she welcomed the surge of strength it sent coursing through her.

"Take it easy, Tate." JT grasped her shoulders, holding her back. Preventing her from moving before Tate realized what she was about to do. "He's not going to do anything. His lookouts will have told him we're here and he knows we're watching. He has a reputation for enjoying inflicting pain and he's doing it all for show."

"I don't care why he's doing it," Tate said tightly. "What's happening down there is still real. He's still hurting her. And more than likely, Evan believes the bastard's going to kill her."

Tate met JT's gaze, saw the change in his expression, and knew she'd hit a nerve. She stood still a moment longer, lips pressed hard together. But then the adrenaline deserted her and her shoulders sagged as she turned away.

An instant later, JT's radio squawked, and they received the clearance they had been waiting for to proceed.

JT hesitated before moving. "Don't let this get personal, Tate. And don't give Khalid the excuse he needs to turn this into anything other than a straightforward exchange. We go in, we get your girl and Walker, and we get the hell out. Nothing less, nothing more."

Tate didn't trust her voice, so she simply nodded. Without another word, she followed JT's footsteps back to the Humvee, and after a short delay, the convoy began its infernally slow progress toward the settlement.

They stopped when they were within thirty feet of their targets—a group of insurgents and two battered and weary pilots who seemed unaware their rescue was at hand. It was Khalid, with his weapon mere inches from Evan's temple, who signaled for them to stop.

"We're going to do this slowly and carefully," JT cautioned one last time. "Stay calm, no matter what happens. Don't make any sudden movements and don't make eye contact."

Sudden movement? Eye contact? Tate would have laughed, but she couldn't actually breathe anymore. Her hands shook, betraying her as she fought to appear steady and unaffected. And as they exited the Humvee, Tate realized she had shifted into a kind of surreal state where nothing really registered anymore.

Except for Evan.

They were close enough that she could hear Evan's breathing—harsh and labored. See her face, flushed beneath the bruising and covered with a thin sheen of perspiration. Observe how she was holding herself in a way that told Tate she was favoring one side.

But Evan remained silent, motionless. On her knees, eyes closed.

Tate's fists tightened. She refused to allow herself to think or feel or imagine as she saw the burns on her neck and throat just above the rope holding her tethered. Saw the blood coming through the filthy bandage on her arm and on the leg of her flight suit.

Sweet Jesus, what have they done to you?

❖

Something was happening.

Kneeling in the sunbaked dust, with the hot wind buffeting her face, Evan could feel the escalating tension and hear the incessant whispers from the group of men huddled nearby. Watching but initially unable to clearly hear their conversations, all she could do was wait.

How long, she couldn't tell. Time had long since ceased to mean anything. But there were instances when the voices were raised, and one particular moment when she thought she heard the mention of an exchange.

That got her attention. Was this what Khalid meant when he said they were out of time? Was he finally going to do what he had threatened? Was he going to execute them and trade their bodies back to the Americans?

Be careful what you wish for. She'd allowed herself to get her hopes up the last time this happened. She had dared to think a trade between cells might bring them closer to going home. Instead, they had landed with Khalid in a place where pain ruled and life had little meaning.

But surely nothing could be worse than what she'd experienced during the past few weeks. Not even death. And at least it would provide some measure of closure for her family. And Tate.

Several lengthy heartbeats passed before Khalid pulled his weapon back and walked away from her. Her shoulders dropped wearily and only one thought held her focus fast—surviving. She tried to remain perfectly still, but as she struggled to breathe, she thought she heard the scraping sound of footsteps approaching from the road.

She turned toward the sound, her senses jumping. But her eyes felt like sandpaper and the pain in her head left her vision hazy. It was like watching shadows approach through a fogged window. Still, she hoped what little she could see and hear was real and not a further sign of delirium.

Ignoring the pain, she concentrated on listening to Khalid speak. And then it happened. She heard an unfamiliar voice, clearly male and using a local dialect. But he was speaking with an unmistakable American accent.

As a surge of energy coursed through her, she heard the American say something about releasing the prisoners. In the silence that followed there was an unmistakable squawk of a radio, but she couldn't make out the garbled words as a voice responded.

Apparently satisfied with whatever had just transpired, Khalid returned to her side. Evan could feel the weight of the hostility in his face as he stared at her, and she raised her head to meet his unsettling gaze. He continued to regard her silently for a long taut moment that rattled her more than she cared to admit.

She couldn't back down. She just wasn't sure she had it in her to engage in another skirmish so soon after the last one.

Unexpectedly, Khalid broke the silence, issuing a barked order to one of the guards holding Deacon.

Jesus, did she just hear him say—

The guard immediately dropped the rope he was holding. Releasing Deacon. Telling him to move.

Oh God, this was really happening.

Evan watched Deacon take a couple of faltering steps forward, then stop and turn in her direction. He obviously didn't want to leave without her. He wanted to help her. But it was equally apparent Khalid wasn't going to allow it. He shook his head and swung his weapon closer to her head.

Seeing the uncertainty on Deacon's face, Evan gave a quick shake of her head. *Don't do it.* She winced as she saw one of the guards further discourage Deacon with a sharp push that sent him stumbling awkwardly. Away from her.

Khalid watched and smiled.

Evan felt a sinking sensation in her chest and her eyes burned with regret as she watched Deacon move farther away from her. But she consoled herself with the knowledge that at least he would be free from this never-ending nightmare. He would make it home again.

Just before Deacon reached the tall American, something caught her eye. At first uncertain, Evan blinked. She tried to clear her vision and for several seconds she willed herself to see more clearly.

But then slowly, like an overlay in her memory, the image became clearer and she stared in disbelief, certain she saw Tate standing there, less than twenty feet away.

❖

Tate stayed back, watching JT walk a few feet ahead of her and begin quietly talking to Khalid. She could hear Khalid's responses but didn't understand what was being said or know what language they were using.

Briefly she wondered what game he was playing. But then she made the mistake of glancing at Evan, at her freshly bruised and bloodied mouth, and reasons no longer mattered.

A dozen different emotions swept through her and she stopped breathing, stopped thinking. She stood aware only of the blazing Afghan sun overhead, blinding and hot. And how much she suddenly detested the sound of Khalid's soft, emotionless voice.

God, she wanted this to be over. Sinking her teeth into her bottom lip, she forced herself to remain silent and waited for JT and Khalid to finish speaking. Finally, as if by mysterious command, the conversation ended and JT spoke softly into his radio.

Behind her, she felt more than heard movement, and then the eight prisoners involved in the exchange shuffled past her, while the soldiers in the convoy maintained a state of heightened vigilance.

A moment later, Khalid issued an unmistakable order. Tate had no idea what he'd said, but the rope attached to Walker was released and he was pushed forward. Limping badly, he paused as he drew alongside Evan, who remained on her knees. He appeared uncertain, and then turned as if to help her.

Khalid shook his head and swung his weapon closer to Evan. At almost the same time, Evan looked at Walker and gave a slight shake of her head just as one of Khalid's men yelled and gave Walker a shove that sent him stumbling.

Khalid smiled. He kept his attention—and his weapon—clearly fixed on Evan. And as Tate stared at the weapon, she suddenly understood all too clearly that luck, like time, could run out at any moment. The realization struck her like a fist.

Once Walker reached where she stood, Greg Turner and a young army medic materialized and helped him into the Humvee. But Khalid made no move to release Evan, holding her tethered to him, his weapon at the ready. Tate stared at her helplessly, willing Evan to remain strong.

Come on, baby, look at me. Stay strong long enough to come back to me. Please.

As if responding to her silent entreaty, Khalid finally spoke. He gestured with his weapon, then watched as Evan struggled to her feet. Her face was pale and drawn but determined, and her legs shook unsteadily. It was apparent she was trying to keep as much weight as possible off her right leg.

Tate wanted to go to her, needed to help her. She didn't even realize she'd taken a step forward until she felt JT reach out and tighten his grip on her arm, holding her back. She held his gaze, fighting an overwhelming urge to disregard him. But she knew he was right and remained where she was.

Turning back, she could see Khalid staring at Evan as if measuring her determination. Then he muttered something only Evan could hear and pulled hard on the rope that bound her to him. Evan lost her balance and dropped hard to her knees.

JT scowled and swore under his breath.

But not even the air moved as Evan sat back on her heels, breathing hard and looking to steady herself. She didn't flinch, not even when Khalid raised his weapon and brushed it against her face as he whispered something to her.

And then, in spite of the pain she had to be in, she said something.

Tate had no idea what it was. It certainly wasn't in English. But Khalid's response was immediate. He pushed the barrel of his weapon under Evan's chin and forced her head up until their eyes met.

And then he started to laugh.

Tate heard JT choke back his own laugh. "What the hell did she say to him?"

JT turned and gave Tate a quick assessing look. "She's got a far better grasp of the local language than I'll ever manage, so I didn't catch all of it."

"Come on, JT. Give me something. What did she say?"

"She said"—he grinned—"the gist is, in the end she wins because she's going home to a beautiful redhead, while he'll only have his goat to keep him warm."

"Oh." Tate's breath seized in her throat and she returned the grin. "She always had a way with languages."

She saw Khalid release the rope, dropping it to the ground as he shrugged and walked away. Watched Evan stare blankly in his wake, appearing momentarily stunned, before shakily getting to her feet. She wavered and seemed to falter.

Tate scrambled forward. Felt Evan's stare and saw the confusion on her face.

"Evan, it's okay. I'm here," she said, purposely keeping her voice low pitched and soothing as she drew near, resisting the urge to move too quickly, to close her arms around her. "I've come to take you home. Do you understand?"

Evan didn't blink. Didn't move. Didn't make a sound.

"Evan? It's all over. Come on, love, we have to get you out of here." A moan this time, soft.

Gathering a deep breath, Tate reached for her. She slid her arms around Evan slowly, pausing as she felt her stiffen.

Her expression dazed and confused, Evan swayed, poised between movement and collapse. But then her legs started to buckle, and as she started to go down, she reached her tied hands toward Tate. Tate tried to absorb her weight while JT rushed forward.

"We need to get her into the Humvee," he said. Without hesitation, he wrapped his arms around Evan and lifted her, carrying her limp in his arms as a pair of marines ran forward to help.

Once inside the vehicle, JT laid Evan on her back and quickly cut the ropes that bound her hands before removing the rope from around her neck. Simultaneously, the doctor began checking her over while a medic set up an IV to rehydrate Evan and deliver antibiotics.

In the gurney across from Evan, Deacon Walker clutched a bottle of water and looked on, his anxiety radiating in waves. "We'd pretty much given up on anyone looking for us, let alone finding us." Walker took another gulp of water, spilling some as he started to shake. "And the past couple of weeks…man, it's been brutal. Evan started getting sick and there was nothing I could do to help. She's going to be okay, isn't she?"

"We're going to do everything we can."

Tate felt something fleetingly brush against her hand. She glanced down and saw Evan, reaching for her with one hand, looking confused, as if she hadn't quite processed what had happened yet. Grasping her hand, Tate looked into her eyes, dulled by pain and the drugs the doctor had just administered.

They were more black than gray, but Tate thought she detected a hint of recognition, and as she squeezed her hand, Evan responded with a ghost of a smile. Her lips moved and Tate bent her head down to hear her.

"Are you real?"

Her voice was strained and hoarse. A stranger's voice. Her words were slurred, and her eyes momentarily drifted closed before fluttering open again, as if she was fighting to stay conscious. For just an instant, her gaze locked onto Tate with a force Tate felt physically, and then Evan murmured something else. But with the terror of seeing Khalid with his weapon at Evan's throat still flashing in Tate's mind, her words were lost.

The Humvee started to move and Tate tightened her hold on Evan's hand. "It's going to be okay, Evan," she promised. "You're safe now and we have all the time in the world. All you need to focus on is getting better. And then we're going to take you home."

There was no discernible response, and it took a couple of seconds before Tate realized Evan was asleep, or unconscious. Fresh fear riddled her, sending chills dancing along her spine, and she looked to the doctor, ready to beg him if necessary.

"Why don't you trade places with me so I can get a closer look at my patient?" he said gently.

Tate reluctantly released the hand she'd been holding and moved to the other side of the vehicle. She trembled as memories washed over her, never taking her eyes off Evan while the doctor got to work.

After several minutes, she heard the doctor swear under his breath. He had just removed the filthy bandage wrapped around Evan's upper arm, and as she peered over his shoulder, Tate could clearly see marks where the bandage had been.

Initially they looked like an intricately designed tattoo. But on closer inspection, she realized they were cuts. A pattern of sweeping cuts, made with a sharp blade.

Oh God, oh God, *oh God.* Tate clenched her jaw and remained perfectly still. Wanting to help and knowing there was so little she could do, she stayed out of the way.

She should have been better prepared, but the realization of what Evan had endured threatened to bring her to her knees. Exhausted and heartsick, she could only stare as Greg lifted Evan's T-shirt. His action revealed another deep laceration, this one several inches in length and badly infected. It started at Evan's ribcage and snaked just underneath her breast.

Evan's eyes fluttered as he examined the cut, but she squeezed them tight and flinched as the doctor continued to probe past a combination of fresh and old bruises and cuts. Tate tried to detach herself as each injury was revealed. But she failed miserably, and she struggled to find a spot on her lover's body that wasn't beaten or bruised.

"Her knee's a mess," Greg said quietly. "But we won't know the extent of the damage until we can get her into X-ray."

"She hurt it when she ejected," Walker informed them. "It never really healed and then Khalid kept forcing her to use it. Kept making her stand or walk, knowing how much it hurt her."

Tate closed her eyes and remained silent until the doctor finished assessing Evan's injuries. "How is she?"

"Bad enough. In addition to the knee injury, there's a GSW— sorry, a gunshot wound—in her right thigh." He paused as he adjusted the flow of the IV. "She's also got contusions and lacerations, and a definite case of malnutrition. The wounds themselves won't kill her and she's already survived the shock and blood loss. But the infection that's set in…that's another matter."

"She got shot when we tried to escape a couple of nights ago," Walker said quietly, never taking his eyes off Evan. "She should have gotten away, but I fell and Evan came back to help me. I told her she should keep on going, but she just laughed and came back anyway.

That's when they tagged her. She was bleeding pretty badly, but the bastards wouldn't do anything to stop it. They just literally dragged us back to their camp and spent the next ten hours beating the shit out of us just for fun—no offense, ma'am."

"Not to worry, I've heard the word before." Tate tried but couldn't stop herself from asking, "Can I ask why?"

"Why what, ma'am?"

"Why would you try to escape when the prisoner exchange had already been negotiated?"

Walker turned dark eyes in her direction, his lips pressed together in an expression Tate could only interpret as anger and regret.

"Khalid told us we'd stopped entertaining him. He said in case we were too stupid to understand, it meant we'd outlived our usefulness. Then he told us about the exchange. But what he said was we were going to be executed—decapitated—and he'd arranged to exchange our bodies for some prisoners currently being held near Kabul. His idea of a joke, I guess."

He swiped with one hand at the sweat on his face before he continued in a flat voice. "But even if he hadn't told us his plans, we already knew we had to try to get away. Khalid was killing Evan, slowly but surely, one cut at a time."

"To what end?"

"I honestly don't know, ma'am. He took some kind of perverse pleasure in bleeding her, and Evan—she was getting weaker with each day that passed. Then she started running a fever, for maybe a week or so, and it got so she couldn't keep down what little food they gave us when they remembered to feed us. Neither of us knew how much longer she'd last."

Tate listened with increasing dread. She stared again at the rope burns around Evan's throat, wrists, and ankles, at the cuts on her arm. And she wondered about the extent of the damage she couldn't see.

"It turned out that bastard Khalid had the last laugh. He set us up. He made it possible for us to escape just so he could hunt us down like animals."

Evan shifted suddenly, shuddering in pain. Groaning and flinching away from the doctor's touch, her eyes opened and she stared at Tate before saying something in a soft, pain-filled voice. Tate couldn't make out the words and waited impatiently until Greg finished what he was doing. "What did she say?"

"She asked me if she was dead."

"What the hell would make her think she'd died?"

"That's easy." Greg smiled for the first time since they'd landed in Afghanistan. "She looked up and saw you and said she thought she'd seen an angel."

Chapter Eleven

Landstuhl, Germany

Shortly after one thirty in the morning, Tate closed her eyes, fighting as yet another wave of fatigue swept over her. It clawed at her. Threatened to pull her under. She held her breath and tried not to drown. She'd managed to get some rough sleep on the long flight from Kandahar, and earlier she'd caught another hour or so while waiting for Evan to come out of surgery. But too much had happened. There were too many emotions to deal with. And as the adrenaline high that had kept her going over the last few days wore off, she found herself struggling to stay awake.

It wasn't that she couldn't sleep. And in any case, a doctor with a sympathetic face had offered to give her something. But Tate had refused, knowing it wouldn't help.

She wavered on the cusp of madness.

She wasn't suffering from an inability to sleep. She was awake simply because she was too afraid to fall sleep. She felt strangled by an all-consuming, irrational fear that if she went to sleep, Evan would somehow disappear. She was afraid she would wake up to discover it had all been a dream. A product of her mind's inability to accept the truth.

She would discover Evan had really died on that cold and lonely mountainside in Afghanistan.

So she'd pulled a chair next to Evan's bed and sat with one foot hooked on the side rail. It left her within inches of Evan, and her body sparked with memory. But she didn't trust herself to move, barely trusted herself to blink, as she pushed her hair out of her eyes with an unsteady hand and watched Evan as she slept.

There were changes, of course.

Evan's face was thinner, honed by her recent experiences into sharp planes and angles. Her cheekbones were more pronounced and there were lines where none had previously existed. What she clearly needed was time. Time to heal. Time for swelling to recede and the bruises to fade along with the memories.

Tate marveled at the combination of softness and strength, saw the ghosts of laugh lines by her eyes, and longed for the moment when those storm-gray eyes would open. Reaching out, she touched Evan's hand, lacing their fingers together.

Almost immediately, the contact settled her. Grounded her. Evan's skin was warm to the touch, and if she moved her fingers slightly, she could feel her pulse beating strong and steady.

Not that she needed to. If she wanted, she could simply look up and watch the numbers and lines dance across the array of impersonal machines monitoring Evan. But she preferred the real connection she found and the feeling of Evan's heart beating beneath her fingertips.

Evan had been asleep since they'd brought her up from recovery, two hours post-op. Sedated, bruised, and bandaged, with intravenous lines running into both arms while another tube provided oxygen. But she was alive and that was what Tate focused on as she touched her gently and let her know she was there.

A nurse came in, but she didn't say anything other than acknowledge Tate with a nod. She simply went about her business. Hung a fresh bag of clear fluid and adjusted the intravenous flow. Checked Evan's vitals and made notes in her chart.

Tate checked the time and wondered where Alex was. She knew Althea and Robert were on their way, Althea having called when they'd landed at Ramstein Air Base. But there had been no word from Alex.

He had to know Evan had been rescued. Hell, he probably knew as soon as it happened, if not before. Twin telepathy, he and Evan called it. Of course, now that she thought about it, maybe that connection helped explain why Alex had such a difficult time believing Evan was really dead. He'd said he couldn't feel her gone.

At the time, no one had understood what Alex meant. But after the proof of life video surfaced, Tate wondered if perhaps they all should have tried a little harder to listen and understand what Alex had been saying.

❖

For the next hour, Tate watched with growing unease as Evan's temperature started to climb. Her hair, already sweat soaked, grew tangled as she thrashed back and forth, gripping the sheets at her hips with tight fists, while soft sounds of distress fought their way past her bruised throat.

Reacting instinctively, Tate whispered her name, trying to call her back from the nightmare that held her. "You're all right, Evan," she said softly, hoping on some level Evan could hear her and know she wasn't alone. "You're safe now."

Evan mumbled an incoherent response, but she slowly began to settle. Encouraged, Tate continued to talk to her, using quiet words to reassure and gentle touches to chase away the dark shadows haunting her.

And whether it was in response to the sound of her voice or her touch, Evan's body gradually stilled. The tense muscles relaxed, the frown smoothed out, and her breathing slowed, until the covers were once again softly rising and falling with each breath. As if she had found some peace.

"Tate."

Just that, the soft murmur of her name, and Tate's heart stuttered. "I'm right here," she responded and smiled. "Right where I belong."

❖

With a sigh, Tate leaned her head back. She'd been talking to Evan for the past couple of hours, sometimes reading to her from a copy of *Life of Pi* she'd had in her backpack, other times simply talking about some of the places they'd been to and the things they'd done.

One of her favorite memories kept coming to mind: the trip to Chamonix made all the more memorable because it had turned into their official coming out as a couple. When Tate finally admitted to herself what was in her heart, that she and Evan were not simply having an extended fling, they had become inextricably entwined—body, mind, and soul.

Closing her eyes, she smiled as she reminded Evan of that fateful trip and the first time she'd met Alex.

"You went ahead, catching a ride on a military transport as far as Geneva. I followed a couple of days later because I needed to clear up a backlog at work after my trip to Afghanistan. Of course, the extra time didn't help because while I was supposed to be concentrating on work, all I could think about was how we'd be using the holiday to openly acknowledge our relationship. To each other…and to your family.

"You probably knew how nervous I was—especially when it came to your mother—but I was really looking forward to finally meeting your twin. And as it turned out, Alex was the only one up when I arrived ahead of schedule because, at the last minute, I was able to catch an earlier flight. But Alex didn't seem to mind. He just grabbed my suitcase with one hand, waved away my apology with the other, and introduced himself."

Tate stared at her lover for a long moment, and then smoothed Evan's hair away from her face. "As if he could have been anyone other than your brother. Tall and slim like you and just as heartbreakingly beautiful. Mirror images. Except he didn't have to deal with the constraints put on you by the navy, so he could get away with the dark, bad-boy look he was cultivating—the one that drove your mother crazy, with the diamond studs winking in his ear and the scruff covering his jaw."

Momentarily swamped by the flood of memories rushing to the surface, Tate's voice wavered, but she cleared her throat and forced herself to continue, convinced Evan could hear her and determined to maintain the connection. "Alex made it clear he knew there was an ongoing *something* between us, and he gave me such an intense once-over. But obviously I passed because he said your taste in women had improved and that quite clearly I was good for you because you seemed happier than you'd been in a long time. And that even Althea would be able to see it. I knew then and there Alex and I were destined to be friends.

"You knew we would be, of course. But did you have any idea how much your brother terrified me with his talk of ski mountaineering and off-piste skiing?" she asked the still sleeping Evan. "God, when Alex told me you'd made arrangements for all of us to go heli-skiing, I kept picturing myself tumbling and falling headfirst down a mountain and having to wait for a Saint Bernard to come and rescue me. I got dizzy just trying to follow Alex's conversation, never mind coping with the idea of being dropped by a helicopter on top of a mountain, miles from civilization. But just as I was trying to figure out how advanced a skier needed to be to accomplish this horror, I felt you come up behind me."

Tate remembered the sudden warmth that had spread through her body, followed by a brief spark of electricity when Evan's fingers had trailed across her back. Fresh from a shower, with her hair still wet, Evan had smelled of sandalwood soap, clean mountain air, and desire as she'd wrapped her arms around Tate.

"You whispered in my ear and told me not to worry. Promised you'd look after me on the slopes. Then suggested that I could return the favor après-ski."

As if manifested by her thoughts, Tate heard approaching footsteps followed by a cough and turned her head to see Alex standing in the doorway. An apparition so like Evan when he flashed his megawatt smile it left her feeling oddly unsettled. Moving quickly, she rose from her seat and crossed the room to him in three steps.

His presence was reassuringly familiar as she leaned into him, wrapping her arms tightly around his waist and closing her eyes against the sudden rush of emotions. The onslaught left her dizzy, and she felt something crash inside her, fragmenting, forcing her to remain with her face buried against Alex's neck until she was certain her eyes would stay dry.

"God, I'm so glad you're here," she whispered, when at last she was able to speak.

With her senses already on overload, it took a moment longer before Tate felt the tension coursing through Alex's body. Before she noted how anguished his beautiful face looked in the dimly lit room. "Oh, Alex, baby. It's okay. Evan's going to be fine. I promise."

"I know," Alex grumbled. "She'll never let me live it down if she finds out I've been crying like a baby over her."

Knowing him as she did, Tate understood how badly he wanted to be strong. Like Evan. For Evan.

She said nothing while Alex wiped the dampness from his face with the back of one hand while using the other to draw Tate closer to the bed, where he could finally get a close-up view of Evan.

"What the hell did they do to her?"

The horror in his voice was clear, as was the rhetorical nature of his question. Tate was grateful he expected no answer. Bending over the bed, his expression a mix of joy and pain, he pressed a gentle kiss on his sister's forehead and stroked her hair, watching the dark strands sift through his fingers. There was a reverence in his touch, Tate thought, and such exquisite gentleness, almost as if he was afraid that Evan would shatter and disappear.

Or perhaps, like Tate herself, he was having difficulty believing she was really there. Alive. In their lives once again.

Tate swallowed and because it was her nature to touch she reached for Alex's hand. She laced her fingers through his, both wanting and needing his strength and offering hers in return while they both continued to watch over Evan.

She was so wrapped in the moment, in watching Evan, that it was some time before she realized someone was missing. "Where's Nick?"

"He's off trying to find us a hotel room. I told him it had to be a suite, so you can stay with us."

Tate opened her mouth to protest, but Alex stopped her. "You're not spending twenty-four/seven in this hospital, Tate, and one of the nurses told me Evan's probably going to be here at least a couple of weeks."

"But, Alex—"

"Tate, love, you of all people must know that getting her back is only going to be the beginning of a long road home for Evan. We may not want to talk about the elephant in the room, but the truth is none of us have any idea what she's been through these last months when we all thought she was dead."

Tate closed her eyes and saw Evan bloodied and bruised, kneeling in front of Khalid. She thought she'd dealt with it, but it all came back now, all but overwhelming her.

"The point," Alex continued, "is she's going to need all of us—but you in particular—to be strong for her when we get to bring her home with us."

"You're right, of course."

"I know I'm right. And you're toast. I'm sure the doctors in this hospital have seen dead people who look better than you."

"Thanks a lot. I'm well aware I've not even managed a shower in a couple of days." She started to laugh, then realized Alex wasn't joking.

Alex didn't smile back. "I'm not talking about that. I'm saying you need to rest. You should be sleeping. Have you eaten?"

"Alex, it's the middle of the night."

"Let me rephrase that. When was the last time you ate?"

"I'm not sure." Tate shrugged, swallowed, and tried again. "Maybe yesterday morning…no, I was in Kandahar yesterday morning. I think it might have been the night before."

"Tate, you know better." Alex tapped a finger on the line furrowed in between her brows as he continued to watch her. "What's going on in there?"

"I just don't want Evan to be alone when she wakes up." Tate sighed and slid her hands into her pockets.

After a long moment of silence, she looked up at Alex. "It's ironic, but Evan and I…we never got around to talking about what would happen when she finished her service commitment. Whether she was planning to go home. Where home might be." She released a tight laugh. "I had every intention of talking with her about it the day she was due back in Bahrain. I planned to convince her we belonged together. And if that didn't work, I planned to tie her to my bed until I wore down her resistance."

"Kinky." Alex raised both brows, then continued to stare at Evan's face, where the bruises spread across her hollowed cheeks. "Our girl really does look like hell, though, doesn't she?"

The truth was between the blackened eyes, the swollen mouth, and the cuts and bruises, Evan looked nothing like she should. But his remark had Tate's tension cracking open so a smile could slip through. "I don't think your sister would appreciate your comment. And she's still the most beautiful woman I've ever known."

"Ah, Tate." Alex chuckled. "It must be love, because well, hell, the last time I saw Evan looking anywhere near this awful"—he paused and grinned wickedly—"was just after the first time I got her drunk and then dared her to go bungee jumping while we were in Australia."

His comment surprised a muffled laugh out of Tate. "I don't think I've heard that story. When were you in Australia?"

"If I remember correctly, it was the summer we turned sixteen. I didn't believe it was actually possible for a person to turn such an ungodly shade of green."

He grinned again and Tate couldn't help but grin back. "I can always count on you, can't I?"

Another much-needed laugh slipped free. It felt good to laugh, and it was exactly what they were doing when Althea and Robert Kane arrived and found them a short time later.

CHAPTER TWELVE

A quick glance at Althea—face pale, eyes red rimmed and shadowed, mouth drawn into a thin, grim line—was all it took. Tate felt a flash of anxiety and unconsciously took a step back from Evan's bed, coming up hard against Alex's chest. His hands immediately moved to steady her, and she could feel the reassuring beat of his heart, strong against her back.

With a conscious effort, she tried to regroup. She slowly released a long, silent breath and rubbed her arms to chase away an unexpected chill. At least her hands weren't shaking and she was remembering to breathe. Most of the time.

Althea regarded her silently and gave her a brief nod before turning her gaze to rest on Evan. She didn't weep. But as she looked at her daughter, Tate saw a spate of tears willed away and wondered what that level of control cost her.

"Oh God, what did they do to her." Althea reached out and caressed the side of Evan's face before pulling back and covering her mouth with her trembling hand. But as she continued to stare at Evan, it seemed to Tate as if Althea had been waiting for this moment and this chance to beg, to promise, to do whatever it took to set things right again with her daughter. To put Evan squarely back in her life.

Robert looked as exhausted as his wife, his expression shuttered. Tate watched as he lowered his head and pressed a kiss to Evan's forehead. "I've missed you, baby," he said, his voice barely audible. When he straightened, he reached for Althea's hand, drawing her near to him.

"Thank you, Tate," he said. "For bringing Evan back to us. I'll not forget."

His words caught her off guard, and Tate remained silent while a wave of conflicting emotions crashed through her. From somewhere deep inside she pulled the last of her resources, and though the world beneath her shifted, she squared her shoulders, raised her head and looked at him. "I would have done anything." Her voice was only slightly breathless. "But as it turned out, I didn't have to do much."

Robert raised a brow, and his eyes—so like Evan's—reflected the smile that graced his lips. "Somehow I doubt that."

"I'm just glad I was able to help in some way."

After a moment, he nodded. "Has she woken up at all?"

"No." Tate shook her head and gripped her hands together. "Not since we flew out of Afghanistan. She was in a fair bit of pain, so the doctor kept her sedated during the flight. And then they took her into surgery almost immediately after we arrived."

"What have the doctors said?"

Tate allowed her frustration to briefly come to the forefront. "I've not actually seen or talked to anyone since they brought Evan up to the room post-op. I'd also like to find out how Lieutenant Walker is doing—I'm sure one of the first things Evan will want to know when she wakes up is how he's doing. But I haven't had any luck in that regard, either."

Further conversation was interrupted by a knock on the door. Turning, Tate saw a tall, thin woman wearing a white lab coat over pale green surgical scrubs.

"You must be Commander Kane's family. Perhaps I can answer some of your questions for you. I'm Commander Kelsey Grant, and I'll be Evan's doctor for as long as she's here with us," she said with a slight smile.

The doctor had short dark hair framing an attractive, intelligent face and a no-nonsense air Tate found appealing. She also appeared remarkably calm.

"How is she? What can you tell us about Evan's medical condition? What's being done—" Robert and Althea began firing questions in unison.

Alex quickly stepped in to quell the situation before it got out of hand. "I'm sorry, Commander Grant, my parents are both litigators." He offered an apologetic smile. "But you're right, we're Evan's family. These are my parents—Althea and Robert. I'm Alex, and this," he added, without missing a beat, "is Tate. And we'd all like to know how Evan's doing."

The doctor smiled wearily before pushing her hands into the pockets of her lab coat. "Well, I'm happy to report Evan is doing much better than anyone could have expected given the circumstances she's been living in for the past few months."

"What can you tell us about the extent of her injuries?" Robert asked, all trace of his earlier weariness disappearing.

The doctor picked up Evan's medical chart and glanced at it briefly. "We operated on Evan shortly after she arrived," she began softly. "The most serious of her injuries were to her right leg—a penetrating wound to her thigh and blunt force trauma to her knee. We were able to repair the muscle damage caused by the bullet wound, but her knee required extensive reconstructive surgery."

"But she'll recover?"

The doctor nodded. "Her long-term prognosis is really very good. We'll have her out of bed on crutches ASAP, and it'll probably take about three weeks for her knee to resume weight bearing. But it's too soon to predict when she'll be cleared for active duty."

Before anyone else could respond, Tate spoke up. "Actually, Evan had completed her service commitment before she was shot down. She was scheduled to go home."

"Her deployment was extended?"

"Yes, stop-loss."

"In that case, once she finishes physiotherapy, Evan's greatest challenge will likely be clearing airport security systems. We used titanium staples and a number of screws to hold everything in her knee together."

The doctor's comment brought momentary smiles to tired faces.

"Having said that, our more immediate concern is Evan is severely undernourished and has a number of infected lacerations—on her right side, on one arm, and on her back—which have left her in a weakened condition."

The frown on Robert's angular face deepened as he stared at the doctor. "What does that mean?"

"In short, she's going to need time to recover. But Evan is young and I've been told she was remarkably fit prior to her ordeal. It's clearly what enabled her to endure what she's been through and makes her prognosis excellent. Still, there is only so much we can do. The rest will be up to her."

As she listened to the conversation, Tate felt her throat tighten. Lowering her head, she stared at Evan, willing her to open her eyes. "How soon before she wakes up?"

"Actually, she came around briefly while we had her in recovery. She became a little distraught and asked for you and Lieutenant Walker. Once I assured her everyone was safe, she slipped back under. So rest assured this is nothing that should concern you. Her body simply needs time to heal. Now, if you have no other questions—"

"Did they hurt her?" Althea asked quietly.

To her credit, Commander Grant didn't flinch, and Tate thought the doctor's gaze reflected considerable compassion. "Are you asking me if Evan was sexually abused? If she was raped?"

Althea lifted her chin and squared her shoulders. "Yes."

The room became pin-drop quiet and Tate's heart sank as she watched the doctor's features tighten. *Oh, Evan.*

"Before I answer, you should be aware that most women in the military, but particularly women in higher risk roles such as pilots, fully recognize they're engaged in a high-risk, no-margin occupation. They accept there is a small but very real threat of capture, physical and psychological torture, and even death." Commander Grant exhaled softly. "Having said that, I can tell you we found no evidence of any recent sexual trauma. But as you're aware, Evan was in captivity a number of months, and it's impossible to say what she may have endured early on. Only she will be able to answer that particular question. And you have to be prepared that she won't."

Althea flushed, straightened, blinked. But if the doctor's response had not been enough, she clearly had the grace to accept it was all she would get.

"When can we take Evan home?" The question came almost simultaneously from Tate and Alex and earned an encouraging smile from the doctor.

"We'll need to clear up the infection and get her feeling better first," Commander Grant said as her smile widened. "She'll also need to gain some weight. She'll probably be ready to go home in a couple of weeks, possibly sooner. It really all depends on her recuperative powers."

"If that's the case, you'd best start filling out her discharge papers because she'll be out of here in less than a week," Alex said with a grin.

The doctor spread her hands, palm up. "Anything is possible, but you must also be prepared. The effect of captivity is unique to each individual and this isn't going to be easy. Evan will need to come to terms with what happened to her, and to do that she'll need your patience and understanding."

❖

"I'm really not hungry," Tate grumbled, as temper and assorted other emotions hummed equally in her blood. Stiff, sore, and feeling every minute of what had been a very long week, she leaned back in the chair, pushed aside the bag Alex was holding, and stared up at him. She wasn't in the mood to eat, and it didn't really matter that she'd barely eaten in two days. Nor had she slept more than a few hours in the last seventy-two. But that was not the point.

Alex was looking at her with a clearly troubled expression. "How are you going to remain strong for Evan if you don't eat anything? You need to eat something, and then get about twelve hours of solid sleep." Not waiting for an answer, he continued to speak as he opened the bag. "Now, I've brought you a sandwich from one of those machines in the cafeteria. Mystery meat, by the look of it, and it was going begging, but still, it's all there was, it's better than nothing, and you need to eat. So you'll eat at least half of it for me, okay? I also got you a coffee."

After a long, silent minute, Tate gave him a bland look, allowing humor to ghost around her mouth. "Mystery meat? Fine, as long as you eat the other half. Do we have a deal?"

Alex grinned and nodded. "You're worse than my sister, you know that? That's why you're so good together. By the way, I managed to discover Deacon Walker is just down the hall and doing rather well. I popped in to see him, and once sleeping beauty here decides to wake up and rejoin the living, I've promised Lieutenant Walker I would arrange a reunion."

Twenty minutes later, the remains of Tate's half of the sandwich lay abandoned on the bedside table, while she sat by Evan's bed, her half-drunk coffee in her hand. Nick was stretched out in a chair with his feet on the end of the bed. And Alex was once again regaling them with humorous stories about Evan from when they were growing up.

Some of the stories Tate had heard before, from Alex or from Evan herself. Still others were new. Mostly, they kept her interested and entertained and stopped her from dwelling on the fact Evan was still unconscious.

Althea and Robert had graciously declined Alex's offer to share the food he'd gotten and had left to find something more substantial on their own. With Althea's connections, Tate was certain they would be well taken care of.

She took another swallow of the lethal coffee and sat quietly, impatiently waiting for Evan to come back to her. She smiled and listened as Alex recounted yet another tale—of Evan taking a math exam for him. One he needed to ace so as not to get tossed off his high school basketball team. Even in the room's dim light she could see his smile.

"How old were you?"

"Fifteen. For some reason, Evan understood numbers, while I just wanted to paint and play basketball," Alex said, a wry grin on his face.

"And really, all we needed was for her to wear a pair of old ripped jeans, a hoodie, and a baseball cap. No one looked twice. Certainly not close enough to notice the differences, not that there really were many."

"He was older...but I was smarter...and taller."

Tate froze at the sound of Evan's voice, then turned abruptly toward the bed to find a pair of smoke-gray eyes looking back at her. Glassy, bloodshot, and faintly confused. But they were the most beautiful eyes she'd ever seen.

"Evan?" The tremor in her voice betrayed her as her breath caught in her throat. Tears stung her eyes and her heart hammered hard in her chest. "Oh my God, *Evan*."

Alex's whoop of joy echoed in her ears as he grabbed Nick and hugged him in celebration.

Evan looked from Nick and her brother to Tate and tried to smile, but her movements were stiff and sluggish, quite clearly slowed by pain. She blinked slowly, but as she let her vision adjust to the light, Tate could feel the apprehension brewing behind her eyes.

"I thought I saw you...with Khalid. Knew that wasn't right. Couldn't be right," Evan said hoarsely, a thread of wonder in her voice. "I was so afraid I'd dreamed you...you came and went in my head like a damned ghost...so many times. But you're really here. Please...tell me you're really here."

"Oh God, yes, I'm really here. So are Alex and Nick." Tate's gaze locked on Evan's as she tried to reassure her. She feathered her fingers over the abrasions on Evan's face and noticed despite the warmth, she was shivering again. "And your parents. The medical people said you'd sleep straight through until morning. But they'll be back in a few hours."

"My parents?" Dazed, Evan didn't seem capable of registering what Tate was saying, and as she fought to understand, Tate could see her anxiety level increase. "Tate, you shouldn't be here. It's not safe. What are you doing here? Where's Deacon?"

"Take it easy, Evan. You're safe, I promise. You're in the hospital." Tate took Evan's right hand in hers and for several long seconds she sat there holding it. Staring at the scraped knuckles, the bruised and swollen fingers, the rope burns on her wrist. Finally, she brought Evan's hand up to her lips and gently pressed a soft kiss against her open palm.

"Let's try this again. You're in an American military hospital in Germany. Lieutenant Walker's here too, in a room just down the hall. He's going to be fine. You'll probably be able to see him as soon as you're feeling better. Maybe later today. And I'm here because you're here, which makes it where I need to be. The same goes for Alex and Nick. And your parents."

Evan drew in a deep breath and nodded. A groan worked its way from somewhere deep in her chest.

"You doing okay?" Tate asked softly.

"I probably look worse than I feel…and I feel like hell." It came out in barely a whisper. Evan licked her lips, then swallowed and winced. "My throat hurts. And my leg. Actually, everything hurts."

Tate gazed tenderly down at her. She could see Evan was already starting to fade and was fighting to stay with them. It was also clear she was in pain as her eyes drifted closed. "How about we get a nurse to give you something for the pain? And see if we're allowed to give you something to drink or some ice chips. In the meantime, you need to rest and heal, so the best thing you can do now is sleep. We'll be here when you wake up."

"I'll go get a nurse," Nick volunteered and slipped from the room.

Evan visibly struggled to open her eyes one more time. "I heard you talking to me earlier. That's how I knew I was still alive…I've missed you."

Tate smiled. "I've missed you too, love. Now all you need to do is get well. Don't fight it. You're safe here—with us."

"Don't go," she murmured. She was clearly too foggy to stop the needy words that were so out of character before they slipped from her mouth. "Please."

"I'm not going anywhere, Evan," Tate assured her, leaning close to her ear. "I promise."

"I dreamed you so many times that I'm scared. I'd see you when you weren't really there, but it seemed so damned real I swear I could hear you breathing," Evan whispered. There was a world of pain in her words—words that threatened to break Tate's heart. "And now…now I'm afraid I'm going to wake up. I'll wake up and you'll be gone again. You'll be gone and I'll be back with Khalid in his little corner of hell."

Tate's smile faded. "Never," she breathed in reply. She pushed Evan's hair off her temple and watched the dark strands sift through her fingers. Felt an irresistible urge to gather her up and hold her until every horrid memory disappeared. "Go back to sleep, love. You need the rest. And I'll still be here when you wake up. I promise."

Evan started to murmur something, then gave up, sliding into sleep.

Tate watched her drift off with the comfort of that promise echoing in her mind, until she knew nothing at all. She leaned down and kissed her mouth softly while she slept. And then kept watch over her.

CHAPTER THIRTEEN

Evan struggled, aware enough to know she was dreaming. The images were in her mind, blurred but still there and still menacing, and she was unable to break free.

In her dream, she opened her eyes with a low moan. In the span of a heartbeat, terror came at her in suffocating waves, and it took a long breathless moment for her to recognize the cacophony of sound as the beating of her own heart.

She gritted her teeth and struggled to roll into a sitting position. It was a simple move under normal circumstances. But it was made more difficult by the rope binding her hands and the constant pain in her head.

The heat was cloying and sapped her strength. Beads of sweat trickled between her breasts, and her T-shirt clung at the small of her back. Leaning her shoulders against the wall, she stared at the mud wall on the opposite side of the small room and tried not to think.

She didn't know how long she'd remained unconscious this time. Daylight was visible through a small gap in the roof, but that didn't tell her if it was still the same day. She had no way of knowing how much time had passed. Not that the time of day seemed to matter much to Khalid.

From the moment she and Deacon had been traded to his cell, her captivity had become a series of meaningless stretches of unaided recovery bookended by painful one-on-one sessions with Khalid. And his visits were becoming more frequent.

Initially, his favorite form of entertainment had been his own variation of waterboarding, repeatedly holding her head under water, then pulling her out for brief respites. Almost but not quite long enough for her to draw in a full breath before he submerged her again.

Just remembering brought a fresh wave of nausea, and Evan breathed slowly as she waited for it to pass. Khalid had quickly grown bored with the water games, and she discovered he preferred a much more personal touch. He had switched to using the razor-sharp blade he carried at all times. It didn't get more personal than that.

Not that it really made a difference. It had all become a blur—a continuous cycle of sleep deprivation, questions, and pain. For reasons she couldn't fathom, Khalid was determined to break her. And he was very close to succeeding. The grim truth was he'd taken her to the very edge of death on at least four previous occasions. And she knew one of these times she wouldn't make it back.

She was covered with bruises and cuts. She knew she needed food, although she no longer felt hunger. She also needed to sleep and was desperately thirsty. She licked her lips and tried to swallow. She grimaced when she heard the outer door scrape open and saw three figures come into the room. Khalid, the tallest of the three, stepped forward.

"Stand up," he said in perfect, unaccented English.

She wasn't sure she could stand, knew she had no choice but to try. She got to her feet through sheer force of will. An instant later, one side of her face exploded as he struck without warning. Her world spun madly and her mouth filled with blood.

"Do you know what American and Afghanistani intelligence do to detainees to get them to talk, Commander?" he asked softly. "I do. I have been learning how to make people talk, and today you will talk to me. No matter what I ask, you will tell me whatever I want to know. Or you will die."

Exhausted and hurting, Evan had no choice but to let him drag her out of the small room. Determined she was not going to die today. Not if she could help it.

I'm dreaming. I'm dreaming. Evan successfully trapped the scream in her throat before it could escape, but for a lingering second or two, she had no idea where she was. She only knew the nightmare still lurked on the edge of her awareness, the dark memories still casting shadows. She bit her lip then realized her mistake when it hurt like hell.

As the echoes of Khalid's voice faded, the pain slowly diminished, and she concentrated on regulating her breathing, trying to clear her head while her eyes carefully scanned the room.

The blinds were closed and she didn't know what time it was. But focusing on the clean lines of the walls and the assortment of medical equipment helped. It provided a much needed level of assurance she was no longer in Afghanistan. She was safe, with nothing to fear but her memories. And she would find a way to ward them off.

A sniff of the air brought the first faint smile to her face. The room carried the scent of springtime, aided by the abundance of flowers that were providing a riot of color.

She knew her parents had brought most of them in an attempt to brighten her surroundings. There was a vase from Deacon's parents holding more brilliantly colored blooms, most of which she didn't recognize. But it was the small arrangement of lilies and roses in varying shades of orange and gold that caught her attention and caused her smile to widen.

Tate.

As she glanced around, Evan suddenly realized it was quiet in the room and she was very much alone. The knowledge should have reassured her. She wouldn't have been left alone if she hadn't been showing signs of improvement. But instead, the solitude had the opposite effect.

The smile on her face faded. Anxiety swirled unchecked and her mind began to fill with random uncensored images, flickering like an old silent movie. She forced herself to remain perfectly still, to keep breathing. Fighting the needles of panic as disparate emotions came together, blending and flooding her senses with thoughts of Khalid.

Damn him. He doesn't get to win. She'd already lost too much time. More than four months. She'd be damned if she was going to let him take more.

It was then she saw him.

Standing in the doorway, an ominous silent silhouette.

"Commander," he whispered. "Did I not tell you? Or did you not believe me when I said this thing between us wasn't finished?"

Evan heard a quiet whimper, a choke of horror. She realized the sounds were coming from her own throat but could do nothing to prevent them. She stared at her hands, shaking with panic, and knew she had to pull herself together. Knew if she waited just a moment or two longer, she could get the roaring in her ears and the hollowness in her stomach to pass.

"Commander?"

"No"—she swallowed convulsively—"you can't hurt me any-more."

"Commander?"

"You're not real."

"Commander, look at me."

"No." She screamed.

"Commander? Commander Kane."

Evan struggled to think, tried to speak. Tried to breathe. But too many threats and too much pain had left her tired and numb, unable to fight back any longer. She felt hands touch her and discovered she was too weak to do anything but let them hold her down.

She let her head fall back, closed her eyes, felt the sharp prick of a needle, but was beyond caring. And then she felt nothing.

❖

Tate hadn't been gone long.

She'd turned down an invitation from Alex, who was taking Nick and his parents out for dinner. Instead she had opted to make a quick trip to the hotel. Just long enough to grab a shower, a bite to eat, and a fresh set of clothes.

Her senses went on immediate alert as she stepped off the elevator and looked down the hall toward Evan's room. It was the dinner hour and the hallway was bustling with staff distributing food trays. But her eyes focused only on Evan's doctor and two nurses coming out of her room. Their expressions were grim.

Everything else faded in a paroxysm of fear. She should never have left Evan. Not even for a minute. She quickened her steps, sprinted toward them. "Is Evan okay?" Not waiting for a response, she tried to move past them and into the room, only to have the doctor step in front of her.

Tate hadn't known she could get this angry so quickly. But Evan was behind the closed door and she was being prevented from reaching her. "Get out of my way."

"Ms. McKenna…Tate, please listen to me. Commander Kane's not in any danger."

"Then why won't you let me see her?" Something in the doctor's gentle tone seeped through the haze brought on by her fear and concern, and Tate momentarily stopped struggling. "I need to know what's wrong. Evan was sleeping when I left and I wasn't gone that long."

"She had a nightmare. A particularly bad one. One of the nurses heard her screaming and went in to check on her, but Commander Kane became confused and seemed to believe he was one of her captors. She became quite agitated and had to be sedated to prevent her from hurting herself. She should sleep through until morning."

Tate had never felt so helpless. Dimly, she heard the clearing of a throat. She swallowed, stared at the doctor. "She hates how the drugs make her feel."

"I understand. Truly. But we need to control the pain Commander Kane is in and help her body conserve energy so she can heal. I assure you by morning she should be quite lucid."

"I still want to see her now. Be with her. She shouldn't be alone."

"Actually, she's not alone. Lieutenant Walker's with her."

"Deacon?"

"He was in the hallway when he heard Commander Kane scream and offered to help. Said he knew how to calm her and bring her down from a nightmare better than any sedative we'd administered. He was right."

The doctor indicated to one of the nurses, who opened the door to Evan's room. Stepping in, Tate saw Deacon Walker sitting in a chair by the side of the bed, holding Evan's hand while singing softly to her. The door swung shut noiselessly behind her, but she must have made a sound because he looked up and smiled.

"Told them this would work," he whispered. "When things would get bad with Khalid—after he would finish with Evan—sometimes singing was the only way I could reach her, get her to calm down."

That his voice was slightly off key didn't matter. As he resumed singing, Tate could see Evan relax, sinking deeper into the bed.

When the song was finished, Deacon pulled a second chair toward the bed beside him. "Do you know 'Into the Mystic'?"

Tate nodded.

"Great, it's one of Evan's favorites. You can sing it with me."

A small groan escaped from Evan's lips as she moved restlessly, stirring and mumbling in her sleep.

Tate immediately gravitated toward the bed, reaching for Evan's hand. "I'm right here, Evan. Right beside you. Everything's all right. I've got you. You're safe."

For several minutes, she continued the litany of assurances. Sliding her fingers through a lock of dark hair, she watched it curl around her finger, and then she leaned in and softly kissed her mouth. As if on cue, Evan's features slowly went slack, her clenched fist unfurled, and she melted into the bedding as she drifted deeper into sleep.

"That's bloody amazing. She normally doesn't listen to anyone, but she listens to you even in a drug-induced sleep."

Shit. She'd forgotten about Deacon.

"I'm sorry." He blushed and looked hopelessly young. "I didn't mean to embarrass you. I just thought you should know I'm okay if you want to hold Evan's hand or...do whatever."

"What do you mean?"

"During the last four months, Evan didn't really talk much, but when she did it was mostly about you. I believe the thought of getting home to you was what helped her survive everything Khalid did." As he paused, he blushed once again. "But for the record, I knew about Evan—and about the two of you—long before what happened in Afghanistan."

She glanced at Evan's sleeping face. "Evan told you?"

"Yeah, but I'd already guessed. I mean she's gorgeous, you know? But she never showed an interest in any of the guys that were always sniffing around after her like a pack of dogs, starting all the way back in flight school. So when we both ended up assigned to the same strike group, to the *Nimitz*, I finally just asked her."

"You're kidding."

Deacon shook his head. "I think when you spend months living in each other's back pocket during your first deployment, or keeping each other focused through first night landings or first landings in rough weather, some things fall by the wayside. And Evan and I—we'd already become friends. Anyway, that's when she told me."

Tate tried not to laugh. "Wait. Let me see if I understand this correctly. You asked Evan if she was gay. Is that what you're trying to tell me?"

"Well, yeah. After that it became fun to place side bets on the life expectancy of anyone who pursued her a little too aggressively. Man, she could shrivel a guy's testicles at twenty paces with just one look… begging your pardon."

"No need to apologize."

"Yeah, well after she told me, I realized I should have known sooner, seeing as she had more luck attracting the ladies than any of the fighter jocks in the squadron."

"Oh?"

Deacon coughed. "Of course, there's been no one else since she met you…at the embassy dinner in Bahrain," he added quickly. "I still remember, when I saw her the next morning, she told me she'd met an amazing woman who seduced her with a smile and then had her way with her."

"She said that, did she?"

"She did, and when I saw you in Afghanistan coming to our rescue I saw how right she was," he added with a grin. "You're really hot."

Tate rolled her eyes. "Thank you, Deacon, that's so sweet." She was still shaking her head when a nurse came in and chased Deacon back to his room.

Chapter Fourteen

When Evan next opened her eyes, the first light of day was beginning to bleed through the open blinds. It offered just enough light to confirm she was alone. Again.

Almost immediately, panic bolted through her and she covered her face, not liking the emotions swirling inside her. She felt disoriented. Isolated. Afraid.

Enough, she told herself, fighting to shake off the night, the dreams, and the remnants of fear. She had been given a second chance at the rest of her life. She needed to do something with it, starting now, or she wasn't going to make it.

Suddenly impatient, she threw back the sheet she'd managed to tangle around herself.

A hundred bruises immediately made themselves known. Pain took her breath away. The moisture in her mouth evaporated and her head began to pound. With no other choice, she fell back against the pillow and waited for the pain to subside.

On her second attempt, she moved more slowly. One deep breath followed by another. Every move was an effort, and her battered body screamed, but with equal parts dread and determination she began to slide toward the edge of the bed.

Movement proved awkward, made more so by the brace on her knee meant to help control motion while healing occurred. But in spite of the care she took, pain blossomed in her leg and she couldn't quite contain the groan that came from deep within her every time she inhaled. Her palms grew damp and her stomach threatened to rebel.

That in itself was almost funny because she couldn't remember the last time she'd eaten.

She persevered, and after what felt like a lifetime her feet cleared the edge of the bed. She paused for an instant, braced herself for what she knew was to come. But before she could follow through, a sound stopped her. Voices coming from just outside her room. And then the door swung open.

"Whoa, Commander Kane, now what do you think you're doing?" The rebuke was gentle, almost maternal. Evan watched as the tall, thin doctor moved quickly to the side of the bed. She held both of her hands out as if to stop Evan or catch her should she continue her forward momentum.

"I believe I'm getting out of bed," Evan responded. Her voice was hoarse, raspy. Unfamiliar to her own ears. She vaguely recalled being assured the bruising to her larynx had not caused permanent damage. Still, the weakness irritated her and she felt a stirring of impatience to move beyond her captivity.

"Does your throat hurt?"

Evan nodded, one hand automatically going to her neck, rubbing it absently before she tried again. "But what I really want…no, what I really *need* is a shower." She wrinkled her nose in distaste. "More than anything."

"Well, we can certainly arrange—"

"Please don't say another sponge bath," Evan interrupted sharply. Stopping herself before she could say anything else, she sighed and let her head drop forward. "I'm sorry. That was rude. What I really want, Commander, is a long, hot shower. I desperately want to feel clean for the first time in longer than I care to remember. I want to get rid of the smell of dirt and fear and blood. I'd like to put on some real clothes, preferably something other than a flight suit. And then I'd like you to tell me what I need to do to get released, so I can finally go home."

A wide smile lit Kelsey Grant's face and Evan realized her minor rant was probably what the doctor had been waiting for. A sign of whatever inner strength had enabled her to survive four months of captivity. She watched the doctor's expression soften with understanding.

"All right. Why don't we try this one step at a time, starting with getting you out of bed?"

Not chancing the doctor changing her mind, Evan pushed with her hands and let gravity pull her the remainder of the way off the bed.

As soon as her left foot hit the floor, pain ran like an electric current through her body and she felt herself sway. The room spun, a roaring filled her ears, and her undamaged leg started to buckle. But the doctor proved to be stronger than she appeared.

Unsteady and far from sure of herself, Evan gratefully accepted her support. She sagged in the doctor's arms, stunned by her own inglorious weakness. "Thanks."

"Happy to oblige." The doctor gently reached out and cupped her chin, turning her head from side to side to study her face. "Here's what I think, Commander. I think you're fighting for a sense of normalcy. And if a shower will give it to you, then that's what you'll have."

Evan accepted the scrutiny before raising a suspicious brow. "Just like that?"

"No arguments. Just some basic rules of engagement. You're going to lean on me, keep your weight off your right leg, and take small, slow steps all the way to the bathroom. You're still quite weak and I don't want you to risk undoing all the progress you've made."

The urge to protest came and went. Instead, a hiss of pain escaped Evan's lips as she leaned heavily against the doctor, a tacit agreement. But there was one more thing. She swallowed, licked her lip, considering. "Could I ask one more thing?"

The doctor waited in silence for her to speak.

"Do you suppose you could call me Evan? Khalid...he only ever called me *Commander* and just hearing it makes me..." She shuddered.

"That won't be a problem, Evan," came the soft reply. "I'm Kelsey."

The pain in her leg made it difficult just to stand, and Evan struggled not to groan when they began to move. Baby steps. Slow and laborious. Kelsey offered to get a wheelchair, but Evan stubbornly refused to give in. Breathing through the pain, she quickly recognized she would only make progress if she let the doctor take most of her weight as they made their way.

"Are you all right?"

Evan gritted her teeth and held herself rigid, but it was taking all her energy just to breathe in and out. "I'm good." *Trying not to throw up.*

"Really?"

"Really." Evan's voice grew more strained. "Especially if I ignore the fact that every inch of my body is screaming like a girl."

Her comment was greeted by a muffled laugh. "I suppose I should refrain from pointing out the obvious."

In that moment, Evan discovered she had some life left in her after all. She laughed out loud even though she promptly regretted it. "Ah, Jesus, please don't make me laugh." She made a small, choked sound. "Right now, I'm trying to convince myself I'm still a Lieutenant Commander in the US Navy. You know...strong, disciplined, fit. But damn. Everything hurts."

"Deep, regular breaths, Evan. And try to relax."

"Easy for you to say."

By the time they reached the bathroom less than twenty feet away, Evan was in a world of pain. Emotionally and physically exhausted, she leaned against Kelsey gratefully. An instant later, the breath she'd been holding shuddered out.

"Oh Jesus."

She raised one hand uncertainly and pushed the limp, too-long bangs back from her face in horror as she stared at her reflection in the mirror. A gaunt stranger stared back at her. Dark multicolored bruises marred her face and neck, while both of her eyes still showed signs of having recently been blackened. Swallowing painfully, she slowly lowered the hospital gown, but the story didn't get any better. Every inch of skin she revealed was covered in cuts and abrasions.

"Oh God." She remained rigid for a moment. Not moving, not even breathing. "Shit, Kelsey, my family…Tate…they've all seen me looking like this. I've seen roadkill that looks better than me."

"Your family understands, Evan." Kelsey made a sympathetic sound. "I know it looks bad, but believe me when I say you look a lot better than you did when you first arrived."

Evan touched her face with one hand and winced as she continued to stare into the mirror. "Is that even remotely possible?"

"Not only possible, it's the truth. And in a few more days, you'll start to recognize the face in the mirror. I promise."

"I'll have to take your word for it," Evan said. She broke off, closed her eyes, and in the lengthening silence felt herself fade.

"They worked you over pretty good. Does that account for all of your injuries?"

"No." The question caught her by surprise and she made an effort to pull herself back. "I'm pretty sure I had some kind of head injury"— she absently rubbed her forehead—"that goes back to when I got shot down."

Evan felt the gentle pressure of Kelsey's gaze and realized the doctor was waiting for more of an explanation. She shrugged apologetically. "I took a blow to the head," she said. "Or at least I think that's what happened. Something shattered my visor and dented my helmet not long after the canopy blew. Dented my head too, but my recall after that's a little fuzzy. I think I got hit by a piece of debris from my aircraft—or maybe it was something from Deacon's. Impossible to tell, really. I was already on the ground by the time I regained consciousness, but it meant I had a less than controlled landing and somehow buggered up my knee."

"How long were you unconscious?"

"No idea. I was—"

"Unconscious, I know."

"Right. It wasn't too long before we were captured, and after that…" The thought of Khalid caused a darkness to pass over her, like a cloud occluding the sun. Her hands began to shake and she felt dangerously close to crying. She could feel her eyes sting, her throat burn. But there was no release because she never cried. She was, after all, a Kane.

Taking a deep breath, she rubbed her dry, burning eyes and tried to pull some of her normal self-assurance back around her. She almost succeeded. But then she started to shake again. It started slowly, faintly, and then grew in intensity until she was trembling uncontrollably. Kelsey would probably tell her it was a normal enough response. A physiological reaction. But knowing it was normal didn't make her reaction any more tolerable. She tried wrapping her arms around her body. Images flashed in her mind. Quick and harsh, one after another, and she couldn't get them to stop.

"I can't breathe," she whispered, doubling over, gasping with a sudden primal need for air.

Kelsey's arms came around her, strong and comforting, holding her trembling body with a surprising gentleness. Her touch stroked Evan's scattered emotions, and she struggled against the impulse to bury her face against the doctor's strong shoulder, wanting to hide away from the horrifying memories that had slipped to the surface while she wasn't looking.

But there was no place to hide.

Kelsey continued to hold her until her erratic heartbeat slowed its racing tempo. Until the tension began to ebb from her body. Briefly Evan wondered how long she could stay in this cocoon, while another part of her simply wanted to run away.

She wouldn't, of course. She was stronger than that. A Lieutenant Commander in the US Navy. Robert and Althea Kane's daughter. She just needed a few minutes to pull herself together.

Lifting her head, she met Kelsey's gaze. "I'm sorry. I don't know where that came from." She felt her face heat, but Kelsey remained silent. Watching her, but not saying a word.

Evan straightened awkwardly. Feeling exposed and uncertain, vulnerable, she closed her eyes, effectively shutting the doctor out. But with her eyes closed, she was once again plagued by recollections.

Tate's hands on her body.

Khalid's fist striking her face.

She tried not to recoil. Remembered that during the past four months, she'd become adept at disappearing, mentally and emotionally.

She had used it as a pain-coping mechanism, letting her mind drift free until there was nothing left of her, until she could find oblivion.

With her eyes still closed, she gathered the darkness around her, waited for the Zen-like calm to envelop her. A moment later she found herself standing on the deck of a sailboat, cutting through the crystal-blue waters of the Mediterranean. Overhead, the sky was cloudless, a vast and endless blue. The sun was warm on her face, the wind teased her hair, and only the creak of the mast, the snap of the sails, and the waves slapping against the hull intruded on the blissful silence.

❖

"Evan..."

Evan shuddered and slowly raised her head. Became aware her mind had wandered off to a beautiful place. Gradually she recognized she was still in a military hospital in Germany and Kelsey was still there. Still watching her.

"I'm sorry," she said but wasn't sure why.

"Don't worry about it." Kelsey watched her a moment longer. "Is that how you did it, Evan?"

"Did what?"

"Survive what they did to you. Did you close your eyes and dream yourself away?"

Evan couldn't help but smile. "That's pretty astute of you. Or does the mind reading come as part of the medical degree?"

"Of course." Kelsey smiled back.

In that moment, any thought of protest or denial died. "The answer to your question is yes, I guess. I suppose I would dream myself to anywhere but where I was whenever I could. Unfortunately, it wasn't possible all the time. But even half the time was certainly better than the painful reality I found myself in."

"You really need to talk to someone about what happened to you," Kelsey said softly. "You know that, don't you?"

The gentle voice insinuated itself in Evan's lacerated psyche, and she felt it soothe her even as her throat tightened with regret. "Yes, but all in good time. Just not right now."

"Fair enough. I'm guessing you'll also need to have a serious conversation with Tate before too long."

Evan's shoulders tensed, her back burned, and she shifted restlessly as a shaft of remembered pain shot through her. Knowing Kelsey was right didn't make things any easier. She moistened her lips before finally meeting her gaze. "That conversation will definitely have to wait until I have some idea how to approach it."

"Do you think you'll be going home with your parents when we release you?"

Evan thought about it for a moment, then shook her head and shrugged. "Actually, I've no idea where I'm going, but I strongly doubt it'll be to my parents' home. For far too many reasons."

"Okay, let's approach this differently. What would you have done if you hadn't been shot down?"

"Four months ago? I planned on staying with Tate in Bahrain. Maybe convince her to take a holiday with me while I figured out what I was going to do in my post-navy life. At the time, I had a couple of ideas floating in my head. Now, suffice to say I'm not really sure of anything."

"As you said, all in good time," Kelsey said, and there was a thoughtful expression on her face. "The reason I'm bringing it up is that like you, I've served my time and I'm due to go home soon. Depending on where you end up, my partner is a psychiatrist."

"Your partner?"

Their eyes met for a brief moment before Kelsey continued. "Jenna. Dr. Jenna Nolan. She served in Iraq and has a private practice in Seattle. She gets a lot of referrals from the naval base on the peninsula and has extensive experience dealing with PTSD."

Evan tensed and remained silent for a moment. "You're suggesting I need to talk with her?"

"I'm suggesting what happened to you in Afghanistan is now a part of you, and Jenna—or someone like her—can help you deal with it," Kelsey responded calmly. "And I'm offering to help if you ever find yourself out our way and want an introduction."

"I'll keep it in mind."

"Good. Now let's get you into the shower."

Leaning on Kelsey, Evan allowed herself to be guided toward the shower while the implications of their conversation rained down around her. She sighed, and as her tension slowly ebbed, she lifted her gaze.

"Thanks, Kelsey," she said softly.

CHAPTER FIFTEEN

It was late morning by the time Tate returned to the hospital. The sun was warm on her face, the sky was a deep and cloudless blue, and it promised to be a truly glorious day. The kind of day she would have reveled in under normal circumstances, perhaps dragging Evan along while she browsed through the many quaint alley boutiques Landstuhl had to offer, then stopping at one of the outdoor cafés for a glass of wine and some excellent people-watching. As they relaxed and watched tourists and locals pass by, Evan would inevitably provide humorous commentary. Tate would laugh and reach for Evan's hand, amazed how she could never keep her hands to herself and wondering if she would always feel like this—in lust with Evan. Knowing the answer was yes.

But instead, she was hurrying toward the bank of elevators, irritated and with a frown on her face as she waited impatiently for one to arrive.

She had spent the night dreaming of Evan, and the memories surfacing out of the dream had left her wet and needy. She was annoyed with Kelsey Grant, who had refused to allow her to spend another night at the hospital, sleeping in the chair she had placed by Evan's bed. The night before, Grant had casually mentioned her plan to get Evan out of bed in the morning and suggested Tate might want to be there to help her. But before Tate could become too excited by the prospect, the doctor had one caveat. Tate needed to get a good night's sleep, away from the hospital, so she could be refreshed and alert.

Tate had argued that Evan was better served having her stay close. The nights seemed to be particularly difficult for her, and Tate's presence—her voice, her touch—seemed to help Evan ward off the nightmares she slipped into all too frequently.

But the doctor had held her ground, and Tate had conceded she could use a break.

Unfortunately, she hadn't planned for what had happened. By the time she stumbled back to the hotel, her eyes were nearly closed. Mumbling good night to Alex and Nick, she entered her room, kicked off her shoes, and fell facedown across the bed. She was asleep in seconds. And whether from exhaustion or an adrenaline crash wasn't relevant. What mattered was she forgot to set her alarm.

She awoke hours later to the unhappy realization she'd overslept. She couldn't believe it. Worse, she couldn't believe Alex had allowed it to happen, this morning of all mornings. Even if she'd slept like the dead, as he cheerfully pointed out, because it was exactly what her body demanded.

On a day when she had wanted to be at the hospital early, knowing he was right didn't alter the facts, and it was almost ten o'clock by the time she was showered and dressed.

The hospital room was deserted by the time she got there. Tate heard the door softly close behind her while she stared at the neatly made bed and tried to make sense out of what she was seeing. The IV hookup was gone. So were the monitors that had kept track of Evan's progress. Only the profusion of fragrant flowers remained as a silent reminder Evan had been there.

Knowing it was irrational, knowing there was no reason to think Evan had taken a turn for the worse, didn't stop the sudden trickle of uneasiness blossoming in Tate's chest. Fighting to contain the echoes of remembered pain, she turned to leave just as the door opened.

Evan stood there, leaning awkwardly on a set of crutches, attempting to maneuver around the door and maintain her balance while wearing a brand new wrist brace. Her brow was furrowed and the tip of her tongue poked out as she concentrated.

It was a sight Tate knew she would never grow tired of seeing. The first—the only—miracle she would ever need in her life. Releasing a soft sigh, she allowed herself the pleasure of simply looking at Evan, adding to the images already stored in her memory.

This morning there were noteworthy changes. Evan's hair, clean and shining, was gathered in a loose knot piled high on her head, stray wisps falling against her face, and she was wearing the clothes Alex had left for her the previous evening. Better still, for the first time since pulling her out of Afghanistan, Tate thought Evan looked bright and alert, and the lines carved by pain had begun to ease from her face.

The downside? The T-shirt and sweatpants riding low on her hips did little to hide how thin she was. Nor did the clothing conceal the crisscrossed cuts on her arm. And although the healing process was well underway, the livid marks left no doubt they had been deliberately made.

Tate bit back a flash of rage along with a desire to go back to Afghanistan. To find and hurt the bastard who had done this to Evan.

The emotions startled her. Not the fierce protectiveness, but the desire for revenge. It was not only out of character, she knew the rage she was feeling would do little to help Evan heal and move beyond whatever she'd experienced at the hands of her captors. Struggling to contain her anger, Tate concentrated instead on how the sweatpants had slid dangerously downward, revealing an enticing bit of skin.

She must have made a sound because Evan looked up at that moment and saw her. The frown disappeared, and a slow, disarming smile tipped up the corners of her mouth. The smile was all it took to chase every vengeful thought out of Tate's head.

It was the kind of smile that could shatter hearts.

Or make them whole again.

"Hey, beautiful lady. I was wondering when you'd come along."

Her voice was still hoarse, still sounded weak, but it didn't matter. Tate hadn't realized how much she'd missed just the sound of it. After months with nothing more than memories to hold on to, Evan's simple greeting rocked her. It breathed life into her, permeating her dormant senses.

She found herself needing to touch Evan, if only to make certain she was real. But she buried that along with other needs fighting to be released. Slowly letting out a breath, she shook her head and grinned, drawing pleasure from the strength of the ever present electrical current she could feel running between them.

Tipping her head back, she met Evan's gaze. "Hey, yourself. It's terrific to see you up and moving around. But what's with the brace on your wrist? Can't I trust you on your own for just one night?"

She watched Evan stare down at her wrist for an instant, her eyes widening in mock surprise as if seeing the bright blue brace for the very first time. But when she lifted her head to meet Tate's eyes once again, it was with an unmistakable look of humor on her face. For the first time since leaving Afghanistan, the dimples in her cheeks were in full evidence, and a genuine grin flickered and spread across her expressive mouth.

Having Evan's mouth so close, so tempting, nearly proved to be Tate's undoing. Her throat tightened, and any questions she might have entertained were forgotten as she completely lost her train of thought.

There were women, she knew, who were first attracted by another woman's eyes. Still others who were invariably drawn to various parts of the female anatomy. Breasts or legs or a sweet heart-shaped derriere. Tate could appreciate all those things, but when it came right down to it, she knew she would always be drawn to a woman's mouth. Especially a mouth made for long, slow, deep kisses.

And Evan's mouth—God, it was sinfully sensuous. With considerable effort, Tate swallowed and drew her eyes away from the tantalizing mouth. "So, Commander Kane, are you going to tell me what happened to your wrist?"

"Can you believe it? I fell on my ass during my first physio session," Evan confessed with a mildly embarrassed half grin. "I have to admit it wasn't the most auspicious beginning. It also begs the question what the hell happened to the coordination I used to have that enabled me to fly an F/A-18."

"Or dance the tango."

"My point exactly." The grin widened. "Not to worry, though. As luck would have it, there was an emergency department with doctors in it close by. And I'm pleased to report the wrist's not broken, just a mild sprain."

Tate couldn't help but laugh. She drew nearer and touched Evan's arm just above the line of the brace. "I'm glad to hear that. But I bet this makes using those crutches an absolute bear." She reached out with a hesitant hand, gently brushed back a fall of dark, silky hair, and tucked some loose strands behind one ear, breathing deeply as she drew in her scent. "You smell nice."

Evan chuckled, momentarily leaning into Tate's touch. "Thank God I had a shower, then. You wouldn't have wanted to get this close to me if you'd been here earlier. In spite of the sponge baths the medical people were giving me, I was starting to offend myself. Khalid's goat came to mind."

"Have I ever told you I have a fondness for goats?" Tate asked softly. She suddenly realized no one else was around. This was the first time she had found herself alone with an alert and fully conscious Evan in forever, and she edged closer still, until they were as near as they could get without actually touching.

But not for long. With slightly trembling hands, she reached up and cradled Evan's face. So eerily beautiful despite the evidence of violence. She noticed for the first time a faint crescent-shaped scar on her forehead, just above her right eyebrow, and a thousand questions sprang to mind. She wanted to know what had happened. She wanted to ask how she was doing. What she was feeling. And thinking.

She felt a deep, aching familiarity and allowed herself to be caught up in the intense pull of their undeniable chemistry. It left her wanting to do something to prolong the moment. Her heart thundered in her chest and her pulse skyrocketed as awareness shimmered between the two of them, and she began to wonder why she was waiting, resisting, when the attraction was so obviously strong.

And oh God, it's been so long.

More than anything, she desperately wanted to reacquaint herself with Evan's beautiful mouth. To taste her lips, her tongue, her skin. Just the memory made her mouth water.

Held captive by Evan's proximity, overwhelmed by the intensity of her longing, Tate struggled to hold back. Lulling Evan's senses with her touch, she skimmed her fingers along her cheek and continued to play with the loose strands of black hair, hoping she wasn't moving faster than Evan was able to handle.

"Have your parents been by to see you this morning? Are they around?"

"Hmm, no." Evan's voice was distant. Distracted. "One of the nurses said Althea called earlier to check up on me. They assured her I was fine. Told her I was up, and in fact, I was scheduled for my first physio session. So Althea said something about making a leisurely morning of it with Dad and asked the nurse to tell me they'd come by this afternoon. I think she may start avoiding me now that I'm fully conscious and capable of responding coherently when she talks to me."

"It's possible...but they're not around? We're actually alone?"

Evan nodded her head. Her smile was absolutely devastating.

"Thank God. Because I've been waiting to kiss you since forever."

Tate knew she was dreaming. She'd fantasized about Evan's mouth, but not a single fantasy could prepare her for the reality of kissing Evan again. A wave of heat washed over her as the familiarity of Evan's body slid past her defenses, and she captured Evan's lips with exquisite tenderness.

Holding her, touching her, kissing her with all the passion of pent-up longing. Indulging in something she'd done only in her dreams for much too long. This was what she'd been aching to do. To hold her, to feel her warmth, her softness and strength, as she tightened her arms around her.

Her heart sang and her blood heated. She buried her hands in the fragrant softness of Evan's hair. She tried to speak, tried to tell Evan what this moment meant, but all she could say was her name, over and over again. She heard Evan's soft intake of breath. Then the rest of the world faded, and for the first time in months, Tate felt whole.

I thought I'd lost her forever.

She gripped Evan tighter and wished they could be somewhere else. Anywhere else. She knew she couldn't live without her, without this, and the reality of having Evan back in her arms was so much better than good. It was everything.

How many nights during the last few months had she stayed awake, reliving Evan's touch? How many times had she remembered how Evan felt beneath her? Above her? Inside her?

How many times had she remembered her taste? Imagined her scent?

She'd longed for this, hungered for this, in so many ways. And this was no dream. This was real. Evan was warm and alive and in her arms. Her lips were still soft and sweet, just as she remembered. She tasted of peppermint and joy. And she was kissing her back, responding to Tate's passionate assault with soft moans and a deepening, sensuous kiss that went on forever, conveying a need as powerful as her own.

There'd never been anything quite like kissing Evan Kane. In part because of how Evan responded. Tate loved knowing she could make her breathless. Equally loved how Evan could turn a kiss into an act that said everything.

She could feel Evan's heartbeat quicken. Every touch, every sigh just made her want more, and she moved her arms around her neck, pulling Evan closer still. The loose knot holding her hair started to unravel and she threaded her fingers through the tendrils that were drifting down, tangling her hands in the dark, silky strands.

On some level, she realized Evan was weaving slightly on her crutches. But she couldn't help herself. Couldn't stop herself from prolonging the embrace as her mind simply stopped functioning and her body took control. Want and need collided, and a small sigh escaped as Tate tugged gently at Evan's bottom lip with her teeth. Evan's mouth parted, warm and inviting, and she took full advantage, deepening the kiss until she felt Evan melt, going limp in her arms.

They fit against each other so perfectly. As good as—no, better—than she remembered.

She felt as much as heard the rough groan that came from deep in Evan's throat. And then she was lost. Lost in the feel of Evan against her, in the taste of Evan, in the memories. Lost in everything that was Evan.

She knew this was what they had both needed.

A kiss of remembrance.

A kiss of healing.

CHAPTER SIXTEEN

Tate had no idea how long she and Evan remained lost in a heated embrace before awareness slowly returned. Reality intruded as a sound coming from somewhere near the door. It brought her back into the present with a jolt, and she ended the kiss, abruptly pulling away. Evan swayed awkwardly and one of her crutches clattered to the floor. Tate immediately reached for her, felt her sharp intake of breath, and held Evan steady while trying not to add to the bruises already covering most of her body.

Struggling with her composure, Tate caught her breath. What the hell had she been thinking? How could she have forgotten where she was? In a military hospital, for Christ's sake, with Robert and Althea Kane due at any moment. But she hadn't been thinking, had she? She'd simply been reacting, her body going into hyperdrive, just as it had always done whenever she found herself anywhere near Evan.

"I'm sorry. I'm an idiot," she murmured and gave herself a mental headshake. "Are you all right?"

Evan held on to her and rested her head against Tate's shoulder. "Working on it," she said as she closed her eyes. "And I'm not sorry at all. But whatever you do, please don't let go, because right now, I think you're the only thing keeping me off the floor, and I've already done that once today."

"Not letting go," Tate reassured her softly. "Not a chance."

With the memory Evan's scent and taste filling her mind, Tate settled Evan's body against her once again. Cupping the back of her neck, she gently pressed Evan's head to her shoulder, instinctively tugging her closer in a protective gesture. Holding her there, sheltered in her arms, before she finally looked up.

She felt a nearly instantaneous burst of relief when she saw Alex and Nick. They were standing in the doorway like bookends. One light, one dark, each leaned against a side of the door frame wearing similar expressions on their faces.

"You two believe in living dangerously, don't you." Nick smiled as he strode into the room.

Alex had a slight grin of his own as he followed Nick. "Dad and Althea could be standing here. The two of you really need to remember where you are."

"My thoughts exactly," Tate mumbled apologetically and threw a wry grin of her own.

Alex stopped just in front of Evan, and as he surveyed her carefully, his smile slowly widened. "Hello, little sister," he said. "You still look like shit, but you certainly smell a hell of a lot better than you did yesterday."

"My thoughts exactly," Evan repeated. Amusement flitted across her face and there was a hint of laughter in her voice. "By the way, thanks for the clothes, big brother. This is a huge improvement over the hospital gown they had me in, and I loved the thong. But maybe next time you could aim for something that fits a little bit better."

"Then maybe you should try eating something because if you ask me, you're too damned skinny."

Evan tilted her head to one side and narrowed her eyes. "Actually, I believe it was one of Althea's people who once told me a woman can never be too thin. I think I was fifteen at the time."

"Hey, I remember her," Alex said. "Wasn't she the skinny bitch who said you needed to wear skirts because otherwise we looked too much alike and it confused her?"

Tate bit her lower lip and tried not to laugh, watching and waiting as brother and sister stared at each other for a long, silent moment. And then Alex did something he hadn't been able to do in months. He pulled Evan out of Tate's arms and into his own, holding her close.

"I can't say I care much for what you let them do to our face," Alex said, placing a kiss on the tip of Evan's nose.

"I can't say I care much for it, either." Evan sighed. "But the doctor assured me I'll be recognizable in another couple of weeks."

Alex moved back slightly and touched his hand to her face, trailed his thumb over the deep bruise marring the curve of her cheek. "That'll be good. Almost as good as seeing you awake and talking, even if you do look like hell." His expression grew somber as he continued to stare at her.

Evan felt the intensity of his gaze. "What?"

Unexpectedly, Alex started to shake. His hands. His body. His voice. "Fuck. I promised myself I wouldn't do this. That I wouldn't fall apart."

The warmth and humor Evan had seen just a moment earlier vanished instantly and she found herself staring into Alex's face. A face she would have said she knew as well as her own, but suddenly couldn't read.

"Alex? What's going on?" Trying to reassure but not certain what to do or say, Evan released the remaining crutch she'd been holding, letting it bounce against the bed before it fell to the floor while she looped her arms around her brother's neck.

Aware she had always been the stronger of the two, she placed a kiss on his cheek, another on his brow. She could feel Alex's heart beating hard and fast but couldn't identify the cause for his obvious distress as a heavy, awkward silence saturated the air. Gently, she rubbed his neck with her uninjured hand and held him close to her.

"Whatever it is, it'll be okay," she whispered softly. "Just tell me what's wrong and we'll fix it together. Same as always."

Alex closed his eyes, breathed deeply, and said nothing. When he finally opened his eyes, his expression was uncharacteristically serious and his voice was thick with emotion. "I'm pretty sure I told you I'd never forgive you if you let anything happen to you."

"I'm fine, Alex, so there's nothing to forgive."

"Yeah, I can see that," Alex responded harshly. "Do you honestly think I can't guess what it's been like for you? I mean…damn it all, I know you went through hell. You don't need to tell me, I just have to look at you to know that. I can see it in your eyes."

"Nothing much happened to me."

"Right, nothing much happened. That's why we all went to your funeral. Because nothing much happened to you. Dad couldn't say your name without getting choked up, and I actually caught Althea holding your picture and crying. I've felt so damned guilty every time anyone looked at me, knowing it was my fault. Christ, I haven't been able to pick up a paintbrush in over four months."

Evan felt suddenly cold. Every nerve in her body became still and she struggled to draw a deep breath. "You went to my funeral?"

"Jesus Christ, Evan. Of course I went to your funeral. You're my sister. What the hell do you think? Me, Nick, Tate—we all went together."

Evan turned to look over her shoulder, automatically seeking out Tate with her eyes. Desperately wanting her to say it wasn't true, to offer some kind of denial. Some kind of explanation. But when she saw the expression on Tate's face, she knew what she was getting instead was confirmation. She swallowed and looked away.

She could feel her body start to react and fisted her hands. She suddenly felt weak and tired and vulnerable, and prayed—no, begged—

for Alex to stop talking. To stop saying things she now knew she wasn't ready to hear. But the twin telepathy failed her.

"Don't get me wrong," Alex was saying. "We're all beyond thrilled with how everything's turned out. Being told it was a mistake and you weren't really dead. Being told you'd been captured and the powers that be were negotiating your release. It was un-freaking-believable— like a dream come true. But don't you see? It's all so damned surreal, and I'm just finding it a little difficult to take in, that's all."

Time remained suspended as Evan tried to put all the disparate pieces of what Alex was saying together into a cohesive story. "Alex?" She tilted her head back, feeling dazed, and in spite of all the evidence to the contrary, she held out a faint hope she had somehow misunderstood. "Do me a favor and slow down a bit. Please?" Her voice was strained, barely a whisper, and she tried to clear her throat. "I'd really like to understand. Now, can we try again? What are you talking about?"

His face flushed, Alex moved Evan back a little, holding her at arm's length. "When the navy told us you'd been shot down, that you'd been killed, I didn't want to believe them," he said softly. "Part of me believed you had to be alive. You're my twin, for Christ's sake. I would have felt something if you were really dead, wouldn't I? But I didn't. I didn't feel you gone and I should have forced the issue. I should have made them go back and keep looking for you until they found you."

"Alex—" Tate said softly, but Evan stopped her before she could say anything else.

"No, let him finish," she said flatly.

Alex blinked and seemed confused. "There's not much more to tell. About a month after you were shot down, we were told there was nothing else to be done. The navy said they weren't going to be able to recover your body. So we buried an empty casket with full military honors and blindly moved on with our lives, not knowing any better. Don't you see?"

No. No. *No.* She didn't see.

"That's what's making this so damned hard. Seeing you and the way you looked after Tate brought you here. Imagining what had been done to you."

Alex's words sent chills up her spine. *This wasn't happening.* Staring without really seeing anything, Evan could feel something twist inside her and swore softly.

Alex clearly misunderstood and smiled at her. An achingly sweet and tender smile she hadn't seen for much too long. "Exactly, little sister. But now, well, now we've got you back." He gave her a squeeze that was no doubt meant to be reassuring. "And as soon as the doctors tell us you're able to travel, we're going to take you home. Wait until you see—"

Evan caught Alex off guard when she suddenly pushed herself out of his arms. She took an awkward step back and nearly stumbled in the process, her leg screaming with the strain, her muscles threatening to liquefy. She would have fallen but for Tate's quick move to catch her and hold her steady.

Almost as quickly, she pulled herself away from Tate's arms with a surprising show of strength that came with a harsh price. But she used the pain radiating from her leg to help her withdraw into herself, desperately trying to shut everything out even as it hit her. All the horror, emptiness, and pain that had filled her life for the past few months.

"Evan? What is it?" Tate asked, watching as Evan stood unsteadily with arms wrapped tightly around herself and her bare feet planted on the cool tile. "Talk to me. Tell me what's going on. I can help."

"You can't fix this. No one can."

The words were whispered so quietly Tate almost missed them. But she didn't miss the look of defeat in Evan's face, superimposed over the signs of illness and violence and strain that still marked her. Before she could turn away, Tate glimpsed the raw emotions swirling in Evan's eyes.

She tried replaying what had just happened and then it dawned on her. "Oh God. You didn't know. No one told you."

"Know what?" Alex asked, radiating bewilderment. "What the hell is wrong? What didn't she know, Tate? Evan? God damn it, somebody talk to me."

Tate saw the stunned expression in Evan's eyes, watched her throat work, and knew she couldn't answer. She didn't even flinch. She was frozen, mute, as if she'd just had another shock. Her face grew as shuttered as it had been when Tate had first sighted her in the settlement. In Afghanistan with Khalid. It was as if a light had been switched off somewhere inside her, leaving her in a dark and pain-filled place.

And then Evan abruptly looked away.

"She didn't know the navy reported she'd been killed in action," Tate answered for her. "She didn't know about the funeral or how we all thought she died when she was shot down."

"Jesus," Alex said. "Is that true?"

Tate was close enough that she thought she could read the expression in Evan's face, and for a second, she wondered if Evan would answer Alex. Or if she'd even heard the question. Her eyes were intense and simmering with something Tate had never seen before. But then Evan turned her head slowly to look at her brother.

She stared at him, and as she blinked, shock and disillusionment were etched on her face.

She closed her eyes and drew a deep breath, but it seemed as if it hurt her to do it. "I guess it explains why no one came looking for us."

"It wasn't like that," Alex said. "There was a video—it showed you and Lieutenant Walker getting blown out of the sky."

"A video?"

Alex nodded. "It was released by some group claiming responsibility for taking down two navy jets. The damn thing went viral. It was all over the news and the Internet. We all saw it, Evan, and after that, there just wasn't any reason to hold out hope. Jesus, I'm sorry. I know this has to be a shock, but it never occurred to us you might not know. I mean, surely someone from the navy or maybe one of the doctors—"

"Don't." Evan cut him off. "Not now." She bent awkwardly to retrieve her crutches, stopping Tate with just a look when she tried to help her, and then moved out of reach toward the door. "I think I'd like to be alone for a little while. I'm going to get some air." There was no anger left, just fatigue and an unrelenting determination to get out of the room.

Tate remained motionless. Torn. Staring at Evan. She looked lost and vulnerable. There was a bleak chill in her eyes, a look of utter desolation on her face, and a distant and polite smile on her lips. Her conflicting emotions created a palpable shield around her. A barrier so thick and intense Tate could feel it from where she stood.

Her heart told her to stop Evan. This was no time for her to be alone. *Go to her, wrap her in your arms and hold her tight. Don't let her go.*

But her head said the opposite. Said to let her go. *Give her the space and time she so clearly needs.*

"Of course," she said, her voice shaking slightly and her fists clenching as she met Evan's gaze. What words could she use to penetrate this kind of hurt, this kind of pain? "Take as long as you need. We'll wait for you right here, if that's okay."

Evan tightened her grip on the crutches as she maneuvered herself to the door. Looking eerily calm, she patiently waited while Nick held it open for her, then quietly fled the room.

CHAPTER SEVENTEEN

The US Navy had declared her dead.
Don't think about it, just walk, one step at a time.
It should have occurred to her, especially when no SEAL team ever arrived to rescue her and Deacon. But it hadn't, and Evan was having a difficult time making sense of it all. Trying to piece together how she'd ended up here.

She'd been declared dead. There'd been a funeral.

She repeated the words in her head once again, but it still couldn't make them seem real. Because it wasn't just accepting the reality of the statement, it was accepting her family had actually believed she was dead. A shudder ran the length of her spine.

Tate had believed it.

Once she could move beyond the immediate shock of Tate's revelation, Evan had been prepared to feel a deluge of emotions. Disbelief certainly. Add anger. Hurt. Even betrayal. And yet, at the moment, she felt very little. In fact, she was past feeling anything at all. She was totally and blessedly numb, and that actually suited her because she didn't really want to think about what any of it meant.

Feeling too restless to stop once she left her hospital room, she realized all too quickly she had nowhere to go. Nowhere she *could* go, she corrected. She had no identification, no passport, no money, not even a credit card.

Shit. She had nothing. She stared at her bare feet, and as the realization dawned on her that she didn't even have shoes, she started to laugh.

Just how far can I get dressed in ill-fitting clothes and bare feet before someone stops me?

If nothing else, it made escape problematic.

Ignoring the pull of the stitches and the constant pain in her leg, she eventually found herself standing in the hospital's rooftop garden.

With her face lifted toward the sun, her eyes fixed on the contrails of three military jets cutting across the brilliant blue sky.

God, she desperately wished she could be there with them. Free. Flying high above the clouds with all the unbelievable power and lethal grace of an F/A-18 at her fingertips.

But even as the thought took shape, she felt an instant pang of regret, knowing she would never again experience the thrill of flying a state-of-the-art navy jet. It didn't matter that the medical people would probably never clear her to fly, given the damage to her leg. A return to the navy was simply not in the cards. It hadn't been an option since she'd made the decision not to extend her service commitment more than ten months before. She'd gone into her last mission knowing it would be the last, knowing she would be heading home once it was over. Or, in actuality, to Tate's.

The longer she thought about it, the more she realized the irony of her situation. She had left home so certain of her course of action. That it was the right one. One that would allow her to both help her brother and satisfy family honor and obligations. She had also left home certain of her place in the world.

That girl—the confident, self-assured one she had been ten years earlier—was long gone. The woman who stood in her place had traveled extensively, could speak eight languages fluently, and had seen and done things she previously could only have imagined. She had also managed to survive the destruction of her aircraft and her subsequent captivity.

But she no longer had any idea who she was or where she belonged.

Her first priority had to be untangling the bureaucratic nightmare she expected would be necessary to get her life back. And then what?

Thomas Wolfe said you can't go home again.

Evan somehow wanted to prove him wrong. She just needed to figure out who she was first and where home might be.

With the sun warm against her face and a soft breeze in her hair, for the first time in days the feeling of disorientation faded and Evan felt some of the tension churning inside her begin to dissipate. She could breathe a little easier, inhaling as deeply as her injured ribs would allow, and as she released a breath on a sigh, she found a measure of calm.

Swaying slightly on her crutches, she stood taking in the sun like it was a drug. It felt good. Better than good. It felt wonderful, and she couldn't help wishing she was miles away on some sunny beach in Barbuda.

But then reality intruded. She heard the soft sound of footsteps coming up behind her and she braced herself for what was to come.

"I thought I might find you here."

Evan felt the pounding of her heart in her throat and started but didn't turn around. She had known it would be Tate who would come and find her. She just didn't know if it would make things easier or more difficult.

"Do you mind if I stay here with you for a while?"

She managed a small shrug with one shoulder but remained silent.

"Thanks, I think I will." A minute or two passed, filled only with the sun and the wind and silence. "I can only imagine what's going on inside your head. Do you want to talk?"

Evan shook her head. For some reason, Tate's steadiness was not having its usual soothing effect on her. Tate must have sensed it as well because Evan felt her move closer, felt her warmth, and watched as Tate reached with the tip of one finger to trace her jaw.

Damn. The touch called up sensations she didn't want to think about. But for a split second she shut her eyes, letting Tate know she wasn't unaffected by her touch. And with her emotions still in turmoil, Evan leaned into Tate before she could stop herself. Found her mouth for a whisper of a kiss.

"Damn, Tate," she murmured, her breathing ragged.

Tate's mouth twitched. "Damn?"

"Just damn." Her voice caught on the wind and seemed to echo back to her. Evan gave her the barest of smiles before briefly finding Tate's mouth again.

"Evan?" Tate asked a few moments later. "What can I do to help? Tell me what you need. What you want."

Nothing. Not one damn thing. Actually, that wasn't true. She wanted her life back. And if she couldn't have it, then at the very least, she wanted a clean slate. Without ghosts. Without reminders. Without dreams of Afghanistan and Khalid as he lovingly drew his knife over her flesh.

Because in her dreams, he didn't stop. In her dreams, she bled to death.

She took an audible breath. But before she could speak, she heard another set of footsteps fast approaching.

"I see you found her."

Evan groaned on hearing the familiar voice. She remained facing Tate, and for a moment she said nothing before opting to use indifference as a protective cloak. "Where else could I go? It's not as though I have a lot of choice."

"Evan," Tate whispered, the fingers of one hand wrapping around her forearm.

But Evan wasn't finished. "And even if I knew where I wanted to go, I have no means of getting there. It's not like I have a passport or money. Or clothes. Or shoes. Hell, I don't actually exist, do I?"

"All those things will be fixed, Evan. It's just going to take a little time."

"And you're still the fixer, is that it, Althea? Now, there's breaking news." Evan avoided looking at Tate as she turned around and met her mother's gaze head-on, her anger surfacing beneath the veneer of manners. And if her icy composure was cracking, she was thankful the tension between them seemed to help steady her, giving her some sense of control.

"Evan." Tate's whisper was more urgent this time.

Evan experienced a twist of regret when she saw Althea flinch, but couldn't have contained the biting frustration in her voice if she'd wanted to. As they regarded one another silently, she thought she saw more emotion flicker across her mother's face than she'd seen in years. Possibly since she was a child.

An instant later, it was gone. Then again, she could have been mistaken.

"Someone—we should have told you. I see that now. But there was a concern you weren't strong enough, and your father and I agreed."

Evan swallowed back an anger that was both immediate and real. "I was strong enough to survive."

"I can see that. And it's something for which I'll always be grateful." Althea regarded Evan calmly, her expression once again both familiar and unreadable. "Do you want to return to the navy? Is that what you want?"

"I'm not really sure about anything right now." Evan looked at her mother and felt precariously close to the edge. Uncomfortable and frustrated, and fighting the years-old emotional hurt that blossomed deep inside, she turned away abruptly. Her abdominal muscles contracted with the sudden move, and she tried not to let the pain get to her. But still she flinched.

"If you're going to stay here and talk, why don't you at least sit down?" Tate said softly.

"I'm fine," she responded, her back stiff and her head held high even though part of her wanted to do nothing more than follow Tate's suggestion.

"Evan, for the love of God, when was the last time you got a good look at yourself?"

"As a matter of fact—"

"You're hurting," Tate snapped. "Do you think I can't see it? Don't you know I can't stand to think of you hurting more than you've already been hurt?"

The seconds ticked by as she met Tate's unwavering gaze. "I'm sorry," she murmured. She expelled a long sigh and moved without another word to sit on a bench. The moan of relief remained trapped in her mind, but she had no doubt Tate heard it. She steadied herself, then turned back to face her mother.

"Not that I feel I owe anyone an explanation, but just so we're clear, it's not that I want to go back to the navy." She paused, needing a breath. "It was never how I defined myself and I knew I was done months ago, when I set out to fly my last mission."

"Then what is it you want?" Althea asked.

Evan tried to summon a tentative smile before giving a quiet, shaky laugh. "What I'd *like* is to go back just over four months in time and for all of this to have been a dream. A really bad dream." She paused. "But I know that can't happen. As to what I want...I just want to understand."

Althea drew in a soundless breath. "Understand what?"

"Why everyone gave up so easily." She felt Tate's hand tighten on her forearm, drew strength from it and persevered. "I need to understand why Deacon and I were left in that hell for so long."

She watched the color fade from Althea's face. "Evan—"

"You asked what I wanted. Well, that's what I want. I want to know why no one came looking for us."

"I'm just not sure this is a good idea."

"Why not?"

Althea sighed. "Evan, to be honest, I'm not entirely sure you're up to it."

"Not up to it?" Evan repeated numbly. "Do you have any idea how it felt? What it was like to realize no one was going to help us?"

"Hurt? Angry? Betrayed?"

"Bingo." She bit back a curse, knowing she needed answers and her mother was the most likely source of accurate information. "You couldn't help me then. Help me now. I really need to know."

The strained silence lengthened uncomfortably before Althea finally nodded and began to softly speak.

Evan had thought she was ready. And although it was apparent Althea was choosing her words carefully, as she spoke of getting a call in the middle of the night from the Secretary of the Navy, Evan quickly realized she wasn't ready at all.

She sat without moving while her mother spoke. But as she listened, other images flashed in her mind.

Smoke pouring into the cockpit. Hurtling through the darkness after ejecting just as her F/A-18 exploded. Feeling hopeless rage as she lay beaten and staked to the ground.

The memories pushed her emotions to the surface. With her palms damp, mouth dry, and her heart racing, she struggled back to her feet, holding the crutches like a lifeline.

Tate moved to stand beside her, a look of intense understanding on her face. Not touching, and yet lending her strength. "Evan?"

"I'm okay." She regarded Althea quietly. "Do you know what happened to my personal effects? And what happened to my plane? The Tiger Moth? I had it in storage in San Francisco. I know you hated it. Please tell me you didn't get rid of it."

Althea paled and tight lines appeared around her mouth. Evan recognized her lack of trust had cut her mother deeply. Belatedly, she chastised herself for her knee-jerk reaction.

"You'll need to speak with your brother. Since he was already storing everything else you owned, Alex took the things that were sent back from the *Nimitz*. And in accordance with the provisions in your will, control of everything else was turned over to him, including your plane, your trust funds and investments, and your bank accounts. Everything."

Evan nodded. For a moment she wondered how things might have turned out if she hadn't been shot down. If she had simply finished her service without incident and had gone back to Bahrain as planned.

But *what if* was a pointless game at the best of times, and Evan pushed the thoughts aside. The pain in her leg was almost to the point of forcing her back onto the bench, and she hoped they could begin to make their way back to her room before that happened.

Althea met her gaze, watching her through the silence, and Evan made a mute appeal with her eyes. But to no avail.

"About a month after the funeral, Jim Stephens came by the house."

"Oh?" Uncertain where the conversation was leading, Evan bit her top lip. "How is the admiral?"

"He wanted to personally deliver your medals to your father and me." Althea paused. "Why didn't we know you'd been awarded those medals?"

They both heard the unspoken question. *Why didn't I know?*

"There was no need for you to know. It was my personal business."

"That's not good enough."

Evan felt her temper flare and looked at the horizon. Her fight-or-flight response was as sharp as it had ever been, and capable or not, she wasn't into running anywhere. "If you want to go a couple of rounds with me on what I consider to be personal business, fine. Let's do it." Turning back, she squared her shoulders as she met her mother's eyes. "If I remember correctly, you told me I was throwing my life away by enlisting in the navy."

"You were barely twenty."

"I was an adult. Forgive me if I thought you'd see the medals as nothing more than the navy's way of encouraging me to continue to throw my life away."

"Twenty is still more child than adult." Althea sighed. "Don't make light of this, Evan. You were commended for extraordinary heroism under enemy fire. For risking your life beyond the call of duty."

"Believe me, I was there and I'm not making light of anything," Evan responded in a quiet voice. Cool fingers suddenly pressed against her neck, and for an instant she was conscious only of Tate, her fingers gently circling, easing away some of the tension. She closed her eyes. "It's just that at no point in time was I actually trying to be exceptionally brave or courageous. I simply tried to remain true to what and who I was raised to be by you and Dad and did what I believed was the right thing to do. I just did what was in my DNA."

Althea stilled, regarding her without speaking for more than a minute with an unreadable expression on her face. Her curiosity piqued, Evan watched as her mother waded cautiously into the vast space between them—a space that harbored ghosts and seemed filled with more haunting echoes and detritus from the past than either knew how to deal with.

As she drew closer, Althea placed a tentative hand on her shoulder, and Evan could read the surprise on her mother's face when she didn't flinch or pull back from her touch. Feeling encouragement from Tate's mobile fingers, she smiled wryly and consciously allowed the connection.

"You've changed."

"Well, there's a news flash," Evan shot back. She tried to summon another tentative smile and hoped it would soften the sharpness of her words. "But it's been some time since you and I last tried to talk, and it was bound to happen sooner or later, don't you think?"

She said it softly, simply. As if it was the only truth she knew for certain in her currently tangled and upside-down life. Which of course it was. So much time had passed. So many things had changed. Including both of them.

Althea stood for a moment longer, gazing at Evan with a look that spoke of both pride and sadness, and Evan knew instinctively what she had to be thinking. Other than those few days in Chamonix, this was the longest conversation they'd managed to have since Althea had discovered her daughter had enlisted in the navy. She found herself holding her breath again, afraid at any moment something would happen to destroy the delicate accord.

"You should know I've done a lot of soul-searching," Althea said, as she finally broke the silence. "Since Jim Stephens first called to tell me you'd been killed, but even more so since we were advised you were still alive and I saw you on that video."

"Althea—" Evan started but couldn't finish. Instead, she was left to hope the expression on her face relayed her discomfort with the direction the conversation was taking and her desire to have it end. She could see her mother was obviously torn between a desire to respect Evan's unspoken wishes and whatever internal compulsion was driving her to speak. But it became equally apparent Althea wasn't going to allow this moment to pass.

"Please, Evan, this needs to be said."

Evan faltered, conceded. "Then say whatever it is you think you have to say."

"I don't expect you to understand what I said and how I reacted when you joined the navy. And I know we still need to get you home. I know you need time to heal and to reconnect with your life."

Evan shifted uncomfortably and looked up to the clear blue sky as the headache she'd forgotten about started to pound. She wanted to speak, but finding no words, she sighed and turned back to her mother. She could feel Althea hesitate and heard her take a deep breath.

"I need to tell you—Evan, you need to know—I'm so very, very proud of you. Of what you did for your brother, of all you've accomplished on your own, and especially of the woman you've become."

Evan was stunned. Humbled by her mother's comments, she could feel the years peel back, leaving her exposed. As she absorbed the clearly heartfelt words, she felt tears pooling in her eyes and blinked to hold them back. "I—I don't know what to say."

"You don't need to say anything." Althea gently squeezed her tense shoulder and smiled as her own eyes welled up and spilled over. "You've been through so much already, and right now, you just need to concentrate on getting well. Everything else can wait. We've got time now, and I'm certain we can work it out."

Chapter Eighteen

They were finally alone.

On a day that already resembled an emotional minefield, no one who looked at Evan could think her capable of handling much more. But maybe it also had something to do with the twin telepathy, because after some initial awkwardness when they returned to the room, Alex came to the rescue.

With his gaze fastened on Evan, her pain reflected clearly on his face, he suggested they get to work reestablishing Evan's life. The Pentagon and State had already started the ball rolling on the high-level process, but there would be mounds of paperwork and granular details the four of them could start sifting through. And of course, Evan needed clothes.

More importantly, Evan needed room to breathe. And even if, at best, it was only a few hours, Tate would gladly take them.

She wasn't by nature a patient woman, but experience had taught her the value of strategic silence. So Tate said nothing while Evan quietly gazed out the window, repeatedly clenching and relaxing her hands, dull incredulity still evident in her eyes.

A full twenty minutes passed before she spoke.

"I feel like I've been in hell." She seemed a bit surprised at the notion. "I'm still trying to find my way back, but I'm not sure how."

"Tell me what I can do to help."

Evan momentarily looked as though she was having second thoughts about revealing too much. But then she shook her head and sighed. "I'm sorry. I don't seem to be operating at top speed. My biggest concern right now is putting one foot in front of the other and making it to that bed without falling on my ass again. If you could help with that and maybe…do you suppose they've got any aspirin around here?"

Tate choked back a laugh. "I'll see what I can do about aspirin after we get you horizontal."

Evan nodded, held her hand up, and let Tate pull her unsteadily to her feet. Tate tightened her grip and saved her from further damage. "Careful. There are already enough bruises on you." She watched Evan's eyes shift toward the bed as if measuring the distance. "Are you okay to continue?"

"I'm a bit dizzy." Her face relaxed into amusement and something more. "I think you should hold me in your arms a little longer…just in case."

Tate hid her surprise. "Brat," she said, reaching out to grab Evan's crutches and move them out of harm's way. But as she settled Evan onto the bed, she couldn't help but notice how pale her face was. Bending down, she gently cupped Evan's cheek. "No offense, love, but you look like hell. Should I go find your doctor?"

The mere hint of another medical intervention quickly added some color to Evan's face. "That won't be necessary," she said, and Tate fought back a smile. "I've overdone it is all. For some reason, everything I do seems to require a minute or two to catch my breath."

"It's to be expected, Evan," Tate chided gently.

"I guess. Maybe. But this"—she turned her face and pressed a kiss into the palm of Tate's hand—"I think I need more of this."

Evan leaned her head back against the pillow, glancing around as if to confirm there really was no one else present before she turned back and looked at Tate. "Can we try this again?"

"Try what?"

"Hello, beautiful lady."

Tate watched her in silence for the space of several slow breaths, felt her blood begin to stir, and shook her head helplessly. "Hey, yourself."

She started to move toward the chair when she felt Evan reach for her, an eyebrow raised in invitation. Her hands were cool against Tate's skin—the emotions they stirred, anything but. Tate felt something tighten inside her, and in spite of her better judgment she let herself be pulled to the bed.

"This isn't very smart," she said. "You're in pain and need to rest."

"Shh." Evan touched a fingertip to her lips. Then, with her eyes still on Tate's, she raised her head, bringing her mouth closer until it was a mere inch away.

What I need…what I want…is you.

The words hovered unspoken between them, and without another thought, Tate surrendered. She removed Evan's finger from her lips, closed the final distance, and covered Evan's mouth with her own.

As her mind emptied, she forgot where they were. Forgot about the hospital staff and the possibility of Evan's parents returning. Forgot how to do everything but feel.

She felt Evan's hands fist in her hair, felt her lips open on a shuddering breath.

Swallowing Evan's groan, she let the kiss play out, hot and greedy, imprinting Evan's scent, taste, and texture into memory. *Oh God, yes. More.*

Only half-aware of the needy sounds coming from her throat, Tate lost track of time, conscious only of pervasive warmth wherever their bodies touched, of Evan's heart beating strongly beneath her fingers. It was all so achingly familiar, and yet she couldn't help but notice the familiarity seemed mixed somehow with a sense of newness.

With her eyes still closed, Tate rolled onto her side and stretched out on the narrow hospital bed, content to drift and catch her breath. She didn't need to look at Evan. She was acutely aware of every breath Evan took, every beat of her heart, the scent of her skin, the warmth of her hand as it burned through the thin material of her T-shirt.

She felt the familiar rush. But she was keenly aware Evan was physically and emotionally spent. Inhaling deeply, she tried to calm her heart and clear her mind. "I should get up."

"Mm-hm."

But Evan seemed disinclined to release her. A moment later, she felt Evan run an index finger in a slow, sensual glide along the side of her jaw before she leaned in and inhaled, as if absorbing Tate's fragrance.

"Awesome," Evan said, nipping lightly at her bottom lip. "I knew it would be the perfect scent for you when I bought it."

Tate stopped breathing. Need arose like a craving, a living, breathing thing, and she found herself wanting to lose herself in the reality of having Evan in her arms. Solid, real, flesh and blood. Alive.

"Oh God, Evan, I've missed you so much," she whispered, the words pulled from her. "Over the past few days, sometimes I catch myself looking at you and I can't believe you're really back in my life. It feels so much like a dream."

Tate's words hit her like a blow, the pain sharp and instantaneous.

Evan froze. Her entire body became numb and so cold she feared she'd never feel warm again. Unable to look at Tate, afraid of what she might see in her eyes, she rolled away, struggling to sit up.

"Evan? What is it? What's wrong?"

For a fleeting moment she couldn't answer. She bit her lip and in the silence heard her own breathing, rapid and uneven. Thrusting a surprisingly steady hand through her hair, she pushed aside the dark strands obscuring her vision before finally looking back at Tate.

"Shit," she managed to say. "I'm so damned sorry. I've been completely self-absorbed, feeling sorry for myself. And I haven't stopped to think about what you must have gone through, or how you must have felt."

"It's all right—"

"No, damn it, it's not. I should have stopped to think what all of this did to you, but I didn't. I hate that you were hurt. Christ, I haven't even asked how you found out."

"Jillian." Tate stopped for an instant, swallowed, and her eyes grew distant. "She knew I was waiting for you."

She broke off, and Evan could see she was determined not to expose the extent of her pain. But her face was heartbreakingly expressive. Wordlessly, Evan waited, encouraging her with a silent entreaty. She could feel the emotions swirling between them but allowed the silence to stretch.

Finally she was rewarded as Tate began to talk, quietly explaining what had happened that fateful February day and in the days and weeks that followed. And though she knew Tate tried hard not to let it show, she could hear the residual hurt in the calmly spoken words and wished she could undo the pain. Pain Evan knew she had caused.

Focused as she was on what Tate was saying, Evan was caught off guard when an onslaught of breath-stealing memories suddenly pushed her present reality aside and began running like an unending video loop in her head. She tried to still her mind. Could still see Tate's lips moving. But for a moment she couldn't hear her words over the roaring in her ears as memories flashed in her mind.

It probably only lasted seconds. Or at least that was what Evan hoped as her mind cleared and her focus returned to the present. Back to Tate who had paused, tilted her head, and was studying her gravely.

"I'm sorry." Emotion had her voice wavering, a ragged whisper that was barely audible. She hesitated, knew she was on the verge of hyperventilating, and wondered what she could say to make things right. "I never meant—"

"No, don't." Tate pressed her fingers momentarily against Evan's lips to stop her. "Nothing that happened was your fault. But you know all those lines about time healing wounds?"

Evan nodded.

"They're just that. They're lines. Because the truth is, missing you never got easier. It would have been easier for me to quit breathing."

Evan felt a tremor run through her. "It was like that for me too. I missed you. So damned much, I was positive I'd created you out of a fevered dream when I saw you in that godforsaken settlement." She stopped, needing time, but only closed her eyes briefly before continuing. "And though I was certainly happy to see you, Althea should have never asked you to go. She put you unnecessarily at risk. Jesus, Tate, you barely got out alive the last time you were in Afghanistan, and it was too dangerous for anyone to ask you to go back—no matter the reason."

"Evan," Tate responded with quiet certainty, "the truth is Althea didn't have to ask. Because once I knew you were still alive, all I cared about was finding you and getting you out. Bringing you home. Nothing else mattered, and no one could have stopped me from going there. You have to know after months of believing you were dead—after four months when I couldn't breathe without it hurting—I would have gone to hell and back if it meant bringing you out alive."

They looked at each other somberly before Tate continued in a quiet voice. "I also want to be perfectly clear about one more thing. When I saw that bastard hitting you, I could have killed him and would've had no trouble sleeping afterward. But I was there to get you out safely. It was all that mattered."

Evan grabbed hold of the certainty in Tate's voice and tried to quell the turmoil she was feeling. She discovered it helped. Raising an eyebrow, she stared at Tate for a long heartfelt moment before she licked her lips and let out a slow breath. "Okay," she said. "So you're telling me Althea actually did right by me. Go figure."

Kelsey dropped by later to check on her. She greeted Tate, then turned to Evan and asked, "How's the wrist?" Evan thought she was trying not to grin.

Evan shrugged and plucked at the brace. "It's good. Does that mean I can go home?"

Kelsey regarded her intently. "I know you're anxious, but it really depends on several things."

"Like what?" At Kelsey's pause, Evan added, "You can speak freely in front of Tate."

"Mostly what I see when I get your last test results back." Kelsey glanced at her chart, wrote something down before studying Evan more closely once again. "But you're also going to need someone to help you while you recover, and as I recall, you said you're not planning to go home to your parents. Do you have anyone who can help look after you?"

Evan almost said Tate but remembered in time it was a conversation they still needed to have. Restless and uncertain, she stared past the doctor's shoulder and remained silent.

"I can provide whatever help Evan will need since she'll be staying with me," Tate said quietly. "It's what we were planning had she come home in February, although back then she would've been coming to stay with me in Bahrain. But I should think Puget Sound would be more conducive to rest and recuperation, and Alex and Nick are nearby and can help."

Evan turned and looked at Tate, forgetting for the moment that Kelsey was still in the room. "I guess that's something we haven't gotten around to talking about. You're not in Bahrain anymore?"

Tate shook her head.

"Can I ask why?"

"Bahrain got to be too much, well, too much Bahrain. It was hard enough to keep going after what happened in that convoy with the IED. But after you were shot down...after the funeral, I knew I couldn't do it anymore. Couldn't chase any more stories."

Evan's earlier headache returned and she released a small sigh. "And you're living on the island near Alex and Nick?"

"About a mile down the road," Alex informed her as he and Nick returned. Pulling up one of the arm chairs, he moved it closer to the bed. "If you're talking about where Tate lives, does that mean they're letting you out of here?"

"Soon, I hope."

"We just need to be certain everything's healing as it should," Kelsey cautioned as she paused by the door. "I'll get back to you as soon as I get the results of your blood work back. In the meantime, try and get some rest."

Evan grinned faintly and watched the doctor leave the room. "I think she really just wants to be sure I'm a little steadier on the crutches, so I don't keep ending up in the ER."

"Well, going home can't happen soon enough," Alex said. "And you're going to love Tate's house. In fact, I think you'll find it to be everything you hoped it would be."

Something in Alex's voice had Evan's eyes narrowing until they were mere slits. But in that moment, somehow the confusion began to clear and she turned to Tate. "Damn," she said, but it was without rancor. "You bought the property on the point, didn't you? The house with the huge deck built out over the water."

Tate gave an uncertain nod.

When Tate remained silent, Nick stepped in. "After the funeral, Alex and I thought you'd want us to look after Tate, so we brought her to stay with us."

Evan felt her eyes burn as her emotions drew perilously close to the surface. "You were right. Thank you."

Nick nodded. "She fell in love with the area like we knew she would, and when the house on the point became available, she jumped at the opportunity to buy it."

Evan took a deep breath and sighed, letting her head drop forward, aware Tate was watching her quizzically.

"I'm not sure why, but I get the impression you have a problem with my having bought that property."

But before she could formulate a response, Alex jumped in once again, his face alight with humor. "She's just jealous. Evan had her eye on that place ever since Nick and I moved to the island. She even went so far as to contact the owner. Before she shipped out, Evan arranged for him to let either Nick or me know if he ever wanted to sell. She promised to meet his asking price without question in return for right of first refusal."

Tate stared at Alex as comprehension dawned. "That's how you knew it was going on the market before it ever got listed?"

"I don't suppose I could interest you in making a quick profit," Evan interjected with a wry grin.

Tate gave a quick shake of her head in polite refusal. "No, not really. But you're welcome to stay as long as you like," she countered softly.

"Sounds like you're making plans for going home," Althea said from the doorway. "That's wonderful news, Evan. Do I take it you'll be staying with Tate on the island?"

Evan nodded, uncertain what to say.

Tate squeezed her shoulder reassuringly. "You don't need to worry about Evan. There's a really good medical clinic in town and we can always hire a nurse if that's what Evan needs. Or we can get help through the naval base on the peninsula."

"I'm not worried," Althea said mildly as she approached the bed. "But we still need to fatten you up, so we'll have to plan a celebratory dinner. Something with all of your favorites. What do you think you would like?"

"A barbecue," Evan answered immediately, suddenly feeling poignantly young as one of her favorite childhood memories flashed into her mind. It stood out in a sea of countless functions and events dictated by politics. A private family holiday and a barbecue at the lake on the Fourth of July when she and Alex had been ten or eleven. "I'd love to have barbecued chicken, apple pie, and a gallon of champagne. And music. I've really missed listening to music."

Althea brushed the hair away from Evan's face with a slightly uncertain hand. "Then we'll arrange to have a barbecue as soon as you're comfortably settled."

Evan nodded and rubbed her temple. Maybe she could just plead a headache and deal with everything else tomorrow.

"Are you feeling all right, Evan?" Althea had continued to watch her closely. "You look like you're in pain. Should we get one of the nurses to give you something for it?"

Evan considered her mother's offer briefly. "Actually, it's only a headache," she said, "and I think I'd rather try a couple of aspirin and see if that works. Maybe with a cup of strong black coffee and some apple strudel."

"I understand the patisserie downstairs serves excellent strudel. Shall we go down and see if they have some?"

"That would work." As Evan began to relax, her mouth curved into a smile. "But maybe first, if it's all right with you, we could stop by Deacon's room. I understand he's going home today and I promised I'd stop and say good-bye."

CHAPTER NINETEEN

A t first she thought it was a dream.

She was drowning in waves of hopelessness and pain, trapped in a world without light, without air. In a state of near panic, her mouth grew dry, her heart pounded frantically, and her eyes burned. Except she wasn't asleep. She was awake. And even with her eyes wide open, the air in her hotel room remained charged, and Tate had the unshakable feeling something was horribly wrong with Evan.

Intellectually, she knew it made no sense. She had left Evan ensconced in her hospital bed, safely tucked in for the night, albeit restless and bored.

But the feeling Evan was in danger hit her like a blow. With her head between her knees, she breathed slowly until the pain eased and she could think more clearly. Having just found her again, there could simply be no disregarding unexplained feelings. No matter how illogical.

Raking a faintly shaking hand through her hair, she gave in to the inevitable and headed to the shower.

When she stepped out of her bedroom, showered and dressed, she was startled to see Alex moving quietly out of the shadows. With unspoken questions between them, she walked across the suite toward him, rubbing her arms with her hands. Nick stepped out from behind him and she saw both were fully dressed.

"The twin telepathy can be a real bitch," Alex said with a faint smile and handed her a large coffee.

Humor. She hadn't expected it, but under the circumstances she certainly appreciated it. And if nothing else, it told her at least Alex still had his balance. That was a good thing. A necessary thing. "I feel like Alice in Wonderland and I've just fallen down the rabbit hole," she admitted. "What the hell is going on?"

"I was coming to wake you up and let you know Nick and I were going to pop over to the hospital. See if you wanted to come along. But then I heard your shower running and figured you were ahead of us. I should have known you'd already be up. You felt it too, didn't you?"

"The twin telepathy?" She focused on sipping the top inch from her coffee and tried to come to terms with what he was saying. She'd certainly read about twins sharing an uncanny connection. How it could produce an intense sense of empathy, strong enough to generate physical sensations, such as feeling pain when a twin was hurting or in crisis. But still…"I don't know about this, Alex. It makes no sense. I'm her lover, not her twin."

"Doesn't seem to matter much at the moment, does it?"

"It probably means nothing." But why waste time arguing? Not finding any ready answers, Tate shrugged.

"Are you all right?"

"I don't know. I don't think so." She gave a shaky laugh. "Shall we go?"

The moon was a silver sickle, its light faint and thin as it guided her into the hospital less than twenty minutes later, Alex and Nick following closely in her wake. She had all but convinced herself she and Alex were suffering from a shared delusion, brought about by the unrelenting stress of the past few months.

But as she stepped off the elevator, Tate was confronted almost immediately by a disturbingly too-real sight. Kelsey Grant stood just outside Evan's room with two MPs while a nurse gestured with her hands.

She hated this. Hated feeling helpless. Hated being so frightened she couldn't breathe. But she was functioning on only caffeine and nervous energy, and as she tried to ignore the obvious implications of the military police presence, her chest began to ache.

Oh God, not again. Let Evan be all right.

What the hell could have happened? Every nerve in her body began screaming for her to run as fast as she could. Remembering to breathe, she sprinted forward and braced herself for the worst. "What's happened? Where's Evan?"

"She's all right," Kelsey replied, a line forming between her brows as she took a careful look at both Tate and Alex. "She's in her room."

"She wasn't hurt," the nurse added.

Tate felt a hysterical laugh bubble up to her throat as she clenched her fists and fought for control. "What does that mean?"

"Tate, I'm going to ask you to stay calm. Evan's all right," Kelsey reiterated.

"I'm as calm as I'm going to get. What happened?"

"Earlier this evening we had a situation—an intruder got into Evan's room. One of the nurses thought she heard something, and when she went to check and saw what was happening, she called for the MPs."

Tate's head reeled and her blood turned to ice.

"How the hell did this happen?" Alex asked. "And where is this intruder now?"

"All I can tell you is he was dressed in scrubs and a lab coat and looked like he belonged. He escaped before he could be caught. The MPs are still searching for him, but he's most likely long gone. In the meantime, we're trying to contain the situation and have stationed two MPs at Evan's door. They'll be there until she's discharged."

"Damn straight they'll be there," Alex said, his tone caustic. Turning, he tried to push his way into Evan's room but was stopped by the two much larger MPs. Alex sent them a glowering look. "Give me a fucking break. Listen, I don't give a rat's ass—"

Before Tate could determine how to defuse the situation, Kelsey intervened. She quickly stepped between Alex and the MPs and looked directly into Alex's eyes. "I'm sorry Alex. I know you want to see your sister, but we can't let you in just yet. Dr. Patterson is in there with Evan, and right now she's what Evan needs. Trust me."

Seeing the determination still shining brightly in Alex's eyes, Tate put a restraining hand on his shoulder, squeezing gently. Alex raised an eyebrow and exhaled heavily but didn't persist.

"Who's Dr. Patterson?" Tate asked.

"She's a psychiatrist. We just want to make sure Evan's okay emotionally after what happened. If you could give them a little more time, I'm sure you'll be able to see Evan once they finish."

Something in Kelsey's tone had Tate swallowing uncomfortably. "Did Evan say anything? Did she know who the intruder was? Could she identify him?"

Kelsey seemed to weigh her answer before she spoke. "Evan knew him. Said his name is Khalid."

Tate felt her throat close, could see the beginnings of horrified understanding on Alex's face. "This isn't some manifestation of PTSD, is it? Evan didn't imagine any of this?"

Kelsey shook her head. "He was very real."

"Did he do anything to her? Did he hurt her?"

Before Kelsey could respond, a petite woman with wavy hair generously laced with silver stepped out of Evan's room. Knowing this could only be Dr. Patterson, Tate quickly turned toward her. "How is she? How is Evan?"

❖

She found Evan sitting by the window, staring out at the night sky. The only light in her room was a night-light blending with what little spilled in from the corridor. But the darkness surrounding her did nothing to obscure the shadows clouding her eyes and the paleness of her skin.

"Hey," Tate said softly. "Is it okay if we come in?"

At first Evan appeared not to hear her. But after several painful seconds passed, she turned her head toward them. One look had Tate's level of concern escalating. She appeared confused. Almost as if she didn't know them. Didn't recognize her twin brother and his partner. Or her lover.

Tate moved a step closer. "Evan?"

Evan stared at her a moment longer before Tate saw her features slowly relax. "Hey. What are you doing here in the middle of the night?"

"For some reason, we thought you could use some company."

Beside her, Alex laughed. "You were sending out pretty strong distress signals earlier," he said, and when Evan's eyes swept over Tate, Alex added, "Yeah. Tate picked them up too."

Evan's expression inexplicably altered. Instead of laughing, her eyes darkened and traces of tension and unhappiness appeared on her face. She didn't move, but Tate felt her pull away. She felt the distance between them stretch and could almost see the barriers closing around her.

What the hell happened? She tried to relax her body, tried to ignore the sharp ache in her chest. Tried to remember to breathe. "Evan? What is it?"

Evan shook her head. "Pointless what ifs."

What ifs? Clarity struck Tate like a bolt of lightning. "You're wondering why we picked up on your distress tonight but failed to pick up anything during the months you were held captive. Is that it? You're wondering if you might have been rescued sooner if we had—before Khalid happened."

"Something like that."

It was a question Tate wasn't prepared to ask herself. "I can't answer that any more than I can pretend to understand what happened earlier tonight. I just know I've never experienced anything like it. I'm only sorry we didn't get here sooner. But we're here now and I promise we're not going to let anything else happen to you." *I'm not going to let that bastard hurt you again.*

As if hearing her thoughts, Evan looked down for a second, blinking. "I don't think you'll be able to stop Khalid. He won't let anything stop him."

"Oh, Evan." Tate wanted to reach for her, to touch her so badly she ached. But she hesitated. Afraid to startle Evan who was clearly on edge. And even more afraid of being rejected.

Shadows had infiltrated the room, secluding them in a silence broken only by the occasional sound of voices and movement of the hospital staff in the corridor beyond the door. After a minute or two passed, Evan looked up and held Tate's gaze steadily.

"We need to talk about this…about what happened this evening."

"I agree," Tate responded calmly. "But I get the feeling we're talking about having two very different conversations."

"What do you mean?"

"I mean I think we should talk because you're already holding in much more than is healthy. You've been through hell and you need to start letting some of it go. But that's not why you want to talk, is it?"

Evan shook her head. "No. I think we need to talk because I'm thinking this…my going home with you and Alex…my staying with you…I don't think it's going to work. I think we're making a mistake."

"What are you saying?"

"I'm saying Althea is heading to the UK, but Dad's flying back to DC and I think you and Alex and Nick should catch a ride back with him."

Tate felt a flash of something hot and painful deep in her chest. Anger or hurt, she couldn't be sure. She found her throat suddenly dry and she was no longer certain she could say anything. She made an effort to swallow, knew her heart was breaking. The best she could manage was to keep her voice calm when she spoke, even if it was only one word.

"Why?"

"Because I don't think my going with you is the right thing to do. Not right now, anyway."

Tate waited only an instant before shaking her head in disagreement. "That's not good enough," she said, and some of the hurt she was feeling seeped into her voice. "After all this time and everything we've been through, don't you think I deserve more of an answer? At the very least, I think I deserve the truth." She didn't need to look at Evan. She knew by the silence she'd made her point.

Evan pushed her hands into her hair and held her head. "Christ, Tate, I don't know if I can handle much more tonight, and I'm not sure I know how to explain, but I really need you to understand." She lowered her hands and blew out a breath.

"Understand what?"

"Don't you get it? Khalid found me. He was here this evening. This isn't PTSD. I didn't imagine him and he's as mad as a hatter. He's obviously still working on some agenda I'm not sure even he understands, but quite clearly he needs me to be part of whatever he's got going on. And that makes it dangerous for anyone to be around me."

"That's bullshit," Tate responded sharply. "There are MPs stationed outside your room even as we speak and they'll be there until you go home. If that's not enough, if we need more, then we'll get them. And once we get you home, we'll do whatever we have to do to protect you. We can get security systems, security guards. Whatever."

"She's right," Alex spoke for the first time. "For Christ's sake, Evan. Our mother's the bloody secretary of state. Don't you think Althea's got enough resources she can call on to protect you—to protect all of us if need be—until they can find and put a stop to this guy? You're obviously not thinking straight."

Evan exhaled tiredly. "You're right. I'm not thinking straight, and that's part of the problem."

"What do you mean?"

"I mean I'm a mess, physically and psychologically. The doctors want me to gain weight but food is the furthest thing from my mind. I can't sleep for the nightmares, and when I'm awake, I'm having flashbacks I can't control. Don't you see?"

"What, Evan? What do you want me to see?"

"That this whole situation is completely fucked up because the truth is the Evan Kane you knew didn't survive. She died in Afghanistan." She paused and released a harsh laugh. "Jesus, listen to me. A psychiatrist would have a field day with me on a couch."

"Evan—"

"No, don't." As she continued, her voice grew calmer, became softer. "Don't get me wrong. I know I'm getting better every day and I'll heal physically. I'd also like to think I'm still mostly sane, in spite of everything that's happened. But right now, I'm the last thing I figure is good for any of you the way I am. I'm not sure I have anything to offer, not while I'm like this, and I don't know if anyone can fix what's broken."

"What the hell are you talking about?"

Evan stiffened, but before she could respond, Alex quietly inter-rupted. "Listen, it looks like the two of you really need to talk, so why don't Nick and I head out of here? Tate, do you want us to wait for you?"

Tate shook her head. Trying to remain calm, she watched Alex and Nick leave before turning back to face Evan. "Now, do you want to explain what's going on in that head of yours?"

"Tate," she whispered uncertainly.

"I'm not going anywhere, Evan. So you might as well talk to me."

For a moment she didn't answer. She wanted only to be left alone. To protect her world and to be left alone inside it. But as quickly as the desire crystalized, she knew Tate wouldn't let her be. "You and I," she began. "We've always had a very active…a very physical relationship."

"Is that the problem?"

"Not exactly, no. The problem is right now I'm not sure I can handle any level of intimacy."

"And you think that's going to be a problem for me?"

Evan leaned her head back, closed her eyes, and took a long, deep breath before finally lifting her gaze back to Tate. "I don't know. Maybe. All I know is this—everything that's going on between you and me has the potential of hurting you, and that's the last thing I want to do. But there's so much inside me right now, churning, and I don't know what to do. Every time I close my eyes, I see Khalid. Holding that damn knife of his. Cutting me. And I know one of these times, he's going to succeed. He's going to kill me."

"Evan, no, listen to me. He can't kill you. You can't die. They're just dreams. You've got to believe that. Say you believe me."

"Except that wasn't a dream in my room tonight. Was it?"

Tate took her time studying Evan's face and wary expression. Kelsey Grant had warned them Evan's reintegration into everyday life wouldn't be easy. But what words could she use to penetrate the kind of fear Evan was feeling? What words would begin to undo all the damage that had been done?

Then she looked at Evan's face again and all her carefully planned speeches slipped quietly out of her head. "I spent four months believing you were dead."

"Damn it, Tate, do you think I don't know that?"

Tate tried not to flinch at the raw hurt evident in Evan's voice and hated knowing she was adding to her pain, but she stood her ground. Was she doing the right thing? She answered her own question almost immediately with a resounding yes and pressed on. "Then try to understand my life was empty without you in it, and I'll gladly take you however you are, even with Khalid in the wings coming after you, rather than not have you in my life at all."

She paused and held Evan's gaze briefly as she thought about what she was going to say next. What she needed to say. "I know it was a long time ago, but do you remember the night we met?"

For an instant, Evan frowned. But almost as quickly, her expression became wistful. "How could I not?"

"Then perhaps you'll remember asking me what I thought was going on between us," Tate recounted softly. "You said you wanted the chance to find out, but you already knew, didn't you? You knew we had a chance for something special. And then in the letter you left for me—in your just-in-case letter—"

"Oh Jesus." Evan paled. "I forgot about that damned letter."

"I haven't," Tate said forcefully. "You told me in the letter that you had three regrets. The first was not having made things right with your mother. I'd like to think you've already started making those course corrections. Not to say everything is right between you, but at least you're both trying. As for Alex, he'll tell you he stopped grieving the moment he was told you were still alive."

Evan nodded, closing her eyes for an instant. Momentarily retreating as the color slowly returned to her face. "Tate—"

Tate quickly stopped her. "No, let me finish. As to your last regret, I'd like to think you and I are finally in the right place at the right time and we're being given a chance to find out what's possible between us. Without my bureau chief sending me dashing off to Tripoli or Tel Aviv chasing some damn story. Or the navy sending you into a war zone on an extended deployment. Or insurgents shooting you down and making you disappear from my life for months."

"Yes, but—"

"But you need to stick around for that to happen, don't you think?" She paused as a different thought occurred to her and she felt her heart stop for an instant. It didn't bear thinking about, unless…"Unless what you're really trying to do is tell me that's not what you want anymore. I'm not what you want anymore."

Evan swore softly and swiftly pressed her fingers against Tate's lips, effectively silencing her. "Trust me. It's not that I don't want to be with you. I may not be sure about much but that much I'm sure of," she said. "But I don't think you understand. There's still Khalid and I'm not sure if you've realized it yet…I'm not who I used to be."

Tate understood how Evan might believe what she was saying. But it didn't mean she agreed. "We'll get help to deal with Khalid. As for you not being who you used to be, we've both been changed by what happened."

"I can see that. You never used to argue with me so much in the past." A ghost of a smile touched Evan's lips. Then it was gone again, as if Tate had imagined it. "But first and foremost, I need to know you'll be safe. You and Alex and Nick. You don't know Khalid. You don't know what he's capable of."

Tate nodded. "Like I said, we'll get help."

"I also need to know what you want, what you can live with. And I need to believe I can give it to you."

"I can help you with that. We just need to be open with each other. Tell each other how we're feeling and what we need. We can start by giving you your own room, some space and time to heal, and then see where that takes us."

"And you're sure you'll be okay with that?"

"Oh, Evan, of course I will. I'm not saying I won't miss sleeping with you, making love with you, or holding you while we sleep. But we're about so much more, and I see this as simply the next part in your recovery. Short term."

Evan closed her eyes again, inhaled deeply, and appeared to concentrate on regulating her breathing as a heavy silence settled between them. When her eyes opened, her expression remained sober. "This isn't going to be easy," she warned softly. "What I have left may not be enough. Ever. You know that, don't you?"

Almost weak with relief, Tate released a heartfelt sigh. "I'm not looking for easy." She met Evan's gaze head-on. "All I ask is for you to be honest with me and not shut me out. If you do that, I think we can both get through this. It's worth a chance, Evan. We're worth a chance."

Tate could almost hear Evan thinking, weighing her options. But she waited her out, vacillating between doubt and hope, wishing it wasn't so but knowing she would gladly accept Evan under any terms and conditions.

"What if this doesn't work?"

"What if it does?"

Evan wrapped her arms around her chest like armor and lapsed into a brief silence before flashing a rueful look. "If we're seriously talking about trying to make this work...making us work"—she tilted her head to one side as she paused—"then I think you should know the kitchen is not my natural habitat."

Tate felt some of the tightness in her chest begin to loosen. "Why doesn't that surprise me? But as it happens, I'm a pretty good cook, and I'm sure, given time, you can learn to make your way in a kitchen without endangering any lives. And if not, well that's okay too, because you probably come with other talents that will more than compensate for your woeful lack of culinary skills."

"I can think of one or two." This time a real smile appeared. "I guess if you're still willing to take the risk, then we should see where this takes us."

"Absolutely." It suddenly became hard to concentrate because Evan's smile took Tate's breath away. She leaned closer and touched her lips to a fading bruise on Evan's face. There was still more to say. Questions she still needed to ask. But they would have to wait. She didn't think Evan could handle more. And she felt too drained to try.

"You know what else I think?"

"What's that?"

"I think you've had a pretty hellacious night. On top of that, you can barely keep your eyes open. In fact, we're both exhausted. What do you say we try to get some sleep and pick this up in the morning?"

"Sounds good, but I'm not sure if I can sleep."

"Try anyway." Tate stepped back. "I'll be back before you have a chance to miss me." She was surprised when she felt Evan reach for her hand, linking their fingers. "Do you need anything before I go?"

Evan swallowed. "Don't go."

"I'll stay with you for as long as you want," she murmured. "For as long as you'll have me."

CHAPTER TWENTY

Tate held Evan as she slipped into a blessedly dreamless slumber and was holding her still when she awoke two hours later. Turning her head, Evan saw the new day was beginning to break. She had managed to survive the night and knew the horror was receding because of the woman beside her. And not just last night's.

"What are you thinking?" Tate murmured.

"That I can't believe you came to Afghanistan and found me." Evan's words came out in a tumbled rush. "After so long, I still can't believe anyone came. But you came. You put it all on the line for me and I don't know how to begin to thank you."

Tate gave her a serious, assessing look. "You've got to know thanks aren't necessary." She reached for Evan's hand and studied her face for a full ten seconds, as if debating her next words. "But you know we've never actually talked about it...about what happened."

"In Afghanistan? There's not much to tell." It was there in her voice. A faint tremor. The faint edge of fear and a hesitation so slight as to be barely noticeable. But if she could hear it, chances were so could Tate. Her suspicions were confirmed when Tate continued.

"Hey, I'm on your side. But I understand this has to be hard for you, especially after everything that happened yesterday. So we don't have to talk about it now if you don't want to."

She remained quiet for a moment, recognizing the out Tate was giving her if she chose to take it. It would be so easy. "No, it's okay." Pushing herself into a sitting position, she considered how much she could share. How much she'd be able to say without getting sick. "I know I owe you some kind of explanation."

"You don't owe me anything," Tate corrected. "I'd just like to understand and be able to help if I can."

Evan shifted uncomfortably. "It's funny," she said at last, "because it occurs to me that in all the time you and I have known each other, most of our deep, soul-baring conversations have taken place without the benefit of our actually being in the same room…or in the same country."

Tate laughed.

But it was the truth. Conversations between them, whether of the soul-baring variety or any other kind, had taken place to a large extent via e-mail, by phone, and sometimes, if they were lucky, by Skype where they could at least see each other. Whether by accident or design, face-to-face time seemed to have been reserved for touching. Kissing. Tasting.

"Would it help if I left the room?"

"No." Evan reflexively tightened her hold on Tate's hand, her smile faint. "But I hope you understand. I hope you won't be too disappointed if there are some things we don't talk about."

"Can't or won't?"

Evan felt herself flush. "Both, I guess." It was the best she could offer. The only question remaining was whether Tate could live with it.

"I'm good with that," she said as she reached over and gently twirled a finger in Evan's hair. "Maybe we can go back to the beginning."

Evan thought about getting up, moving around. She really didn't want to be sitting for this conversation. But she knew her leg wouldn't allow her to pace like she needed to. Frustrated, she leaned back against the pillow and stretched, deliberately not meeting Tate's eyes. "You want to know about my last flight?"

Tate nodded.

"All right. It was meant to be a straightforward reconnaissance mission, tracking insurgent movement through the mountains. The intel we were gathering was supposed to help map out the various routes being used to transport both insurgents and weapons from Pakistan." She felt an odd shiver along her spine and straightened her shoulders, refusing to be intimidated by her own recall of events. *You can do this*, the little voice whispered in her head. *You need to do this*.

"The reports I saw indicated you got called to support some NATO troops pinned down under heavy fire," Tate prompted.

"When the call came from control, Deacon and I were the closest available support. They wanted a show of force. Just come in fast and low and loud and drop flares."

"Shock and awe? Isn't that what they call it sometimes?"

"Yeah, that's another name for it."

"So what went wrong?"

"They…they were waiting. They were counting on someone getting called to provide air support and do what we did." Evan closed her eyes while the scene replayed in her mind. Just like it had a thousand times before. Each time she prayed the missile would miss her, but each time it turned out exactly the same. The ending never changed.

"They were set up on a break we had to pass to gain access to the valley. And in the blink of an eye, the bastards took down two state-of-the-art military aircraft with some fucking shoulder-launched missiles they bought from a warehouse in Karachi for a few hundred dollars."

Tate's eyes narrowed. "What are you saying? That it was bullshit luck?"

"Because of their limited range, shoulder-launched missiles are normally more of a threat to low-flying aircraft."

"You mean like helicopters?"

"Yes, although during Desert Storm, one was used to bring down an F-16. Another brought down a civilian airliner outside Mogadishu. They're aviation's dirty little secret. There's no warning prior to launch and they can't be effectively jammed after they're launched. They're also resistant to most conventional countermeasures. And because we were coming in low, we made it easier for them to target us."

She swallowed hard on the nausea rising in her throat, took a breath and exhaled unhappily. Tate squeezed her hand. "Are you okay?"

"Yeah," Evan said distractedly. "No warning meant there was no time to react and made for a rather ignominious ending to what had been a stellar naval career, don't you think? Who would have guessed Althea was right when she told me I was throwing my life away by enlisting. Go figure." She paused, lowered her eyes, and faltered. She felt off balance and acutely conscious of how rapidly her heart had begun to beat. Hammering so hard she was certain Tate could hear it. And maybe she could because almost immediately, she felt Tate's hand begin to slowly stroke her arm, reassuring and soothing her.

"Your mother couldn't have been more wrong, Evan," Tate said softly. "And sometime, I'll be quite happy to debate the point with you. Why don't we put it aside for now? Tell me what happened next."

"I got hit first. The missile struck my starboard wing and I had just enough time to recognize I was in trouble, but not much more. Every warning light in the cockpit suddenly started flashing. But they were warning me about things I already knew."

"Were you—?"

"Afraid?" Evan shrugged and smiled wanly. "I was losing altitude and I knew I was going to have to punch out. I also had a pretty good idea of what to expect from the terrain below me, so quite frankly, I didn't rate my chances of survival very high."

"What about Deacon?"

"He stayed close. He wanted to confirm I made it out and then be in a position to provide the coordinates so a search-and-rescue mission could be launched as quickly as possible."

"Before you could be captured?"

"Before I froze my ass off," Evan replied, laughing humorlessly before her smile faded. "But any luck to be had that night was entirely on the other side. Deacon had no chance to communicate anything to anyone before he got hit. Instead, we both got ringside seats and watched our jets light up the night sky like the Fourth of July."

"Deacon said he landed badly and was in trouble, but you saved him. Even though you were bleeding rather badly."

"He was my wingman. My friend." Her voice was dying now, a rasp of a whisper that hurt. "I'd known him since flight school and I wasn't about to leave him hanging on the side of a mountain without doing everything possible to help him. And he was in no position to help himself."

"Is that when you were both captured? When you were taken prisoner?"

"Yes."

She shuddered for an instant as she felt a chill pass over her. There had been snow near the mountaintop and she remembered being unbelievably cold. She couldn't keep her balance, couldn't seem to stay on her feet, and after using the last remnants of energy to haul Deacon up the side of the mountain, she had pitched forward, too exhausted and numb to care.

The hands that picked her up were rough, but she didn't protest. She was only vaguely aware they were dragging her across the rocks and snow, bruising her, hurting her, but she wasn't in any position to protest or complain. She lost all sense of time and direction, and then, mercifully, everything receded and she felt nothing.

Until later, when she found herself *wishing* she could still feel nothing.

"What did they do to you, Evan?"

Evan shook her head, shuddered out a painful breath, and fought the rising tide of panic that began to set in. Pulling her hand away from Tate, she folded her arms across her chest to hold back the nerves beginning to snake through her once again.

I can make the pain stop, Commander. Just answer the question.

Oh Jesus, she thought and knew she was losing whatever calming distance she'd managed to achieve.

I can also make it worse.

Evan didn't want to think about it anymore. Tired beyond reason, she was having difficulty focusing on anything. She didn't want to remember, in fact wanted desperately to forget. She tried to shut down. Tried to find the place that made it all seem bearable.

But it was almost as if when the dam holding everything back had been broken, it had somehow destroyed her ability to escape. Everything she tried failed to work. She remained firmly trapped in reality. And it wasn't until Tate brushed a finger along her cheek that she realized she was crying.

Silence prevailed, insulating them.

Evan had been staring sightlessly for several minutes, lost in her thoughts, when Tate finally broke the silence. "Do you want to stop?" Her expression was tender, filled with compassion. But then Tate, no doubt, saw straight through her.

What did they do to you?

It wasn't the first time she had been asked that particular question since arriving in Germany. But this time the question was deeply personal, and for the first time since she'd been rescued, Evan acknowledged she would eventually have to provide some kind of cogent response. Especially if she wanted to prove she had achieved a satisfactory level of psychological recovery. Enough for them to let her go home.

What did they do to you?

In the span of a few seconds, Evan debated and then decided to consider this a dry run. Almost immediately, she felt the rough grip of tension easing from her shoulders. Looking up, she met Tate's eyes once again. "They did what we were warned to expect in the event we were ever captured," she said. "But they don't prepare you for what it's really like. They can't. No one can show you how it feels to have absolutely no control over what's happening to you."

The words were out before she could call them back, and Evan was surprised she had managed to get them out without stumbling. Still, she considered it a hollow victory because what she couldn't say—the bitter truth she couldn't get out—was that they also hadn't taught her how to go on once she was twisted and broken inside.

Tate regarded her intently through narrowed eyes. Concerned. Able to recognize the depth of anguish Evan's words held but uncertain how she was supposed to respond. In the prolonged silence that followed, Evan closed her eyes and rolled over onto her side, turning her back to Tate. Lying perfectly still.

It looked almost as if she was waiting.

Tate didn't wait to reach the count of three before crawling closer, until Evan's back was pressed firmly against her chest, and she had her arms tightly wrapped around her. "I'm so sorry they hurt you, Evan," she whispered. "I'm so sorry for everything you had to go through. But you're here now, safe, and I'm here with you. For you. Now or whenever you want to talk. The when doesn't matter, I'll still be here."

Evan didn't reply. Didn't make a sound. But after a minute or so, whatever pent up emotions kept her stiff and unyielding began to dissipate, and Tate heard her sigh. Felt her relax into the embrace.

How long they remained in that position, curled up against each other on the narrow bed, Tate had no idea and she didn't really care. She was content to remain there until Evan wanted to move, providing her with whatever comfort she could find in their embrace and allowing everything else to fade.

She listened to the ambient sounds of the hospital—the hum of the ventilation system, the muffled voices of the staff as they went about their business, the sound of a helicopter as it came in to land on the helipad. All the pockets of activity that filled the world just beyond the room with life and noise.

As she listened, it occurred to her that for the first time in months, she was at peace. Content to simply hold the one woman who meant more to her than anyone ever had. Or ever would. Drowsy, she almost missed the next words Evan said.

"The first ones—the ones who captured us—they wanted information. They were angry about a drone strike from a week earlier. They claimed it had killed some civilians from their village. They kept asking who was responsible as if we could give them a name. Point a finger at someone. And pain is a wonderful incentive to talk. Except we had no real information to give them, so it just prolonged the pain."

Evan rolled over onto her back, stared at the ceiling. And although it looked as if she had more to say, she bit her lip and fell silent, lost in painful memories once again. Tate gave her time to regroup, and then gently nudged her forward.

"What about later? Kelsey said some of your injuries…she said some are much more recent than the others. And I'm not just talking about the bullet wound in your thigh."

"Khalid."

"He interrogated you?"

Evan shook her head. "You could call what he did many things, but interrogation wouldn't be one of them. By the time he traded for us, there couldn't have been anyone among the insurgent cells in the area who didn't know we had no information to give. Or that anything we might have once known was now too dated to be useful."

"Then why did he trade for you?"

"Khalid was different," Evan responded. "He…one time he laughed and admitted he was working both sides of the line. He'd help the insurgents, and then sell bits and pieces of the information he happened to collect along the way. Whatever he thought might be of interest to the CIA. The thing of it was, when he traded for Deacon and me, he knew exactly what he was getting and it suited his purpose."

"I don't think I understand." Tate could feel the tension thrumming through Evan. She could feel her slip painfully into some recent memory, and watched her intently. Knew the moment she started to shake, the vibration evident everywhere their bodies touched.

Evan swallowed nervously. The walls of the room began closing in on her and she felt on the verge of suffocating. "Khalid doesn't like people in general—and women specifically."

For an instant, she remembered all too clearly the brutal feel of his hands on her and couldn't control a shudder. Anger flared and became the dominant emotion in her voice as she continued. "He had a fondness for playing with knives. And he liked to cause pain. He only intended to hold us long enough to make his sadistic little soul happy. Whatever condition we happened to be in by the time he finished playing wasn't really important because his intent from the start was simply to allow the CIA to recover our bodies. He knew they would be grateful and not question too closely the condition our bodies were in."

"Then why did he make the trade?"

"I don't honestly know," she said, her voice a mere hint of sound. "He's a sociopath with no remorse and he was ready to move on anyway. Find another place to ply his trade as a bomb maker. Pursue his personal interests."

Tate stared at her without saying a word. Finally, she sighed softly and said, "Look at me for a second, will you? Can I ask you one last question?"

"What?" Evan responded warily, as she turned to face her.

"In the settlement in Afghanistan, just as he let you go, Khalid said something to you. I know he did. I could see it in your face. What did he say?"

Evan bit her lip. "He said we weren't finished. That he and I— we'd have another go. There would be another time and another place, and then he would finish things. I wasn't sure if I believed him or not, until last night."

"He's never going to get another chance to get that close to you," Tate countered with finality. "I need you to believe me when I tell you we will do whatever we need to do to protect you until he's caught. Until he's permanently out of our lives."

Evan didn't argue the point. And for a while, Tate wasn't inclined to break the silence. Instead, she listened to the steadiness of Evan's breathing, felt the rhythmic beating of her heart, and briefly wondered if Evan had fallen asleep.

But then Evan looked at her, and she saw the flash of doubt that shadowed her face and turned her eyes nearly black. "I don't want to talk about it anymore," she whispered. "I don't want to think about it or remember any of it. Can we do that, Tate? Can we not talk about it anymore?"

Tate watched her try to gather her fraying composure. Tears welled but never fell and it broke Tate's heart. "Of course, love. Whatever you want."

"What I want?" Her voice started to break. "What I want is to run barefoot along a beach with you. I want to eat crab cakes and drink wine while we wait for the sun to sink below the water. And then I want to watch as the sky fills with stars. What I want—" Evan covered her face with her hands.

"What, Evan?"

"What I want is for you to tell me you missed me. Please, Tate. I need to hear you say it. Tell me you're glad I'm still alive. Tell me you're glad you came to get me."

Tate didn't know what fear had suddenly triggered those words. Evan had always been so strong. And so very good at hiding her emotions. But she could hear the quiet desperation in her voice and in her words. For now, she wanted nothing more than to allay Evan's fears. To have her feel safe again. Secure again.

"I've missed you, Evan. More than I can ever say. Christ, I used to talk to you like you were still around." Her throat tightened. "The truth is, I've only been half-alive without you. I managed to get through denial, anger, bargaining, and depression, but somehow I never found my way to acceptance. And coming to find you was as necessary to me as breathing."

CHAPTER TWENTY-ONE

Evan stared out the small window at the cloud formations in the gathering darkness. She was finally going home. She should be thrilled at the prospect. Elated to be flying above the clouds once again.

Instead, she simply felt...tired.

Although it hadn't been a particularly arduous day, it still didn't take much to wear her out. Truthfully, she didn't understand it. She'd been through worse. There had been times during deployments when she'd gone days on mere moments of sleep. So why the hell was she so damned tired?

Her leg throbbed dully, a constant reminder of what she'd been through. But she resisted taking anything for it. She was tired of pills and determined to work through the pain without having to rely on any further chemical interventions. Mostly, she just wanted to get back to some semblance of normal.

Moving gingerly, she stretched her injured leg on the leather sofa, looked around, and was forced to acknowledge this was an entirely different kind of flying experience from anything she'd experienced over the last few years.

She had always loved to fly—everything from gliders to her tail dragger Tiger Moth to jets. But this—this wasn't flying. This was cruising in the lap of luxury, seated in the dimly lit cabin of the well-appointed Gulfstream V that was part of the small fleet owned by her father's law firm.

Tipping her head back, Evan closed her eyes as a soul-deep weariness washed over her. She shifted restlessly, felt inexplicably cold, and wondered if she'd ever feel warm again. Whole again. She noticed the slight tremble in her hands and swore under her breath. But she wasn't surprised at the emotional toll her body was reflecting.

She hated good-byes.

Five days earlier she'd said good-bye to Deacon, who was heading home to Chicago to reunite with his extended family and a girlfriend he planned to marry. That particular good-bye proved to be even harder than she'd anticipated.

She and Deacon had been there for each other for so long. Other than Tate and Alex, Evan couldn't think of a single soul who knew her as well. Nor could she think of anyone else she'd let get that close and knew she'd miss him like crazy.

There had also been a good-bye of sorts with her parents, who had flown off in different directions. Neither had wanted to leave before she was discharged, but Evan had watched them both clearly struggling to deal with mounting external pressures from their busy professional lives. When Althea began to uncharacteristically hover and fuss, she finally convinced them it was time to go, assuring them she'd be fine and would be in touch once she was settled at Tate's.

But surprisingly the most difficult good-bye turned out to Kelsey Grant, a woman she'd known for only a short time, but someone she'd connected with and had come to rely on emotionally. Ever observant, Tate gently suggested her surprise stemmed from not being used to developing friendships with women.

"From what you've told me, your closest friendships while you were growing up and during your time in the navy were almost exclusively with men and were segmented around shared interests and activities—sports, school, flying," Tate observed. "But what characterizes friendships between women is closeness and emotional attachment. A willingness to share feelings and thoughts. And you did that, Evan. You allowed Kelsey in."

Evan found herself bemused, not so much by what Tate said as by the fact that it was such a revelation. At least that farewell had been tempered by the knowledge Kelsey herself would be heading home to Seattle soon. And that would put her just a short ferry ride away from Tate's island home.

She smiled for a moment as she thought of the business card Kelsey had given her. The one with her contact information. The one that came with a heartfelt promise both Kelsey and her partner Jenna would help see her through the tough days and weeks to come.

It made saying good-bye more palatable, but the residual sadness left her withdrawn from the others and unable to sleep.

In the soft glow of the courtesy lights, she could see Alex and Nick, sprawled in a set of side-by-side recliners. They had crashed shortly after takeoff, having spent two hellishly long days running through the endless loops deemed necessary for her to be properly outfitted with legal documentation prior to leaving Germany. Tate was also sleeping, taking advantage of the privacy offered by the bedroom in the forward galley.

More than anything, she wished she could sleep like the others. Wished she could stop thinking about Afghanistan.

But Khalid was always there, in the shadows between reality and her nightmares. Recently, there'd been times he'd seemed so real she was convinced she had seen him again on the hospital grounds.

The hospital, however, had assigned MPs to protect her around-the-clock, so it was unlikely he was still around, making her sightings somehow more disturbing. Still, she was taking no chances the medical people would decide she wasn't psychologically fit to go home. So she told no one, promising herself she'd deal with it Stateside.

During her captivity, memories of home had kept her going. When Khalid had driven her half out of her mind with fear and pain, pushed her beyond endurance, it had been thoughts of Tate that had enabled her to survive. Now she was finally going home, determined to make up for lost time and get on with her life, and Tate was less than thirty feet away.

So what the hell was she waiting for?

Reaching for her crutches, she slowly made her way to the bedroom. The door opened silently and allowed the muted light to stream in, falling across Tate, stretched out on the bed. The sight caused Evan's mood to lighten and she found herself faintly smiling.

Still she hesitated, even as a distant part of her wanted Tate to wake up, to see her standing there. What if she did? She rocked back slightly, stunned to realize if Tate awoke, she didn't know what she'd do or say.

❖

Tate normally awoke in stages, aided by caffeine. In this instance, Evan's presence in the doorway had her suddenly and completely awake. Not because Evan had made a sound but because of the way the air always seemed to stir whenever she was near.

"Hey," she said, sitting up and watching Evan. In the past, Evan would have been humming with energy. But not today. Actually, not since Afghanistan. Instead, she was regarding her solemnly—her face pale and vulnerable, her eyes dark. "How're you doing?"

"I'm okay…well, maybe not exactly okay," Evan allowed when Tate tilted her head and looked at her more closely. She looked haunted. Lost. Possibly broken.

In the blink of an eye, Tate was standing beside her, guiding her into the room, closing the door behind them.

"I'm sorry. I don't know what's wrong with me and I certainly didn't mean to wake you up."

"Oh?" Tate gave her a teasing look. "Then what did you mean to do?"

Evan swallowed. "Actually," she said softly, "I thought I might crawl into bed beside you."

The dim light deepened the hollows in her face, casting her eyes in shadows. But as Tate's gaze traveled slowly upward from Evan's mouth, she found herself fascinated by the gleam that momentarily lit her gray eyes.

"What took you so long?" she murmured on a sultry laugh.

Evan gave her a quick look and a small smile hovered on her lips as she placed her crutches against a table. But Tate also saw uncharacteristic nervousness in her deliberate movements and in her expression.

"Evan? What is it, love? You're shaking."

She didn't immediately answer. Instead, she threw her arms around Tate. Burying her face into her neck, she breathed her in with a hint of desperation. "I'm sorry," she said softly. "I'm not sure what I'm doing. I think I just needed to be with you."

"That's good, because I can't think of a better place for you to be." As Evan started to pull back, Tate reached out and rubbed the frown line between her brows with her thumb. "I've got an idea. Why don't we go with your first impulse? Come lie down. Let me take care of you for a little while."

Evan sucked in a soft breath. "I'm not sure I know how to do that anymore."

Tate heard the sorrow in her words and wondered if Evan realized how much she revealed with that statement alone. "It's going to be okay, love," she whispered. "Sometimes it's okay to lean on someone and just let things happen."

Evan made a slight sound, but Tate had no idea whether it was acceptance or denial. It didn't matter. Pressing a kiss against her forehead, she helped Evan onto the bed, then slid in beside her, covering them both with a soft blue blanket.

After waiting a moment, she reached one arm across her waist and anchored Evan, holding her close in the semidarkness. Guarding her. Protecting her. Hopefully keeping the ghosts at bay. "Is this okay? Will you be able to sleep like this?"

"Yes."

It was a lie and they both knew it, but neither of them acknowledged it out loud.

Evan shivered slightly. She still felt oddly disoriented, her entire body strung so tightly she was afraid she would break apart at the slightest touch. But Tate's embrace felt warm and cocoon-like, enclosing her in a safe and quiet intimacy. Turning onto her side, she sighed when Tate curved her arm around her, allowing Evan to rest her head on her shoulder as fear and comfort briefly commingled.

She forced herself to try and find a place where she could escape the nightmare that hung thick in the air around her. But even as she drifted into sleep, she couldn't escape, couldn't shut out the sounds. And in the end, she should have known what was coming.

The blade cut into her, the pain searing as blood ran freely. "What's your lover's name, Commander?"

She hadn't known pain could be this bad and she tried to lash out, but her hands were securely manacled by the ropes and he held her back easily. Laughing. Bruising her as she tried to fight him. In her present condition, he was stronger than she was. But she continued to try, continued to struggle.

He backhanded her across the face, a casual blow that snapped her head back. She heard a strangled cry, but it took some time before she realized it had come from her. He seemed to like it and hit her again. She felt another scream well up inside but knew it was what he wanted. To stop herself, she bit her lip so hard her mouth began bleeding again.

"You haven't answered my question." He leaned closer, inhaling the scent of blood and fear and pain as he made another cut. "Tell me your lover's name. Surely you understand I won't stop until you answer. So the sooner you tell me, the sooner this will be over."

She closed her eyes.

"Tell me her name."

The pain grew, became intolerable. "You'll tell me her name before we're through." His eyes were calm as he looked down at her, drawing the knife slowly across her skin. "You'll beg me to let you say it."

She saw the blood shining on the blade as he brought it up. Ready to cut again. She bit down on her lip, but there was nothing she could do to stop it. Except...

"Her name is—"

"—Tate."

In the darkness, she heard the echo of the scream ripped from her throat with a violence that left her shaking. Struggled to breathe. And then Tate was there. She must have felt something of her desperation. Tate reached out with one hand and began to slowly rub comforting circles on her back.

"You're safe," she whispered soothingly. "It was only a dream."

Evan hunched her shoulders and immediately tried to pull away.

"Evan? Baby, what is it?"

Evan narrowed her eyes as light suddenly spilled out from the small bedside lamp Tate had switched on.

"Nothing." Her mouth felt wooden, stiff, as she mumbled her response. Scrambling out of reach, she sat up on the bed and cradled her head in her hands, tension radiating through her body. Dark, haunting images flickered across her mind and she took several deep breaths to calm herself. "I need a minute. Please. Just don't touch me…I just need a minute."

Tate jerked back as if she'd slapped her and there was a strained silence between the two of them. Clearly uncertain, Tate sat back, staying just within reach.

"I won't touch you," she said quietly. "But be careful. You're on the edge of the bed, and one more move in that direction and you'll end up on the floor."

Evan nodded and tried to focus on steadying her breathing and keeping panic at bay. Her hands were shaking, her head was spinning, and as she turned away, a dark curtain of hair mercifully fanned down the side of her face, cloaking her. But there was no real place to hide.

"I can't think straight and I've got the shakes," she said unnecessarily, her voice whisper-quiet. She was appalled by the tears burning her eyes and the recognition that she was on the verge of falling apart.

"You've had a pretty rough time of it these last few months. You're entitled to let go. You don't always have to be strong."

It took several more minutes, but slowly the ice around her began to break up and dissolve, and the need for warmth and a human touch finally took precedence. Blindly, she reached out and clutched Tate's hand, a lifeline she could use to reel herself in.

"I'm sorry," she whispered. Her breath hitched and she bore down. It wasn't Tate's fault that her life had undergone an unplanned metamorphosis. Nor was it Tate's fault she hadn't explained everything.

She wanted to close her eyes, to go into the dark, but instead she forced herself to keep them open and on Tate. "I should have told you sooner. I have some cuts…on my back. Kelsey assured me, like everything else, they'll heal, but right now they're hypersensitive and I overreacted."

Tate inhaled sharply. She could count the seconds between heartbeats as she remained motionless, stung and confused.

Evan was a lousy liar. And she was unquestionably lying, or at the very least withholding something. What Tate couldn't understand was why. She might have cuts on her back—Kelsey had said as much—and those cuts might be sensitive, but that wasn't why she had pulled away. There was something else at play and knowing that much left Tate no closer to understanding what was going on.

"You don't need to apologize." She worked at keeping her voice soft, unemotional, but it was killing her by inches. Because all she wanted to do was hold Evan close and try to figure out what was really wrong. "I know about the cuts on your back—Kelsey told us they were there. But I didn't realize how much they were bothering you."

"What exactly did Kelsey tell you?"

"It was when you first got out of surgery. Kelsey came by your room and spoke to your parents, and Alex and me. She gave us a rundown of your injuries and mentioned you had a number of cuts—on your arm, side, and back," Tate said before adding, "I'm sorry I hurt you."

"You couldn't have known."

The silence stretched. "Are you okay now?"

"As okay as it gets."

❖

They both slept, tangled together for what proved to be the remainder of the flight, until the sound of the jet's landing gear being lowered awoke Tate. Opening her eyes, she realized that she was holding Evan so close she couldn't tell where she ended and Evan began.

That was nice. But even better, she could see that Evan slept on, her face more relaxed than it had been for some time, her breathing even, her mouth soft. She looked so young, so innocent even after all she had seen and done and been though. As Tate stared down into her sleeping face, she felt her heart catch.

Beyond the healing cuts and bruises, Evan was still—would always be—the most beautiful woman she had ever known. Deciding she deserved at least thirty seconds more to enjoy the view, she tilted her head back and continued to watch Evan sleep until, at last, she saw her begin to stir.

Evan floated to the surface very slowly, still dreaming about Tate. She was conscious of someone lying in the bed next to her and she fought an unshakeable sense of being trapped. Disoriented, she turned her head but quickly realized it was Tate who lay wrapped around her.

Slowly, her panic receded as she listened to the pilot advising them they were beginning their descent into Seattle.

"Hello, beautiful lady." She stared at Tate for an instant longer. Saw her smile and then, slowly, she smiled back. It seemed impossible not to. "I don't know if you're real, or if I'm still dreaming. But if this is a dream, please don't wake me."

Tate's smile widened at that. "I'm very real, love. And on a different occasion, I would be happy to prove that to you. But as much as I'm enjoying lying here with you, we really should start thinking about getting ready."

"For what?"

"For landing."

"That was fast."

"You slept."

That was a pleasant surprise. "I couldn't have done it without you so thank you"—she touched Tate's hand and shrugged helplessly—"and I'm sorry."

Tate looked at her, ran the back of her fingers along Evan's cheek. "It's okay, Evan. I expect we'll probably stumble a few times before we get it right."

Evan closed her eyes for an instant. "I expect we will."

When she opened her eyes, Tate was still smiling. "I'm not sure he told you, but Alex has arranged to have a private floatplane take us out to the island. More comfortable than a long drive or taking the ferry."

"That's good."

"The only question is how long it'll take to clear Customs. Any ideas?"

Evan arched a brow and shook her head. "I think you've forgotten whose private jet you're traveling in." Her voice trailed off as she stretched her arms high to work out a dozen stiffened muscles. "We're talking about the queen of connections and the king of control."

Tate laughed at the descriptions.

"Laugh all you want, McKenna. It may have driven Alex and me crazy when we were kids, but clearing Customs should be a breeze."

❖

As evening faded into night, he trimmed a wire on the improvised explosive device he'd assembled, a device which would be used to detonate a truck filled with explosives. With his part of the job finished, he smiled at the two students who'd been watching him. Following his every move, taking meticulous notes.

Fools, he thought but didn't let it show. Caught up in romantic notions of revolution and anarchy, they believed they'd be able to replicate what he'd done. He knew better, of course. Knew they'd be lucky if all they managed to do was lose a couple of fingers the first time they tried to duplicate the kind of magic he could create with his eyes closed.

But the splinter cell he'd hooked up with in Germany served a much-needed purpose, so he masked his disdain. Knowing that in return for building pipe bombs, tilt fuses, and other incendiary devices, they would provide him with the means to get back to America.

Running a hand through his recently shorn hair, Khalid walked away. The students forgotten, his thoughts immediately turned back to her. The pilot.

He had felt a first spark of connection without ever having seen her. But nothing could compare to what he'd felt the first time he'd cut her. The first time he'd made his knife sing as it sliced through her skin. The first time he'd heard her choke back her cry of pain and watched her blood drip from his blade.

He knew now he'd been wrong to try to see her in the hospital. He should have exercised more control. As it was, that bitch of a nurse, showing up when she did, had almost undone everything.

But the commander was in his blood, and the fear he had seen in her eyes had been more than worth the risk. He owned her. She was his. She'd know that soon enough if she didn't already.

He smiled again, feeling better as he began to imagine how good it would feel the next time.

CHAPTER TWENTY-TWO

W e're almost home."
From her seat, Evan heard the excitement in Alex's voice as he leaned forward and watched the water rush by. A few minutes later, the pilot deftly maneuvered the aircraft up to the dock jutting out from the island. Adrenaline coursed through her as she gazed out the window at what would be her home for the foreseeable future while the ever present scent of the sea reached out to welcome her.

The plane bobbed slightly as the door was swung open and Nick was the first to jump down, moving quickly to tie off the mooring line. Tate and Alex exited close behind.

Evan hesitated, staring at the water lapping against the floatplane's pontoons. Within the narrow confines of the plane, she'd been unable to use her crutches and she felt momentarily trapped. But by using the seat backs to support her weight, she slowly made her way to the open door.

"Come on, Evan. Grab hold of my hand."

After the relative dimness of the plane's interior, the sun immediately blinded her, hurting her eyes and forcing her to rely completely on Alex's assistance. With a muttered curse, she steeled herself and did as Alex suggested. She reached out and grabbed his hand. Alex held her with a sure grip and in no time had her standing solidly on the long wooden pier. He produced a pair of Ray-Bans from his shirt pocket and slipped the sunglasses into place for her. He then tipped her chin up with a fingertip and examined her face closely.

"You doing okay?"

"I'm good." After being cramped in the small plane, even for a short hop, it felt good to stand up and stretch. She gave him a smile meant to reassure and nodded to where Tate and Nick were busy unloading their baggage and groceries they'd picked up in Seattle from the plane. "Go help them. I'm okay here on my own. I promise."

Of course, not a lot of what was being unloaded was hers, since she didn't have much to call her own beyond the silky warm-up pants and T-shirt she was wearing and a couple of spares. But she wasn't particularly worried.

Alex had promised he would drop by later with the clothing he'd been storing for her, including everything shipped home from the *Nimitz*. Among the flight suits and dress uniforms she would no longer need would be things she could use, including some of her favorite jeans and T-shirts.

Half listening as Nick and Tate teased Alex about something, she made her way to the end of the pier and onto a well-worn but not entirely crutch-friendly footpath that cut through the property. It led down to the dock from the house and appeared to follow the shoreline, veering and disappearing from view as it went around the point. She followed it with her eyes and determined she would explore its length before too long.

And oh, the house.

The house was everything she remembered. It had been custom designed to take advantage of the views through expansive windows in almost every room, as well as from the huge wraparound deck built out over the water on two sides. And the views, she knew, were truly spectacular, with the snowcapped Olympic Mountains providing a backdrop for the channels, inlets, estuaries, and islands that made up the Puget Sound waterways.

Pushing her sunglasses down her nose so she could get an unobstructed view, Evan drew in a deep breath. The air felt good against her skin and was scented with the clean fragrance of the cedar and pine trees as well as the salty tang of the sea.

Turning back toward the water, she looked out at the waves rolling gently onto the shore. Watched the working boats and pleasure boats go by. Time evaporated. There were no schedules to keep, no missions to fly. She could simply stand here and listen to the lap of the water against the rocks along the shore, or watch a bird—some kind of hawk, maybe an osprey, she wasn't certain—as it flew just above the thick stand of trees near the waterline.

For the first time in a long time, she felt good. Surprisingly good. Almost at peace with herself. In the distance she could hear the distinctive sound of a ferryboat's horn, but it in no way detracted from the quiet. It was peaceful here. Tranquil. No IEDs or bombs. No insurgents waiting to blow aircraft out of the sky. And no twisted sociopaths.

Tate had been right. The island was a bucolic paradise and would be the perfect place to heal.

Thinking of Tate, she turned once again to look for her and found her standing with Alex who had his arm swung around her shoulder. She liked seeing them together, liked witnessing the very real bond of affection that had developed between them.

Tate's face was flushed and she was laughing, a sound Evan found particularly appealing. And she looked casually sexy, dressed in a pair of khaki shorts and a navy blue polo shirt. The slight breeze was stirring her collar-length hair and Evan paused in her perusal, admiring the way the sunlight brought out the varying shades of red and gold.

Conflicting emotions surged inside her, leaving her confused. She wanted to walk over to them. To be part of their laughter and share in their joy at coming home. She knew that was what Tate wanted.

But she was barely hanging on, and she knew Khalid was still out there. Waiting for the right moment to strike. How could she bring Khalid's threat to Tate's doorstep? For that matter, how could she bring the empty shell of the woman she once had been?

Tate deserved so much more than a woman who couldn't make it through each day, let alone each night, without falling apart. A woman who couldn't make love with her because she was afraid to discover sex—a primitive, primal response—was all she had left to give.

Tate looked up in that instant, suddenly aware Evan had been watching her. She waved and flashed a smile as she and Alex approached.

"How're you doing?" she asked softly when she reached Evan's side. "Ready to check out your new address?"

Evan felt a flash of panic, afraid Tate had sensed the direction of her thoughts. But Tate smiled gently and Evan somehow managed a tentative smile in response before she turned and concentrated on the last stretch of the path that led to the house. "You lead the way and I'll follow."

They slowly made their way along the path, Tate occasionally glancing back over her shoulder. But Evan remained reassuringly close behind and something—Evan hoped it was the confident ease with which she was moving in spite of the crutches—stopped Tate from hovering or offering to help.

Once they reached the house, Tate unlocked the front door and deactivated the alarm system, and they both said their good-byes to Alex and Nick. They were borrowing Tate's SUV to transport their luggage and groceries to their own home, a mile away as the crow flew. Both were anxious to get there after being away for so long.

Still, there had been a moment, just before he got into the passenger side, when Alex grabbed and held onto Evan's arm with a none-too-steady hand. Leaning close, Evan brushed Alex's hair out of his eyes. "You know I love you, right? And I'm not going anywhere. You need to go home and paint. I'll be right here with Tate whenever you need me."

"I know that. Otherwise, Tate will just have to go find you again and bring you back home." Alex's expression softened. "And I love you too."

Watching Alex and Nick drive off, Evan shook her head fondly. "I'm surprised Alex lasted this long. I can't remember when he's been away from home for such an extended period of time, constantly surrounded by people, without being able to lose himself for a while in his painting. At least not since he was fifteen and going through the throes of his first crush on the local tennis pro."

"He was totally lost when he thought you'd died. He said he'd literally lost a part of himself, and I think he's a little afraid to let you out of his sight in case you disappear again."

Evan didn't know how to respond. She could also sense that Tate was anxious to show her this house—her home. Pushing everything else aside, she set a smile on her face and said, "Come on, beautiful lady. Show me your home."

After years of living in navy housing abroad or in cramped, noisy quarters on an aircraft carrier, Evan felt a wave of pleasure as she stepped inside the huge, open-concept space that made up the lower level of the house. Looking around slowly, she tried to take in all the changes Tate had made—changes from the one time she'd seen and fallen in love with the house.

The huge stone fireplace, soaring beamed ceilings, and gleaming hardwood floors were exactly as she remembered. So were the majestic views visible through the floor-to-ceiling windows that looked out over the wide expanse of island-dotted water that stretched beyond forever.

But gone was the clutter of the previous owner which had threatened to overwhelm the beauty of this particular island home. In its place, Tate had created clean open spaces. She had painted the walls a soft cream and utilized beautiful handcrafted tables Evan recognized instantly as Nick's work and colorful art produced by the local Suquamish Tribe to give the home life.

"Absolutely amazing." Her mouth curved into a wistful smile. "You've made this place every bit as beautiful as I had imagined it could be."

"Thanks." Struck by the note of pleasure in Evan's voice and the soft light in her eyes, Tate slowly exhaled as she continued into the kitchen. Until that very moment, she hadn't realized how important Evan's reaction to her home had been. Her heart was still beating a little too fast, but the tension which had been building inside her began to slowly recede.

"As soon as I put the food away, I'll give you the nickel tour and we can get you settled. Wait until you see the main bathroom. It's the only room I've completely remodeled so far and it's now got a giant whirlpool tub that can comfortably accommodate small groups." She laughed softly at the images that entered unbidden into her head. "And then I hope you're hungry. I thought I might grill salmon with some vegetables, and I have a nice Pinot Noir to go with it."

When Evan failed to respond, Tate retraced her steps to the living room, where she found Evan looking inexplicably pale and shaken, leaning heavily on her crutches. Her eyes were distant and wide, her mouth slightly open, and Tate could hear her shaky breaths. She stopped short so as not to startle her.

"Evan?" she called softly. "Is everything all right? Did you overdo it? Are you in pain?" When Evan still didn't answer, Tate moved closer, touched a hand to her shoulder. Evan shrugged it off, tried to move away, but Tate persisted. "What is it, love? Tell me what just happened."

The silence stretched before finally Evan responded, her voice reed thin. "I was just standing here, enjoying the view. I was thinking about how I would have bought this place if I hadn't been shot down, but it was still okay because we both wound up here anyway."

She stopped, plucked at her crutches. "And then, I don't know. Suddenly, it was like I was back there on that godforsaken mountain in Afghanistan, cold and bleeding. I could hear Khalid talking…just before he cut me the first time."

"What did he say?"

"He said—" Evan closed her eyes, swallowed. "He said I would consider myself lucky if I died before he finished with me."

Tate hurt for her and knew there were no easy answers. "You're going to have to believe me when I tell you what you're experiencing is normal. Give yourself time to heal."

"But that's just it. I'm not sure how much time I have. I know I sound crazy, but Khalid's still out there. He's still coming, and I don't know how much time he'll give me."

Tate watched Evan turn away, her shoulders slumped. Damn Khalid. Experimentally, she rested her hand lightly on Evan's shoulder and waited to see if she would pull away again. When she didn't, Tate felt a wave of relief. "Evan, listen to me. No one's going to hurt you again. If Khalid comes here, we'll be ready for him. I need you to believe me."

Evan took a deep, uneven breath. "I'll try."

Tate gave the tense shoulder under her hand a gentle squeeze. "We're going to work through this. And if you remember, you promised Kelsey you would contact her partner once you were settled. So why don't we concentrate on getting you settled?"

Accepting they'd gone as far as they were going to for the time being, Tate picked up her suitcase and Evan's backpack off the floor. "The master bedroom's on the main floor. And that's a good thing since I'm guessing it'll be a while before you can manage the stairs."

Dropping the luggage just inside the room, she rubbed at the headache that suddenly seemed to have laid siege behind her eyes. She started to back away when Evan's hand caught hers in a surprising show of gentle strength. Leaning precariously on her crutches, Evan drew her closer.

"I'm sorry," she said against Tate's cheek, her voice soft and husky. "Are you sure you're still okay with this?"

"I want to do what's best for you. I'm just not sure what it is."

She knew she should move away. Create some distance. But she continued to stay where she was for a few seconds longer, perversely enjoying having Evan's body pressed tightly against her own.

"You're what's best for me." Feeling the intensity of Tate's scrutiny, Evan remained quiescent, almost not daring to move. Everything that had happened to her was still too close, too raw. It still lived and breathed in her nightmares.

She thought about the cuts on her body and the conversation that still needed to happen before they could begin to move forward with their interrupted lives. And if she was honest with herself, she was afraid of how Tate might react. "This is what I was trying to tell you in Germany."

"What's that?"

"That I don't have a clue how to deal with anything that's going on in my head. In my life. With how I'm feeling from one moment to the next. I guess I haven't dealt with it well. Obviously I'm making things difficult for you and I don't mean to. I don't think I'm very good around people right now."

Tate's smile was sad. "But you and I—we're not just people, are we?"

Evan shook her head. "No, we're not. But right now, I need to know I can trust myself not to shatter into a thousand pieces every time I see something or hear something that reminds me of Khalid...of Afghanistan...and I can't."

She paused again, only this time she leaned in closer and pressed a searing kiss against Tate's soft lips, their texture and taste reminding her all too briefly of what had been. "I know I'm making a total mess of this and I don't mean to. But I need to work through some things. So perhaps it would be better if you just let me go."

"Oh, love, I can't do that," Tate whispered. "Ask me anything but that. Just tell me how I can help."

Evan shrugged helplessly. "I'm not sure. All I know is when I'm with you I feel safe, and without sounding totally needy and self-absorbed, the truth is I'd *rather* find my way with your help. With you beside me. But there are things I haven't worked through yet, things I don't fully understand myself, let alone how to explain them."

"Take your time. There's no hurry."

"I will—I have no choice. But can you handle this?"

"Yes," Tate said. "Don't you know I'm here for you, love? I'm not going anywhere. I'll be here with friendship and caring and support and whatever else you may want or need to help get you through this. All I ask in return is that you don't shut me out. That you tell me what you want."

"Thank you."

Tate brushed her lips against Evan's and smiled. "You have nothing to thank me for. I'm just doing what feels right—in here." She placed her hand over her heart. "Now why don't we get you unpacked?"

Evan closed her eyes tightly against the dull ache she was feeling, against the memories that were still too near the surface. "All right."

"After we're done in here, how about an early dinner?"

That got the slightest lift in the corners of her mouth. "You're going to keep trying to feed me, aren't you?"

"Damn straight."

❖

Evan leaned back in one of the Adirondack chairs on the deck, listening to the ocean and the shorebirds while watching as the sun began sinking low. It was a beautiful evening. The breeze had picked up, causing the wind chimes that hung from the eaves to dance and whisper. Stretching her long legs and propping them up on the railing, a suddenly carefree feeling made her smile.

There was soft music coming from the stereo speakers, she had a glass of wine in her hand, and fresh air, rich with the scent of pine and the sea, was gently brushing over her face. Three things she thoroughly enjoyed, all of which had been missing from her life for too long. And when she factored in the beautiful woman standing less than ten feet away, life didn't get much better than this.

"What did you say you were going to feed me?" she asked.

Standing in front of a giant barbecue, Tate glanced up and sent her a smile. "I'm grilling salmon and asparagus, and I made some wild rice to go with it. Why, are you trying to tell me you're actually hungry?"

"My stomach thinks my throat's been cut." Evan grinned and continued to watch Tate work, her hands moving quickly and efficiently with a skill she quite possibly would never acquire. She paused in midthought to admire Tate's long, slender legs, highlighted at that moment by the slanting rays of the sun. She lingered for an extra moment or two, marveling at the sweet heart-shaped derriere she knew lay just beneath the soft khaki shorts, before working her way up Tate's slim torso.

It wasn't until she reached her face that she realized Tate had been aware of her scrutiny all along, and she felt herself blush like a schoolgirl.

"If I didn't know any better, I'd swear you were just cruising my ass," Tate teased.

"You'd be right," Evan admitted sheepishly. "I'm sorry. I couldn't help enjoying the scenery."

"It's really all right, Evan. Trust me, I don't mind. In fact, I think I'm flattered."

Evan shook her head wryly and tried to stifle a laugh before she shrugged and gave in to it. "I think I spent too much time in the mountains, away from civilization. I've lost whatever finesse I may have once possessed." She paused and tossed another grin in Tate's direction. "Although you have to admit, it's a mighty fine ass."

It was Tate's turn to laugh. "It's nice to know you still appreciate it."

Evan arched a brow. "Oh, I appreciate it. Never doubt that," she said, the husky tone in her voice becoming more pronounced.

Tate took a moment to enjoy the relaxed posture of Evan's body, and the fact that her lips were curved into a sexy, disarming smile. She didn't let on that she was surprised at finding Evan more than happy to flirt with her. Because this was good. Very good. She'd missed seeing Evan's smile, hearing the sound of her laugh. And she looked like a dream with her silky black hair tousled around her face and her eyes clear and shining.

Their laughter set the tone for the evening. Determined to keep their conversation from veering into anything that might dim Evan's spirits, Tate ensured the subjects were light and was able to keep Evan distracted. Or at least, Evan allowed herself to be distracted while they sat on the deck and watched as night descended.

The shadows lengthened then disappeared, melting into the darkness, and it was nearly midnight by the time they decided to call it a night. By then, Evan had probably consumed one glass of wine too many and her mood had become subdued. But it had still been a very enjoyable evening. A good start.

Tugging Evan to her feet, Tate decided to forgo the crutches. Instead, she suggested Evan lean on her. She teetered and happily complied. But that was no surprise. Tate knew she hated the crutches and would be grateful for any opportunity where she didn't have to use them.

"What about all of this?" Evan indicated vaguely at their wine glasses and the coffee cups still on the table.

"I'll come back and deal with it once I get you settled."

Evan looked as if she was about to argue, but then shrugged tiredly. "Okay."

Helping her into the bathroom, Tate unwrapped a new toothbrush and left Evan leaning against the double sink with instructions to wait for her before attempting to get into bed on her own.

Returning to the deck, Tate finished gathering their remaining dishes, filled the dishwasher, then locked the doors and activated the alarm before making her way back to the bedroom. She only half expected to find Evan waiting in the bathroom, so she wasn't surprised to see her curled under the wedding-ring quilt in the middle of the four-poster bed.

"Sorry, I didn't wait for you," Evan mumbled, her voice husky and sleepy. She lifted one eyelid and gave Tate a glimmer of an unrepentant smile. "But I was fading fast, and I figured since it wasn't that far, I could make it just fine on my own."

Tate shook her head with affection and smiled. "Obviously your leg's getting better. But try to remember I'm just down the hall and promise you'll call me if there's anything you need."

"Okay." Evan nodded drowsily and burrowed deeper into the bed. "You know I could get used to this. So easily."

"That's the idea, love," Tate murmured softly. "Welcome back, Evan. Welcome home."

CHAPTER TWENTY-THREE

Tate's words continued to echo as Evan lay in the darkness, more relaxed than she could remember feeling at any time in the recent past.

She had loved her life on board the *Nimitz*. But the noise level could be bone jarring and the continuous cycle of launch and recovery made it difficult to think, let alone sleep. With each launch, the catapult sounded like a cannon going off, while landing aircraft came in with engines at maximum power.

In the hospital too, the air had been filled with constant sounds. Helicopters routinely took off and landed on the helipad, monitors beeped, pagers went off. The ever-present hum of people's voices, talking softly in the corridors.

As for Afghanistan…well, there was nothing peaceful about her time there.

And now—now Evan was looking forward to sleeping to the gentle song of the water lapping against the deck pilings. She just didn't want to dream.

She deluded herself into thinking she was too tired to dream. And that Tate's presence nearby would keep the dreams at bay. She should have known better. As she willed herself to sleep, the dreams drifted around her. She could feel them. Couldn't stop them.

She could hear him coming.

Please, no.

And then he was there.

Khalid stood over her. He moved closer, so close she could feel his breath against her skin and his face filled her vision.

He swung out in an almost lazy arc, his fist slamming against her. Hitting her with a blow that sent her sprawling. Swimming in and out of focus, he leaned over her, smiling as he pulled out his knife. Laughing as he began to cut her. Each time daring her to cry out.

Almost instantly, her world turned red and filled with pain.

Evan lost all sense of time. She was trapped, smothered by the heat and darkness. The smell of her own blood was all around her, the air so thick with it she could no longer breathe, while the pain stole her ability to think. All she could do was feel.

Feel the pain and know she was going to die at the hands of a sadistic monster.

She accepted the knowledge there was nothing she could do to alter her fate. But she was damned well not going to give him the pleasure of hearing her scream. At least she could deprive him of that.

"I want to hear you, Commander. Do I need to remind you? If you cease to entertain me," he said, bringing the knife up to her throat, "you will leave me with no alternative but to finish you now. And that would be a shame, don't you think?"

At least then it would finally be over, she thought, as she began free-falling into the darkness.

Tate came awake instantly to the sounds of screams. They were anguished, tormented screams that shattered the stillness of the night, and it took a moment for her to fully understand they were being ripped from Evan's throat.

For seconds, she couldn't move. And then she was stumbling from her bed, her heart hammering fiercely in her chest as she fumbled with a light switch and ran to the master bedroom.

In the light from the hallway, she could see Evan tangled in the bedding and automatically reached out. The chill of Evan's skin shocked her. "It's all right, Evan. It's just a dream," she whispered repeatedly. "You're all right."

Whispering reassurances had worked in Germany. It didn't work this time.

Evan didn't seem to hear her. She screamed again, snarling and twisting frantically, and came up swinging. Releasing a low, feral growl she used her nails, slashing and raking Tate's arm, and as she swung out, her fist connected solidly with Tate's jaw.

Momentarily stunned by the strength of the blow belied by Evan's weakened appearance, Tate found it impossible to hold on to her while trying to protect herself from further damage. She managed to move her head aside and avoided the follow-up swing, taking it instead on her right shoulder.

Her arm became instantly numb. Abandoning any further attempt to hold Evan, Tate scrambled to avoid another strike, dodging a flailing elbow as she landed hard on the floor.

Evan immediately retreated to the corner of the bed, crouched into a defensive position. She released a cry that sounded more animal than human and wrapped her arms around herself while staring at Tate with wild, unseeing eyes.

"Evan, it's all right. You were dreaming. You're safe now. It was only a dream."

Keeping her distance, Tate carefully repeated variations of the words, telling Evan over and over again she was safe. She whispered phrases meant to calm and reassure. Phrases meant to drive away the darkness that held her in its grip. In a struggle not to reach for her, she clenched her hands into fists. Anything to keep from touching her.

Because she wanted to help her. Oh God, she simply wanted to hold her in her arms.

At that moment, she remembered something Deacon had said. *"Sometimes singing was the only way I could reach her, get her to calm down."*

And with nothing left to lose, she began to sing.

It might have taken minutes or hours, but finally the flow of Tate's soft cadence began to have some effect. She didn't know whether it was the songs or just the gentle sound of her voice, something was beginning to get through, and Evan showed the first signs of relaxing.

As the nightmare released its grip on her, she shuddered convulsively then curled into a tight fetal position. And after a few more minutes, she fell asleep, her hands tucked beneath her chin, her breathing deep and regular, dark hair fanned across the pillow.

Tate watched Evan for a minute or two longer, waiting until she was reasonably certain she was safely asleep before making her way to the bathroom. She quickly took a couple of ibuprofen and splashed water on her face. She then set about cleaning the scratches on her arm and pressed a cool damp cloth against her aching jaw which would be bruised by morning.

Finally, when the sound of Evan's screams stopped echoing in her head, she turned the light off. Letting her eyes adapt to the darkness, Tate silently made her way back toward the bed. Evan hadn't moved and her breathing remained steady. As if in response to Tate's presence, she groaned faintly.

Praying she was making the right decision, Tate slid into bed and reached down to pull the blankets over them both. Almost immediately, Evan's hand blindly reached for her, grasping her hand and lacing their fingers together. Tate stared at their linked hands and then tentatively gathered Evan into her arms.

She held her. Just held her. Stroking her hair, murmuring words of assurance, her touch as gentle as her words. She felt helpless and alarmed, shaken to her core. But she continued to stroke her and watched her chest rise and fall with each breath until she was certain the last tentacles of Evan's nightmare had loosened their grip and slid away.

Only then did she let go, giving in to the pull of exhaustion and followed Evan into sleep.

❖

Evan awoke between one heartbeat and the next with the memory of her nightmare still clinging to her. The rational part of her mind told her she was safe, assured her Khalid had only been present in her dreams. But the dreams had been among the worst, the most vivid she had experienced since her release, and she swallowed to contain the fear clawing at her throat.

She lifted her head slowly. Cautiously opened her eyes and blinked several times, trying to get some sense of where she was. As she waited for the pounding in her head to settle, she pushed herself up on one elbow, suffered through an additional wave of disorientation before she was able to bring her surroundings into focus.

She realized several things simultaneously. She was in Tate's bedroom. It was still quite early, as the sun was not yet evident through the open curtains. And Tate was sleeping beside her.

Relief edged past residual fear. She managed to draw a shaky breath and started to ease out of bed. But before her feet could hit the floor, the pounding in her head increased to match the staccato beat of her heart. Groaning softly, she froze and breathed through her mouth, willing her heart to slow down. After taking several deep breaths, she struggled to stand on unsteady feet. The room spun and her leg threatened to buckle. But her only concern was keeping one foot in front of the other, and with a concerted effort she made it into the bathroom.

Once safely ensconced behind the closed door, she sank down to the floor. She sighed with relief, dropped her head into her hands, and tried to clear the images crowding her mind.

Dr. Patterson, the navy psychiatrist who had cleared her to leave the hospital in Germany, had said it didn't matter whether she was actually dealing with PTSD or simply experiencing an all too human reaction to trauma.

She had been advised to expect the nightmares and flashbacks. They didn't make her crazy.

When your sense of safety and trust are shattered, it's normal to feel crazy, disconnected, or numb.

And she had also been told not to expect to feel a little better with each passing day. That in fact, she could actually start to feel worse.

Got it.

Dr. Patterson had also stressed the importance of exploring her own thoughts and feelings about what had happened to her rather than avoiding any reminders. Her mind and body were in shock. And it was only when she began to make sense of what happened and processed her own emotions that she would start to come out of it.

Right. This is normal.

Fuck.

A hot shower would probably go a long way toward making her feel more human and remove the vestiges of the night still clinging to her skin. A hot shower, some aspirin, and several cups of coffee.

Rising shakily to her feet, she slid the sweat-dampened T-shirt she was wearing over her head and dropped it to the floor, then released a muffled laugh. After the spartan and overcrowded facilities on the *Nimitz*, Tate's bathroom renovations appealed to the hedonist in her. The shower was enormous, almost the equal in size of the Roman tub. And yet it somehow managed to combine high-tech and tasteful without being ostentatious.

Turning the shower on, Evan released a heartfelt moan as hot water and steam enveloped her in a loving embrace. She made the water temperature as hot as she could physically tolerate, then stood with her head bent, letting the pulsing force of the water pound her. This was sheer bliss, and she remained with her eyes closed until some of the residual tension left her body.

It wasn't until she stepped out of the shower nearly half an hour later that she remembered she hadn't brought any clothes to change into. She felt a sharp jolt of panic and found herself fighting an uncharacteristic sense of desperation. Still, there was little she could do other than wrap herself in a thick bath sheet before walking back into the bedroom.

She hoped to find Tate still tucked in bed, sleeping soundly.

But luck was not with her.

Tate had obviously used another bathroom—her hair was damp from the shower and she was just finishing making the bed. She turned, and Evan could see the shadow of a bruise on Tate's jaw, the long scratches on her arm. In the span of the next few seconds, it became horrifyingly clear what had happened.

Guilt swept through her. "Oh Jesus, did I do that to you?"

"It's all right, Evan," Tate responded quickly. "You had no idea what you were doing and I should have known better than to try to restrain you. But I was afraid you'd hurt yourself."

Evan closed her eyes, not wanting to see any further evidence of her own madness. "I'm so sorry. You've got to believe I would have never knowingly hurt you," she whispered, aware her apology was inadequate. "Worse, I don't remember any of it. I sometimes think I'm back in Afghanistan with Khalid, and I get a little crazy."

Tate remained quiet. But then, Evan mused, what could she say? All the wishing and hoping wouldn't make the evidence of her madness go away.

Evan swallowed and started to turn away, remembering in the nick of time she was wrapped in just a towel and was barely covered. Uncertain what to do, she crossed her arms protectively across her chest only to feel Tate's eyes land automatically on the pattern of cuts on her upper arm.

"I forgot to grab a change of clothes before I had my shower," she explained needlessly, clutching the towel and praying Tate hadn't glimpsed the marks on her back as she awkwardly circled the room.

"Not a problem." Tate's eyes continued to follow Evan as she moved, her expression shifting to mild concern. "But hold off before you get dressed. Kelsey gave me some ointment before we left Germany. She wanted me to make sure you used it until all those cuts you have are fully healed. She said it would not only help the skin regenerate, it would also help the scars fade more quickly."

Evan froze. A shudder went through her as memories crowded in from every direction, leaving her defenses in tatters. She had no choice but to meet Tate's gaze but stalled, pushing back the hair from her face while she struggled to school her expression and keep it acceptably blank.

Tate picked up the backpack that had held the few possessions Evan had brought back from Germany and retrieved a green tube. "Why don't you come and sit on the bed near the light," she said. "It'll make it easier if I can see what I'm doing when I apply the cream so I don't accidently hurt you."

"No." Evan winced as her refusal came out louder than necessary. She tried again. "Really. Thanks, but I can do it myself."

"Don't be silly," Tate countered and held out her hand. "I promise to be gentle and it'll be over before you know it. Besides, you'll never be able to reach the cuts on your back, and you said they've been giving you trouble."

Evan felt her face flush and shook her head helplessly, biting her lip to keep from speaking and saying the wrong thing. Finally, from somewhere, she found her voice. "Don't do this, Tate," she pleaded. She stepped back and avoided contact with Tate's hand, all the while hating herself for being a coward.

Startled into silence, Tate studied Evan carefully. She was visibly shaking. Her face was ice pale while her eyes were dark, filled with shadows and a fear so deep it shimmered. Her physical retreat was also troubling. It clearly indicated a lack of trust. An unwillingness to let her in. Emotional fatigue. Probably all of the above.

Don't do this. Don't shut me out. Don't turn me away.

"Evan," she said quietly, "I don't know what's going on inside your head, but you are going to have to decide pretty quickly whether or not you're going to trust me with it. As in right now."

"Tate—"

"No, I'm sorry, but you know I'm right. Because it's pretty obvious something is seriously troubling you and the only way we're going to be able to deal with it is to get it out in the open. Unless you've decided you *don't* trust me, and if that's the case, then I don't know what the hell we're doing here."

Evan stared at her for an interminable moment. She swallowed. Then, without saying another word, she dropped the towel she had wrapped around her body to the floor and went to sit on the side of the bed.

"Thank you," Tate said. Exhaling as a wave of intense relief flowed through her, she followed Evan with her eyes, watching her as she moved. Evan's body bore only a slight resemblance to the one she had been familiar with in the past. She was much too thin, and there were too many signs of recent physical trauma. Too many healing cuts and fading bruises.

Tate hurt just thinking about what Evan had gone through. But she was here and that was all that really mattered. She slowly approached the bed, picked up Evan's right arm and examined the series of cuts before she began to apply the cream. She was pleased to see how well they were healing.

"Let me know if anything I do hurts you."

"I'm not worried. I trust you."

Tate's throat tightened and she could feel the sting of tears. Aware of the faint tremors in her hands, she focused doubly on keeping her touch gentle.

Working silently, she tried without much success not to think about how much pain Evan had endured. Found it impossible not to think about the man who had inflicted the damage. A man whose primary purpose in holding both Evan and Deacon Walker had been seemingly driven by an inexplicable need to cause pain.

It made no sense, and she wanted to ask Evan more about what had happened to her. Wanted to learn more about the man named Khalid. And perhaps now they could talk more candidly rather than ignoring the elephant in the room.

A shift in Evan's posture and an increase in the tension under her fingers brought her attention back sharply and caused her to freeze in midmotion. Evan's back muscles were going to spasm if she didn't relax, but as Tate narrowed her gaze, she could find nothing to account for the sudden change. Was she doing something wrong?

Concerned, she tilted her head to one side and glanced at Evan's face, wishing she could read what she was thinking at that moment. "Are you sure I'm not hurting you?"

"I'm sure." It was the only thing she said, and she clearly struggled to get out the words.

"Then try to relax, Evan."

"I can't—I'm sorry."

Tate heard the near-panic in Evan's voice, saw her shoulder muscles further tense and tighten, felt her pulse begin to race beneath her fingers. But she remained baffled about what was causing her mounting distress. She finished applying the cream to her arm and gently lowered it.

"I'm going to need you to turn to your left so I can get a good look at your back."

In that brief instant when Evan looked up at her, her eyes so dark they were nearly black, Tate saw a flash of something indecipherable in their depths. In the next moment, Evan turned to the left as asked without saying a word.

Tate stared, looking at the series of deep cuts that had been carved close to the center of Evan's back. At first, she was unsure what she was seeing. But then, with horrifying clarity, she recognized what she was looking at.

Letters.

Her name in bold, blood-red letters.

TATE.

"Oh God. Evan?" She looked at Evan and swore softly under her breath. Acting on pure emotion, she crouched down until they were eye to eye, and then reached for Evan's hands. They were ice cold, but she held them anyway and wished she could somehow warm them. "What did that bastard do to you? Why? For God's sake, talk to me."

Evan looked away, refusing to make eye contact and refusing to answer. But after a long and interminable minute passed, she finally turned her head and looked back at Tate. There was no color left in her face and her eyes were half-closed. But for one brief moment, it was impossible not to see the wealth of pain and heartbreak now clearly evident in her face.

"Evan." Tate tightened her grip on Evan's hands and pulled her closer. "Stay with me."

"I'm trying," she said unsteadily. "Khalid…he enjoyed hurting. Causing pain. He liked to feel the blood, hot on his hands. He said it was why he used a knife. It excited him."

She lapsed into a long silence, lost in some private hell while Tate waited. Hoping Evan would be willing to say more. Praying she wouldn't. Wondering if she could.

When a couple of minutes passed and nothing else was forthcoming, Tate spoke. "When Khalid's name first came up in the negotiations for your release, it turned out the CIA already knew him. Quite well, as it turned out. They had checked him out when he first surfaced in Afghanistan offering to sell them information and had a file on him."

The calmly offered information drew Evan back from wherever she'd gone. She shifted restlessly. Her hand flexed. "He said his father was American and that he'd spent some time with him when he was a teenager."

"Actually, he grew up not far from here. His mother's family sent him to live with his father around the time he turned ten, and he stayed with him until his eighteenth birthday. In Portland, Oregon. But it turned out the kid was a handful. Started getting into trouble early, and his father had to bail him out on a number of occasions."

Evan swallowed. "What kind of trouble?"

"Just truancy, initially. But then it began to escalate. He got more aggressive, bullied smaller boys. He was also suspected of killing a teacher's dog after he was suspended for beating a much younger boy. But they could never prove it."

"A baby sociopath."

Tate nodded. "He got caught setting fire to a neighbor's garage after a noise complaint and was suspected of being responsible for a couple of other fires. But his father intervened, paid all the damages, and somehow managed to get the charges dropped."

"How?"

"I'm not sure. Then, just before he turned eighteen, he beat a young female navy ensign pretty badly." She paused for a moment. "He used a knife on her. His father's lawyer intervened one last time, but he still did eleven months in juvenile detention."

Evan briefly closed her eyes. "Do you know how he ended up in Afghanistan?"

"He apparently made some connections while in juvie. After he got out, he had ties to an anarchist group suspected in a number of church bombings. It's believed they were the ones who helped get him out of the US. He later surfaced in south Asia, which was where he adopted the name Khalid."

Evan stiffened. "His real name's not Khalid?"

"No. His name's actually John—John Anderson."

"John?" Evan stared at her. "The bastard's name is John?"

Tate shrugged. "Named after his father." She watched Evan closely as they talked, but her expression remained unreadable. "You okay?"

Evan nodded and they both were quiet for a moment. "Sorry, you were saying—"

"Khalid, right. He apparently drifted through south Asia, then worked his way to Afghanistan where he discovered his bomb-making skills were in demand. It helped he could speak the language and pass himself off as a local, thanks to his mother."

Evan frowned as she regarded Tate through half-closed eyes. "It makes sense. Afghanistan gave him the freedom to do as he pleased. It was in a state of chaos. A war zone. He could build his IEDs and kill or maim people with impunity. And when he wanted to get up close and personal, another mutilated body was unlikely to draw much attention."

"But why did he—?" Tate caught her lower lip between her teeth, effectively stopping the question she wanted to ask.

Evan answered anyway. "I don't know. I never fully understood what drove Khalid. I always thought he was damaged somehow. Or maybe he really is just a sociopath." Her voice faltered. "I just know he was carrying a lot of old anger. Somewhere along the line, somewhere in his past, something happened to him and he became convinced all women in the military were lesbians."

"Do you suppose it had something to do with the navy ensign in Oregon? Maybe she was gay."

"It's possible. *Pardus maculas non deponit.* A leopard doesn't change his spots." She shrugged her shoulders. "The truth is it was a gross stereotype on his part. He just happened to be right about me, and because of it, he intended to teach me a lesson."

Evan fell silent, her face taking on an introspective look, but Tate didn't press her to go on. Willing to let her tell the story at her own speed, she waited and thought about what Evan had said.

Just listening was proving to be difficult enough. She knew Evan's wounds, both physical and psychological, were still raw, and she wished it was possible to spare her from talking about what had happened. But not talking wouldn't prevent Evan from reliving everything in her mind. As she clearly did every night in her dreams.

"Every day...every single day without exception...he would come and get me," Evan continued at length as if there had been no stoppage in the conversation. "For whatever reason, he kept asking me what my lover's name was."

"Oh God—"

"Somehow, I don't think any God had anything to do with Khalid and what went on in Afghanistan. Most of the cuts on my arm...they were for each time I failed to give him the answer he wanted...and to teach me about pain."

"Why didn't you just tell him, love?"

"I honestly don't know. For some reason, it seemed important not to. When I finally couldn't hold back any longer—" Her voice caught and she visibly struggled to continue. "When I told him your name, he laughed. And then he said if I somehow managed to survive our encounter and ever saw you again, I should thank you."

The room suddenly felt very cold and Tate shivered, aware only of the roar of the blood rushing to her head as she tried to breathe. She had long since finished applying the medicated cream to Evan's back, and she realized she was still clutching the tube in her hand. She quickly set it down on the bedside table.

"Thank me?" she asked. "Whatever for?"

"For having such a short name. I think he was disappointed there were only four letters."

Chapter Twenty-four

Over the next couple of weeks, Tate kept hoping Evan would begin to move on. Hoped they could begin rediscovering some of what they'd had and somehow lost. Especially after Evan had finally opened up about Khalid.

But two things changed the course of her progress.

The first was a newspaper article in the *Washington Post* featuring the remarkable story of two navy pilots' return from the dead. That one of the pilots happened to be female and named Kane only served to drive circulation.

From a journalistic perspective, Tate thought the story had been reasonably well written. It was as factual as possible given Evan's refusal to be interviewed and included comments from Deacon's family who hailed Evan as a hero for saving their son's life. The others who were quoted—old school chums, former teachers, fellow pilots, and Evan's commanding officer from the *Nimitz*—said all the usual things.

She was a bright and popular student.

A first-class athlete.

An amazing pilot.

A damned fine officer with an outstanding service record and a chest full of ribbons.

Tate knew Evan was media savvy. Had probably been so since birth, given who her mother was. She had to know in a sound-bite culture, it was only a matter of time before something else—another political scandal or financial crisis—came along and the story faded from prominence.

But Tate knew Evan hated having any part of her life put on display for everyone to see. Worse still—

"At least Khalid won't have any difficulty figuring out where to find me."

The implication terrified Tate, but Evan refused to discuss it. Instead she became progressively more subdued, more withdrawn. She stopped initiating conversations and showed little interest in anything beyond the physiotherapy sessions she'd started and making use of Tate's home gym. She was also barely eating, at a time when she was meant to be regaining the weight she'd lost, and though they still went to bed at night in separate rooms, Tate knew what little sleep Evan got was troubled and filled with nightmares.

It was almost as if she was waiting for Khalid to arrive.

And then Tate caught a tiny newswire item, only hours old, about the firebombing of a church in Vancouver, British Columbia. According to police, they had one suspect in custody—a self-described jihadist with outstanding warrants in the US. They were reportedly seeking two others. He had been captured as he attempted to board a ferry that would have taken him to Port Angeles, Washington.

The elements of the story were disturbingly familiar and sent Tate searching through her files until she found what she was looking for. The suspect in the Vancouver bombing had been listed in the dossier she'd obtained through Althea prior to going to Afghanistan. He'd been a person of interest in previous church bombings in the US. He was also a known associate of John Khalid Anderson.

Port Angeles was only two and a half hours out of Seattle. Too close for comfort and possibly too much of a coincidence. Uncertain what to do, Tate sought out Alex and asked his advice.

❖

"Whoa. What are you talking about? What's this about Khalid?"

"Before he released her, Khalid told Evan things weren't over between them. He said he'd find her again and finish what he started." She paused just long enough to make sure Alex understood what she was saying. "He reiterated his threat when he managed to get into her hospital room in Germany."

"Jesus. Are you trying to tell me you believe Khalid had something to do with what happened to that church? That he's this close?"

Tate sighed wearily. "I'd like to think Khalid's living in some dark cave in Afghanistan, but the bombing in Vancouver can't be disregarded. And Evan believes he's coming after her. It's probably why her nightmares have been getting worse instead of better. But she won't talk to me about them. She's barely sleeping—"

Alex sat back and regarded her. "And that means you're barely sleeping."

"I know I look awful." Tate self-consciously raised a hand to her face and grimaced.

"Tate—"

"It's okay. It's not important. What matters is Evan, and we can't ignore the probability Khalid is coming after her."

"You really think that's going to happen?"

"He's crazy. Crazy enough that he chanced confronting her in a military hospital." Tate swallowed. "So yes, I believe he's coming after her and we can't just wait for him to show up. We need to make plans. We need to do something. I don't know how much more Evan can handle."

"I could talk to Althea and dad, but they'd insist Evan return to the ancestral home, where they'd surround her with state troopers or FBI agents until Khalid's caught."

In spite of Alex's sarcasm, Tate found some merit in his suggestion. "At least she'd be safe."

Alex quickly shook his head. "No, she'd go crazy, making it more likely she'd take off. Go somewhere alone where we couldn't help her if she needed us."

"Then what are we supposed to do?"

Alex thought for a moment, then said, "First, I think you need to get Evan away for a couple of days. She's a sailor. It shouldn't be that hard to convince her to spend some time on the boat, and maybe once she's on the water, she'll relax a bit, maybe get some sleep and be in a better place to deal with things."

Tate stared at Alex as hope sprang. "That's actually not a bad idea. And second?"

"While you're off sailing, I think I'm going to talk to our local sheriff. Maybe see if he can offer any suggestions on how we can keep Evan safe. At the very least, I'll alert the sheriff's department to the possibility Khalid may be heading this way."

Tate considered, tapped her fingers restlessly on her leg. "I don't know, Alex. It's not that I think it's a bad idea. But why not have Evan be part of the conversation with the sheriff?"

"I'd like to talk to him alone first and see what he thinks. Unless he's been living under a rock, he'll already know who Evan is and have a pretty good idea what she went through. And I don't want Evan upset if he thinks she's suffering from PTSD and disregards what we have to say."

"And if he does?"

"Then we'll have to pull out the Kane family connections. But let's hope it doesn't come to that because none of us will be able to move without tripping over someone with a gun until this is over."

Tate laughed at the image and Alex gave her an encouraging smile. "Hang in there, Tate. The good news is Kelsey will finally be coming home in a few days, and if anyone can help us with Evan's state of mind, it'll be Kelsey."

The conversation helped defuse some of Tate's fears. Now all she had to do was convince Evan to spend some time on the boat.

❖

The following morning, Tate sipped her coffee and stared out the window at the promise of a beautiful day. But she still wasn't comfortable keeping the truth from Evan, even if it was for a good reason.

Before she could give in to the doubts assailing her, she walked out onto the deck prepared, if necessary, for a confrontation. "Let's take the boat over to Seattle for the day."

Arms wrapped around her legs, chin on her knees, Evan continued to stare out across the water without responding. But Tate held her ground, and Evan finally looked up, a wary expression on her face.

"What's in Seattle?"

Raising an eyebrow, Tate bit back a caustic reply. "I thought we could start with a visit to the Pike Place Market," she said with a calm she was a very long way from feeling. "Maybe we can pick up something interesting for me to cook that might actually entice you to eat. But mostly, I thought it would be nice to get out of here for a while and spend the day on the water."

Evan turned and stared at the horizon for what felt like forever, but probably only amounted to a heartbeat or two. "Fuck," she said succinctly.

Tate saw the signs—the tightening of Evan's jaw, the flash of heat in her eyes—and braced for a fight. But Evan surprised her.

"I'm sorry." She licked her lips, cleared her throat. "It seems all I'm doing lately is apologizing to you, but I've been so wrapped up in my own head I haven't stopped to think how I'm making all of this impossibly difficult for you. But I am. And I don't really mean to."

Tate felt a small measure of relief knowing there would be no confrontation today. "I know you don't."

"I know I haven't said it, but I really am grateful for everything you're doing to help me."

"I don't need your gratitude, Evan."

"You have it anyway." Evan looked up. "And you may be on to something. A day on the water could be just what the doctor ordered.

My natural habitat, and all that. That's if you think you can stand to be cooped up in close quarters with me for so long."

"Sometimes you make me crazy," Tate said softly. But she smiled as she said it, and as she took and held Evan's hand, she could feel a little of the tension between them ease. "In case you've forgotten, let me remind you. I've always enjoyed being in close quarters with you."

Evan closed her eyes.

"Now get your ass in gear. And just so we're clear, you may be the former navy officer, but the boat's mine, which makes me the captain." She leaned in, keeping her eyes open as she brushed her lips over Evan's. "And you, Commander Kane, are paying for lunch."

"Got it."

Less than half an hour later, Tate sat comfortably at the controls as she reversed the cabin cruiser that had come as part of the house sale. Dozens of other vessels dotted the waterways, confirming what she'd thought all along. It was an idyllic day for boating. Not too hot, the perfect mix of wind and sun. The morning air was clean and clear, while overhead the sun was burning through the early-morning coastal haze, its light sparkling brightly on the water.

Piloting the boat with a sure and steady hand, she soon had them making headway toward Seattle over the calm water, leaving an expanding V behind them. Beside her, Evan rested a hand lightly on her thigh, her eyes on the scenery rolling by as they cut through straits and eased past the rocky forested shores that made up this part of the Pacific Northwest. She'd seemed almost happy once they got out on the water, and Tate silently berated herself for not having done this sooner. She'd swear she could all but feel Evan's heart rate slow down, could almost see the tension begin to drop away.

The sun warmed them as they walked to the market after leaving the boat moored at a slip in the marina.

Covering nine acres, the market was home to numerous shops and stands selling everything from regionally grown fruits and vegetables to handmade crafts, antiques, and collectibles. It was a Seattle institution, and Tate had fallen in love with it. She enjoyed watching as shoppers mixed with street buskers while the air was filled with the competing scents of fresh baked goods, herbs and spices, and coffee beans.

They wandered at a leisurely pace, Evan constantly distracted, Tate watching her with amusement and steering her around obstacles she threatened to run into every time something new caught her eye.

They paused in front of a display of sun catchers, and Evan chatted with the artist.

Tate tilted her head and enjoyed looking at her, remembering how good it felt to be with her. Evan had always been able to take her breath away. And when she smiled, it could make her weep. She continued looking, her gaze skimming long enough to admire how Evan managed to appear tempting in a simple indigo henley and well-worn jeans.

Very nice. Very nice indeed, she thought, and though she willed herself not to, she felt her body automatically respond. Christ, but she wanted Evan. More than she'd ever wanted anyone else. More than she wanted to take her next breath. She stared at Evan's lips, soft and parted, and all she could do was remember just how they tasted.

She hesitated and considered chucking the entire shopping excursion, finding the nearest hotel room, and making love to Evan until she couldn't fight her anymore.

She wanted to take her hard and fast until they were both exhausted and sated. Then she wanted to do it all over again, only slower this time. She wanted to touch every inch, explore every curve, taste every hollow, and reconnect with Evan in a most elemental way.

As if sensing her thoughts, Evan flashed a quick searching look in her direction. She smiled—a mischievous curving of the corners of her mouth, a flash of dimples—then winked and returned to making her purchase.

Tate laughed softly and let out her breath in a long sigh, reminding herself that where Evan was concerned, patience was the only virtue that mattered. She had promised she would be patient and give Evan the time she needed to feel comfortable with any level of intimacy. It meant she would need to rein in her thoughts and her libido. But it was hard—so very hard—not to make the demands her body and soul and heart craved.

Just as it was hard to believe they were making any progress when there was no evidence to support it. When most of the time, Evan continued to look at her with distant eyes, a near perfect stranger, and Tate feared she'd all but forgotten the links that once bound them.

When there was nothing Tate could do about it.

Evan returned to her side a short time later. The sun catcher in her hand was streaked with purple, red, and blue hues and had an evening sky feel to it. "It reminds me of flying over the Arabian Sea just as the sun was setting," she said as she handed her acquisition to Tate. "I thought you might like it."

Accepting the gift, Tate held it up, appreciating the craftsmanship and beauty, but especially what it represented to Evan. "Thank you. It's beautiful and I'll treasure it."

"You'll enjoy it even more after I get you up for a sunset flight in my Tiger Moth. When Alex took me to physio the other day, he told me he's got it in a hangar at a local flying club on the island."

"Oh my God, your biplane. I'd totally forgotten. If I remember correctly, you once promised to take me flying when you got home. When do you think we can go?"

"I'm not sure. I guess it'll depend on how quickly my leg heals. You actually use your feet as much as—if not more than—your hands when you're flying a Tiger Moth. But my physiotherapist seems pleased with the progress I'm making, so hopefully it'll be soon."

The faintly wistful note in her voice and faraway look in her eyes had Tate momentarily forgetting the crowd milling around them. She lifted her hand and skimmed her fingertips lightly over Evan's face. "You miss it, don't you? The thrill and excitement of flying a Super Hornet and landing on a tiny runway in the middle of a vast wind-tossed ocean."

"Yeah, I do," Evan admitted. "But before you get too sad on my account, you need to remember before I got shot down, I was already at a place where I was okay with walking away from it. I did what I set out to accomplish, and I'll always have the memories of everything I got to experience." An instant later, the warmth returned to light her eyes and banish the momentary sadness. "But more importantly, I'm looking forward to taking you up on your first open-cockpit flight. And teaching you how to fly."

"I can't wait for my first ride in your plane." Tate smiled before slowly narrowing her eyes. "But I'm not too sure I'm in any hurry to learn how to fly."

Reaching for her hand, Tate drew Evan along so they could watch the workers at the fish market. Evan laughed as their antics drew reactions from the crowd, and she gave some thought to pulling out the sketch pad she had tucked into her backpack.

Not that she could, of course. She knew realistically she would never be able to manage the pad and pencil while leaning on the cane Nick had carved for her to replace the crutches. For the time being, she contented herself with cataloging the images and faces in her mind.

There was the man leaning against a wall, relaxing as he read the *Seattle Times* before making his selections from the catch of the day. He had an interesting face. Weathered and lived-in. The kind of face that told stories.

Or the pair of hormonally challenged teenagers, maybe fifteen or sixteen. Holding hands, oblivious of the crowd as they exchanged a tentative kiss. God, had she ever been that young?

And of course, there was Tate. Casting a quick glance over her shoulder, her eyes soft and alluring, she sent Evan a smile that lit up her face before she resumed shopping with a single-minded focus.

Evan nodded and smiled back. Glad she had readily agreed with Tate's decision to come here today, she settled contentedly to wait for her while continuing to watch the ebb and flow of people and activity with interest.

It was the sense of being watched that pulled her abruptly out of her thoughts. A subtle, subconscious warning. Evan stiffened and stood without moving for ten seconds, then twenty.

Being watched wasn't a particularly unique experience for a woman who'd grown up with two high-profile parents. But this felt different, and as the awareness intensified and the disquieting sensation lingered, she turned nonchalantly in a slow circle and looked back into the crowd, hoping to discover Tate watching her.

Her brief moment of optimistic hope sputtered and died when it became quickly apparent Tate was no longer nearby. It took a minute longer of searching the faces in the growing throng before she finally spotted her. Maybe thirty feet away, she had wandered near the produce stalls and was engaged in an animated conversation with a vendor, adding fresh fruit and vegetables to her growing load of groceries.

Finding herself alone and feeling inexplicably vulnerable, Evan reached for the pair of aviator sunglasses she had tucked into the collar of her T-shirt and slipped them into place. The sunglasses helped restore a much needed sense of anonymity and after a few seconds, she casually glanced around again. Watched people go by.

No one seemed to be paying any particular attention to her. But she still couldn't shake the feeling, the sense of imminent danger, and the people milling around her suddenly seemed less friendly, less entertaining.

Perilously close to an unreasoning panic, Evan struggled to pull in a deep breath. She quickly decided what she needed was some fresh air. And she didn't want to wait for Tate to return.

Actually, she couldn't wait. Not for a second longer. Moving as swiftly as her leg and the crowded venue would allow, she edged toward one of the exits before suddenly coming to a stop, her heartbeat accelerating.

She didn't know how long she stood there, unable to move, unable to breathe. Because for a fleeting instant, she thought she'd seen a familiar face out of the corner of her eye. She inhaled sharply and felt her heart stutter. Her eyes frantically searched the area, but as she scanned the crowd once again, she realized she had to have been mistaken.

It just wasn't possible.

It was a trick of light.

A flashback. PTSD.

The sensation of being watched persisted, and knowing it was her imagination playing tricks on her didn't help.

Fear sat in the back of Evan's throat. She could taste it as she swallowed. As the fear strengthened its hold, a wave of dizziness swept over her, and her knees almost buckled. Only her reflexes as she grabbed for a door prevented her from falling.

She didn't draw a full breath until she was through the door and back in the sunlight. Stumbling as she got outside, Evan moved quickly to lean against a nearby wall, allowing people to pass her as she tried to regain her equilibrium. Her heart was hammering so hard she could hear nothing else, and she was all but hyperventilating. But she would not lose it here. Not if she could help it.

Just the thought of seeing Khalid—even in a flashback—triggered an onslaught of painful images she couldn't restrain, and it took several minutes before she could restore any semblance of calm and composure. Lost in a dark world of swirling memories and emotions, she felt arms slide around her waist, and her body recognized Tate's touch before her head did. Groaning softly, she felt her heart catch as Tate's breath brushed against her skin, and she gratefully absorbed the strength Tate offered as she pressed against her back.

Tate's presence served to ground her. It reminded her life could still be safe. Warm. Vibrant. But her body was still trembling and Evan reached instinctively for Tate's hands, lightly grasping them. Breathing in her warm familiar scent as she wrapped herself tightly in Tate's embrace.

"Hey, what's going on?" Tate's tone reflected concern.

After a brief hesitation, Evan turned within the circle of her arms until they were face-to-face. "It's nothing."

Tate continued to hold Evan in her arms. Tilting her head back, she regarded her until their eyes met and held, and Evan could see the flicker of disquiet in Tate's face.

"Come on, I can tell something's wrong," she chided gently. "And you should know you can tell me anything."

"I know—but it was stupid."

"What was stupid?"

Evan shifted uncomfortably under Tate's scrutiny and stared at the ground. The question remained in the air between them and she bit the inside of her cheek. If she was being honest with herself, shouldn't she be honest with Tate?

"For a moment—for a moment I'd swear there was someone standing in the crowd watching me," she admitted uneasily.

"Someone?" Tate stiffened.

"Okay, Khalid. I thought I saw Khalid."

"You thought you saw—"

"You don't need to say anything. I know it's impossible, it's just PTSD. The doctors warned me this could happen, and now my mind's playing games—" She stopped and groaned in frustration, not knowing how to continue.

"Don't say that." Tate gave her a gentle squeeze as she looked around. "Listen, I've got an idea. Why don't we get out of here and head back to the boat?"

What she wanted, Evan thought, was to be left alone in a dark room. To fade into the void she'd discovered in Afghanistan, where she could escape the pain of reality.

No, not this time.

What she wanted was to turn back the clocks to a time before she'd been blown out of the sky. Before she'd discovered just how real monsters could actually be. And then she wanted to lose herself in Tate's arms.

Thinking of Tate brought her abruptly back into the present. What had Tate suggested? Something about canceling their plans for the day and heading back to the boat? She shook her head and forced herself to smile.

"That's not necessary. Really," she quickly added in response to the look Tate was giving her. "I overreacted and got a little lightheaded for a second or two, but I'm okay now. I guess I'm not used to crowds anymore."

Tate raised an eyebrow and regarded her thoughtfully. "This from a woman who lived on an aircraft carrier through how many deployments?"

Evan shrugged. "Yeah, I guess it's kind of funny when you think about it, but the worst is over and I'm already feeling better. Why don't you finish the shopping you wanted to do while I sit here in the sun like a lazy cat? While you're gone, you can think about where you want me to take you for lunch."

"I've got a better idea," Tate countered. "It just so happens I picked up enough that I could make us a picnic. I've got deli meat, salmon, cheese, salads, and sourdough rolls. Why don't we get you and the groceries back to the boat where you can relax away from the crowds? I'll find us a secluded spot and we can have lunch out on the water."

"That sounds like a terrific idea if you're sure you don't mind." Catching hold of Tate's hand, Evan gratefully pressed a kiss into her palm. "Did you by chance also pick up something sweet for later?"

"As a matter of fact, I got fresh strawberries because I seem to remember how much you like them. And some—"

"Chocolate?"

Tate laughed. "Could I possibly pick up groceries and not buy chocolate?"

"You've got a point."

He'd dreamed of her last night.

He groaned as he remembered how his knife had danced across her bare skin leaving a trail of dark red blood in its wake. He allowed the memory to play out in his mind a while longer. Glorious, he thought, but no longer enough.

He hadn't anticipated running into her in the market. It had happened so unexpectedly he'd had no time to think things through. For a moment their eyes had locked, and his body tingled as his mind slipped into a dangerous fantasy, imagining grabbing her there and then. In a crowded public venue. The anticipated thrill almost overwhelmed him, almost overrode his sense of caution.

Almost.

He laughed when he thought about how she turned ghostly pale and stumbled out of the building, fear clearly stealing her breath in her rush to get away from him. He gave her retreating back a cheerful wave, taunting her even though he knew she couldn't see it.

Slipping through the crowd, he followed her. Contemplating his next move as he watched the other woman approach. Her girlfriend. *Tate.*

He saw them talk quietly, then followed them with his eyes as they walked toward the marina. When they disappeared from view, lost in the maze of pleasure craft, he raised his long wickedly sharp knife and pressed his lips against the cold steel.

His hands ached, his fingers itched. As he fingered the knife, already he could feel the warmth of her blood, smell its coppery scent. See the horror and pain in her eyes. It would be so good. And it would have to be soon.

CHAPTER TWENTY-FIVE

While Tate got Evan settled on the boat and prepared to make way, the possibilities circled in her mind. Evan's experiences in Afghanistan had left her hypervigilant. Of course she would sense someone watching her. Following her.

Was it possible? Was Khalid actually in Seattle? Had Evan really seen him or was it a symptom of PTSD?

Both scenarios were fraught with pitfalls.

If it was PTSD, then Evan's current mental state was more precarious than she'd thought.

But if it was even remotely possible Khalid had been at the market, then Evan was in real physical danger. It meant she needed to get her away from here. Fast.

In that moment, she made a conscious decision to do what she should have done in the first place. Not wait and tell Evan everything. About the bombing in Vancouver, the suspect who had been arrested, and his past connection to Khalid. About her fear Khalid might be making his way to Seattle. About Alex arranging to meet with the sheriff.

She didn't want Evan unaware of any potential danger she might be in or get caught by surprise should Khalid suddenly appear. And she didn't want Evan to think she was going crazy, seeing apparitions.

It would be a difficult conversation. If she was honest, she wasn't looking forward to the eventual fallout when Evan realized she'd gone behind her back to Alex. And when she learned of Alex's plan—

But it was the right thing to do. The only thing to do.

It didn't take long before she had them back out on open water, but Tate was unable to relax until the Seattle skyline was receding in the distance. She knew her anxiety showed—Evan looked at her curiously on several occasions but, mercifully, didn't ask any questions.

Tate didn't allow herself to relax until she guided the vessel to a secluded cove on the leeward side of one of the many uninhabited islands. The water was calm, the sun was warm, and they were alone except for the gulls aloft in the gentle breeze. A good place, she decided, to have a leisurely lunch. And a good place to have a heart-to-heart conversation.

She turned and looked around for Evan. Not because there was any immediate reason to worry now that they'd left Seattle behind. Mostly, she just didn't feel comfortable having her out of her line of sight, not for a single moment.

She expected to find her enjoying the passing scenery. Or possibly, she could hope, asleep beneath the brilliant blue of the sky. Instead, she was astonished to see her sitting on a bench seat on the deck, one long blue-jeaned leg curled under her, while she carefully balanced a sketch pad on her lap. Her head was bent, her eyes fixed on the pad, and her attention was focused intently on the image she was creating.

Moistening her lips with the tip of a tongue, Tate continued to watch her. *When did you take up drawing?*

That there were facets to her lover she had yet to discover was not surprising. They'd spent so much time apart, and there was much they both needed to learn about each other. But Tate was still left feeling disconcerted.

The ease and comfort with which she was sketching told Tate drawing was nothing new to Evan. Her hand moved with obvious confidence across the page, and she appeared to have effectively shut out all extraneous distractions as she concentrated on what she was doing to the exclusion of everything else.

What Tate couldn't discern from her vantage point was if, like her brother, Evan had serious talent or whether drawing was simply a way to pass the time. Knowing Evan, she would hazard a guess there was talent.

She made a mental note to ask if she could see her sketches.

❖

While Tate was busy finding the right location to moor the boat, Evan put her sketch pad away and went below to select a bottle of wine to go with their lunch. Finding Tate's well-stocked cooler, she chose a Pinot Noir and was still in the galley searching for glasses and a corkscrew when she heard her cut the engines and drop anchor.

Tate had been in an odd frame of mind since she'd told her about the flashback. It was possible she'd revealed too much too soon and

Tate was now worried about her mental health. Not entirely without cause.

But after everything Tate had been through because of her, she'd be damned if she'd let her brood. She just needed to come up with an idea or two to get her out of her somber mood.

Heading back up a few minutes later, she joined Tate on the flybridge and half filled two glass tumblers before setting the wine bottle down on a table. Without the steady rumble of the boat's engines, the silence settled upon them like a benediction, broken only by the sound of the water hitting gently against the hull.

Breathing in the salty air, Evan let the rhythmic motion of the waves lull her. Much as she suspected had been Tate's intention, the combination of being out on the water, the rugged splendor of the coastline, and Tate's gentle presence had lifted her spirits. She held a glass out for Tate then raised her own glass in a toast to the beauty and peace that surrounded them.

She kicked off her running shoes, then dropped onto a cushioned seat. She inhaled deeply once again and let the water, sun, and wind blur the remaining edges of tension churning inside her, allowing what had turned into a picture-perfect day to soothe and heal.

With one elbow propped on the table and her jaw in the palm of her hand, she alternately sipped from and played lazily with her glass, swirling the wine and admiring the way the sun's light sparkled in the translucent liquid. She remembered reading how someone had described Pinot Noir as sex in a glass. She took another sip and felt a heated rush as the wine flowed through her body.

Almost orgasmic, she thought and grinned.

For no discernible reason—or possibly because of the direction her wayward thoughts had taken—an image flashed in her mind. A moment out of the past. A hotel in Amsterdam.

She had been lying in bed with Tate, taking her time as she explored every inch of her soft, warm, and inviting body. Absorbing her heat and tasting her sweetness. Breathing in her essence and getting lost in the wonder of the moment while Tate writhed and begged for more.

How long she stayed revisiting that singular moment in time wasn't clear. She was lost, lost in a pulsing heat and aching want that had somehow coalesced into one woman for her.

Tate.

With her focus slowly returning to the present, Evan felt shaky as she looked across the deck at Tate. Truly saw her for possibly the first time since she had been rescued from her own personal version of hell. And in a moment of perfect clarity, she realized she had never been more physically and emotionally aware of or drawn to another human being.

A shiver rippled through her and she found herself suddenly consumed with wanting—no, needing—Tate. Needing to touch her. Needing to kiss her. Needing to wrap herself around her and lose herself in Tate's welcoming heat. And just maybe she would discover the missing pieces of herself in the process.

She opened her mouth to say something but closed it again without uttering a word. She didn't know what to say. She remained frozen, conscious only of an ache buried deep inside her. Then Tate looked up and smiled at her and she lost all ability to think.

Jesus.

Her heart began to race and she found herself standing at one of life's crossroads, knowing some decisions were smarter than others, and some were long overdue. Something shifted inside her as if a knot had unraveled, and a sudden awareness too strong to be denied helped Evan push past any lingering doubts and indecision. Digging deeper, she found and gathered her misplaced courage.

The light breeze ruffled her hair, sending a few errant strands across her face. She absently brushed it back and stood up before she could change her mind. She felt a wave of vertigo sweep over her but ignored it and walked toward Tate who had turned and was looking at her quizzically.

"Do you need something, love?"

Yes.

She was keenly aware of Tate's eyes following her, watching her attentively, searching her face as she closed the remaining distance between them. She stepped close enough to brush her index finger in a slow sensual glide over Tate's cheek.

She saw the quickening of the pulse at Tate's throat, felt the heat radiating off her body, saw the fire-flash of awareness in her eyes. Followed by the wariness.

The air sparked with supercharged memories and she reacted to the moment. Slowly, very slowly, she eased against Tate until their bodies touched at the one spot where she knew both of them ached.

Tate's eyes widened and she stared as Evan pressed closer. She eased back, looking shell-shocked, her face reflecting an endless array of conflicting emotions. Nervously twisting the wine glass in her hand, Tate watched Evan warily, offering shades of both resolve and surrender.

Evan didn't fully trust herself to speak. Acting swiftly before she could say or do something that might somehow alter the moment, she took Tate's face in her hands, settling her fingers against the curve of her cheeks, and looked at her. Just looked at her. And then she lowered her mouth, taking Tate's lips with exquisite tenderness. Putting everything she had into it.

The kiss was no tentative brushing of lips. Instead, it unleashed a maelstrom of yearning. Her tongue teased and danced until Tate opened for her, and the kiss quickly became a mating of lips and tongues. Sensuous. Hungry. A fierce and vibrant thing.

She wanted this.

Needed it.

Craved it.

The flavor of Tate's mouth tasted achingly familiar and for an instant, Evan took it deeper. She tasted the wine on her tongue and savored the softness of her lips, plundered the sweet white heat and felt the sheer magic of it.

Finally, with her heart still thundering and her blood boiling from the heat of the kiss, she drew back. Just far enough to stare wordlessly into Tate's eyes.

She saw want there. Need. Raw hunger.

Or maybe she saw a reflection of what was in her own eyes.

"Evan?"

Evan gently took the wineglass out of Tate's hand and put it on the table, shaking her head in wonder as she pulled Tate close once again. She found herself struggling to breathe. Her lips were still tingling. But something deep inside her settled to a level of contentment she had not known in months as she held Tate in her arms.

"I've missed touching you." Tipping her head back, she closed her eyes, letting the breeze cool her overheated senses. "I used to love waking up in the middle of the night to find you next to me, naked and warm. You were always so receptive. And after…after I got shot down, after I was captured…I would wake up shaking after I'd dreamed of you. I'm shaking now."

"Did you think I wouldn't understand?"

"Maybe. I don't know. I'm not sure about anything right now."

Tate slipped her hands around Evan's neck. "Be sure about this, Evan. Please," she whispered.

Evan remained silent, instinctively knowing there was more and waiting for Tate to finish.

"When I thought I had lost you, I didn't know how to go on without you. I survived those months by dreaming you were still with me, touching me. Loving me. But this…all I know is my fantasies could never live up to the real thing and I'm not sure I can deal with it if you—"

Evan placed her index finger gently across Tate's lips. "Don't go there. Maybe we're both dreaming. But if we are, I don't care. All I know is this feels real. You feel real." She shuddered convulsively. "Since I've been back, I thought what I wanted—what I needed—was space. Distance. Time. But it turns out that all along, this is what I've really wanted. You're what I've needed. You. I really want you...I really need to be with you."

Tate smiled but appeared to be still caught somewhere between desire and the need to proceed with caution. "What about lunch? Didn't you say you were starving?"

"I am. Can't you tell?" Evan picked up Tate's hand, kissed her fingers, one at a time. Licking. Biting. Absorbing the scent and the taste of her. Oh yeah. She was starving. With a hunger only Tate could satisfy.

Clearly wavering, Tate made one last effort to slow things down. "But I thought you wanted to—"

"Whatever I thought before, I was wrong. I want you. I want my mouth on you. I want to be in you. Right here. Right now." Evan paused and grinned. "Have I told you how much I like the T-shirt you're wearing?"

"My T-shirt?" Tate's confusion was evident in her face. "You like my T-shirt?"

"Yeah. I think I'll like it even better when it's on the floor."

Stepping back for an instant, she grasped the T-shirt by the hem and deftly pulled it over Tate's head with a sweeping motion before dropping it to the deck. "Are you okay with this? Or would you prefer some other place?"

Her mouth formed the words against the curve of Tate's neck. Without waiting for a reply, her lips slowly and tantalizingly began to trail over her. Brushing against her face, her throat, her shoulders. Skimming her teeth against Tate's skin, she stripped away her control as easily as she'd stripped away her T-shirt.

"You can have me, Evan. Anywhere. Anytime," Tate responded with obvious delight. "The only question left is what are you going to do with me now that you have me?"

Evan pretended to ponder the question for a moment. "Enjoy you, of course."

Tate didn't need any further incentive. With a soft sigh, she opened herself to Evan, welcomed her, let her in. Making her feel like she had finally and truly come home.

She moved her hands to undo the button at the waistband of her shorts. But almost immediately, Evan stopped her, catching her fingers and bringing them up to her lips.

"It's been a while and I might not remember how to do everything perfectly, but I'll let you know if and when I need any help," she said, her voice hoarse with barely controlled passion. Her nimble fingers moved to Tate's waist and deftly unhooked the button. She then tugged effortlessly on the zipper and laughed when Tate's shorts slid past her hips to join the T-shirt on the deck. They were quickly joined by her silk briefs.

Evan's laughter rippled like music over Tate's skin. It was a throaty, sexy sound, and she realized how badly she'd needed to hear her laugh again. She stared at her sensuous, smiling mouth and suddenly desperately wanted it on her.

As if reading her mind, Evan drew closer. "I'd almost forgotten how beautiful you are." Her fingers moved to catch and caress nipples already taut and straining for her touch. "I'm not sure you're aware, but I have this fantasy."

"Oh?" Tate arched her back and gave her better access. "And what does this fantasy of yours entail?"

"Kissing you until you scream." Evan released a groan as she closed her mouth over Tate's breast. She dragged her teeth across sensitive flesh, flicking a hard tip with her tongue and drawing out sensations before feasting with greedy abandon first on one breast, then the other, while her hands moved slowly, enticingly, lower and lower.

Tate shivered and felt the knot of emptiness and despair that had formed deep inside so many months ago finally begin to dissipate. "Where…where are you planning on kissing me?"

"Everywhere."

Totally powerless, Tate whimpered when Evan momentarily drew away, but she was gone only long enough to shed her own clothing. And then her hands and fingers and mouth were back. On her. In her. Finding her hot and wet and wanting. Arousing her until she could barely stand up any longer. Until she thought she would go absolutely mad with wanting.

"Oh God, Evan," she whispered thickly as the scent of her own arousal mixed with the erotic fragrance of Evan's skin. "I feel like my brain just short-circuited. If you keep touching me like that, this will be over far too quickly."

"Not to worry, we'll have plenty of time to do it all again, only more slowly." Evan laughed once again. "But trust me, not right now."

Slow, Tate discovered almost instantly, wasn't going to be an option for either of them. The next touch of Evan's lips proved that. It was as if she had been waiting far too long for this moment and she couldn't wait a second longer. With mouths still fused and legs no longer capable of supporting their bodies, they tumbled, pulling each other down to the deck.

Tate didn't care. She was on the verge of shattering.

A sensual fog swept over her, clouding all reason, as Evan's body covered every inch of her, and it suddenly felt as if Evan was everywhere, stroking her with hands and mouth and body. Tate groaned in response, the sound rising from deep in her chest. Her mind emptied, and as Evan continued her sensual assault, she was helpless to do anything other than whimper and writhe.

Tate heard the soft cries of pleasure and dimly recognized them as her own. But the realization had no meaning as she gave herself over completely and begged Evan to take her. Harder. Faster. Higher.

For an instant, she teetered on the edge. The next moment, all she could do was ride out the surging tremors shuddering through her body as those talented hands she remembered so well continued to move in a primal rhythm, shooting her to a staggering climax.

Gasping for breath, she lay limply on the deck, disoriented and delirious. A moment later, she felt Evan's hot and clever mouth replace her fingers, claiming her. "Sweet Jesus Christ, Evan. I don't know if I can—"

But Evan would not be dissuaded and kept her movements achingly slow. "Sure you can. You're already so close. Relax and let me do this," she whispered and began to trail kisses and nips across her abdomen, tracking a warm, wet path across her hip.

Tate was slick and swollen. Pulsing with need. As Evan sucked lightly, and then used her tongue and teeth and lips to draw out her pleasure, Tate arched beneath her touch, once again longing for release.

"Have I told you that I love how you feel, how you taste? It's always made me hungrier. Made me want you more." Evan's husky whisper was like her mouth—maddening, searching, caressing. Velvet heat. She touched her open mouth to her hip bone in a caress that made Tate shiver.

And Evan's hands were everywhere. Exploring her. Stroking languidly. Running over her abdomen. Tugging on her nipples. Caressing her every curve, seeking out her every shadow. Sending expanding waves of pleasure through her, until she was spiraling out of control.

The need arose in her so fast it burned. Heat and fire spread and consumed her. Strangling on a moan, unable to stop herself, Tate reached down and grabbed Evan's head as the sensations pushed her to the edge of control.

Thrusting her fingers into dark silky hair, she desperately pressed Evan's mouth against her throbbing clitoris, bowing her back and opening herself up as Evan slid two fingers inside her. And as she wondered how she'd ever lived a single minute without her, she peaked once again, even higher than before, and her breath released in a sob that became Evan's name.

❖

For a long time Tate was aware of nothing but a silky lassitude. She stirred slightly and moaned, muscles protesting. Her body still trembled with almost every breath, and she was floating in a haze of euphoria, an aftereffect of the pleasure Evan had given her.

Her first thought when her mind finally cleared was the realization she was lying on the deck of the flybridge. Naked. The sun was unrelenting in the sky, but the breeze off the water provided a measure of relief, cooling her heated skin.

She was still holding on to Evan and in no hurry to break the contact. Evan's body was resting between her thighs, her face damp and pressed against her neck. *Mine, all mine,* Tate thought, and she laughed softly, marveling at how unbelievably well they fit together. Always had. Always would.

She finally began to understand how much of herself she'd been living without. Evan was the missing piece of her life, and she would always be incomplete without her.

Reluctantly, she loosened her embrace. "Evan," she whispered. "There's a huge bed down below in the aft cabin. Why don't we go there now so we can continue this more comfortably?"

"That probably requires getting up from here," Evan responded, her breath hot against Tate's skin. "And I don't know about you, but I'm not sure I can move."

Laughing softly, Tate reached down with one hand, sliding it between their bodies. Watching Evan though half-closed eyes, she parted her hot, sweetly swollen flesh and brushed her fingers lightly over her clitoris. Evan's response was immediate, as her stomach muscles clenched and she moaned her need and arousal.

"No problem. We've got a floor right here. For you and me, I believe that's about all it's ever taken, and I'm pretty sure I can do what I want to here just as easily as down below."

"Tate," Evan whispered in a hoarse voice. Her face flushed, and she raised herself up on her elbows and looked at Tate with need-filled eyes a deeper gray than the water beneath the keel of the boat.

"I thought you'd never ask." With a triumphant laugh and very little effort, Tate rolled Evan onto her back before moving over on top of her, pinning her body to the floor. Straddling her, she reached down and cupped her face in her hand. Evan turned her head and kissed her palm.

"Let me have you, love."

Bending toward her, Tate reached for her mouth. They exchanged long, slow, intimate kisses before she slowly trailed her lips across Evan's throat. She traced her thumb lightly across her rib cage, sliding over a small firm breast, brushing delicately over the dusty pink tip. She felt it harden as Evan reflexively arched into her, and then trailed her mouth lower.

Her lips traveled across her chest as she rediscovered the taste of her skin. The only trace of control was in the gentleness of her lips as she kissed the healing cuts that bore silent witness to everything Evan had suffered.

She tasted every inch, teasing her with soft kisses and slow, deliberate caresses. Tormenting her. Pleasuring her while enjoying the deep sensual heat of her response. Her skin felt incredibly soft and smooth under her exploring mouth.

"You're so damn gorgeous," she said. "You take my breath away."

She loved Evan's body. The long, lean lines, the sleek muscles. As she absorbed the taste of her skin, every memory of touching her, the hours spent in pursuit of endless pleasure, came back to her, and she acknowledged Evan was a craving she would never get over.

She could barely breathe as she slid her hands possessively, watching Evan's face as her head fell back and her eyes closed. She gasped for air as Tate took her with her mouth and with her hands. Driving, hot, and insatiable. Then again, smoother and slower.

And as her tempo increased once again, she recognized the tension building in Evan's body, heard her rapid breathing. This was what she wanted. She wanted her wild. Wanted her thrashing.

"Let go, Evan. I'll catch you. I promise."

Evan let the moment wrap around her and let everything else disappear. She arched, enjoying Tate's touch and ready for more as she let go of all the stress and fear and anxiety, and focused only on the woman above her. "Tate," she whispered. "Please. I need you." A roaring started somewhere in her head. For so long, she had refused to feel or think or dream. Now it was as if the dam had burst and the floodgates were wide open.

Tate teased her with a slow, rhythmic intimacy that unraveled her. Waves of desire—hot, strong, and pounding—surged through her, driving her to the very edge of madness. And Tate held her there, suspended, stroking her with her tongue and working her with her fingers as she shuddered helplessly.

It was sweet, it was hot. It was maddening. She gasped with pleasure and then her gasp became a moan as liquid heat spread through her body. She felt dizzy with it, and as she cried out Tate's name, Tate moved swiftly up her body and took possession of her mouth once again. Swallowing her cry of release as she shattered and broke apart.

"What do you suppose would happen if we took the boat out into the Pacific and just kept on going?"

"I don't know," Tate said, laughing. "I guess someone would eventually notice we were missing, your brother more than likely, and send out search and rescue."

Evan raised an eyebrow. "But I wonder how many times we could make love before they found us?"

It was a delicious thought.

Chapter Twenty-six

They spent the afternoon moored in the quiet cove. Reconnecting. Kissing. Touching. Making love whenever the need overcame them, which was often. Old memories faded, new ones taking their place.

There was no need to talk. Instead, Evan let her body say all the things words never quite covered, and Tate seemed content to accept the answers her silence provided.

Perhaps no words were needed. The thought brought a smile to her face, nearly made her laugh out loud. It might be an illusion, but it was a nice illusion and Evan was just as happy to prolong it.

Joy was an emotion that had been foreign to her for too long, but she could still remember how it tasted, how it felt. It felt exactly like this. She recognized it in the feelings swelling deep inside her and in the smile she couldn't keep off her face.

She was happy to find this chance to reclaim the life she feared she'd lost.

Deliriously happy to discover her connection with Tate was stronger than ever.

And sated beyond belief.

The rocking of the boat in the gentle swells lulled her as she braced her legs on the gunwale. Taking a sip of wine, she watched the clouds in the sky chase shadows and listened to the wind whisper secrets to the universe.

Inevitably, her gaze was lured across the deck until it settled once again on Tate. The rays of the late-afternoon sun were slanting across her, bringing out the highlights in her hair. Her eyes were soft and her cheeks and nose glowed faintly pink.

After a moment, she lowered her eyes appreciatively to Tate's mouth. Her lips looked like they'd been thoroughly kissed and the corners were lifted in a hint of a smile—

Jesus.

She felt a stirring of renewed desire and wanted to make love with her again. All night long. Over and over again. She wanted to kiss every inch of Tate's body. She wanted to hear every sound she made, every gasp, every moan that escaped her lips. She wanted to breathe in her scent and absorb her taste. And then she wanted to watch her as she came apart in her arms.

Evan chewed her lower lip. She felt her face flush and her pulse throb as need sparked and she was breathing erotically charged air once again.

"Not before you have something to eat."

Evan hadn't heard her cross the deck. Hadn't heard her approach and place a tray loaded with food on the table. The last time she'd looked, Tate had been pulling a meal together out of the various foodstuffs she'd bought at the market. Now she was standing beside her. Quite obviously reading her mind and quite clearly trying not to laugh.

Tate watched her for a second or two longer before lowering her head and pressing her lips against the pulse near Evan's temple. She then picked up a tidbit of cheese and nibbled on it.

Evan grabbed a bite-sized morsel of poached salmon from the tray, dropped it on a cracker, then popped it into her mouth. She sighed in utter contentment. "That's okay. I'm not sure I can actually do anything right now. You've destroyed me."

Tate laughed. "I meant to. Now have some more to eat. You're going to need to build up your strength. I have plans for you for later tonight. We need to feed the beast."

That made Evan grin.

Tate leaned in and teased Evan's smiling mouth with her own before retreating. Replaced her mouth with a piece of buttered roll, laughing when Evan caught her fingers and licked them clean. Tate's smile widened in amazement as she fed Evan another morsel.

Good God, Tate had found a way to get her to eat, Evan acknowledged wryly. All she'd needed was a little distraction. Who knew?

They fell into a comfortable silence as Tate continued to feed Evan, finishing off their impromptu meal with the strawberries and chocolate, while the sun dipped closer to the horizon. It wasn't until she was pouring the last of the wine that she remembered the question she'd wanted to ask earlier.

"Can I ask you about the sketch pad you were working on earlier?"

Evan let out a half laugh of genuine surprise, a startled expression on her face.

Tate raised both brows. "I noticed you were sketching this afternoon. Considering your brother is a renowned artist, I couldn't help but wonder how strong the artistic gene is in the Kane family. Would you mind if I took a look at your sketch pad?"

"Now?"

"Sure, why not?"

Tate thought she detected a glimmer of uncertainty before Evan got up and retrieved her backpack. Pulling out a well-used sketch pad, she wordlessly passed it to Tate. But she kept one arm wrapped reflexively around her midsection in an obviously self-protective gesture.

It was the only sign of nerves Tate could discern. Still, it was enough to make her hesitate. She searched Evan's face intently a moment longer and wondered if that was a hint of distress in her eyes, but she received a nod of encouragement. Turning her attention to the sketch pad, she slowly absorbed the mesmerizing quality of Evan's work.

The sketches began in the hospital in Germany. Tate recognized the faces of the medical staff. The view from Evan's hospital-room window. Robert and Althea captured in a quiet moment as they leaned into each other.

It was also quickly apparent Evan was good. Very, very good.

"You are full of surprises, aren't you," she murmured, half to herself. As she turned the pages, the chronology of sketches moved into more recent times and included views of Puget Sound and the Olympic Mountains. An osprey resting in the trees near the dock.

Out of the corner of her eye, she saw Evan watching her, both arms now folded across her chest. And then Tate found herself staring at her own face, sketched in exquisite detail, making her appear…beautiful. She jerked her head up.

"Jesus, Evan. That's not—"

"Don't argue. It's how I see you."

Tate swallowed and tried to form a coherent sentence. "Discounting, for the moment, your obviously biased vision, your talent is unbelievable. How long have you been doing this?"

"Since I was twelve." Evan grinned slightly. "If you're really interested, I can show you sketch pads covering the last ten years or so. They're in one of the boxes Alex was storing."

"If I'm interested? I'd love to see them—wait a minute. Twelve?" Startled, Tate turned to her. "Why have you kept this talent of yours hidden?"

Evan gave her a long, level look before she shifted and looked away. Tate tried but failed to interpret the look. "Don't feel you have to tell me anything if it's going to make you uncomfortable."

"It's not that, not really. It's just awkward explaining it to anyone."
She paused then flashed a wry smile. "When Alex and I were kids,
everything seemed to come easy to me."

"You're kidding?" Tate grinned at her and Evan rolled her eyes.

"Of course, it didn't hurt having staff around all the time, hovering,
watching. Always ready to report any transgressions, making sure we
didn't cast a negative light on the Kane family name. It was a powerful
motivator for me."

"I can imagine."

"Alex, on the other hand, never gave a damn about getting
anyone's approval, but for some reason he struggled to find a direction.
So when he showed both interest and an aptitude, a genuine talent for
art, I pushed mine into the background. I didn't want anyone making
comparisons or saying anything that might derail him. It wasn't that
big a deal to me. It was simply how I relaxed. But to Alex, it quickly
became everything."

Tate touched her lips to Evan's cheek. "Does Alex have any idea
what an amazing sister he has?"

"He'd better." She managed a faint smile before dropping her
head, nestling it in the curve of Tate's shoulder. "He's not just my
brother—he's my twin. How could I not do that for him?"

Tate brushed Evan's bangs back and kissed her forehead. Gently,
almost reverently, she brushed kisses over her eyelids, her temples,
her cheeks. She kissed her mouth, a mold of lips and tongue that sent
desire flaring through her. A moment later, the sleek curve of her throat
beckoned and she pressed her mouth there, feeling the pulse beneath
her lips.

Raising her head again, she traced a fingertip under Evan's eye.
"You look beat. You should rest for a while. Maybe catch a nap."

"You keep kissing me like that," Evan smiled hazily, "and neither
of us will ever sleep again."

"What about touching?" She leaned close once again, her warm
breath ghosting over Evan's ear. "Can I keep touching you?"

"Same thing."

Tate felt a quiver of response as she ran her hand low over Evan's
abdomen and lost her train of thought. Something about kissing her again.
But at some point she pushed past the growing need and remembered
the shadows under Evan's eyes and how fragile she still was.

"God, Evan, I'm sorry. I'm like a kid in a candy store. I've
absolutely no self-control where you're concerned, and right now, it
doesn't seem to matter how often you let me have you. I just keep on
wanting you until I can't think of anything but having you again."

Evan's breathing wasn't steady. "Don't be sorry. Show me."

❖

It might not have started out that way, but it had turned out to be a perfect day. Far beyond anything Tate could have or might have hoped. But a shadow persisted, hovering over them like a storm cloud, and she knew it wouldn't go away until she did something about it.

"Do you think we could we talk for a few minutes?"

Evan settled back and looked at her. "Does this mean you're finally going to tell me what's been bothering you?" She laid her hand over Tate's.

Tate found herself short of breath at the contact. "I've never been good at keeping things from you, have I?"

"I'm shocked and amazed to hear that." Evan smiled a little, but it quickly faded, leaving a troubled look. "What is it, Tate? Are you worried because of what I told you? About thinking I saw Khalid at the market? Are you afraid I'm losing it?"

"God, no."

"Then what is it?"

Tate was silent for a moment, then said very quietly, "You're right that I'm afraid." She could see Evan watching her in utter stillness. "But it's not what you're thinking. I'm afraid because I believe you might have really seen Khalid."

Evan briefly closed her eyes. "You believe me?"

Tate heard the note of hurt surprise in Evan's voice and had to force herself to continue when what she really wanted to do was comfort her—and not have this conversation. "Yes, I believe you. And I'm terrified to think he could have gotten so close to you. I'm scared to death he might try to hurt you again before we can do something to stop him."

"Why?"

"Why am I afraid or why do I believe you?"

"Both."

"That's why we need to talk. There are some things I need to tell you, things I have to explain, but I want you to hear me out before you say anything. Can you do that for me?"

"Okay."

She was stalling. "I also really need you to understand it was never my intention to upset you or make you angry. But some of what I'm going to tell you will likely piss you off."

"Tate, it's not like you to prevaricate." Evan's expression grew turbulent. "Are you planning on getting to the point any time soon?"

Nodding, Tate drew in a shuddering breath. "A couple of days ago, a church in Vancouver was firebombed," she began and didn't stop until she'd told Evan everything.

She told her about the suspect the authorities had in custody. About his past connection to Khalid. About his arrest as he attempted to reach Port Angeles and her fear Khalid might have done the same, only with greater success. And she told her about Alex's plan to contact the sheriff's department.

She folded her arms across her chest and talked until there was nothing left unsaid. Until every thought and fear she'd had was set free. Then she lowered her head and waited for Evan to react.

There was dead silence except for the sound of the waves gently slapping against the hull and the keening cry of the gulls as they circled overhead.

"I'm not sure what you want or expect me to say," Evan said after a long moment had passed. "If you knew all of this, I don't understand why you didn't talk to me. You asked me to be honest with you, but then—"

"I know and I'm so sorry." Tate swallowed painfully. "I know I'm the one who preached about open and honest communication. Then I got caught up trying to protect you and forgot to talk to you. Forgot to involve you in decisions. But you need to understand, it wasn't long ago we all thought you were dead and I don't ever want to go through that again. Not if I can help it. So I'll do whatever I have to do to protect you."

Evan raised a brow. "It sure as hell doesn't sound like you're all that sorry."

Her voice was cool, but her expression was fiery. Tate felt her face grow hot knowing Evan was right. "Would yelling at me help?" She waited for a response, but got none. "I can take it, you know. I remember once having to interview your mother when she was in a foul mood over a story I broke in the media. If I survived that…" She thought she saw Evan try to suppress a grin. Encouraged, she reached for her hand. "I really am sorry, love." A minute drifted by. Then another. Then she heard Evan release a soft breath and felt the knot deep inside her start to come loose.

"It's all right, Tate. I understand."

"You're not angry?"

A flash of heat. "Oh, I'm pissed, don't think I'm not. But I guess I can understand why you did what you did. I lived with it every day after I woke up in the hospital in Germany and it scared me. Knowing what Khalid did to me. Wondering when he was going to show up to finish things." She shrugged. "So I don't have to like it, but I can understand."

Tate tightened her grip on Evan's hand. "I can't bear to think of Khalid getting his hands on you again, hurting you again."

"Not going to happen, is it?"

"No, it's not," she agreed. "Because we're not going to let him… one way or another."

"Probably more my way than another, don't you think?"

"Absolutely." Tate bit her bottom lip, leaned closer. "Are we okay?"

"Yes, we're okay." The gentle response was in total contrast with the wicked grin that appeared unexpectedly. "But if I were Alex, I'd be nervous."

❖

The sun had long since set and the indigo sky was studded with brightly gleaming stars while the moonlight reflected off the water and danced across the boat. Not wanting to go below, Tate had brought blankets out on the deck and was leaning against a stack of cushions and pillows while Evan sat on the floor, reclining in the vee of her thighs. Gazing up at the stars.

Peace slowly seeped into her, and when Tate brought her hands to settle on Evan's shoulders and began a slow, deep massage, her muscles relaxed and she willingly gave herself over. In mere seconds her head dropped forward, a low moan escaping her parted lips.

"Does that feel good?"

The words were only breathed in her ear, just a whisper of sound. "Mm-hmm," she mumbled as she sank into the sensual bliss Tate was creating with gentle fingers. She felt her body grow limp even as the energy flowed between them and seemed to crackle in the air.

When Tate finished, it took Evan a minute or two to come back down to earth. And a couple of minutes longer than that before she could begin the other conversation she wanted to have.

"Tate?" With an unsteady laugh, she pulled away from the warm sanctuary Tate provided and ran a hand through her hair as she turned to face her. "I've been thinking."

Something in her voice, probably the indecision or possibly the sudden nervousness had Tate sitting up straight. "Is something wrong?" she asked warily. "Did I do something wrong?"

"No," Evan answered quickly. "Nothing's wrong. It's just that, lately, staying with you, being with you reminded me of who I used to be, and I realized…that is, it occurred to me we've never really dated."

"Dated?"

"Yeah, dated." Evan blew out a breath and gave a soft laugh. "Couples do that. I mean, I know we've gone skiing in France, been to Amsterdam, and there was that time in Germany, although I don't know if that counts because I don't believe we ever left the hotel room. But we've never actually…been a couple, planned stuff together. We've simply made our own ways and met up wherever we could."

"Evan, what are you talking about? I always understood why we couldn't—"

"I know all the reasons. But that was then, this is now, and all those reasons no longer matter."

"What does that mean?"

"I think"—there was a hint of humor in her voice to match the smile on her face—"I *think* what it means is I don't believe I've ever taken you out on a real date and I'd like to correct that oversight."

Tate blinked and tried to speak past the sudden tightening in her throat. "You're asking me out on a date?"

Evan gave a quick nod. "I'd like to take you out someplace where life is normal. Where people get together to eat good food, drink good wine, and enjoy a good time. I'd like to hold your hand and maybe hold you in my arms while we dance a little. And then I'd like to walk you home and spend the night making love."

"Oh."

"So what do you say, Ms. McKenna? Would you do me the honor? Would you go out with me?"

"There's no one else I'd rather go out with," Tate responded, hoping her expression showed Evan exactly what was on her mind and in her heart. "Do you have something in mind for this occasion?"

"Actually, I was talking to Alex, and he led me to believe the Harbor House Inn meets all my prerequisites. I was thinking we could go there Friday night. After all, isn't Friday supposed to be date night?"

"You talked to Alex about this?" Tate's eyes narrowed. "And what do you mean Friday night? This coming Friday night? As in days from now?"

Evan chuckled at Tate's aggrieved sigh. "Yes and yes. Why? Did you have something else planned?"

"No. Just answer one question for me."

"What's that?"

"Why are we waiting so long?"

Evan laughed. "Anticipation."

❖

He hadn't intended to go near the house.

It was a mistake, he knew that, but his self-control wasn't as sharp as it needed to be. As it was, he'd had to force himself to wait until the cover of darkness before finally moving closer, using the trees surrounding the property as cover.

But as it turned out, he needn't have worried. The boat wasn't tied down by the dock and the house stood empty and dark.

Maybe karma and not a mistake, he thought. This would give him a perfect opportunity to check out the surrounding area more thoroughly. Time to plan his next moves like a military mission where reconnaissance, surveillance, and target acquisition were the keys to success.

He tried to stay calm, to quiet his racing heart. But it was difficult. Near impossible. From the moment their eyes had unexpectedly met at the market, he'd been wire tight, filled with anticipation. He could feel his blood coursing hot and fast in his veins, while the recurring fantasy of their next meeting played out in his mind.

He knew she would be feeling uneasy. Anxious. Wondering if he would come for her, when fate would catch up to her. She didn't know he planned to play with her a little longer.

He wanted her to know it was inevitable, but not when or where or how. Only he would know. Because he had the power. He was in control.

He closed his eyes and savored the possibilities, wondering what it would feel like when she finally looked into his eyes and realized there was nothing she could do to stop him.

Somehow he knew it would taste sweet.

CHAPTER TWENTY-SEVEN

Evan shifted and stared balefully at the narrow shaft of pale light slanting across the room through the partially open curtains. Too damned early, but more sleep was simply not going to happen.

Accepting the inevitable, she gave up trying, taking care not to awaken Tate as she eased out of bed. She could see the day was emerging gray and cool, knew from yesterday's marine weather reports a storm was brewing somewhere off the coast.

Terrific, she thought, her mood matching the dismal weather.

The rain wasn't supposed to hit until midday, but as she stood by the window watching the gathering clouds, she doubted it would wait that long. She could already hear the roll of thunder, the wind carried the sweet pungent scent of ozone, and the water surrounding the house had become choppy, white foam capping the crests as they formed.

Still, inclement weather had its compensations.

Her physiotherapist had given her clearance to start running again, and today seemed like the perfect day to put her leg to the test. Maybe a run, even one taken at a slower pace than she was used to, was just what she needed to empty her mind and shake off her mood. And the promise of bad weather all but guaranteed the solitude to do both.

She could only hope.

Ignoring the dull ache in her head, she got ready quickly, tugging on shorts and an old sweatshirt and grabbing her new Nikes before slipping out of the house. With any luck, Tate would just be rising by the time she returned. Maybe they could sit on the deck and watch the storm blow through.

The moist, salty air hit her like a tonic as soon as she stepped outside. And much to her delight, only the seagulls ubiquitous to the shore would be keeping her company on the five-mile trail.

Blowing out a breath, she walked for the first few minutes, gradually lengthening her stride before breaking into a slow jog. As she ran, she tried to concentrate on the signals her body was sending. She knew her leg was doing better, but she had no desire to experience a setback of any kind.

Still, from time to time, she caught herself looking at the potential challenges presented by some of the trails intersecting the main footpath. Another time, she promised herself.

Falling into a comfortable pace, trusting her leg, allowed her to gradually relax. She was moving easily and everything was in harmony. The sound of the waves crashing on the rocks was strangely soothing, and by the second mile the remaining whisper of her earlier headache had begun to ease. It was also the first time she'd come this far along the trail, and a natural curiosity in her surroundings kept her moving forward even as her energy began to wane.

She had just reached a sweeping turn where the relentless wind and water had carved a slice into the island when the skies opened up and the rain began to fall. It had a surprising bite to it and didn't augur well for her continuing run as the path quickly grew slippery.

There was a half beat of hesitation as she contemplated turning around, heading back to the house. Tate would make coffee, strong and hot, and maybe light a fire to ward off the unseasonable chill in the air. The temptation was unquestionably there. But after peering through the rain at the gray, listless sky, she opted to push just a bit farther, wanting to see what lay just around the bend.

As luck would have it, the intensity of the rainstorm increased over the next few seconds. Laughing at her own misfortune, Evan had just decided to turn back when she felt a tickle at the back of her neck. The gulls fell silent and time slowed down.

A touch of fear crept along her spine then clawed at her throat with razor-sharp talons.

She had learned long ago not to ignore gut feelings. They were usually right. Reacting instinctively, she skidded to a stop. The rain became a metronome, an aural pulse beating a steady counterpoint to the harsh sound of her breathing and the hammering in her chest. Wiping the rain from her eyes, she cast a quick look around.

In that instant, a bolt of lightning cracked the sky, illuminating the dark shape of a man. Wavering into focus, he appeared to be watching her from the top of a nearby rise. And for a moment, she saw him quite clearly.

Khalid.

Without a doubt.

Her muscles froze. Her heart jolted and her breath caught at her throat. The logical side of her brain automatically rejected what she was seeing. Argued it wasn't real. But it grew more and more difficult to question when he was clearly visible just a short distance away.

He was standing beside an enormous pine. Watching her. His stillness added to her discomfort, and although she knew it was her imagination kicking into overdrive, she swore she could almost see his eyes. See the predatory gleam in them.

She bit down on her lip so hard she could taste blood. The copper taste blended with the fear that filled her mouth and paralyzed her for what seemed an interminable few seconds while she stared at him. Her mind clouded and her vision tunneled.

Swiping the rain from her face, her eyes caught and held on the vicious-looking knife in his hand. She took an involuntary step backward. She had no way to protect herself from him and her retreat was instinctive.

She remembered the knife all too well. She could still feel the sting as Khalid drew the tip of the razor-thin blade across her skin. Could feel the beads of warm blood form and trickle down her back.

She remained frozen in the past for an instant longer before her instincts kicked into high gear. And then, ignoring the storm, the mud, and the dull ache in her leg, she turned and ran. On adrenaline, self-preservation instincts, and a healthy dose of fear.

Behind her, she was positive she could hear new sounds as her worst nightmare became reality. She could hear labored breathing. Heavy footfalls splashing in the muddy track. Drawing closer. She could all but feel his breath, hot against her skin. All but sense his hand reaching for her. Bringing her down.

She cursed as she stumbled. Tried to maintain her balance, but lost her footing on the slippery path and went down hard, planting her face in the mud. A sharp, stabbing pain knifed through her along with an explosion of fear as her breath left her. She'd banged her chin and scraped her hands and knees, adding blood to the rivulets of rain and mud.

Out of breath and grimacing, she rolled to her feet, heedless of whatever damage she'd just done to herself. Fear closed like a vise around her throat as she lifted her gaze, but she'd run as far as she could. Unable to go any farther, she turned to face Khalid, turned again, then stopped.

She wiped her face with a mud-caked hand.

No one was there.

If Khalid had ever really been there, he was now gone. And it was a big *if*. There was no sign of him anywhere.

Evan turned in a complete circle, her breath heaving painfully in her chest as she searched for him. But she was completely alone. Her knees threatened to buckle and she felt a chilling wave of shock sweep over her.

Jesus. Jesus. *Jesus.* Maybe she was as crazy as she'd secretly feared. Maybe Khalid had succeeded in destroying her, after all. Because there was no one else on the trail with her. Quite clearly she had imagined the whole thing. And if this was a flashback, she was in serious trouble.

Stepping off the trail, paying scant attention to the mud, she sank to the ground. Leaning her back against a tree, she pressed her head between her knees and tried to breathe more slowly.

There was nothing but fear left inside her. She felt isolated. Alone.

Evan wasn't sure how long she sat there. When she finally opened her eyes, her clothes were soaked through to her skin, her teeth were chattering, and she was shivering violently. All she knew for certain was that the rain had stopped, the air was cool and damp, and the sun was trying to peek through the thick pewter clouds.

Like dreams, fears faded with sunlight. The horror she had experienced—real or imagined—dulled, and the thin edge of fear receded. Years of military training kicked in and she forced herself to get up. To move.

Breathe, she told herself.

Her movements were sluggish, each step an agony of cold, wet, and muddy clothes. Her knee felt stiff and sore, and there were a few aches where she'd banged herself when she'd fallen. But the adrenaline that had been driving her was gone, leaving her running on empty. She swallowed as she looked around. And then with her hands trembling, she turned back toward the house.

For over an hour, Tate had been staring out at the rain. She had gotten up with romantic rainy-day notions in mind, but as she glanced at the clock, romantic thoughts faded and her mood shifted to concern.

Where the hell was Evan?

She'd already been gone much too long. And that was without knowing just how early she'd actually left the house. She grew more uneasy with each minute that passed.

As she leaned back and listened to the rain coming down, the pragmatist in her reasoned Evan might have simply taken shelter from the rainstorm. Even now, she could be making her way back, having waited for the worst of the storm to pass.

So why did she have this disturbing sense of unease? Tate couldn't shake the feeling something was wrong. Something had happened. The last time she had felt such a strong sense of premonition was—no, she wasn't going to go there.

Instead, while she waited, she tried to write. But after several abortive attempts to make progress on her book, she pushed away from the laptop. She tried putting on some music but managed to listen for less than a minute before turning it off.

Unable to concentrate, she paced over to the rain-spattered window, only to find herself wondering yet again where Evan was and asking herself what she'd expected. There were times when she was certain she could see all the way to Evan's soul. But there were other times when she seemed more of an enigma than ever.

She reminded herself that, in spite of the recent progress they'd made, Evan still needed both space and time to deal with everything that had happened to her from the moment her jet had been shot down.

To hell with space.

She cursed herself for being an idiot but found herself reaching for a jacket and heading for the door. She threw the door open only to stop abruptly as she came face-to-face with Evan, shivering and soaked to the skin.

She looked lost and more than a little in shock. Her hair was plastered against her face as water dripped from the ends. She had mud everywhere. And there were traces of blood on her face, her hands, and on her legs.

"Evan?"

She gave Tate a weak smile and laughed shakily. "I fell."

Tate's eyes quickly skimmed over Evan's face, sizing up the damage. Evan was breathing hard, not from having been for a run, but from the obvious tension and emotions swirling around her— frustration, anger. Mostly fear.

Tate could see the lines of strain on her face. Recognizing the weariness in those two words, she nodded. "Yes, I can see that."

Standing mere feet apart, she could still detect the enticing scent of the sandalwood and vanilla soap Evan loved, mixed with fresh rain emanating from Evan's skin. But she resisted the urge to touch her. For reasons unknown, in spite of her attempt at levity, Evan looked as if she might shatter at a single touch.

Tate allowed the air between them to fill with questions for as long as she could before asking softly, "What happened, Evan? Are you all right?"

Evan gave a mirthless laugh. "Am I all right?" she repeated. She shrugged and looked away. "I'm fine. I got caught in the rain and slipped on the path. It's just a couple of scrapes and bruises."

Her voice was casual and she *almost* passed for fine. Almost, but not quite, because she couldn't prevent the tremor that visibly ran through her.

She tried to pull away when Tate finally reached for her. But ignoring her unspoken protest and mindless of the mud, Tate pulled her inside the house and gathered her close.

"Tate, I'm a mess."

"I don't care." Tate's control slipped for an instant as she cupped Evan's face in her hands, listened to her breath catch. "Don't you know I'm crazy about you?"

Her hand came up quickly and caught Tate's wrist. Her fingers were cold. Despite that, they felt wonderful, electric. In that moment, she couldn't have moved away even if she'd wanted to—and she didn't want to. Heat flared between them, as bright and strong as ever.

But Tate couldn't read what she saw in Evan's eyes.

"I was worried about you."

Trapping Evan within the inviting warmth of her embrace, Tate brought her mouth closer. She briefly nipped at her full bottom lip before embarking on a slow and gentle exploration of Evan's mouth, drawing out an incoherent sound as her hands drifted down her back, then lower to cup her buttocks. She tasted rain, the cold of Evan's lips contrasting with the heat of her mouth, holding her with fierce strength as she plundered and explored.

By the time she pulled back, the worst of the shaking had subsided. Tate breathed, calmed, then said, "You're still a mess and your chin is bleeding." She brushed Evan's hair back from her face before dropping a kiss on the tip of her muddy nose. "But at least your color's back."

"I don't doubt that for a minute," Evan muttered in response, but there was an odd catch in her voice as she softly added, "Please don't be worried. I know I look like a train wreck, but honestly, it's just a few scrapes."

Her words belied the pain evident in the tightness around her eyes and mouth. "I'm supposed to believe that?"

"Comes from planting my face chin first into the trail." She breathed a ragged sigh and briefly pressed her mouth against Tate's. "I've gotten you muddy and wet. Let me clean up while you change, and then maybe we can have something to eat, okay?"

Tate sucked in a breath. For no discernible reason, she feared something had just happened and she was losing the connection she'd reestablished with Evan. She could almost see her pulling the barrier walls down around her, closing herself off.

Nonplussed, she simply nodded. "Call me when you're done in the shower. I'll put some of that ointment Kelsey sent home with you on those scrapes."

Letting Evan limp to the bathroom on her own, Tate forced herself not to watch her retreat. But she could still feel her silently drawing farther away with each step, each breath, each heartbeat, as her footsteps receded.

Hearing the soft *snick* as the bathroom door closed, she released a deep sigh. She stood there staring at the door, then turned quietly and made her way to the bedroom.

❖

Evan began stripping off her mud-caked running gear before the bathroom door had fully closed behind her. The cold made her movements stiff and she stumbled awkwardly, nearly falling in her rush to turn on the water, wanting desperately to feel warm again.

Almost immediately, the bathroom began to flood with a moist and welcoming heat. But she was shivering uncontrollably, her teeth chattering by the time she managed to step into the shower. Letting the near-scalding water stream over her body, she released an enormous sigh. Slowly the numbness began to recede and feeling returned to her body.

As her brain began to thaw, her thoughts returned to Tate. She didn't like the look of insecurity she had seen on Tate's face. She especially didn't like knowing she was responsible for putting it there. But she didn't know what to do or say to make things right.

Once again, circumstances had forced them into a position where they needed to talk. Somehow she had to find the words to tell Tate about the flashback. About Khalid. She needed to tell her what had happened. And then somehow she needed to explain her very real fear—that she was losing her mind.

As the blood and mud were washed away and warmth returned, her mood shifted and gradually fear gave way to a low burning anger.

Damn it. When had she become a coward? She should have confronted Khalid, not turned rabbit.

Assuming it was Khalid, a soft voice reminded her.

But if she hadn't turned tail and run away, then at the very least she would know whether the apparition on the hillside was real or she had become completely certifiable. Disgusted with herself, she ducked her head under the spray and let it pulse for a few minutes before reaching for the shampoo.

By the time she stepped out of the shower, the near-debilitating cold and accompanying tremors had finally dissipated. Steam from the shower filled the bathroom and Evan stared through the condensation into the mirror.

Shoving her wet hair behind her ears, she saw a stranger looking back at her. But something—a glimmer in her eyes, perhaps—gave her hope that maybe something of the old Evan had survived Afghanistan and was waiting for the right moment to come out.

That was how Tate found her a short time later. Still damp from her shower, with a bath sheet draped around her and tiny beads of water glistening on her skin. She had wrapped her arms around herself, her eyes were shadowed, and she stood in front of the sink frowning as she stared at her reflection in the mirror.

"Evan?"

At first Evan didn't answer, but then she turned toward the doorway. The troubled expression on her face shifted and she managed a smile. "Hey, beautiful lady."

She knew every plane and angle of that amazing face. And although there were still shadows beneath her eyes, there was also something different. Tate could sense it as she watched Evan.

Stepping closer, she brushed a soft kiss on Evan's damp shoulder before catching her chin gently with two fingers. She tipped Evan's head back, looked at her face, and examined the fresh scrape. And then, disregarding all of her previous arguments with herself, she pulled Evan into her arms.

Evan shuddered almost convulsively as she curved and melted into her. Sinking into the embrace, she closed her eyes and held on to her as if she would never let go.

"Hush, baby. It's okay." Tate rocked her gently and pressed a kiss to her damp temple. "You can tell me later. Whatever it is. Right now, just hold on to me. Just hold on."

Evan offered no resistance when Tate led her back into the bedroom and wordlessly helped her dress. And then she followed her out onto the deck, where they shared hot soup and pieces of chocolate. Afterward, she sat cradling her head in her hands, her hair falling forward, shielding her eyes.

"Will you tell me what's troubling you?" Tate asked. "Will you let me help you?"

She wasn't at all surprised when Evan didn't immediately respond. She really hadn't expected an answer. But a moment later Evan began to talk.

She started in a soft halting voice, but as she told Tate about the thoughts plaguing her, with each word her voice grew stronger and more certain. For the first time since being pulled out of Afghanistan, she opened up without reservation. She told Tate what had happened that morning. About seeing Khalid on the path with a knife in his hands. And about how he seemed to disappear into the rain and mist like a wraith.

She held nothing back, including her very real fear she was going crazy. She was seeing things. Seeing Khalid when he wasn't really there. Didn't that mean—?

"Evan?"

Evan sat back, staring at nothing.

"Don't do this to yourself, don't beat yourself up. And thank you. I know how hard this was for you to do. Now let me tell you what we're going to do. On Monday, you and I are going to call Kelsey's partner and arrange to go and see her. Together. And together, we're going to get you through this. I'm not saying it's going to be easy. But I am promising I'll be with you every step of the way."

Evan swallowed. "Okay."

Tate hesitated for an instant. "We're also going to check in with Alex, see how his conversation with the sheriff went. See if he thinks we should upgrade the security system in the house. Just in case."

"All right."

"Is there anything I can do for you right now?"

"Kiss me."

Tate smiled. Leaning toward Evan, she touched her lips with a soft kiss. Then more firmly, capturing her lips, feeling her mouth open. Hearing her whisper.

"Don't stop. When you kiss me, I can't think of anything else."

Chapter Twenty-eight

Tate stood in front of the full-length mirror and studied her reflection critically. She had already changed four times and had passed the point of being exasperated with herself. This was Evan, she reminded herself. If she hadn't impressed her by now, nothing she wore or did or said tonight would make a damn bit of difference.

But she knew this evening was important to Evan and she wanted to do her part in making their date perfect. So in the end, she chose her current version of the little black dress she'd worn the night they'd met.

As her thoughts turned to Evan, she wondered where she was and what she was doing. Alex and Nick had picked her up earlier in the day. When she'd questioned where they were taking her, Alex had rolled his eyes.

"You'd think the girl would have something nice to wear on a date, wouldn't you? Preferably something between Versace and US Navy issue."

"You're taking her shopping?" Tate's eyes had widened and she'd tried hard not to laugh. She could only imagine what it had taken for Alex to convince his sister to go shopping, knowing how much Evan hated to shop.

And while she acknowledged Alex had impeccable taste when it came to women's fashions—he had, after all, taken her shopping on a number of occasions—Tate didn't think it would matter what Evan wore. From jeans and T-shirts to dress whites to Alexander McQueen originals, Evan Kane would always walk into any room and easily be the most compelling woman there.

Of course, that was only her opinion. But since she was Evan's date, it was the only opinion that counted.

The doorbell interrupted her musings. Adding a last-second dab of perfume and inhaling deeply to calm her curiously unsteady nerves, she made her way to the front door and opened it. Tate immediately felt her mouth go dry.

Evan stood there, slender and elegant in unrelenting black, from the light silk jacket and matching slacks to the thin camisole that hugged her body. She held out a single red rose before leaning in and pressing a delicate kiss on Tate's lips.

"Hi," she said softly as she pulled away. "You look beautiful."

Taking the flower, Tate pressed the petals to her lips as she met Evan's eyes. "Thanks. I…" She had to stop for a moment. "It's beautiful. You look amazing."

"Alex and Nick." Evan smiled and shrugged nonchalantly, then held out her hand. "Thanks. Shall we?"

Tate nodded. "Let me put this in water, and then absolutely."

Harbor House Inn was a charming fishing captain's estate perched near the mouth of the harbor. Since moving to the island, Tate had developed something of a friendship with the two women who owned the inn, and she was looking forward to introducing Evan to them.

Evan, she believed, needed those connections. Needed to be connected to friends, to the community, and to the island. It would help her feel more grounded, and just maybe, it would help reassure her that this was where she was meant to sink roots.

"Randi and Grace have an amazing kitchen," Tate remarked as they walked hand in hand toward the front entrance.

"Oh?"

"I'm talking fresh Dungeness crab, Penn Cove mussels, and they also do an incredible cedar plank salmon. And for dessert, they have a crème brûlée that can make you weep."

Evan grinned. "I'm thinking you'll have to order for both of us."

Tate laughed, but before she could respond she heard someone call out her name and saw a familiar face fast approaching. White teeth flashed in a wide smile as the woman took hold of her hand and drew her closer before kissing her lightly on both cheeks.

"Tate, you look absolutely wonderful. In fact, I think you're glowing. What have you been doing with yourself? I saw Alex at the market yesterday and he told me you had dinner reservations for tonight, but I checked the book and couldn't find your name. I figured he had to be mistaken."

"That's because the reservation wasn't in Tate's name. It was in mine." Evan smiled faintly. "I'm Evan—"

"Kane. You could only be Alex's sister. You're the spitting image of him, right down to those delicious dimples. But then you're twins, aren't you?"

Releasing Tate, she took Evan's hand and shook it enthusiastically, the smile on her handsome face widening. "I'm Miranda Taylor, Randi to my friends and one of the owners of Harbor House. I'll be your hostess for this evening. I have to tell you, I was hoping to meet you sooner rather than later. Alex has done nothing but talk about you, never more so than since he found out you were..."

Still alive?

The words remained unsaid and Randi stopped abruptly before Tate could intervene. It was as if she suddenly realized the conversation had taken a turn down a dangerous path. Her dark-chocolate eyes closed for a brief instant, and she shook her head. "Forgive me. My wife will tell you that sometimes my mouth gets the better of me. Gracie was an army medic in Iraq, and I couldn't be happier now that she's home for good and I don't have to worry about her all the time."

Evan flushed. "It's all right."

"Please understand. Grace and I got to know Alex and Nick quite well when they first joined our community, and more recently we've started getting to know Tate. They had a difficult time of it when they thought they'd lost you, and I sometimes think what they went through brought back all the fears I had for Grace. But we couldn't be happier knowing you've come home. That you're here safe with Tate." Randi's eyes skimmed along Evan's length speculatively. "Tell me, do you play softball, Evan?"

"She'll stop talking eventually," a new, much softer voice interrupted dryly. Turning, Tate saw Grace Taylor approaching them from the dining room. Quiet and fair, she was the polar opposite of the dark and gregarious Randi in every way.

"I'm Grace Taylor," she said to Evan, her hand soft but strong. "Welcome to Harbor House. Now let me get you settled and get a drink in your hands. I'm thinking champagne is in order. I'll send some over on the house. And Tate, you might want to keep a close eye on your date. We're expecting a full house tonight."

Evan glanced over quizzically, but as Tate caught Grace's wink, her throat tightened with suppressed laughter and she was unable to respond. She knew Harbor House always drew a crowd, especially on weekends when they brought in live entertainment and there was dancing. Tonight was no exception.

Much as Grace had indicated, the room was already more than three quarters filled, mostly with women. And then she thought of Evan unleashing that sexy smile—the one that lit up her eyes and caused women from eighteen to eighty to fall under her spell.

It was going to be a very interesting evening.

Momentarily concerned Evan wouldn't feel comfortable with so much attention and feeling somewhat possessive, Tate reached for her hand and gave it a quick tug. But Evan had quite clearly taken the lessons she'd been taught at Althea Kane's knee to heart. She continued to hold Tate's hand as she moved easily through the crowded room and appeared oblivious to any attention she was garnering.

Thanking Grace once they reached their table, she held out a chair for Tate then took her own seat across from her. Tate suppressed a laugh but swore she heard sighs from the women seated closest to them.

Their table was by the window and offered iconic coastal and mountain views, but Evan looked only at her. There was something different in the way Evan's gaze played over her and as she smiled, Tate let herself bask in the warmth and affection she saw and felt.

They were interrupted briefly when a waiter appeared with the champagne Grace had promised. Evan watched silently while he placed the bucket beside the table, opened the bottle, and filled their glasses. Once he was gone, she handed a glass to Tate before reaching for her own glass and raising it.

"I believe a toast is in order—to our first date," she said, then added softly, "I'd like to toast what I believe will be the first date of many."

It's not a one-night stand. I'd like to think of this simply as the first night of many.

Tate heard the echo of the words Evan had spoken after their first night together and felt her heart skip a beat, driving every other thought from her mind.

True to her word, Tate chose their meal while Evan made their selection from the inn's rather eclectic wine cellar. Although Evan barely noticed her food and drink, the date was perfect and exactly what she wanted.

To talk and laugh with Tate as they had in the past. To remind herself of what her life had been like. And to set the tone for what life would be like as she moved beyond Afghanistan and Khalid.

Eventually a group of local musicians set up in one corner and music began to fill the night air, enticing numerous couples onto the small dance floor. It had been a long time since she had been dancing, but Evan was already feeling the music. The rhythm and the sultry beat. The heat. It felt so good.

Her body humming with fierce energy, she reached for Tate's hand, brought it to her lips. "Dance with me," she said as she drew Tate to her feet and steered her toward the crowded dance floor.

Tate laughed, probably as much from surprise as uncertainty. "If you remember, I'm not much of a dancer. And I'm most certainly not in your league."

"I don't believe the band's going to break into a tango anytime soon," Evan teased her with a smile. "And you've always worried too much. Anyone can dance. You just have to let yourself feel the music." Not giving her the chance to resist any further, Evan pulled Tate into her arms and held her motionless for an instant as their eyes met. Tate laughed again, more relaxed this time, and when Evan began to pull her farther onto the dance floor, she followed her lead with a loose-limbed grace.

That was all it took. Evan was instantly bombarded with sensations. Tate's subtle scent was like inhaling a tropical forest. Cool and inviting. The swell of Tate's breasts pressed against thin silk sent delicious chills along her spine. And the heat radiating from Tate's body everywhere it brushed against her was pure promise. It made her heart pound and her blood boil.

She raised her hand and brushed the back of her fingers against Tate's cheek before sliding them down toward the pulse beating visibly in her throat. And then in a move driven by instinct, she allowed her senses to be inspired by both the music and the woman.

She moved her hands to Tate's waist and slowly began to move her hips. The people crowding around her disappeared, and as their bodies swayed sensuously close, she transformed her movements into something so much more than dancing.

Just as the band moved effortlessly from one song to the next, she knew the moment Tate felt the change. Knew the moment she became aware Evan's moves had shifted into something suggestive and arousing and infinitely more intimate. She stumbled briefly and locked eyes with her, but gamely continued to follow her lead.

They remained on the dance floor until the band took a break. By then Evan's leg was starting to ache, but she wouldn't have missed dancing with Tate for anything. Except maybe getting her home, where she could peel off Tate's dress and devour every inch of smooth skin with her mouth.

Tate pressed her face against Evan's shoulder, catching her breath. "That was unbelievably…hot," she said. "Why don't you get yourself a drink while I go freshen up?"

Drawn out of her thoughts, Evan raised an eyebrow. "Are you trying to ply me with wine so you can have your way with me?"

Tate tilted her head back slightly and gave her a wicked grin. "Is it working?"

"Actually, forget the wine. You can have your way with me anytime." She grinned back and pushed away a lock of hair that was clinging to the heated dampness on Tate's face. "Can I get you something from the bar?"

"I think ice water would be great right about now," Tate responded. "And try not to let any of these women steal you away. I have plans for later which involve your active participation."

"I wouldn't have it any other way—"

Tate's mouth was on hers before she could finish. "I can feel you wanting me. Do you have any idea what that does to me?" she whispered and then she was gone.

Tate was still thinking only about the lingering taste of Evan's mouth. Enthralled, her body and mind in a different place and time, she was only vaguely aware of someone calling out to her.

"Tate? Tate McKenna?"

Tate looked up and frowned as a woman stopped in front of her. An instant later she broke into a smile. "Oh my God, Kelsey. I'm so glad to see you. I didn't think you were due in until sometime next week."

"I wasn't, but you can thank Robert Kane for my being home early."

"Robert Kane? Evan's father?"

"None other." Kelsey nodded happily. "He came through and arranged to fly me home yesterday in a private jet, rather than the military transport I was scheduled to take next week. Talk about a different kind of flying experience."

"I know what you mean. That's how we came home as well. But—"

"He said it was just a small token of his appreciation for my part in taking care of Evan. I tried to tell him it was a team effort and I was just doing my job, but he said Evan insisted on it."

Tate couldn't hide her surprise. "Evan?"

"Yeah, you remember Evan, don't you? Tall, dark hair, gray eyes? Navy pilot? She and her father made it possible for me to come home early and surprise Jenna."

Kelsey's smile widened as a striking woman with close-cropped prematurely silver hair, a youthful face, and pale blue eyes approached them. "Perfect timing. Tate, this lovely lady is my partner, Jenna."

Jenna smiled warmly as she held out her hand. "Kelsey has told me about you and Evan. Dare I hope she's here with you tonight? I'd love to meet her and thank her in person for helping to bring Kelsey home in style."

"Of course. We came for dinner earlier and stayed for the dancing. I was just heading back to our table."

Jenna's smile wavered. "I don't want to intrude on your evening. I can always meet her some other time."

"Don't be silly. Evan has been looking forward to meeting you, and I know she'll be thrilled to see Kelsey again. Come and join us for a drink. Please."

"If you're sure—"

"Absolutely."

"How's she doing, Tate?"

She considered Kelsey's question for a moment. "Physically, I'd say she's doing great. I can tell when her leg bothers her, not that she'd ever admit it. But it's not as often and the physiotherapist she's been working with has been terrific. He finally gave her the go-ahead to start running again this week."

"That's good to hear," Kelsey said gently. "Now what aren't you telling me?"

Tate sighed. "She's still much too thin. She used to have a healthy appetite, and I know she's trying, but some days it's a challenge getting her to eat."

"What else?"

"She's still having nightmares. She's also been having flashbacks, at least a couple that I'm aware of, where she's convinced she's seen Khalid. The most recent was just yesterday while she was running."

"The bastard who tortured her?" Kelsey's temper visibly flared before Jenna casually placed a hand on her arm. "Sorry."

"That's not all," Tate said. "The deeper problem is there's a real chance Evan's not having flashbacks. There's a real chance Khalid's actually here in Washington."

"How's that possible?"

Tate briefly explained, before adding, "The situation's left Evan uncertain whether she's having flashbacks or seeing Khalid for real."

"Maybe I can help her," Jenna offered.

"I sure hope so, since we were planning on contacting you on Monday," Tate responded with a wry smile. "But enough serious talk for the evening. Come on, Evan's probably wondering where I've gotten to, and it's really not safe to leave her alone this long in a room filled with single women."

Kelsey grinned and Tate knew she'd caught her first glimpse of Evan. "After meeting Alex, I had a pretty good idea what she probably looked like underneath all those cuts and bruises, but she cleaned up nicely, don't you think?"

Tate snorted and Jenna rolled her eyes.

They were still laughing until just before they reached Evan, when Tate stopped, suddenly overwhelmed with a feeling that everything was far from all right. Evan, she noted with concern, appeared to be leaning heavily on the table, gripping it with one hand and looking as if she needed it to keep herself upright. There was no light or warmth in her face. Instead she seemed distant and unfocused.

Something tightened in Tate's chest and she stepped forward quickly. Resting her hand on Evan's shoulder, she immediately felt the tension in the tightly coiled muscles. "Evan, what is it? What's wrong?"

She glanced at a man standing much too close to Evan. But before she could think to ask him who he was and what he wanted, Evan slowly turned toward her and released a weary sounding breath.

"Tate, this is John Anderson. It seems he wants to talk to me about his son." Evan swallowed. "Khalid."

Silence, as thick and palpable as the tension radiating from Evan's body, swallowed the air around them.

John Anderson was a big man with blunt-edged features and deep-set dark eyes. His wide shoulders blocked Tate's view of the room as he extended a large, powerful-looking hand. But his handshake was gentle in spite of the callused skin.

Shaking off the frisson of unease and the sharp bite of anger that accompanied it, Tate met his gaze. "What's this about, Mr. Anderson?"

"I realize I'm intruding on your evening, and I apologize, but I'd been debating whether or not to talk to Commander Kane. When I recognized her in the parking lot, it helped me decide." Anderson's next words were all but impossible to hear as the band returned for another set. "Perhaps we could continue this discussion somewhere quieter so we can talk without having to shout."

Evan pushed her chair away from the table and rose on unsteady legs. "Let's go."

"Whoa, there. Easy." Tate reached for her hand.

Evan stopped, realizing she had no idea where they would find some privacy. But she needn't have worried. Tate took over, leading them to a small library situated just off the inn's main lobby.

On some level, she acknowledged Kelsey's presence. She and the woman with her appeared reluctant to leave but looked equally uncertain about staying. Tate resolved their dilemma by indicating they should come with them.

"I'll get to the point so you can get back to enjoying the rest of your evening, Commander Kane." Anderson's voice was soft and graveled, but Evan was certain she could hear New England roots in his words, regardless of how much time he had spent living in the Pacific Northwest.

"It's Evan." She was aware her breathing had become shallow. *Christ, you sound as if you're coming undone.* Almost as quickly, she felt Tate squeeze her hand, linking their fingers and calming her with her touch.

Anderson nodded stiffly. The muscles in his face tightened and something flickered in his eyes. Discomfort, maybe.

"I thought you should know the FBI came to see me a few days ago," he said a moment later. "Asking me about my son. They said John's the subject of an international manhunt. That he killed a CIA agent near Kabul. And more recently, they suspect he took part in firebombing a church in Vancouver."

That brought her up short. Blowing out a lungful of air, Evan noted his blank expression hadn't changed with the telling, not even a fraction. "What does that have to do with me?"

"I'm coming to that. The FBI told me things got too hot for John in Afghanistan. They know he left about a month ago, but they lost track of him and they suspect he's made his way back into the US. They wanted to know if I'd heard from him. I guess whoever did their background search didn't let them know I'm about the last person John should come to for help."

"Why is that, Mr. Anderson?"

"It's what I told the boy the last time I saw him, after he got into trouble for hurting that girl. I told him he was no son of mine and not to come back anymore because I had no home for the likes of him."

Evan frowned. "I'm still not clear what any of this has to do with me."

"I know who you are, Commander Kane." He emphasized her rank and her name as he studied her. "I read the story in the papers and the two FBI agents filled in a lot of the blanks."

"What exactly does that mean?"

Anderson shrugged but seemed genuinely distressed. "They wanted me to know John was still up to no good, so I wouldn't be inclined to help him. They knew all about what the boy did to that pretty little girl in Portland. The navy ensign. And they wanted me to know he was up to his old tricks. Still cutting girls up, only this time it was some downed navy pilot in Afghanistan. I put two and two together, Commander. I'm sorry for what the boy did."

Evan closed her eyes and reached down to lightly massage her throbbing knee while the cuts on her back suddenly burned. "Thank you, Mr. Anderson, but I need neither your apology nor your sympathy. It's not yours to own. You're not responsible for Khalid."

"Khalid—is that really the name he's using?" He gave her a level look. "No matter. I may not be responsible for the boy, but I can see quite clearly he still lacks any kind of moral center, and no matter what I tried, I couldn't change that in him. That's my failure. I don't hold for torturing women and I felt I owed it to you to warn you."

"Warn her?" Tate interrupted. "Are you threatening Evan, Mr. Anderson?"

"Not at all," he answered quickly and Evan marveled at his neutral tone. "I may not have seen John since he was eighteen, but you need to know I recently heard from him."

"You spoke to him?"

Anderson shook his head. "He left a message on my machine a couple of days ago. He wanted me to know he was back in the area. Said he had some unfinished business to take care of, and if I was interested in seeing him after he was done, I should leave the porch light on."

He ran a hand through his thinning hair and then said calmly, "In case you're wondering, Commander, I smashed the bulb. I didn't want to leave the light on by accident."

Evan knew a bleak moment of despair. "Have you told the FBI any of this? About the call and Khalid's message?"

"No, I'm sorry to say I haven't. I couldn't do it. The boy's not right in the head, but I guess there's a part of me that still thinks of him as my son." He stopped himself and let out a breath. "But after thinking about what he said, I knew I couldn't stand by and just let it happen. I felt I owed it to you to warn you. He's hurt enough people and it has to stop. Before he hurts you again. Or worse."

Chapter Twenty-nine

Tate drove back to the house in silence, conscious of the crosscurrents of tension and the shadows in Evan's eyes. Kelsey and Jenna parked their car a few feet away. She drew an audible breath. "We might as well get comfortable. I've got a feeling it's going to be a long night, and I think we could all probably use a drink."

Evan walked in ahead of her. She disabled the alarm and turned on the lights but didn't slow down as she retreated toward the bedroom without saying a word.

Tate tried not to read too much into what had happened. Or think too much about how it would affect Evan and the progress she'd made. The progress *they'd* made. If there was a light in all the madness, it was having Kelsey and Jenna here. She knew instinctively she could count on their support. Knew they would help her get Evan through whatever was to come.

She stared at the bottles in the bar and suddenly couldn't handle something as ordinary as pouring drinks for everybody. Turning to Kelsey, she smiled apologetically and nodded toward the bar. "You'll find something there to accommodate almost every taste. Why don't you get drinks for Jenna and yourself while I go check on Evan? There's a bottle of Richard Hennessy, if cognac's of any interest. I'm sure that's what Evan will want when she comes back out."

"Let me know if you need my help," Jenna called out softly after her as Tate walked toward the bedroom.

She wasn't sure what she expected to find. But it certainly wasn't Evan dragging her duffel bag out of a box in the closet and placing it on the bed. Tate felt a cold chill descend as she tried to shut out the bleak picture of a future without Evan. Again.

"You're leaving."

"What?"

"I said you're leaving." Unable to stop herself, Tate snapped, her eyes never straying far from Evan's face as she began to pace. She picked up a throw pillow and hugged it to her breast. "At least tell me why, Evan. Why are you letting that bastard win? Why are you leaving without talking things through—with me or, at the very least, with Alex?"

"Tate?" Evan stopped what she was doing. "What the hell are you talking about?"

Tate indicated the duffel bag on the bed. "Are you not ready to start packing?"

Evan stared at her for a moment, her expression suggesting Tate had taken leave of her senses. "I'm not going anywhere and if that's what you think is happening, then we need to have a conversation. A really serious conversation."

Tate felt a rush of warmth but warned herself against reading too much into what Evan had just said. Instead she watched a faint frown touch Evan's face as she reached into the duffel bag. It was gone an instant later—a clear *aha* moment—when she met with apparent success.

"This is what I was looking for," she said mildly, and when she withdrew her hand, she was holding a lethal looking handgun.

"What the hell is that?"

"It's a Sig Sauer P228. It's a nine millimeter with a thirteen-round magazine. A real beauty. Light, compact, and extremely accurate. It's also the weapon of choice as a sidearm for navy pilots because it's got a special corrosion-resistant finish." She looked at Tate and flashed a grin. "More than you wanted to know?"

Tate willed herself to breathe. But she didn't know what to do or say. Christ, she wasn't even sure what she was feeling at the moment. She shook her head, swallowed back the urge to scream, and tossed the pillow aside. "I think I just want to know two things."

"What's that?"

"I'd like to know why that gun was in your duffel bag and why you suddenly felt the need to find the damned thing."

Evan's eyes were serious when she looked at her, all teasing gone. "It was in my duffel bag because once upon a time, in another life, I actually owned a pair. One I had on me when I was shot down. This is the other. It was shipped to Alex from the *Nimitz,* along with the rest of my personal effects, after I was reported killed in action."

Tate winced and discovered she hated hearing those particular words. "That doesn't explain why you felt the need to find it tonight. Why you just went looking for it."

Evan sighed. "I looked for it because it occurred to me that if John Anderson's right and Khalid is close by looking to finish what he started in Afghanistan, I'm not going to make it easy for him."

"What does that mean?"

"It means I'm going to do whatever I have to do to protect myself and the people I care about. It's been a while since I've practiced, but it's like riding a bike, isn't it, and I was always a pretty good shot. I'm also going to teach you how to shoot because I need to know you can take care of yourself if you have to."

Tate stood frozen for a moment, looked away, and the sound that escaped from her throat could have been shock. Or relief. She wasn't certain. Several heartbeats passed while she tried to regulate her breathing. When she finally looked back, Evan was actually grinning at her.

Evan crossed her eyes and made a face. "Well, you've got to admit this is one hell of a first date, isn't it?"

"You do like to keep me off balance."

And then Tate started to laugh.

❖

Evan gently swirled and sipped her drink and pointed out the different constellations in the sky while Tate made a pitcher of mojitos and brought it out to the deck. The night had cooled and she could taste the salt in the air, blending with the vanilla and spice flavors of the cognac. She realized the stars were serving as a mutual distraction. For Tate because she was clearly shaken and looked as if she wanted to run from the fears John Anderson's appearance had raised. And for herself for too many reasons.

"You see that constellation snaking its way between Ursa Major and Ursa Minor? The Big and Little Dippers? That's Draco, the Dragon. You can see the head of the dragon lying directly under the bowl of the Little Dipper."

"All this time and I had no idea you were such a knowledgeable stargazer," Tate teased.

"It was my father who first got me interested. I must have been twelve or thirteen," Evan responded, giving Tate a Cheshire cat grin. "But I didn't get back into it until my second deployment. As I remember, I had just taken off at night over the ocean. Everything around me was black, and as I climbed above the clouds, suddenly I couldn't see anything but stars, the moon, and a bit of moonlight caught by clouds below me."

"It sounds incredible," Kelsey said.

"It was. It started me thinking about all the things my dad had talked about and I just had to learn more. So I took some courses—mostly astronomy and astrophysics."

Tate raised an eyebrow and looked at her with a curious expression. But whatever was on her mind remained unsaid, and instead she gave a nod and asked, "What else can you show us?"

Evan angled her head and stared at the sky. "Well, if you trace a line from the stars at the end of the Big Dipper's bowl, past Polaris, you'll arrive at the top of Cepheus, the King. Can you see it? It looks like a simple drawing of a house. A triangle on top of a square."

"Hey, there it is."

Evan laughed. "Yeah. And sitting just east of King Cepheus is his wife, Queen Cassiopeia. Depending on the time of year and her relative position to Polaris, you can identify Cassiopeia by her shape. In winter, she'll look like a W, while in summer she'll appear as an M."

"I've never been able to pick out constellations before." Tate's voice caught with unexpected emotion and her expression softened. "That's amazing."

"Yeah, amazing," Evan repeated as her smile and voice faded. "I guess this means I'm not really crazy after all, am I?"

She felt Tate squeeze her hand, but it was Jenna who responded. "Is that what you were afraid of?"

"The thought that I was losing my mind terrified me," she admitted. "I think quite possibly it scared me more than thinking I actually saw Khalid."

"Why is that?"

Why? That was the real question, wasn't it? But this time, she knew she had an answer she could give. "Because I can deal with him if he's real. Khalid…John…or whatever he chooses to call himself. He may be a soulless bastard, but I can fight back. But not if he's just a shadow, a specter I created out of my own nightmares. I can't defeat him if he exists only in my head."

She felt her face heat as the words spilled out and closed her eyes. Shifting restlessly, she fought back the urge to get up, to escape the images crowding her mind as she continued to speak.

"By the time Deacon and I ended up with Khalid, we'd been in captivity for almost three months. Any hope we might have had that someone was still looking for us had long since been beaten out of us, and I certainly didn't have a lot of fight left in me. And after my first couple of encounters with Khalid…"

"What, Evan?" Jenna encouraged her when she fell silent for too long. "What happened?"

Evan was suddenly acutely aware of the three women—the psychiatrist, the doctor, and her lover. All three were watching her intently, each waiting to see how she would respond. She remembered the psychiatrist in Germany telling her healing would begin when she started to trust again. When she learned how to trust others as well as herself.

"There was a moment when I just wanted it to be over." She paused, her mouth suddenly so dry it was difficult to get the words out. "And it very nearly was. If Deacon hadn't been there, I'd be dead. Still dead," she corrected, staring at her hands. "He had to revive me the first couple of times after Khalid drowned me."

She felt more than heard Tate's sharp intake of breath. It caused her control to slip slightly, but she kept her eyes fixed on Jenna.

Jenna appeared unruffled by her admission. "I'm so sorry, Evan. You've been through a lot and you're still recovering. Physically as well as emotionally. But you need to be prepared. If his father's correct and Khalid is here, you're probably going to end up facing him. Are you ready for that?"

For an instant, Evan felt there wasn't enough air to breathe as the reality of her life locked back in. She could feel the freshness of old pain again, and she turned and met Tate's gaze briefly before looking back at Jenna.

"Without question." She took another sip of her drink, aware of a burning in her throat that had nothing to do with the smooth cognac. "There's not a moment of my time with Khalid I don't recall with absolute clarity. I can still smell the dust, smell my own blood. I can still hear his voice and feel his hands on me. I can still feel the sting of his knife each and every time he cut me. After a month with Khalid, I understood only too well why an animal would chew off its leg to get free from a trap."

She paused, leaned back and drained her snifter. "But things are different now. He won't find it so easy to defeat me. And this time, it will be on my terms."

❖

It was an easy decision. Kelsey and Jenna would spend what was left of the night in one of the guest rooms rather than drive back to the inn. And while Tate looked after the immediate needs of their guests and ensured they were comfortable, Evan took care of locking up the house and setting the alarm. Routine behavior that was possibly never more important than tonight, and Tate wondered how quickly she could get someone in to install additional security.

She was already in bed by the time Evan made her way to the bedroom. Undressing quietly in the diffused light of the bedside lamp, her skin looked pale. But it felt warm and smooth as she lay down beside Tate and closed her eyes.

Tate shifted, pushing herself a little higher against the pillows. "How're you doing?"

"I want this over."

Even in the shadowed room, she could see the strain around Evan's eyes. Knew she was trying to come to terms with everything that had happened. Not only the encounter with John Anderson but her revelations about what Khalid had done to her in Afghanistan as well.

Tate didn't want to think about that right now. Breathing in her scent, feeling her warmth was nothing short of a miracle.

"It will be over soon, love. And in the meantime, I'd like to start by calling the sheriff's department in the morning. At the very least, they can advise us. And then we need to do whatever they suggest to make sure you're safe." She paused to pull Evan closer until her lips were only a breath away. "I can't believe I'm actually going to suggest this but—I don't suppose you'd consider going to DC and staying with your parents for a while?"

Silence stretched until the air grew tense between them. "No."

Tate wasn't surprised by the answer since she'd expected no different. She dropped a kiss on Evan's shoulder and felt the ridged scars that marred her skin as she trailed her fingers over her back. Felt the faint ripple that coursed through Evan in response to her touch and the corresponding tingle of sexual awareness that danced across her own skin.

"Why don't we put any final decisions on hold until we talk to the sheriff in the morning and see what he has to say?"

"You're starting to repeat yourself." Evan smiled faintly. "I know you're expecting me to argue, but I'm not going to fight you on this. God knows we'll need all the help we can get."

"I know. I just don't want anything happening to you. Did Alex say anything to you about his conversation with the sheriff?"

"He said he thought the sheriff was non-committal but interested in what Alex had to say and didn't blow it off as the by-product of PTSD."

"That's good, isn't it?"

"I guess. And at the very least, the sheriff's department will be able to help me get a concealed carry permit. One for you too."

Tate shifted uncomfortably. "You're serious, aren't you? About the gun."

"Never more so." Evan's intensity was palpable. "I lost more than four months, Tate, and I'm just finding my way back. To you. To my family. To my life. I'm not about to let anything get in the way of that happening. And if it means confronting Khalid, then that's what I'll do. But I'm okay with it because I know you'll have my back."

Tate stared at Evan and wondered if she would ever fully understand her. She didn't say anything because there really wasn't anything to say. She simply nodded and held on to her.

"If you don't mind, I'd rather not talk about it anymore. At least not right now. It can all wait until morning."

Tate started to say something, then thought better of it. Mostly because she couldn't see a way around the truth. The one that said Evan would eventually have to deal with Khalid. A moment later, all thought left her as Evan found her mouth. At first, it was in gentle exploration, but then with an increasing hunger that all but brought Tate to her knees.

Oh God, she's so good at this.

Tate recognized the jolt of desire, hot and sharp. Felt her control slip a bit more, and it suddenly seemed as though too much time had passed since they had last made love. Helpless to stop herself, she covered Evan's mouth with her own, shivering as Evan's hand swept up her spine.

When she pulled back and looked at her, she found Evan smiling a high-octane smile just like the one she'd had in her first memory of her. Sensuous and hungry. Tate didn't think she'd ever seen anything as erotic. Or beautiful. And she wanted her.

"You're a madness in my blood. You know that, don't you?" she whispered. "Give yourself to me, Evan."

"Anytime. Any place. Any way you want," Evan replied, her eyes capturing Tate's soul. "But first—" She released a low, guttural sound as she lowered her head and feasted on Tate's throat. Devouring her as her hand slid provocatively across Tate's heated skin.

It was a sound Tate loved, and she tipped her head back to give Evan better access. Fueling the fire until it consumed them both.

❖

She felt warm and protected, safe, with Tate's body pressed tight against her back. But it didn't stop the dreams, and the nightmare that night was the worst one yet.

It had started with Tate. Making love with her on a beach. But it swiftly changed. Tate was pulled from her and her arms were tied, leaving her helpless and hurting. She could see Khalid, holding his bloody knife. But he was holding it against Tate's skin, and she could feel herself fall apart in jagged little pieces.

Because she was unable to prevent what was happening. She was unable to save Tate.

She called to Tate, screaming her name as Khalid pushed her into the abyss. She scrambled in sheer panic, unable to contain the scream ripped from her throat as she tried to claw her way to the surface.

"Evan!" Tate's voice was distant and strained. "Evan, it's all right. Look at me. You're all right. It's just a dream. You had a nightmare. I'm right here."

Slowly awareness returned, and she sensed when Tate moved closer, stroking, comforting. Her hands were gentle, but firm enough to hold her when she tried to pull away. She could feel Tate's lips pressed against her temple. Hear the whispered words while she shook violently, waiting for the tremors to ease.

❖

Tate glanced at the clock on the bedside table, but it really wasn't necessary. The first pale hints of the new day were already visible through the window, and in the fragile light she could see Evan, sprawled across the bed, facedown and naked. One arm dangled off the mattress, and her sweat-dampened hair partially covered her face.

She was finally asleep. As Tate continued to watch her and listen to her soft breathing, something tightened in her chest. Drawing a shaky breath, she eased out of the bed and slipped into her favorite robe—a short blue silk Evan had bought in Japan—then quietly left the room.

"I'm glad she's finally asleep. Why aren't you?"

Tate started at the voice and turned to find Jenna standing there, concern evident on her face. "I thought I'd make a pot of coffee. After a nightmare, Evan doesn't usually sleep long and, more often than not, wakes up with a headache. Coffee and aspirin are the only things that seem to help. I'm sorry if we woke you."

"It's all right. I heard Evan screaming," Jenna said quietly. "I didn't want to intrude. I only got up in case I could be of some help, but you seem to have it well under control."

"I don't know if I would go that far." Tate released a soft laugh. "But I'm learning as we go. And Evan now seems to come out of it and realize where she is much quicker than in the beginning."

"That's good. Why don't you let me make the coffee while you try and get a little more sleep?" she asked.

Tate shook her head. "Thanks, but I doubt if I could sleep, and besides, the odds are quite high Evan's brother Alex will show up before long. He'll want to hear all about our first date."

"Your first date?" Jenna's confusion was readily apparent. "I'm sorry, but I was under the impression from Kelsey you and Evan had been together for some time. And the chemistry between you—"

Tate laughed as she ground the coffee beans, measured the water. "Chemistry is something we had from the moment we met. A powerful thing. Still is. And Kelsey's right. Evan and I have been together for some time. But we never got around to actually dating." She shrugged and sighed.

"Why was that?"

"Where would you like me to start? She was a lieutenant commander in the US Navy. Her mother's the secretary of state, her father a big-time lawyer. Her twin brother staged a very public coming out while they were still teenagers and is a prominent artist. But Evan never wanted to be a boldfaced name in the gossip columns. So discretion pretty much ruled everything she ever did."

"To think you didn't run screaming."

"Ah, but you had to see Evan in her dress whites." Tate smiled. "She looked so damned hot she took my breath away the first time I saw her. At an embassy dinner in Bahrain, honoring her mother, of all things."

"You fell in love at first sight," Jenna said. "That's wonderful."

"Oh God, I did. I really did even though I fought it at first. I guess I didn't want to admit it to myself, but I finally realized the truth. That in spite of the constant separations brought about by her job and mine, and all the political baggage she came with, every time I so much as thought of looking at another woman, I was always looking for Evan. And none of those women were her."

"That's a good thing."

"Without question, except I've never actually told Evan how I feel and I don't even know why. I mean, it's not as if my feelings could change. Even when I thought she was dead. If anything, what I feel has only gotten stronger."

She felt it then, the stirring in the air indicating Evan was near. *Damn,* she thought, *not like this.* Biting her lip, Tate slowly turned around. Her throat tightened.

Evan stood in the doorway in dark baggy sweatpants and a white tank top. Dark hair carelessly finger combed, smudges under her eyes, pale cheeks, and a resolute set to her jaw.

Tate wanted to go to her. Wanted to erase those shadows and see her smile. But more than anything, she wanted to erase the last few minutes out of existence. Pretend they hadn't happened. She wanted to pretend she hadn't just told a near-perfect stranger she was in love with Evan without having said the words to Evan first.

Jenna cast a quick sympathetic glance in her direction then quietly melted into the shadows just beyond the kitchen as Evan stepped forward into the light. She didn't stop until she was a mere breath away. Silent and intense, she tucked a finger under Tate's chin, lifting her head until Tate had no choice but to meet her eyes.

Tate knew she should do something to break the tension humming between them. Laugh, talk, anything. But she didn't. Couldn't. It was as if she had fallen under some kind of spell. And when Evan lowered her mouth to hers, she automatically parted her lips.

It was the softest of kisses and much too short. She felt a moan lodge in her throat as Evan pulled back, and she wanted nothing more desperately than to bring her mouth back.

"Did you think I didn't know?" Evan's breath was soft and warm against her lips. "Did you think I couldn't see it in your eyes or feel it every time you held me? Did you think I couldn't hear it in your sighs whenever we make love?"

Evan let Tate pull away, watching as she stopped just beyond her reach. Thrusting her hands into the pockets of her robe, Tate looked skittish and nervous. Uncertain. Her shoulders were hunched as if she was cold, but it was more likely from tension. But the silky robe had fallen slightly open, exposing the swell of her breasts, and Evan thought she looked beautiful. Tantalizing. Infinitely alluring.

"You have to know this is not how I wanted you to hear," Tate said after a long silence. "You have to know there were so many times I wanted to say the words to you."

"Tate—" she said, offering a quick smile, wanting to ease the tension.

But Tate continued as if Evan hadn't spoken. "It was just never the right time," she said. "The last thing I wanted was to leave you distracted when you needed every bit of attention focused on surviving your last deployment. As it is, you very nearly didn't." She fell silent, her fatigue and distress evident. But Evan didn't say anything, knowing there was more still to come. More Tate needed to say.

"When I found out your plane had been shot down—when I thought you'd been killed—I couldn't believe I'd let you go without ever telling you how I felt. I couldn't believe I'd allowed so many meaningless reasons to stand in the way of telling you I loved you, and probably had since the night we met." She stopped as her voice cracked and she lost her way. "I wanted to die when I heard. As it was, I was dying without you."

Evan stepped forward and put her arms around Tate, pulling her closer. Pressing her tightly against her body until it was impossible to tell where she ended and Tate began, she felt an incredible calm come over her.

"I'm right here," she murmured softly, her lips close to Tate's ear. "And I'm not going anywhere again unless it's with you. Do you understand what I'm saying?"

Tate nodded wordlessly.

"Good, because when this thing with Khalid is over, I'd like to invite my parents to come for a visit. And your parents. I want to celebrate *us* with the people who matter to us. I love you, Tate. I've been in love with you for a very long time, and I'm planning on spending a lifetime showing you just how much."

She felt the shiver running through Tate and slid her hands inside the silk robe, skimming her palms over her bare skin and setting them both on fire as their lips met.

CHAPTER THIRTY

"If you two are done making out like a pair of hormonally crazed teenagers, some of us are hungry and, at a bare minimum, would like some coffee."

"Alex! I can't bring you anywhere."

Evan and Tate both laughed as Nick tried to pry Alex away from the kitchen door without success.

"Go," Tate whispered. "Take your brother out on the deck and let him entertain Kelsey and Jenna while I get dressed, and then Nick and I will make breakfast."

Still laughing, Evan dropped a kiss on the end of Tate's nose before grabbing Alex's arm and pulling him out to the deck. She got there in time to see the sun slowly creeping over the tall pines, to hear the birds singing and to feel the breeze stirring over the water.

Perfection. She inhaled deeply, enjoying the clean morning air as she watched the day arrive while listening to the waves and the gulls.

"How are you doing, Evan?" Jenna asked softly. "I imagine yesterday was tough. For you, especially."

"I'm doing okay, thanks."

Alex sat up. "Something going on I should know about?"

But Evan shrugged. "Nothing we're going to talk about before I have Tate sitting beside me and at least two cups of coffee in me. You remember Kelsey don't you, Alex? This is her partner, Jenna."

Looking out the kitchen window, Tate watched Evan, sitting in a patch of bright sunlight, her face turned up to the warmth. Listening to something Jenna was saying, Evan stretched the tight muscles between her shoulder blades like a cat and her lips parted slightly before easing into a full, sensuous smile.

God, Tate loved her beyond anything she might have imagined.

"You're burning the bacon."

Nick's words jolted her back to the present, and she grinned sheepishly as she quickly switched the heat off under the pan, removed the sizzling strips of bacon, and placed them on a rack.

"You look happy."

"Deliriously," Tate responded, adding butter and pots of maple syrup and honey to the tray Nick was loading with plates and cups and cutlery. "Can you manage the pancakes and coffee?"

Nick nodded and they went to the deck to join the others.

Evan jumped up to help her as soon as she saw Tate and the pile of food she was carrying. "Think you've got enough food there?"

Tate laughed, just a little breathless. "I'm still trying to fatten you up a bit, and besides, your brother is here. He more than makes up for your lack of appetite."

"Only where food is concerned," Evan whispered and laughed as Tate felt a heated blush spread across her face.

"Be good," she admonished, but there was no rebuke in her tone.

Alex served himself a healthy stack of the wild blueberry pancakes and munched happily before asking, "So, who's going to tell us what's going on? Obviously you two finally figured out what Nick and I've known since the trip to Chamonix. That you're in love with each other. Hallelujah. But there's something else. I can see it in both of you. What's going on?"

With her brother's eyes watching her intently as if he could guess she was about to complicate his life, Evan nibbled on a piece of bacon, drank far too much coffee, and relayed her conversation of the previous evening with John Anderson. To Tate's surprise, she left nothing out. Not even the threat Khalid had made to finish what he had started with her in Afghanistan.

"Have you called the sheriff yet?"

"We thought we'd do that this morning after we finish eating," Tate interjected, trying to give Evan some room to breathe.

"I'd like to go for a run before we make the call," Evan said, placing her napkin next to her barely touched plate. When Tate looked at her questioningly, she shrugged. "I think I'll be in better shape to talk to the sheriff if I can work off some excess energy first. And I wouldn't mind checking out the trail. It's where I last saw him."

"I'll go with you," Alex said, pointing out he was already dressed in jogging pants and a T-shirt. "Plus I still want to hear all about how your date went before your unexpected visitor showed up and derailed it."

"If I can borrow some running gear, I'd like to go with you too," Kelsey added. "We're about the same height, and if you have anything kicking around from before you got skinny, I'm pretty sure it'll fit. God knows I'll need to run a half marathon just to work off all the food I just ate."

Tate felt unseen undercurrents tugging at her. She looked at Evan, close enough that she could see the tiny black flecks in her smoke-gray eyes, and suddenly needed to make sure she understood.

"You do know you didn't imagine him, right?" She waited nervously until she saw Evan respond with a brief nod. "Then what do you expect to find?"

"Maybe ghosts. Maybe nothing. I'm not sure." Her voice was little more than a whisper. "All I know is everyone's trying to give me the space and time to get on with my life except Khalid. And I'm afraid I won't be able to do that—I won't be able to move on—until I settle things with him, once and for all. Maybe he knew what he was talking about. It's what he said, after all. That there'd be another place and time. Now we need to finish things."

"How far will you go, Evan? What are you willing to do to bring things with Khalid to a close?"

"You don't need to worry, love. In my heart of hearts, I will always be a naval officer and my parents' daughter. There are lines I won't cross."

But as she watched her, Tate thought she could see dread creep into Evan's eyes. "Will you at least take your gun?"

Evan nodded, smiling unexpectedly if a little weakly and easing some of the tension out of the moment.

Tate told herself she should be happy about that, even though she wasn't. Still, she *was* genuinely glad to know Alex and Kelsey would be going with Evan. They'd make sure nothing happened to her. They'd bring her back safely.

"Try not to shoot anyone until we get you a permit. Otherwise, the paperwork will be a bear." She leaned closer and their eyes connected. "And try not to be too long. I'm going to call the sheriff's department as soon as I finish cleaning up. It would help if you were here when he arrives."

"Jenna and I will give you a hand cleaning up," Nick offered as he came up behind them. Evan's face remained unreadable, but Tate thought she saw relief wash over her. Nodding gratefully, Tate hooked her arm into Evan's and walked her back into the house.

❖

Anxious and preoccupied, Evan felt increasingly on edge as they approached the trailhead but put it down to too little sleep and too much coffee. The breeze was up this morning, briskly coming across the water and rustling faintly through the trees. She blew a strand of hair out of her mouth as she fastened her eyes on the gravel trail and breathed in the sound of the quiet.

Lifting her eyes to the horizon, she watched a giant blue heron, ungainly looking and yet remarkably graceful as it flew past in the distance before disappearing into the trees. More slowly, she opened herself up to the mournful cries of the gulls, the whisper of the waves lapping against the pebbled shore, the sound of the ferry horn blowing in the distance.

But her throat felt tight, her pulse erratic, and her hands were still trembling from an excess of nervous energy. She was aware Kelsey and Alex were waiting and felt a surge of impatience to get going. But she forced herself to focus on her breathing. Inhaling slowly, deeply, counting to five and then exhaling just as slowly. She repeated the process several times, centering herself with each repetition as she emptied her mind. And then she began to run, slow and steady.

For the first few minutes, she simply enjoyed her surroundings and the feel of the warm air. But inevitably, thoughts of Khalid crept in. When she had encountered him on the trail only days earlier, she had thought him to be nothing more than a creation of her overwrought imagination. Now she knew he was real and felt the stirrings of anger. With each minute, each hour, each day that passed, the horror of her time in Afghanistan receded. But Khalid kept bringing it all back with a vengeance.

She pulled an article she'd once read from the recesses of her memory, something about an age-old tribal ritual of smudging, used for centuries by the indigenous people of both North and South America. The process, as she recalled, was meant to cleanse people, places, or objects of negative energies by burning certain herbs. Sage, cedar, sweetgrass. In theory, the smoke attached itself to negative energy and took all negative influences with it as it dissipated. Perhaps that was what was needed here. Perhaps once this was over, she and Tate could look into having the local shaman visit and cleanse their beautiful island home of Khalid's malevolent energy.

"Are you doing okay?"

Kelsey's question and the faint note of concern in her voice brought Evan back to reality. She realized she'd been setting a pace much faster than was smart, but as she glanced over her shoulder, she was pleased to see Kelsey was having no problem keeping up. Alex on the other hand—she wasn't quite as sure.

"I'm doing good," she replied without breaking her stride. And she was. Her leg was holding up and not causing her any grief. "What about you, Alex? Are you doing okay?"

Alex grunted. "How is it possible that you can run better than me when I know you've got all those staples and things holding your knee together?"

"I had a good surgeon."

Kelsey snorted. "You had a great surgeon. And if you damage my colleague's work by running too hard too soon, there'll be hell to pay, Commander Kane. I've got connections. I'll make sure you pay double if you need a second procedure."

Evan laughed, relishing the moment, the physical exertion, and the company. But she wisely decided not to push her luck and slowed her pace. For the next few minutes, she maintained a steady pace without speaking, using the time to shore up her defenses.

It worked, but only until they approached the hill where she'd spotted Khalid. Her heartbeat began to accelerate and every nerve ending in her body went on high alert.

But she needn't have worried.

As they rounded the bend, it was quickly apparent they were the only ones using the trail. No one was standing on the hilltop. No one lurked in the shadows cast by the trees. And only the waves and the birds disturbed the stillness of the morning.

They stopped as they reached the loop—the point in the trail that circled the hill and briefly wound its way before bringing them back to where they'd started. Alex blew out a long pained breath and sat on the remains of an ancient-looking stone wall, breathing hard, while Evan wandered closer to the shore.

She watched the sun dance on the water and remembered all the reasons she had wanted to move here. Buy the house on the point. Tate's house.

In her mind, this had always seemed a good place to sink roots and become part of a vibrant community. She had fallen in love with the island—the incredible beauty and simple pleasures it offered. Being here with Tate just made it better. It didn't really matter who'd bought the house.

"It's a beautiful spot, isn't it?" Kelsey said as she came up beside her.

"It's quite possibly my favorite spot on the island." Evan breathed out a sigh. "The first time I stood here, the view literally took my breath away. I remember it was fall, the air was cool and clean, and it was so unbelievably peaceful. I didn't think places like this existed anymore, and I'd like to think this would be a good place to heal and begin again."

"And you'd be absolutely right. Other than one little sociopath momentarily darkening the horizon, this place is perfect."

"Maybe. I'm not sure you're aware but I wanted to buy the house Tate now owns," she said. "Funny how things work out sometimes. I keep thinking of the line in that old song—something about getting what you need."

"The Rolling Stones, nineteen sixty-nine," Kelsey answered with a smile.

Evan grinned. "I knew I liked you for a reason."

"Because I like music from the sixties? And here I thought it was for my razor-sharp wit and my amazing medical skills."

"That too." Evan's smile faded just a little. "I've not forgotten how you helped me in Germany."

"I did nothing I wouldn't be prepared to do again. And just so we're clear, in return you had your father bring me home in style and days early. In my book, I'd say that makes us even."

"You drive a hard bargain, but okay." Evan laughed. "That reminds me, I've been meaning to ask about whatever brought you over to our little island paradise. I realize I'm a little slow on the uptake, but I *am* aware you just got home. I hope my mess with Khalid isn't intruding on a romantic reunion for you and Jenna."

"Not to worry. Actually, I came over to see about a job yesterday. There's an opening at the clinic in town, and although I just got home, the opportunity's just too good to pass up, since it includes an option to buy in as a partner. After meeting the other two doctors, Jenna and I talked about it. And since I'm pretty sure I'm going to take it, we thought we'd spend a few days house hunting."

"You mean we could end up as neighbors?"

"Yeah. That's the only downside I can see."

Evan bumped her shoulder against Kelsey's and they both laughed. Lifting her foot onto a knee-high boulder by the water's edge, she stretched her calf muscle.

"Your leg okay?"

"Yeah, just trying to stay loose." She dropped her foot back to the trail. "What about Jenna's practice? I was kind of hoping…" She broke off, uncertain how to continue.

Kelsey's expression told her she knew exactly what Evan was hoping for. "Actually, we'd like to find a place that lets us set up her practice as a home office. And for a lot of her patients, getting here will be easier than trying to get to her current office in Seattle."

"That's good."

"Jenna will see you wherever and whenever you're comfortable, Evan. And between all of us—Tate, your brother and his partner, Jenna and me—none of us are going to let this situation spin you out of control or see you hurt again."

"I don't want anyone else getting hurt, either."

"You let us worry about that."

Evan gave a grudging smile and nodded just as Alex came up to them.

"Everything okay?" he asked as he passed a water bottle to her.

Aware Alex had deliberately hung back, giving her the chance to talk to Kelsey, Evan felt a surge of tenderness. "Everything's good." She took a long drink, then recapped the bottle and handed it back. "Thanks. Ready to hit the trail?"

Both Alex and Kelsey nodded and they set off at an easy pace.

With Jenna's and Nick's help, Tate quickly cleaned up the dishes and tidied the kitchen. She then slipped away to take a shower while Jenna went back to the inn to get a change of clothes for both herself and Kelsey. After thinking about it for only an instant, Tate invited her to check out and bring everything back to the house, but she left the decision up to Jenna.

Twenty minutes later, Tate walked out onto the deck and let her mind sift through the events of the previous evening before making the call to the sheriff's department. As soon as she identified herself, she was transferred to the sheriff himself. Tom Foley had obviously done his homework since speaking with Alex. He'd probably also had a visit from a couple of FBI agents.

He listened without interruption and asked a few sharp questions. After ascertaining there was no immediate danger, he promised to be out with a couple of deputies within the hour.

She was pleased when Jenna returned shortly after she finished her call. She had changed into jeans and a T-shirt and was holding two small suitcases. "I'm taking you at your word that Kelsey and I will be more of a help than a hindrance," Jenna said as she placed the suitcases on the floor. "I know things must be tough for you right now, and I don't want to add any more pressure."

"I'm just trying to wrap my head around what happened last night. What John Anderson said and what it might mean. How it might play out. I just want to keep Evan safe."

Jenna nodded. "The sheriff's department can help you in that regard, ideally by protecting Evan and capturing Khalid. I believe I can help keep her grounded so Khalid doesn't do more emotional damage than he's already done."

Tate's throat tightened, and for a moment, all she could do was smile gratefully. "That may be even more important as this plays out. So thank you."

Nick moved past them as he took the luggage up to the guest room while Jenna followed Tate into the kitchen and helped mix a pitcher of fresh ice tea. When it was ready, they carried the tea and a tray with glasses out to the deck where they joined Nick and sat down to wait.

A quick glance at her watch told her the sheriff was due at any moment, and as she listened to the ocean sigh, Tate found herself wishing Evan would hurry back. She could feel her anxiety ratchet up a few notches, and she shivered against a sudden gust of wind. Picking up a sweatshirt Evan had left on the deck, she wrapped it tightly around her shoulders although she wasn't actually cold.

"She'll be fine," Jenna said sympathetically. "Trust me. Kelsey connected with Evan on some fundamental level when they met in Germany and she's not about to let anything happen to her."

"Neither will Alex," Nick added. "No matter how much time has passed, he still feels responsible. So he's not about to stand by and let her get hurt again."

Some of the intensity Tate had been feeling abated as she focused on what Nick was saying. "Evan would be horrified to think Alex still feels that way."

Nick shrugged and grinned wryly at Jenna. "Do you offer a family discount plan?"

❖

The return loop was easier. Running downhill with the wind at their back always was. They had just made the downward turn to rejoin the main trail when Evan stopped abruptly.

"What the hell—" Alex said as he stumbled into her. He took two additional steps forward before Evan grabbed him by the arm and halted his progress. "What is that?"

"Don't touch it," Evan replied, her voice tight and low as she bent over and pulled out her gun from the ankle holster she was wearing.

"And what the hell is that?" Alex repeated, pointing at the gleaming weapon in her hand.

"Hush, Alex." Holding the gun firmly in both hands, Evan looked around cautiously but could see no one. Nothing seemed untoward—other than the hilt of a knife planted in the middle of the gravel trail a few feet in front of them.

"I'm pretty sure that wasn't there when we came by a little while ago," Kelsey said softly. "Do you think he's still nearby watching us?"

"I'm not sure." Bile rose in her throat, and Evan broke off abruptly as she tried to gather her thoughts. She looked around and listened for a moment longer, but there was nothing to indicate Khalid was close. The birds still sang, the gulls still circled overhead, and as near as she could tell, the bushes on the side of the trail didn't appear to have been disturbed. Nothing looked as if someone had pushed through in an effort to quickly get off the trail.

She lowered her weapon, then took a couple of steps forward and pulled out the knife staked into the ground. It was lethal looking, sharpened to a finely honed edge, its finish marred with brownish stains.

"If we had those stains tested, what odds would you give me that they would match your blood type?" Kelsey asked.

Evan could only shrug as she returned her gun to its holster. "Hard to say. The knife looks about right. For all I know it could be the same one he used on me, but that doesn't mean anything. He wants me to think it's the same one for the same reason he made sure it has what look like bloodstains."

"Why's that?"

"To frighten me."

"Is it working?"

"Oh yeah."

Alex nodded glumly. "Me too."

"I guess it's unanimous," Kelsey added softly.

He watched from a short distance and couldn't help himself. He laughed. And although he knew he was taking an unnecessary risk, he slipped through the dense grove of trees, creeping closer through the underbrush until he could see her clearly.

Only then did he stop, holding his breath as he listened.

Good. He wanted her afraid.

For an instant, the memory of his first time cutting her filled his mind. He remembered watching her blood seep, and seeing both pain and fear in her eyes. But apart from a strangled sound at the back of her throat, she'd said nothing, choosing instead to hold herself rigid. Fighting the pain even as the full effect of his handiwork slowly took effect. Denying him the pleasure of hearing her cry out.

The memory still had the ability to make him angry and he pushed it away, satisfied with knowing he could take her right now. Neither her brother nor the woman with them appeared to be armed, and he was a very good shot.

He knew he could take them both out quickly. The second one would be dead before the first even hit the ground. Before the commander had time to reach for the gun in her ankle holster.

But not just yet.

Soon, he promised. Soon he would have her again, and this time, she would not deny him. He would hear her pain. And as he looked into her eyes, he would know the instant she realized she was his. His creation. His to control.

Even then he would not stop. Not until the moment when she begged him for release. Only then would he finish it.

CHAPTER THIRTY-ONE

Sheriff Tom Foley turned out to be a broad-shouldered, solidly built man with a strong jaw and dark curly hair, cropped short. His square face hinted at a tough attitude while his clear, steady eyes appeared to miss nothing. He was also probably younger than he looked, possibly in his midforties, but there was a competent assurance about him that penetrated the fear that had saturated Tate since meeting John Anderson the previous evening.

The two deputies who had accompanied him were younger, one a beefy looking man with a ruddy complexion, the other a slim, dark-haired woman. Both looked to be in their late twenties and were dressed in identical sharply pressed uniforms. They followed their boss onto the deck and maintained a respectful distance.

But the sheriff seemed to have no reservations and exhibited no concern of running afoul of the Kane family influence. When Evan reappeared, fresh from her shower with her hair still dripping onto her shoulders, he allowed her only the space of two deep breaths before he cleared his throat and began asking questions.

Alex had described the sheriff as a straight shooter. But while Alex's opinion served to reassure her, the sheriff's approach bothered Tate almost from the start. He stood too close, barely giving Evan room to breathe. And the unsmiling expression on his face never changed.

Instinctively, Tate found herself edging closer, caught between frustration and anxiety, ready to end the interview at a moment's notice. "Evan—"

But Evan casually reached for her hand and held her back. "It's okay," she said, then resumed answering all the sheriff's questions with a calm and directness Tate had come to expect of her. Still, for every answer she gave, there were more questions, and as it continued, Tom Foley's conversation with Evan began to more closely resemble an interrogation.

Perhaps it was unintended. Perhaps, being a cop, Foley simply couldn't help himself. But as time went on, the questions began to repeat themselves and sounded a discordant note for Tate. Evan's smile had long since faded and her fatigue was becoming more pronounced, enough that both Kelsey and Jenna moved closer as well and were keeping an eye on her.

Trust your instincts, Tate reminded herself as she battled back both the tug of trepidation and the need to intervene. If she hoped to protect Evan from Khalid, they would need the kind of help only law enforcement could provide. She just wasn't certain what it would take to make Tom Foley less confrontational and turn him into more of an ally.

She'd give the man marks for the surprisingly gentle manner in which he handled questioning Evan about her captivity and her prior dealings with Khalid in Afghanistan. But he showed no such sensitivity once the discussion moved on to Evan's conversation with John Anderson the previous evening and her sightings of Khalid, both in Seattle and again on the trail.

Ignoring everyone else present, Foley kept his gaze pinned on Evan. A flicker of impatience showed on his face as he listened intently. Assessing, probing. Exposing nerves.

"Commander Kane, I know what you've told me," he said. "Now I need you to tell me again. If we're going to find him, I need to understand why this Khalid would follow you from Afghanistan. And if we're going to stop him, I need to understand how badly he wants you and how much he's willing to risk to get what he wants."

"If you're looking for insight into Khalid's psyche, I don't have it to give you. Perhaps Jenna can help, she's the psychiatrist." Evan's voice remained calm but it had become cool. A little remote with just a hint of irritation. "All I can do is tell you he's here. On the island. And I'll do whatever I have to do."

She stopped and left the rest of her thought unsaid.

There was a long silence while Evan stared at Foley and watched him leap to conclusions before latching onto the right one. "I got that when you asked me to facilitate getting you a concealed carry permit," he said as he met her gaze. "More to the point, I've already spoken with the two FBI agents who are heading up the search for this Khalid. Problem with those boys is they want to keep their jobs and they're afraid of what your mother will do if anything happens to you."

"And you don't care about holding on to your job. Is that it, Sheriff?"

Foley shrugged. "Being sheriff's different from being an FBI agent. The people of this county voted me in on a four-year term and they can just as easily vote me out. Maybe I'm wrong, but I don't think there's a whole lot your mother can do about that." His voice indicated he didn't particularly care. "And for as long as I'm doing the job, I have to tell you, I may not be clear about Khalid's intentions, but I don't believe having more people running around with guns is the way to go."

Evan swore softly. "Are you deliberately trying to piss me off or are you just obtuse?" She ran a hand through her hair and gave Foley a long, hard look, then produced the knife they'd found embedded in the gravel trail. Both deputies reacted almost immediately to the appearance of the knife in her hand. Their bodies stiffened in surprise and their hands moved in automatic response toward their holstered weapons. The sheriff only narrowed his eyes, his lips thinning as he watched her with renewed interest.

Evan ignored them all and simply tossed the knife on the table beside her.

"You want to know how much Khalid is willing to risk?" she asked softly. "Then deal with this, Sheriff Foley. Maybe he was good enough to leave his prints on the knife so you can confirm his identity. Then again, maybe not. All I know is he placed this knife where he knew we would find it this morning, so it would seem rather obvious he wants me to know he's here. That he's watching. And that he's coming for me so he can finish what he started in Afghanistan."

Foley's expression was impatient. "You're speculating."

"No, actually, I'm not. I'm the one who's experienced Khalid up close and personal and I'm simply stating the facts."

She felt as much as saw Foley's eyes briefly skim over the cuts still clearly visible on her upper arm, the tightness around his mouth the only hint of any reaction. He knew, she realized and turned away.

She watched a cormorant suddenly dive into the water just beyond the deck, a delicate splash leaving barely a ripple. And just as suddenly, Evan felt as if she'd gained some insight. "Marine Corps," she guessed. "Am I right?"

If Foley was surprised, he hid it well. He gave a terse nod. "Spent some time in Iraq." He bent down and knocked on his right leg. "Got sergeant's stripes while doing my second tour, but it cost me eight months in rehab and my lower right leg."

"I'm sorry. That had to be rough."

"No rougher than getting blown out of the sky and being held captive for four months."

Evan bit her lip. Her shoulder muscles tensed and she felt Tate squeeze her hand as she nodded her head tightly in acknowledgment.

"But you want to know what's really rough, Commander?"

"What's that?"

"What's rough is having a son doing his first deployment on the *Carl Vinson* and a daughter who can't wait to finish high school so she can follow him, instead of going to college like her mama wants her to do." He spoke with a father's mix of love and pride. "My wife's barely speaking to me. She never gave a damn that not all of me came home to her. But she says my kids think I'm some kind of fool hero because of it and now they want to follow in my footsteps. She says it's my fault."

Evan's lips curved in a gentle smile as her eyes closed. "My mother never wanted me to enlist, either. I did it anyway, for reasons far too simple and complicated to get into right now. But in hindsight, maybe she had a point."

❖

Something had changed.

Tate could feel the difference as she watched Evan tilt her head back, her face for the moment in repose as she turned it toward the sun. The sunlight illuminated the contours of her face. Her long lashes cast shadows on her cheeks, while the breeze off the water blew her hair.

She knew Evan had pulled back, was regrouping and trying to focus on what she needed to do next. But while she might appear relaxed, her face was still too pale and her fingers were twisted together, sending clear signs of her agitation.

Moving behind her and placing her hands on Evan's shoulders, Tate began to massage the knotted muscles she found beneath the silky skin, stroking away the tension. Evan hung her head forward, presenting the back of her neck to give Tate better access, and after a moment or two, she let out a low groan and began to relax beneath Tate's touch.

Several feet away, Foley watched. And if he glimpsed the cuts on Evan's back as her tank top shifted, he didn't allow it to show. He remained controlled, focused, leaning against the deck railing, hands buried in the pockets of his uniform pants. His stance was casual, but Tate could see he was watching Evan with an intense level of scrutiny, while she pointedly ignored him.

Both sides appeared to be waiting for something. A word. A sign.

Finally Foley took the lead, attempting to end the impasse with a suggestion.

Tate rolled her eyes and sighed. She stopped what she was doing and moved to take up position beside Evan, keeping one hand on her shoulder while waiting for the response she knew was coming.

Five seconds stretched into twenty, then into thirty and finally into a minute. "Sheriff Foley, I appreciate your suggestion," Evan said, opening her eyes after her long silence. Her voice was low and cool, her tone gave nothing away, but Tate recognized the flicker of annoyance in the set of her chin.

She then did what Tate expected her to do. She refused Tom Foley's recommendation that she consent to being placed into protective custody. She wasn't combative, just firm. She was also polite, but adamant. It was never going to happen.

"What happened in Afghanistan has already cost me more than four months of my life. I'm not prepared to give up another minute. No matter how well intentioned the reasons."

But Foley was undeterred and it quickly became apparent his idea of compromise was having people agree with him. "In that case, Commander Kane, you're leaving me no alternative but to post deputies to watch over you twenty-four/seven until this gets resolved because I'm inclined to agree with you. Everything I've learned tells me this Khalid is coming after you, and I'm guessing he's going to do it soon."

Evan shrugged and looked out over the water with eyes that seemed tired rather than angry. "You do what you have to do, Sheriff. But if I'm going to be tripping over you and your deputies in the dark, then at least call me Evan. The navy declared me dead some months ago and being called Commander is a constant reminder."

As Evan turned away from the view toward Foley, Tate saw they had reached a crossroad. "But just so we're clear, this house and the property around it belong to Tate. She'll have to agree to any kind of law enforcement presence before your people step on this property again without an invitation. Otherwise, I will personally introduce you to both my parents."

Foley swore softly and succinctly. "Your father's the lawyer, isn't he?"

"Actually, both my parents are lawyers," Evan said idly.

As he turned slowly toward her, Tate almost felt sorry for him. Almost.

"You're going to want to think this through very carefully then, Ms. McKenna," he said. "Because everything this Khalid fellow's doing is intentional. He's got to know the CIA and FBI are looking for him. But he still managed to get back into this country and allowed Commander Kane—Evan—to see him. He wants her to know he's coming."

Tate felt a shiver sweep through her. She looked at Evan but could see no indication, nothing to give away what she was thinking or feeling. Nothing that said what she wanted. After waiting a moment, she cleared her throat. "You've got to know I'm going to be willing to do anything to ensure Evan stays safe. And if that means filling my house with deputies from the county sheriff's department or FBI agents, I'll be more than happy to do so," she said. "But I'm not naive enough to think it'll be that simple. Why don't you tell us what you're proposing, Sheriff? And what you think we need to do."

Some of the stiffness eased from Foley's body language. "For starters, call me Tom. As for what we need to do, the first thing is for Evan to help us determine what Khalid Anderson looks like today. The FBI's looking for him based on a grainy photo taken by the CIA about ten months ago in Pakistan. If we have a better idea about what he currently looks like, we can cover traffic coming onto the island via the ferry and the bridge. We can also put out a BOLO—a be-on-the-lookout—in case he tries to hire a boat or a floatplane."

"Not to shoot down any theory you may be working on, but it sounds like you're assuming he's staying off-island," Evan said. "Let's remember he was here on the trail early this morning. Isn't he just as likely to be somewhere on the island? Maybe camping in the woods and biding his time doing reconnaissance while he familiarizes himself with the area? He lived with insurgents in Afghanistan. He's not going to need creature comforts."

Foley nodded and gave her a grudging smile. "True enough. We'll increase patrols through the campgrounds and start checking with the local grocery stores and fast food outlets once we have a composite drawing. He'll need to eat, and we can see if anyone's served someone matching his description in recent days. In the meantime, we'll see about expediting your gun permit. You do know how to shoot, I trust?"

The corners of Evan's mouth twitched with amusement. "Well, at one time I managed to keep everything I fired in the black, but it's been a while since I've used the Sig. At a guess, I'm probably going to be a bit rusty. But if you can point me in the direction of the local shooting range, I'll get some practice in. Until then, I'll try not to accidently shoot you or any of your deputies in the ass."

The air was still warm in the fast fading light as the sun dipped in the horizon and bled into the ocean. Sitting on the deck, Evan lay down the sketches she'd been working on for the better part of a couple of hours. The act seemed to serve as a signal to her brain and she felt the tension that had been churning inside her, haunting her all day, slowly start to dissipate.

After the intensity of her meeting with Tom Foley, she had been more than content to tune out the world while she worked on the sketches. Now she had finished what she needed to do and could begin to decompress. One layer at a time.

She turned her eyes skyward and watched a pair of hawks soaring on the thermals. As she watched their graceful flight, she envied the birds their undisputed freedom to ascend into the endless blue. It was easier to dream about flying than contemplate the reality surrounding her.

Easier than thinking about Khalid.

She had brought him to Tate's doorstep. And her continued presence here was putting Tate at risk. Not only Tate, but Alex and Nick. Kelsey and Jenna. They were all in danger as long as Khalid was hunting her. And while she knew that somewhere on the grounds Foley and his deputies were installing enhancements to Tate's security system, she wondered if it would be enough. If anything would be enough.

Earlier, they had reviewed the existing security protecting the house and Foley had indicated they would need to cover the perimeter of the property as well. Kind of crazy, Evan thought, given the abundance of wildlife in the area. They'd be constantly setting off the motion detectors.

But Foley said he'd arranged for a cousin to come and install wireless cameras. State of the art, high tech gadgets he said would allow for streaming and remote viewing over the Internet.

"In the event a camera's activated, you'll be able to pan remotely and immediately verify what kind of wildlife's tripped the system."

"You mean whether it's the four-legged variety versus two?" Tate had asked with a grin.

The sound of Tate's bright laugh broke through her somber mood. She was talking to Jenna, and they were both smiling at something one of the deputies had said. Evan liked hearing Tate's laughter. As always, it brought a responding smile to her face and she found her mood lifting.

As it happened, Tate chose that moment to glance in her direction. Catching Evan's gaze, she casually sauntered over. "How're you doing?"

"Don't ask. Should I be over there so Deputy Pike can show me how to operate the new security system?"

"No, you don't need to worry about it. We can talk tomorrow about the new technological wizardry Tom's had installed—that'll be soon enough to deal with it. For now, just relax. You've already had one hell of a day." Tate searched her face for a minute. "Can I get you anything for that headache?"

Evan shook her head. Catching Tate's hand, she pulled her closer. "I can't think of a single thing I might need that I don't already have right here."

"Flatterer." Tate laughed, but as she continued to study Evan's face, her smile dimmed, then faded completely. "If it's not the headache, then what's wrong?"

"Nothing—just restless, I guess."

Evan stood up, started to move away and then swore softly as she spun back around, her mouth instinctively seeking and finding Tate's. And if Tate was hesitant, Evan was not. She groaned. All she could think of was how good Tate felt pressed against her.

She deepened the kiss, all passion and heat, driven by an urgency she couldn't begin to explain and fueled by a fire she couldn't extinguish. And then it became difficult just to drag air into her lungs.

Several heartbeats later, she pulled back, suddenly remembering they were not alone.

"God, I'm so sorry. I shouldn't have kissed you like that." She ran a hand through her hair in a distracted gesture. "All of a sudden it's like I don't know who I am or what I'm doing."

"I thought it felt like you knew exactly what you were doing," Tate teased her gently, her eyes still half-closed with pleasure. "Now tell me what's wrong."

Evan swallowed as an unnamed fear tightened her throat. She tried to put words to her feelings, words Tate would understand. "You mean more to me than anyone ever has or ever could. I don't want anything to happen to you."

"Why would you think something's going to happen to me?"

"Khalid. He's not exactly predictable. He's driven by the adrenaline rush he gets from hurting people, and"—she reached with one hand and touched Tate's face—"I've never been more in love with you than I am right at this moment. Until tomorrow, when I know I'll love you even more. But I'm afraid if I stay here, I'm only going to put you at risk. I feel I'm being selfish wanting to be here with you, and I think maybe I should just get the hell out of here until this thing with Khalid is over and he's been dealt with."

An odd expression flickered across Tate's face and then it became suffused with warmth and gentleness. "Evan, love, that's not going to happen. I've got your back, remember?" She smiled uncertainly. "You do know that, don't you?"

"Intellectually, I believe you. The problem is emotionally I'm barely in control."

"That's okay," Tate said, smiling. "You don't always have to be in control. In fact, sometimes I prefer it when you're losing control."

"Maybe you want to rethink that. Do you realize I was this close"—she held up two fingers, less than an inch apart—"to throwing you over my shoulder and carrying you off to bed?"

Tate raised a brow and started to laugh. "How incredibly Neanderthal. Did you think I would have stopped you?"

"No, but my leg probably would have collapsed."

"Oh." Tate sounded almost disappointed. "Another time? Perhaps when your leg is stronger?"

Feeling relief wash over her, Evan drew the first deep breath she had taken since finding the knife on the trail that morning. Pulling Tate gently into her arms, she held her close, breathing in her warm familiar scent. "This isn't going to be easy."

"The important things seldom are. All that matters is I love you," Tate whispered and their lips came together before Evan could say anything else.

The sound of someone clearing their throat brought Tate back to the present. She wasn't certain how long she and Evan had stood on the deck, arms wrapped around each other. But slowly, bit by bit, the world slipped back into focus. The smell of the ocean, the rhythmic slapping of the waves against the pilings, the sound of voices as Alex and Jenna discussed the imagery in a particular painting he'd just finished.

"Sorry to disturb you again so soon. We're finished installing the cameras."

Turning within the shelter of Evan's arms, Tate came face-to-face with Tom Foley. "That's good," she said. "Do you need anything else?"

"I'm hoping we can set up a meeting with the forensic artist we use so we can get a composite of what Khalid looks like today." He glanced at Evan. "Or at least what he looked like when you last saw him."

"That won't be necessary." Evan reached for the sketch pad she'd left lying on the table. Opening it, she passed it to the sheriff. "You'll find several different renditions."

She paused and Tate reached for her hand. "When I knew him in Afghanistan, Khalid had long hair and a scraggly beard. When I saw him in Germany, his hair was short and he had a full beard. Outside the market in Seattle, he had dreadlocks—my guess is he added them to change his look again. In any case, he still had a beard, although it was much shorter. He still had the locks when I saw him on the trail, but he was clean shaven."

Foley leafed through the pad and looked at the sketches she'd made then whistled. "Well, I'll be damned."

"That's the advantage of working with an artist," Alex said softly as he came up behind Foley and stared at the numerous sketches she'd done. Tate edged closer and saw Evan had drawn Khalid in a combination of frontal poses and profiles.

There were versions with both short hair and long. Some bearded, others clean shaven. All different, but Tate realized she could still recognize the man by the shape of his mouth, the chillingly dark eyes. Somehow Evan had managed to capture on paper what were probably the most distinctive characteristics of Khalid's face.

"I've seen your brother's stuff at a gallery in Seattle," Foley said. "I can't understand most of it, but my wife Pam likes it. All I can tell you is—"

"Alex is the artist in this family," Evan said firmly.

"But quite clearly not the only artist." For an instant, Alex's eyes locked with Evan's. "Maybe we can do a joint show sometime in the spring. That would be awesome and it would give you enough time to get some pieces together, don't you think? We could set the West Coast art scene on its head."

"Alex—"

Tate squeezed Evan's hand again, felt it tremble, and sent Alex a pleading look.

Alex smiled. "We can talk about it later, when there isn't so much going on."

Tom Foley coughed awkwardly, staring at all three of them before reaching into his pocket He pulled out a business card and handed it to Evan. "I was also thinking—that is, this is how to reach me if you ever need to talk. Day or night."

"About what, Tom?"

"Life, death, flying machines. Anything and everything or nothing at all. Whatever you want. I won't mind if you wake me up." He looked out over the water. "The doctors tell me I've adjusted real well, but there are still days I feel pain in my right foot."

Evan seemed to understand.

"Things get bad from time to time, and there's this SEAL I met in rehab. Lives in Tucson. I call him sometimes and we talk. It helps," Foley said as he stepped back. "He reminds me to keep my focus on the here and now. Not to think back, or look too far ahead."

"Thanks." Evan started to tuck the card into her pocket. "I'll keep it in mind."

Tate took the card from Evan and placed it in her own pocket. "I'll put it by the phone." She then lifted Evan's arm and slipped under it, holding her close. Evan murmured something to her, but it was too low, too husky for Tate to clearly hear her. But the sentiment was clear and she burrowed closer, seeking and sharing warmth.

CHAPTER THIRTY-TWO

B y the time she crawled into bed, Evan was beyond exhausted. Maybe it was all the talk about Khalid and Afghanistan that had drained her. Maybe she was just tired from trying to deal with too many emotions on too little sleep. Maybe she needed a few hours of sleeping and laughing and loving to chase away the shadows.

Maybe.

She pressed close to Tate, burying her face against her neck, needing the reassurance that came from listening to her heartbeat. Halfway to sleep, she placed her hand on Tate's chest, touched the silky skin above her breasts, and sighed contentedly. And with Tate holding her, stroking her hair, she fell asleep.

The next time she opened her eyes, the gray half-light of the quiet early morning was beginning to seep through the window. She remained perfectly still, her heart pounding and her body taut, while she focused on the reassuring sound of Tate breathing next to her and absorbed the incredible comfort of Tate's arms wrapped around her.

Dreams, she thought ruefully, feeling as though she was still mired in them. Knowing she would not sleep again. But unlike most recent occasions, the dreams that had disturbed her and left her pulse racing had nothing to do with Khalid. Instead, they'd been filled with pleasure. Erotic fantasies. *Sweet Jesus.*

It was difficult to complain when the dreams had actually enabled her to sleep straight through the night. But they had also left her with an insatiable hunger and a deep-seated ache that bordered on physical pain.

She shifted uncomfortably on the bed. The incessant ache reminded her of all the times she'd tried to sleep on the *Nimitz,* in a rack six feet long by three feet wide, with nothing but dreams of Tate to get her through the lonely nights.

To survive the nights when she thought she'd go mad, when not at flight quarters she would go for a run on the flight deck. Otherwise she'd head for the gym where she lifted weights or logged endless miles on the treadmill.

And that's what she needed to do. Right now. Before she pounced on Tate like a ravenous, out-of-control teenager.

With her purpose clearly in mind, she began to ease out from under Tate's arm, which was draped across her midriff. But she'd managed to move only an inch or two when the arm suddenly tightened its hold on her.

"Where do you think you're going? It's still dark and it smells like rain."

"I…I need to go for a run."

Opening her eyes, Tate turned her head and looked at her in the dim light. "You're kidding me, right?"

Evan froze in place.

"Evan, darling, listen to me. Until this thing with Khalid is resolved, there will be no going for a run. Certainly not by yourself. I thought you understood that?"

"I do, but—"

"No buts, love. I know running is how you relax, but it's not safe. Not even if you drag those two deputies Tom left here and make them run with you." She stirred and stretched, then gave a soft sigh. "If you really need to exercise, give me a few minutes to properly wake up and get ready and I'll work out with you. Weights, treadmill, reformer, take your pick."

Feeling foolish, Evan hesitated and tried to choose her words. "It's all right. You need more sleep and it was a really dumb idea." She shifted onto her back and her breath caught when Tate began to slide her hand lower on her abdomen.

"God, you're strung tight this morning, aren't you? What's wrong? Bad dreams again? You're so—oh." Tate's eyes met Evan's and her expression changed. "Oh, baby, I'm certain I can do something that's far better for you as stress relief than exercise," she murmured before she rolled over. Her mouth skimmed over Evan's breast before making a hot wet path across her abdomen. Then lower still.

Evan shivered, ready to go off like a grenade at the slightest touch. Any control she'd been holding on to disintegrated. She tangled her hands in Tate's hair, whispered her name, and stopped thinking.

❖

Rainy days were perfect for thinking—and for being haunted by what had been and what might happen.

Tate didn't want to think about Khalid but found it impossible not to. She didn't want to think about what he'd already done to Evan, but she was reminded every time she saw the cuts on her arm and on her back. Or every time Evan screamed out his name while caught in the throes of a nightmare.

She didn't want to think about the danger that was still waiting somewhere nearby, but she was reminded of it every time the perimeter alarm system was triggered by a deer or coyote or racoon.

That was the problem with rainy days, she thought as she poured herself another cup of coffee. They gave a person too much time to think.

By midafternoon, the rain which had been falling steadily since dawn tapered off. The air was cool and there were tendrils of fog ghosting silently over the rocky landscape. Shifting restlessly, Tate moved closer to the window, scanning the deck until her eyes settled on Evan.

Evan had spent the morning with Kelsey and Tom Foley at a local shooting range. Now she was sitting on the deck in spite of the cool breeze blowing off the water, occasionally sketching and chatting comfortably with Kelsey. In that moment, she laughed at something Kelsey said, dimples flashing, and the sight warmed Tate.

This was more like the Evan she had first met. Relaxed. Happy. And if there was one thing she wished, it was to be able to ease the pain that too often shadowed her eyes. Tate continued to watch her through the window while she prowled around the kitchen and tried to decide what to make for dinner.

"She's doing fine, you know," Jenna said softly as she entered the room. "So much better than anyone has a right to expect, given what she's been through."

"I know. But I can't help it, I'm still worried." Mostly because she knew sometimes, despite everyone's best efforts, things didn't work out the way you wanted them to.

"That's only natural. If it helps, Kelsey said she was impressed with how Evan handled herself at the shooting range. More importantly, she said Evan managed to impress Sheriff Foley. Apparently he thinks Evan's a natural."

Great. Tate wasn't sure how she was supposed to feel about that. She glanced out the window again only to find Evan looking back at her, an expression both amused and faintly weary on her face. *I love you,* she mouthed.

"Evan loves Thai food," she murmured distractedly.

"Pardon?"

Tate smiled wryly at Jenna. "Sorry. I decided on Thai for dinner, but I'm going to have to take a quick run into town to pick up a few things." Especially since the number at the dinner table kept growing. "In the meantime, you should get Evan to show you—she did an amazing series of sketches of Kelsey. Wait until you see them."

"I'll make a point of checking them out. But you know you really shouldn't be going anywhere by yourself. To say nothing of how Evan will react when she hears about it."

It was, Tate recognized, more than a suggestion. But along with a flash of temper came the realization Jenna was right. She blew out a frustrated breath. "Actually, I was going to ask Nick to come along, but maybe I'll take Alex with me as well."

Just over two hours later, Tate sat outside the cozy home Alex and Nick shared, listening to the lonesome sound of the ferry horn while the stereo played something soft and haunting and perfectly suited to the gray, misty day. As she allowed her mind to wander, it drifted back to thoughts of Evan.

She knew loving Evan was as necessary to her as breathing. Okay, love and unmitigated lust, she thought wryly, feeling the warmth on her face that accompanied some of her thoughts. When all this turmoil with Khalid was behind them, she would take her away for a few days.

Maybe Fiji, where they could enjoy the soothing tropical breezes, where Evan could run barefoot in the sand, and where they could see Orion clearly in the night sky.

Or maybe Ibiza. Truthfully, Tate didn't really care where.

A slow smile swept across her face, and with images of Evan going native beneath the stars distracting her, she got out of her SUV, idly wondering what was taking Alex and Nick so long. Intent on hurrying them along so she could get back to Evan, she didn't have a chance to react when a gloved palm covered her mouth and her head was slammed against the side of the vehicle.

Evan jumped when she heard a woman's laugh. For an instant she'd thought it was Tate. But when she spun around with a ready smile, it was one of the deputies who stood there, talking to Tom Foley who had just arrived.

She released a low frustrated groan, felt but ignored Jenna's keen gaze scanning her face. It wasn't as though Tate had been gone a long time. It just seemed that way. And though she was probably being foolish, she picked up the phone and tried calling her cell phone.

Tate normally answered on the first ring. But there was no immediate answer, increasing her level of apprehension, and when the call went to voice mail, she hung up without leaving a message. Her breath quickening, she tried dialing Alex's number. Voice mail.

"Problem?"

Evan met Tom's gaze. "Tate just seems to have been gone longer than necessary and she's not answering her phone. It's probably nothing."

"She's with your brother, isn't she?"

"Alex never remembers to charge the battery on his phone. And Nick refuses to carry one. Says if someone really wants to talk to him, they can find him and talk to him face-to-face."

"Makes perfect sense to me," Tom said gruffly, but his cop eyes narrowed. "Where were they going?"

"They went into town to pick up some groceries," Jenna said. "But they were also planning to stop by Alex and Nick's house to pick up a couple of things before coming back."

"Where does your brother live?" Tom asked. His tone was casual. A moment later, he contacted and instructed an unseen deputy to run a quick check. "You're right. It's probably nothing, but we might as well make sure."

People believe what comforts them, Evan thought. But she wasn't deceived by the sheriff's nonchalance. A moment later it no longer mattered as Nick's battered truck pulled into the driveway.

Moving to intercept it, she saw Alex stumble out of the vehicle before it had stopped moving, his face pale, his eyes wide and filled with dread.

"Evan?" His voice sounded uncharacteristically strained, harsh and laced with panic as he faltered. "Tate's gone."

Evan's world tilted. *Please, make this a dream.*

In the next instant, she caught Alex by the arms and held him until he was steady. "Easy, Alex. Calm down and tell me what's happened."

His voice came back to her in a mere whisper of breath and sorrow. "He's got her. Khalid got Tate."

Hope shattered as Evan felt the chill of Alex's words. Releasing a harsh breath, she held on to her brother, vaguely aware of Kelsey and Jenna moving to stand beside her.

"Alex? What's going on?"

She heard Tom Foley's question as if from a distance. Knew she was holding Alex's arm too tight and had to force herself to loosen her grip. Concentrating on Alex helped.

"Take a deep breath, Alex. Nice and slow," she said softly. "Now tell us what happened."

Alex tried to comply, she could see that, but it was readily apparent he couldn't do it. Clearly seeing his partner's distress, Nick filled the blank spaces.

"We knew Kelsey and Jenna would be going home tomorrow, and Alex didn't want you and Tate to be alone. He asked if I was okay with staying here until Khalid was dealt with. Of course I said yes, and we decided the best thing was to drop him off at the house to pack some things for us while I went into town with Tate for supplies." He licked his lips and started to breathe more quickly. "Jesus…"

"Keep going, Nick," Tom encouraged. "Take your time."

"Alex was supposed to be waiting for us on the porch, but he wasn't there when we pulled up. I told Tate he probably got caught up in some painting…he gets distracted sometimes. I said I'd go in and hurry him along while Tate waited."

He closed his eyes and swallowed. "We weren't very long, just a few minutes, when we heard what sounded like a car kicking up stones in the driveway. We ran out, but Tate's Lexus was already gone." He opened his eyes.

Evan kept her gaze fastened on Nick through sheer will and tried to ignore the sudden dryness in her mouth. "And Tate?"

Nick shook his head.

"By the time we got Nick's keys and got his truck started, there was no sign of where they could have gone," Alex murmured. "I'm so sorry, Evan. She shouldn't have been alone. It's my fault."

"No it isn't." *No, it's my fault.* She looked away, her mind screaming.

"Evan?" Jenna murmured. "You're not breathing."

Evan released Alex, fisted her hands, and took a deep breath. Then another. She turned away, could hear Tom speaking on the phone, but couldn't discern what he was saying. A minute later, she felt him approach. He tilted his head and studied her. And whether military or cop, she recognized the look.

"What is it, Tom?"

"The two boys from the FBI are in town. The fog's too thick right now, but as soon as it clears enough, they'll get a chopper up and see if they can spot Tate's vehicle. In the meantime, they're going to check some of the campgrounds. I've got some of my deputies helping. It's not a lot, but until we get some reinforcements, it's all we can do."

"Thanks for letting me know."

"I'll keep you updated as much as possible. But I've got to tell you, Khalid could be anywhere by now."

Evan shivered. "I disagree. He's nearby."

"What makes you say that?"

"I can feel him." As surely as she could feel every cut he gave her. A frown furrowed the sheriff's brow. "What—"

"He wants me off balance, Tom. That's why he grabbed Tate." Her voice was wound tight with the same tension that held her shoulders in a rigid line. "But it's me he wants, so he won't have gone far. Trust me on that. Timing's everything and Khalid's obsessive. He's not finished dealing with me. And no matter what game he's playing, he won't be satisfied with Tate."

"Then he'll contact you. When he does, we should be able to pinpoint the signal tower and roughly calculate his location. It's not that big an island."

Evan stared down at her hands as she nodded. She reached for and squeezed Alex's hands for a moment, then let Jenna take over, leading him to a chair where he slumped boneless beside Nick while Kelsey brought them each a drink.

Knowing she needed to gain control over the fear welling inside her, Evan walked in the opposite direction and ran a trembling hand through her hair.

"We'll find her," Tom said as he came up behind her. "We'll get her back."

Turning, she held his gaze then lifted her chin in a slight gesture of agreement. "We have to," she said, as she added a silent, anguished prayer.

Please. Oh, please.

Because Tate was her touchstone. It was the thought of Tate that had enabled her to endure her captivity and without her, there would be no life for her to reclaim.

Chapter Thirty-three

Sitting on the deck, Evan frowned. Angry at herself for almost falling apart, she searched the mist hoping to find an answer to the question she kept asking herself.

Could she have done anything differently?

She hadn't taken a full breath since Alex and Nick had brought the news of Tate's disappearance. Because in spite of Tom's confidence, she was afraid. That Khalid wouldn't contact her. That he would hurt Tate. That they wouldn't find Tate in time.

"You're getting wet sitting out here."

Evan shrugged uncomfortably and pushed a hand through her hair, dragging it out of her eyes. "I don't mind. I like the rain."

"Good thing, since you're going to live in this area," Kelsey said and handed her a cup of coffee. "But you don't need to get chilled on top of everything else. Tate won't like it if she finds you haven't been taking care of yourself."

No, she wouldn't like it, Evan thought as she watched the steam rising from the cup. But Tate wouldn't say anything. It wasn't her style. Instead, she'd tell her to take a long, hot shower and help her change into dry clothes before feeding her soup and chocolate. Like the day she'd encountered Khalid on the trail.

She remained lost in thought until she heard heavy footsteps on the deck and turned to see Tom approaching. Something was different, but she couldn't read his expression. Rising swiftly to her feet, she took two steps toward him. "What's happened?"

"Tate's SUV was spotted on a side road near the bridge to the peninsula."

Evan's throat constricted. Dizzy with relief, she swayed slightly, felt Kelsey's hand on her arm holding her steady. "And Tate?"

"I'm sorry, we don't know yet. It looks like Anderson may have pulled off the road to wait until it got dark before trying to make it off the island. For the moment, we're keeping an eye on the vehicle and the FBI agents are on their way. I'm heading out to join them, but I'm leaving two guys parked out front to keep an eye on things here. Just in case."

"Why bother? I'm coming with you."

"No, you're not. Until we have Anderson in custody, you remain at risk, and I won't have you walking into what's likely a hostile situation."

A muscle twitched at the side of her jaw and Evan fought to quell the scream building inside her. Why couldn't Tom understand? She wanted to be there when Khalid was taken down. But more importantly, she needed to see for herself Tate was safe. "Damn it, Tom, he's got Tate. I need to be there."

Kelsey placed a hand on her shoulder, squeezing gently. "Tom's right, Evan, you need to stay here. I'll go with him and make sure Tate's all right then bring her back to you." She then turned toward Tom and added quickly, "If anyone's hurt, you're going to need medical assistance. I'm a doctor and just retired from military service, making me a far better option than any of the local EMTs."

Tom hesitated for only an instant before agreeing tersely. "All right, but you do what I tell you. And we need to leave now."

Evan swallowed, feeling torn, uncertain. "Kelsey…"

Kelsey gave her a quick hug and whispered, "I'll bring her back to you, I promise. Could you let Jenna know where I've gone?"

Evan nodded and listened to the sounds of their footsteps receding on the deck as Tom and Kelsey walked away. Heard the car doors open, then slam. Turning, she watched until their taillights disappeared.

At first, Tate thought she was dreaming. No, not a dream, she realized. Shivering, she forced her eyes open and tried to focus. She was instantly blinded by a searing pain in her head. She was also bound, hand and foot, lying on her side in what appeared to be the cargo area of an SUV.

It was a minute before she tried to move again, and she was riding another wave of pain when it slowly came back to her. She remembered driving to Alex's house. Could remember waiting for Alex and Nick and getting out of the Lexus before being pitched forward into the car door. Then something struck her head and the rest of the world went black.

Fragments of other images swirled in her mind.

A soft voice talking. The sense of being in a moving vehicle. It was impossible to tell how long she'd been in a fog. But her last clear memory was from late afternoon and it was dark now. Minutes or hours?

Oh God, Evan will be frantic.

The thought of Evan's torment and the knowledge she was the cause of it sent her heart racing, and the pain in her head spiked unbearably. Fighting the moan in her throat, she clenched her jaw, aware she had begun to pant, hard and fast.

She swallowed her rage and fear and forced herself to take several slow, deep breaths. She needed to remain calm. She needed to be rational. And then she needed to get herself out of this mess and find her way back to Evan.

As she grew calmer, she began to think more clearly. There was no question in her mind Khalid was responsible for her current predicament. But she didn't know where he was or how long he'd been gone. All she knew for certain was she was alone in the back of a vehicle—her own vehicle, quite possibly, since driving an off-island vehicle would have made Khalid immediately identifiable to police—and that was a good thing. If she was right, somewhere in the cargo area was the tool kit she'd bought for emergencies. In it, along with a tire iron and assorted screwdrivers, was a small utility knife. And if her luck held out and she didn't cut off a finger, she just might be able to cut the rope binding her wrists before Khalid returned.

Working blindly, she wriggled and groped behind her until her hands brushed against a cold metal box. Opening it proved more of a challenge and success came with a price. All her movements had intensified the pain in her head. Bile rose in her throat, and it took several minutes of breathing through her mouth before she managed to conquer the nausea and was reasonably confident she wouldn't be sick.

Once she could move, she managed to get the knife out and manipulated it until she could feel it pressed against the rope binding her wrists, then got to work.

She felt an occasional sting, accompanied by the warm trickle of blood as the blade cut her, and she bit down hard on her lower lip. But she persevered, continuing to work on the ropes without faltering. She hadn't anticipated it would take so long for the rope to fray, and she began to fear Khalid would return before she succeeded. But then, suddenly, her hands were free.

Almost giddy with relief, ignoring the fiery needles shooting up her arms and into her shoulders, she grasped the knife in numb hands. With no time to lose, she bent over and cut the rope that bound her ankles.

She allowed herself only a moment to relish her victory before moving forward, badly wanting to find her keys dangling from the ignition. Her hopes were dashed when she saw the ignition was empty and distantly heard herself groan. But she fought back the panic.

Time for a new plan, she told herself and slid to the rear of the cargo area.

She switched the interior light off before opening the hatch as quietly as possible. An instant later, she eased herself out of the vehicle, praying her legs would hold her upright.

When her feet touched the ground, Tate was forced to grab the rim of the cargo hatch for a moment. Her shoulders ached and her head was throbbing. But she was alive, unharmed except for a few bumps and cuts, and she intended to stay that way. She needed to get away. Tate searched her pockets, but her phone was gone. *Think.*

After being confined in the back of the SUV, the air tasted amazingly good. It was fresh and clean and she gulped it greedily. The rain had stopped, but water still dripped from the canopy of tree branches overhead, and as the wind rustled through the trees, it stirred the fog that skimmed over the saturated ground. Tate shivered as dampness and fear collided. She felt a measure of security in the darkness, but somewhere in the woods she heard creatures scurrying, reminding her that the trees could cloak both hunter and prey. She needed to get away from here. And though she wasn't certain where she was, she knew on some deep primal level survival lay in finding Evan.

For both of them.

She took a step away from the vehicle, then another, the fog snaking around her feet. An instant later, she released a sharp cry as she collided with a wall of muscle, and strong arms wrapped around her.

She immediately began to struggle.

"Tate...*Tate*. Keep still. Are you all right?"

Too numb to speak, Tate could only stare as the shadow holding her morphed into Tom Foley, and Kelsey Grant stepped out of the gloom beside a deputy. She experienced a moment of sheer joy before hearing someone ask the question.

"Where's Anderson?"

Tate's hands began to shake and she had to swallow before she could get the words out. "I don't know. He was gone by the time I awoke and found myself tied up in the back of the Lexus."

Very gently, Tom reached out and cupped her chin, turning her head to one side to study her face. "Did he hurt you?"

"No. I smacked my face against the SUV when he pushed me, then he hit me on the head with something. The rest of the damage I did to myself, trying to cut through the rope. I—I knew what he'd done to Evan and I didn't want to still be here when he returned."

She saw Tom's eyes move to her raw and bleeding wrists, where the frayed rope still dangled. He cursed softly. "How bad are you hurting?"

Tate released a tired sigh. "Like you wouldn't believe." Her shoulders began shaking as control abandoned her, and she buried her face in her hands.

Kelsey gathered her in her arms. "It's going to be all right," she said soothingly and held her while she cried.

When she was a little steadier, Kelsey released her long enough to wrap a blanket around her shoulders and led her to the back of a waiting county sheriff's vehicle. And because she had no choice, Tate sat still while Kelsey poked and prodded, checked her eyes, and wrapped a light gauze bandage around her wrists.

She winced when gentle hands touched her head.

"You've got quite the bump and your pressure's a little low. But you look better than I expected, and at least you don't need any stitches. You're lucky you didn't do more damage."

"I was trying to get away from a knife-wielding terrorist. Losing a bit of skin somehow didn't seem that important." Tate stopped watching what Kelsey was doing when she pulled out a syringe. A moment later, she asked the only question of any importance to her. "Is Evan all right?"

"Your disappearance shook her up pretty hard," Kelsey said gently. "But she'll be fine once she sees you in one piece. After the Lexus was spotted, it was all we could do not to have her come with us. We just couldn't risk it in case Khalid was still here."

Tate's heart began to thunder. "She's not alone, is she?"

"Hell, no. Jenna, Alex, and Nick are at the house with her, and two of Tom's deputies are parked outside the front door. Although Tom and the FBI really thought we'd find Khalid here with you, no one was taking any chances in case he circled back to get to Evan."

The words reverberated until Tate could think of nothing else. "We need to go. I need to be with her."

Tate grew increasingly tense as they drove back to the house. She'd borrowed Kelsey's phone, but Evan wasn't answering. Kelsey and Tom both tried to reassure her Evan was well protected, but every instinct she possessed told her something was very, very wrong. And when at last they pulled into the driveway, she knew she'd been right to be worried.

"Oh Christ," Tom muttered.

They were too late.

A muffled sound was the only warning Evan got. It wasn't loud, but it was enough to alert her. Glancing toward the driveway, she blinked. Tried to focus on what she was seeing. Blinked again and tried to keep her head from spinning.

She could see the big Suburban bearing the county sheriff's seal. The one that had been sitting there all day. Except this time, one of Tom's deputies sat slumped and motionless in the passenger seat, while on the opposite side of the vehicle, the driver's door was open and the second deputy was lying on the ground.

Evan reacted instantly, adrenaline flooding her senses.

"Jenna," she called over her shoulder. "Grab Alex and Nick and get out of here. Go through the master bedroom and get as far from the house as you can. As soon as you're able, call Tom. Tell him Khalid's here. Do you understand?"

Jenna's eyes widened. "What about you?"

"Trust me, I'll be right behind you. Now go."

Evan ran in the opposite direction, intent on following Jenna as soon as she got her Sig Sauer from the top drawer of the foyer table where she'd stored it.

She never reached it.

The front door flew open and she had just enough time to think she should have been better prepared before Khalid slammed into her, knocking her hard against the wall. Thrown off balance, she had no opportunity to defend herself.

His fist caught her hard enough to send her sprawling to the floor. Hard enough that she could feel the pain overtaking the adrenaline shielding her in the first few seconds.

"Commander, how nice to see you. But you really shouldn't have kept me waiting." His soft voice chided her as if she were a recalcitrant child. Then he smiled at her even as he leveled the weapon in his hand, pointing it at her chest.

Memories cued other memories, and for an instant Evan felt trapped between past and present. As if reading the direction her thoughts had taken, Khalid's smile widened, and with his empty hand, he toyed with the knife he had tucked into his belt.

Evan stared at the knife gleaming in the light and fought hard not to shudder. She knew it wouldn't do to show any vulnerability. If he remained true to form, any sign of weakness would only increase his sense of control.

Wiping her mouth gingerly with the back of one hand, she licked her lips and slowly got back to her feet. "Hello, John," she said and had the pleasure of seeing the smile vanish from his face.

"That's a name I no longer use. A boy's name. I'm a man and a man chooses his own name. I chose Khalid." He paused as he looked at her. "Do you know what it means, Commander? Do you understand why I chose it?"

"It means magnificent. Everlasting," she said, feigning a bored tone. "Quite obviously, it shows you're delusional."

He retaliated with amazing speed, lashing out with his fist. Evan went down hard once again, pain lancing through her as her head struck the floor and the air was forced from her lungs. Control? No, he wasn't nearly as controlled as she had believed.

"Get up." The hand touching the knife twitched. "You really don't want to make me angry."

She might have responded had she been able to breathe. Instead, she rolled onto her side, coughing and gasping for breath while the room spun around her.

Khalid scowled. In a show of impatience, he kicked her. Excruciating pain exploded on impact. "I said get up. Have you forgotten everything I taught you? Do you not remember what it felt like each time I cut you? Each time you bled? I'll enjoy reminding you. One cut for every time you fail to do what I ask. Now get up."

Evan remembered. Remembered only too well, but forced the images back. Pressing her lips together, she managed to get to her knees, never taking her eyes off his face. She never flinched. But while she tried to mask the pain, he needed only to hear how labored her breathing was to know she was hurting.

It was ironic, she thought, as she looked up at him. With his hair short and without the beard, dressed in a black T-shirt and khaki pants, he looked incredibly young. Radically different from the half-American insurgent she'd known in Afghanistan.

But she knew this was no innocent, and she could see nothing beyond what appeared to be cold-blooded intent.

"You've got to know help is on the way," she said, hoping it was true. "It won't be long before the sheriff and FBI show up. You killed a CIA agent in Kabul and the two deputies outside. You won't get away."

"Neither will you," he responded. His voice was calm and emotionless, just as it had always been. "But then you already know how this ends." He reached into his pocket and pulled out handcuffs he must have taken from one of the deputies. "I need you to put these on, Commander."

"Why the hell would I do that? Why would I help you? Do you think I'm going to make this easy for you?"

"You'll help me or they'll never find your girlfriend."

"Tate? I hate to disappoint you, but the sheriff's already located where you left her SUV."

Khalid's mouth twisted. "Yes, but they won't find Tate."

"Why not?"

"Because I didn't leave her with the vehicle. I planned on taking your brother. But finding your girlfriend proved even more... enjoyable."

Evan's stomach lurched. She knew he was watching her face as the realization sank in, but she wasn't that good an actress and the thought of Khalid touching Tate sliced through her. "Where is she? What did you do to Tate?"

Khalid shrugged. "I took her somewhere isolated, somewhere no one will find her unless they know where to look, and then I cut her so she would slowly bleed out. But before I left her, I let her know I was coming after you."

Evan squeezed her eyes closed. All she could hear was the thunder of her heartbeat as she tried to push away the image of Tate, bloodied and broken at Khalid's hand. "No," she whispered, but it was still more prayer than belief. "You didn't."

A second...a minute...a lifetime went by.

He snapped the cuffs around her wrist. "You'll never know."

Tate stared at the house as the night deepened. Several feet away, Tom and the FBI agents quietly conferred.

She knew reinforcements had been called in, including members of the Seattle SWAT team. But it was taking too long. Much too long, because somewhere inside the house the woman she loved was face-to-face with a man who had already done unspeakable harm to her. A man intent on hurting her again. Killing her.

"Tate."

She blinked and saw Tom approach her, a rifle in his hands.

"How're you holding up?"

She shrugged and released a sigh. "Do you think you're going to need that?" she asked softly.

"It's a possibility we can't discount."

"Are you any good?"

"I generally hit what I'm aiming at," he answered gruffly. "Can I get your home telephone number? Agent McConnell is going to try and establish contact."

Shortly after Tate reeled off the number, she heard the phone ringing inside the house. A long moment later, the younger of the FBI agents began softly speaking into his cell phone—a brief conversation lasting only a minute or two. When he disconnected, he glanced in Tate's direction before turning to Tom.

"Anderson says he wants a helicopter," McConnell said. "Wants it put down in that field across the way, fueled and ready to go, and he wants us to make sure he has a clear path to get to it. He also said he doesn't need a pilot. Claims Evan Kane's going to fly him where he wants to go, and he'll release her once he's somewhere safe."

The field had been used as a helicopter landing pad once before, Tate recalled, thinking back to the day Althea had landed there and given her back her life. A life and a chance at happiness that were now being threatened.

"Do you believe him? Will he let Evan go?"

McConnell stared at her silently before shaking his head. "There's no way we can let him leave here with Kane. If he does…"

Tate felt sick inside.

Before McConnell could say anything else, his cell phone rang and another brief conversation followed. "Anderson wants a pizza. Says he's hungry. He's testing us, trying to show us he's in control. Let's get him a pizza because that's all he's getting from us tonight."

❖

Nearly three hours had passed since the pizza had been delivered. One hundred eighty minutes without any sign of movement from the house. Without another demand.

The ambulance and coroner had come and gone.

The SWAT team from Seattle had arrived and was now in position, watching the house and waiting.

But Khalid wasn't visible through any window. Nor was he responding to any further attempts to communicate with him.

Tate had begun to pace back and forth, switching directions abruptly like a caged animal, her hands curled into fists at her side. And then she heard it—the distinctive sound of blades chopping through the air as a helicopter approached and landed. Her heart sank even as it began to pound. Nearly dizzy with reaction, she stared in disbelief.

Fury outdistanced fatigue. "What the—Jesus, Tom, you're giving him what he wants?"

Tom turned at the sound of her voice. "No, no we're not, Tate, I promise. We just want Anderson to think we are. The snipers can't get a bead on him and McConnell wants to get him out of the house. Get him paying attention to that chopper instead of whatever he's doing in there."

To Evan. Tom hadn't said it, but then he didn't really need to. It was all Tate could think of—Khalid alone in the house with Evan. "You think he's in there hurting Evan, don't you."

She felt a hand on her shoulder and turned to find Kelsey standing there. "He's hurting her," Tate said with more certainty. "And we're not doing anything to stop it."

"Tate, everything that can be done is being done. But no matter what's happening to her, Evan will get through it. She's a fighter. I knew that the moment I met her. You know it too, and she'll have you to help her. She'll have all of us to help her."

"Yes, but…" She stopped and had to fight back a wave of despair.

"She'll be fine," Kelsey said firmly, and with total conviction.

Tate shoved her hands into her pockets. She needed a minute, just a minute, to settle. To get her emotions under control. But before she could do or say anything, the front door opened and her world narrowed to a single point of focus.

Evan was standing there, dark hair haloing her face.

She could just make out Khalid shielded behind her. He held Evan's hair tightly in his left fist, pulling her head back, while his right hand held a long slim blade pressed to her throat. He wouldn't be able to see the SWAT officers from his vantage point, but he seemed to be measuring the steadiness of the rifle in Tom's hand.

If that was the case, it was possible he didn't like what he saw. His expression altered subtly and he began breathing, fast and audibly. But perhaps he was getting excited at the prospect of getting away and eluding justice once again.

Tate didn't care. All she could see was Evan holding herself stiffly—in a way that had nothing to do with the hand tangled in her hair or the knife at her throat. Her mouth was swollen, while blood streaked the side of her face and ran down her chin.

"FBI, Anderson. Drop your weapon."

"I don't think so," Khalid replied. "I think what's going to happen is you are all going to move back and allow the commander and me to get to that helicopter over there. That was the deal. Otherwise, you can sit back and watch while I kill her. Trust me, it won't take much. Just a little more pressure and she'll bleed out before you can do anything to save her."

Evan ignored the knife pressed painfully against her throat, focused instead on her breathing. Every time she inhaled she felt a sharp stab in her side. Bastard probably busted a rib. She didn't need to look through the glare of lights to know Tom, his deputies, and the FBI agents had taken up firing stances. A show of force.

More importantly, for an instant, Tate's face had wavered into focus.

She was here. Alive.

Evan felt a nearly overwhelming sense of joy, followed almost immediately by the need to go to her. To hold her. To be with her. But to do that, Khalid would have to release her, and she wasn't certain he was willing to let her go, even in the face of overwhelming odds.

"It's over, John. Surely you can see this can only end badly," she said. "Why don't you put the knife down?"

At first she didn't think he'd heard her. But then he leaned his head closer, pressed the knife more firmly, and laughed. The knife sliced into her skin. Fresh blood welled up and trickled down her neck. "Why would I want to do that?"

"You've got to know you're not walking away this time. You've done too much damage. Hurt too many people. No lawyer is going to get you off with just a slap on the wrist this time."

"That's supposed to encourage me to put my knife down? To let you go?"

"Yes, because the good news is you'll still be alive, and where there's life, there's always hope. You taught me that."

He appeared to consider her words. "You're right. And I can still provide valuable information about weapons and drugs moving through Afghanistan. I can still make a deal." His fingers tightened in her hair, the knife pressed deeper. "But it will hardly matter where you're concerned, Commander. Your time's up, I'm afraid. I win."

Evan's mind stayed surprisingly calm as his words crystalized and she realized he intended to kill her. In a second that seemed to span minutes, she saw Tate, met her eyes. She saw Tom, his weapon aimed, waiting for an opening. And having nothing to lose, she mustered her strength and jerked her head to one side.

❖

In a moment of perfect clarity, Tate realized Khalid was going to kill Evan. Realized Evan knew it. Despair swept through her and she turned toward Tom.

Saw him draw in a breath and exhale.

And then he pulled the trigger.

❖

Feeling the heat and the force of the impact, Evan recoiled. She dropped to her knees as the rifle's report echoed, drowning out all other sound.

Then there was only the sound of the waves tumbling endlessly against the shore.

❖

From out of the darkness beyond the glaring lights, Tate rushed forward. Dropping to her knees in front of Evan, she extended a shaking hand, touched her fingertips to the abrasions on her face and her bruised mouth.

"Oh God, Evan, I was so scared. I thought he would kill you before Tom could stop him. I wasn't sure Tom could stop him."

"So little faith," Tom muttered as he reached for the handcuffs on Evan's wrists and unlocked them. "I told you I generally hit what I'm aiming at."

Tate took a ragged breath, turned back to Evan. "Tell me you're all right."

Evan could only nod as her pulse pounded and blood rushed through her veins. In the next instant, all her words evaporated. Trembling, she inhaled deeply, trying to draw in Tate's familiar scent as she ran her hands up and down Tate's arms. Reassuring herself Tate was really there.

She drew in another shuddering breath, but the pressure in her chest wouldn't ease and all she could do was burrow into her, burying her face in Tate's hair. Whispering her name, she gently touched her lips to Tate's brow, her cheeks, her mouth. Tasting salt, but not knowing if it was from Tate's tears or her own.

"Evan?"

"I'm okay. I'll be okay." But she wasn't. Not yet. She couldn't keep her voice steady and gave up trying. Squeezing her eyes shut and digging for composure, she felt the steady beat of Tate's heart. "Just be with me. Just let me hold you for a minute."

"I'm right in front of you, love. I'm not going anywhere without you, so take whatever time you need." Tate tilted her head. "Then we're going to have Kelsey take a look at you."

The ghost of a smile skirted across Evan's mouth. "All right. But not just yet." She drew back for an instant, but only so she could frame Tate's face with her hands. "I know I haven't told you often enough, but I love you."

Tate leaned in and offered her mouth. "I know you do. I love you too. You just need to stop scaring me."

"I promise. And you still need to go flying with me."

"Deal. Now, let's get this over with because I want to take you somewhere."

"Where?" Evan asked as they got to their feet and began making their way toward the others.

Tate looked at her and grinned. "Wherever we can run naked on a beach and make love under the stars."

Epilogue

O h God, Evan, I don't know if I can do this."
      They were standing in the field the local flight club used as an airstrip, where the smell of freshly cut grass mixed with the scent of burning fuel. The dew had begun to disappear in the early morning sun, but the air was still quite cool and carried the distinct feeling of fall.

This was it. They had pulled the bright silver biplane out of the hangar into the light and Evan was about to give Tate her first taste of open-cockpit flying.

Flying had been and would always remain Evan's passion. It defined freedom and adventure. And more than anything, she wanted to be able to share it with Tate.

"You'll be fine once we get up, I promise. There's nothing quite like looking at the world through the struts of a Tiger Moth. And there's nowhere else on earth where you can feel the sun's warmth, the dampness of the clouds, and the swirl of the slipstream."

On her advice, Tate had dressed for warmth. Full thermal underwear beneath jeans, a heavy sweater, thick socks, and a pair of vintage leather flying gauntlets Evan had found at a roadside flea market. She had topped everything with a sheepskin-lined leather flight jacket she had borrowed from Evan. But she continued to look doubtful and stared at the biplane's simple frame with clear distrust.

Evan grinned at her. "I love you, you know."

"I know. I love you too. Now remind me again why I'm doing this."

"Because this is the way we were meant to fly and flying's the thing I love to do the most, next to making love with you."

"Good answer."

Evan watched Tate take a deep breath before putting on her helmet and goggles and stood ready to lend a hand while Tate clambered into the front cockpit. "When you're on the wing, grab the struts, step on the seat, and ease yourself down." She helped strap Tate into the five-point harness and showed her how to hook up the headset and throat mic that would allow them to talk during the flight.

All that remained before taxiing was for Evan to complete the pre-takeoff checks from the rear cockpit. And then, without further ceremony, the small aircraft began to move forward toward the open grass paddock, gently rocking back and forth as they rolled over the slightly uneven turf.

"Are you ready?"

As soon as Tate responded with a fainthearted yes, Evan opened the throttle. The tail lifted within seconds and the biplane effortlessly took to the air. A few heartbeats later, they were slipping through the clear blue sky as they climbed to three thousand feet.

Evan wanted to revel in the sheer joy of being airborne again, but she sat silently waiting, hoping for a sign that would tell her Tate was at least okay with this.

Anything.

Please.

And then she heard her laugh. A joyous, musical sound that filled her head and her heart, followed by Tate's whisper.

"Oh God, Evan. This is amazing. You have to teach me how to fly."

About the Author

AJ Quinn's first novel, *Hostage Moon*, was a 2012 Lambda Literary Award finalist and a 2012 Alice B. Lavender Certificate winner. A transplant from Cuba to Toronto, she juggles the demands of a busy consulting practice with those of her first true love—storytelling—finding time to write mostly late at night or in the wee hours of the morning. An avid cyclist, scuba diver, and photographer, AJ's always willing to travel at a moment's notice.